I0581272

Stumbling Through Life

THREE BOOK COLLECTION

MOLLY O'HARE

Copyright 2018 © Molly O'Hare

All rights reserved. This book or parts thereof may not be reproduced in any form. Stored in any retrieval system or transmitted in any form by any means. This includes, but is not limited to, electronic, mechanical, photocopy, recording, or otherwise. No part of this book may be reproduced or copied without prior consent of the author & publisher. All characters and towns are figments of the author's imagination and bear no resemblance to any person living or deceased if there is any resemblance it is entirely coincidental.

Cover model: iStock photo
Cover art: Wildelake Creative
Editor: Klean Edits
Proofreader: Virgina Tesi Carey

Disclaimer: This title is intended for mature audiences due to adult situations and languages.

Molly O'Hare

First Print: August 2022

ISBN: 978-1-7328338-8-3

Be You Publishing, LLC

www.MollyOHareauthor.com

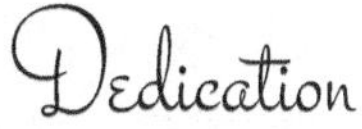

Stumbling Into Him Dedication:
I dedicate this story to all of you. You are beautiful. You are strong. You are a unicorn. Do not let anyone tell you any different. The world is a better place because you are in it. This story goes out to anyone who never felt good enough or looked down upon for any reason. As I said in my last novel, rock who you are. There is only one you out there, so you might as well enjoy every second of it!
Stay awesome. Stay classy. And stay you!

Stumbling Into Forever Dedication:

This book is dedicated to all the Holly's out there looking for your Ben. He's out there. And, for all the Holly's that have their Ben's, Rock on!
Also, in good old Molly O'Hare fashion, you are amazing. You are beautiful, you are special. You are a mother fucking unicorn. Rock your stuff, because no one is just like you and that's amazing.
Go forth and keep kicking ass.
And if no one has told you today, I will: You are fucking perfect.

Xoxo

Stumbling Into the Holidays Dedication:
*This book is dedicated to you. You're what matters in this world
and never forget that. Anyone that tries to tell you differently,
mentally punch them in the face. They don't deserve you.
Keep being a Unicorn.
You're what makes this world a better place.
I promise.
Love you always,
Molly*

Stumbling Into Him

STUMBLING THROUGH LIFE BOOK ONE

Chapter One

"WATCH OUT!"

Holly Flanagan heard a commotion coming from the other side of the park.

Ignoring the shouting, she bent over focusing on picking up her Corgi, Waffles', most recent deposit. With Holly's track record, though, she should have known anyone yelling "watch out," "take cover," or "that's about to fall" was directed at her. Even after years of being the spokesperson for unlucky, klutzy, and clumsy she still disregarded the shouting as she carried on with her dog parent duties.

Before she could register what happened, she was knocked onto her back with a pain radiating from her mouth and nose.

"At least the sky is pretty today," Holly mumbled as she tried to get her bearings. She reached for her mouth as she felt the pain start to spread.

"Ma'am, are you okay?"

Holly closed her eyes as she thought about it.

Was she okay? She'd just been hit with something. She was pretty sure some part of her face, she didn't know which part, but she was sure something was bleeding. Waffles barked uncontrollably, and her head hurt.

So, was she okay?

Holly let out a heavy sigh.

Yeah, she was fine. This was just another day in her life for her. And so far, if being hit by an unknown projectile to the face was the worst thing that happened to her, she'd considered it a good day.

Deciding to face the music she opened her eyes.

Holy shit!

Above her, only a mere few inches from her face was by far the most handsome man she had ever laid eyes on.

He had dark brown hair and deep blue eyes that were richer than the ocean. His jaw was chiseled, with a light dusting of scruff, in the alpha male, I'm in charge here kind of way.

Wonderful. Okay, let's add embarrassing yourself in front of a Greek God to your list of attributes for the day. Hey, it can only get better from here, right?

When she realized she'd been staring at him for what could have been considered too long, she quickly jerked her head forward trying to right herself. Unfortunately for her, though, she slammed her head right into the Greek God's forehead.

Freaking wonderful.

Not only was her mouth hurting, her head now pounded.

Absolutely freaking wonderful!

"Shit," she heard the Greek God say as the wave of pain coursed through her body.

Taking the chance, she opened her eyes again only to see her Adonis holding his head. *Great.* And to make matters worse, Waffles started barking directly at her before looking at his recent deposit still on the ground then back at her.

"For the love of all things, dog. I was trying to pick it up," she growled, before taking her hand away from her mouth to deal with his majesty, *Lord* Waffles. However, the second her hand came into view she saw the blood and screamed.

"Oh shit. Lady, you're bleeding," the Adonis said, putting

his hand under her chin moving it from side to side as he examined her face.

"What happened?" Panic ran through her. *Did I break my nose? Am I unconscious? Am I dying?*

The Adonis tilted her chin back to get a better look. "I was tossing the Frisbee with Ripley, and somehow it veered off course. I tried to warn you with the 'watch out.'"

Typical. Holly groaned. *Hot guy throws Frisbee. Said Frisbee hits me in the face. Hot guy then insinuates it's my fault for not getting out of the way fast enough. I mean, I know I'm generally invisible to men like him, but, damn. You'd think these extra wide hips would make me more visible.* She glared at the Frisbee sitting next to her.

Ignoring the object, she moved her eyes back to the Adonis.

"I can't tell if it's a busted lip or worse." He tilted her head further back like she was a child.

Holly ripped her face from his hand. She'd be able to tell if it was just a busted lip. She'd had too many to count in her life, from falling down, objects to the face, and even falling up the stairs. She reached into her pocket and pulled out the napkin she had stuffed in there from her soft pretzel. She blew off some stray salt and started feverishly wiping at her mouth.

"Let me see," he demanded, before taking one of the napkins from her hand. He then started dabbing at her lips.

She froze.

Well, Holly. This is the most action you've had in months. And, if some hot guy is all over you, you might as well enjoy it while it lasts.

Waffles crawled onto her lap demanding attention and started kissing the underside of her jaw.

Thanks, Waffles, for bringing the attention of my double chin to the Adonis. She rolled her eyes.

"Thanks for trying to help me clean up your mom," the

Adonis remarked before quickly abandoning his job of cleaning the blood off her mouth to pat Waffles on the head.

"He's not trying to help you," Holly scoffed. "He's *trying* to remind me I still need to pick up his poop and then give him a treat."

"Shouldn't your mom be the one getting the treat if *she's* the one picking up your shit?" He cocked his head at her dog.

Waffles, ever the one to argue, looked at the man that now had a mischievous grin on his face, with the most judgmental side-eye he could muster.

No one came between him and his treats.

Ignoring Waffles' attempt at a threat, the Adonis once again pat the dog on the head before moving back to Holly's mouth dismissing him. "I think it's just a busted lip, but your front tooth..." He coughed as he sheepishly looked away.

"My front tooth?" Holly quickly ran her tongue along her front teeth. Shit, she felt a jagged piece. "Oh, crap." She quickly pulled her phone from her pocket and launched the front-facing camera.

As soon as she saw her face, she jerked back. Her hair was all over the place, her face red, there was still blood on her...

You've had better days, Holly. She took a deep breath before he hastily opened her mouth to see the damage.

"Oh no."

Staring back at her was a chipped front tooth along with a busted lip. *Wonderful. Thank you so much, Universe. Thank you, so very much.* She didn't know whether she wanted to laugh or cry. *Clumsy Holly, strikes again. Do you ever take a break?*

As her eyes flooded with tears a sudden cold nose hit her arm distracting her. Realizing it wasn't Waffles she looked to her left and saw one of the most beautifully colored gray and black Australian Shepherds she'd ever seen.

"Aren't you a cutie?" she softly said. Thankfully, her love of animals overrode everything she was feeling.

"That's Ripley." The Greek God chuckled. "I'd thought you'd be more concerned about your mouth than a dog."

Ignoring him, she reached out to scratch Ripley's chin. "You're so pretty." Ripley must have agreed because she barked before kissing Holly's hand.

"Uhh, ma'am, I'm not a human doctor but I think we should pay more attention to your injuries instead of the dogs."

"Human doctor?" Her brows shot up. "As opposed to what, an alien doctor?"

"I haven't worked on any aliens that I know of, but I did neuter a cat named Alien once. Does that count?"

Her eyes widened at the realization. "Oh great, you've got a body of a Greek God, and now you're also a vet. Which of course means you love animals. *Freakin'* wonderful. You're like the most perfect guy, and here I am on the sidewalk with blood pouring out of me with a chipped tooth." She pushed Waffles off her lap and stood. "Please excuse me while I find a place to die of embarrassment."

A corner of the sexy man's mouth lifted. "You're funny."

"And you're hot. So, we've now successfully established which groups we belong to." Annoyed at herself more than anything she angrily started to stomp away from the Greek God.

"Hey, wait up!"

She spun around to glare at him. When Holly saw Waffles sitting at the foot of the Adonis looking up at him, her left eye started to twitch.

Of course, her dog would betray her. She wouldn't expect anything less. "Waffles, come." She pulled on the leash slightly, but the dog wouldn't move. "Lord Waffles, get your butt over here."

The man cocked his brow. "Lord Waffles?"

"Yeah," she answered. "He thinks he's a freakin' king.

Hence the "lord" and I love waffles. Do you got a problem with that, buster?"

The Adonis burst into laughter as he scratched Waffles on the back. To make matters worse, that betraying Corgi rolled over onto his back asking for belly rubs.

The Audacity! *That's it. No more treats for you!* She glared at her dog.

"Who's a good boy?" the Adonis cooed. "You've got a weird name, but you're the best boy aren't cha?"

Holly's eye started to twitch harder.

She stomped back toward her bastard of a dog and the Greek God when out of nowhere her foot hit an invisible rock causing her to trip. Within a split second, she ended up falling right into the arms of the bane of her existence at the moment.

"Whoa, are you okay?"

"I'm fine," she grumbled as she righted herself. *Go ahead and add this to the, "it can only happen to me" list.*

"I feel like you need to walk around with a warning sign or at least a crash helmet," he joked.

"Not the first time I've heard that." Quickly she bent down and retrieved Waffles. "If you'll excuse me. Not only do I really need to find a secluded place to die of embarrassment, I also need to call my dentist, or go to the walk-in. Maybe both." She turned on her heel and started power walking down the sidewalk.

As she passed the spot she'd tripped at, she examined the cement. Figures, there'd be absolutely nothing there. If there were a sporting category on tripping over invisible objects she'd win gold twice over.

"Hey!"

She kept walking, doing her best to hide her humiliation and ignore the Greek God.

Unfortunately, that was short-lived. "Hey, I want to make sure you really are okay," he said, as he caught up to her in two point three seconds.

Stupid short legs! "I'm fine."

"Your lip's still bleeding."

She glared at him. "Wonderful."

"Hey..." He reached for her arm stopping her escape.

"What?"

"Let me help you. My practice is only a block from here. I've got all the supplies to clean up your lip. I can also get a better look at your tooth."

"You're a vet." Her eyes started to twitch again. *Could today get any worse?*

"I am pretty sure if I can surgically remove nuts from an animal I can look at your busted lip." He shrugged before smirking at her.

A laugh escaped her lips. He did have a point after-all. "Thank you for the offer...." she trailed off.

"Ben. The name's Ben Richman." He held out his hand to her.

"Thanks for the offer Dr. Richman, but there is a walk-in clinic not far from where I live."

"Call me Ben. And please let me do this. It'll help me sleep at night knowing the woman I maimed with a Frisbee is somewhat okay." She watched as his eyes pleaded with her. Even Waffles, the jerk, who was still in her arms looked up at her and whined. "Oh, for the love of... fine. Lead the way, Ben."

"Perfect." Ben's mouth curved into a smile. "Follow me."

When he whistled Ripley sat instantly by his side. He quickly bent down and fastened her leash before walking toward the street.

Holly looked at Waffles who was clearly enjoying being carried. "Guess you get an extra trip to the vet."

She couldn't help but burst out laughing when Waffles closed his mouth and glared at her.

Chapter Two

FOR SOME STRANGE reason Ben's heart hadn't stopped racing since the moment he saw the Frisbee head directly toward the lush woman bending over. Thankfully, his clinic was less than a five-minute walk from the park, but right now it somehow felt like an eternity.

He secretly glanced over his shoulder. The woman, whom he had yet to find out her name, held her Corgi in her arms all the while she seemed to be having a silent argument with the pup. He did his best to suppress his smirk. Those two were perfectly suited for each other.

As she was shooting death glares at Lord Waffles – *seriously, who names their dog Lord Waffles?* — he looked at her lip. Fortunately for them, the cut had stopped bleeding. She still had some dried blood on her chin, but that didn't distract from her beauty, though.

She was absolutely stunning. If he had to guess, he'd say she was around five-foot-seven, maybe a little shorter. She also had long dark brown hair that'd been naturally highlighted by the sun. Her eyes were a deep shade of hunter green, a color he'd never seen before.

He flicked his eyes appreciatively over her body. Her

curves went on for days and that was exactly how he liked them.

Ripe and full.

The guy in him couldn't stop his imagination. Her breasts would overflow his palms nicely, and he was sure her ass would do the same. The moment he felt his lower half start to awaken, he scolded himself. *Nice going, Ben. Could you be any more of a creep?*

"Stop glaring at me, Waffles."

He looked at her face before looking at the pup. These two were quite the pair. He laughed.

Her quick wit and fun demeanor were no match for the over-opinionated Corgi.

A soft smile spread across his face. A sense of humor *and* beautiful.

Perfect.

"Yo, Dr. Ben, you got eyes on the side of your face? How do you even know where you're walkin' if you're staring at Waffles and me the whole time?"

Busted.

"Just making sure you're not still bleeding."

She quickly wiped the back of her hand against her mouth. "Am I?"

"Not that I can tell."

"Good. How much farther do we have to walk?" She looked at Waffles. "He takes after his mama. Not the lightest."

Ben stopped walking before turning toward her. His brows drew together.

"What?" she asked.

Did she just call herself fat?

Before he could question her, she tripped over a crack in the sidewalk.

"What the —"

Thank the Universe for his instincts. In less than a second, he caught Waffles who was flying through the sky and was able to use his body to keep the klutzy woman from falling onto her face once again.

"Lady, you've got to be the most uncoordinated person I've ever met."

As she righted herself, she pushed the hair out of her face. "Thanks for the insight, now I can die fulfilled knowing I am once again the winner of the clumsy award." She breathed heavy, making her chest rise and fall. Ben had to force himself to look into her eyes. *Holy shit, even when she's a mess, she's beautiful.*

"How much farther is your office?" she asked before plucking her dog out of his arms.

Feisty. He liked it.

Ben pointed to the sign across the street that read 'Richman Veterinarian Hospital.' He gave Waffles a quick pat on the head, before doing the same to Ripley. "Right over there, Grace."

"That's not my name!"

A smirk appeared on Ben's face. "No? Well, it should be since you're so *graceful*." He held back his laugh as he saw her left eye start twitch.

"My name is *not* Grace." She pushed past him as Waffles sent him the side-eye. "It's Holly. Ya jerk."

Holly walked into the clinic and turned to see Ben staring at her from the front door. His eyes were gleeful, and his smile stretched from ear-to-ear. "Grace suits you better."

She glared at him.

"But, I like Holly, too."

"I'm glad you approve of my name. Now, can we please get this over with?" She tapped her foot.

Holly was still wreaking her brain at the idea there was a vet clinic here. How had she missed it? She'd driven and even walked up and down this street tons of times. Well, in her defense she was usually looking down making sure she wasn't going to trip, but she would have known if she'd seen a veterinarian's office. Ehh, she would definitely need to be more observant. Especially, if hot vets were roaming around in the city.

Ben smirked as he walked into the clinic. "Make yourself at home, Grace."

Instinctively, Holly kicked out her foot while he walked past her effectively tripping him. When he caught himself, he nodded at her, impressed. "Well played."

Holly raised her eyebrows triumphantly. "One point for Holly. Now, Doc Ben, I would like to get this over with."

"Oh, you sure are a fun one." He shook his head with a chuckle. "Do you think you can walk back to exam room one without breaking an arm?"

"Very funny." Holly ignored him as she made her way towards the room marked one. Unfortunately for her the weight of Waffles in her arms, combined with his panic of being at a vet's office unbalanced her. Before she could adjust her dog, she ended up falling into the door which swung open. "Oh for the love of—"

"I thought you said you could do it without breaking something?"

Holly righted herself before putting Waffles on the floor. "I didn't break anything!"

Ben's eyebrows arched as he walked into the room behind her. "Yet."

"I don't have to stand here and take this." Holly bent at her waist to retrieve the shaking Waffles. "Let's go, baby. We can head to the urgent care."

Before Holly even touched her dog a warm hand grasped her shoulder. "Hey, I'm just joking with you. You know, trying to lighten the mood in what could have been a terrible situation."

After a few seconds, she sighed. He was right. She was taking her anger out on him and he didn't deserve it. Even if he did call her Grace.

Her shoulders sunk in. No matter how many lucky pennies she carried or good luck charms she had Holly was always the one at the short end of the stick. Plus, she had so many other worries rolling around in her head. Now adding the busted lip and chipped tooth did not help anything.

Taking a deep breath, she did her best to center herself. All this man was trying to do, was help her.

Plus, she couldn't really blame him for poking fun at her. She was a walking disaster ninety-nine percent of the time. "You're right."

Ben stared at her like he was studying her. When he reached out for her chin, the intensity she saw in his eyes caused her to swallow.

"I'm always right, or at least I try to be," he spoke softly.

He gently stroked her lip with his thumb.

This had to be a dream or some weird reverse Hollywood movie. The kind where the hot guy falls for the unpopular and unattractive girl.

Ben removed his thumb from her lip and slowly traced it down her chin never once breaking their gaze.

Then she heard it.

The telltale sign of one, Lord Waffles, marking his territory. Holly snapped her face around. "Really, Waffles, really?" She glared at her dog trying to regroup. *I know the lust in his eyes was all in my head, but did you have to bring me back to reality so soon, Waffles?*

Ben barked out a laugh. "Gotta love dogs." He lowered himself to his knee, which caught Waffles' attention. Within less than a second, that betraying bastard was at Ben's side begging for belly rubs.

Holly's eyes narrowed on her dog. *No piece of bacon for you! Ever again.*

"It's okay, boy," Ben laughed while he scratched Waffles. "Us men need to mark our territory."

"Men do *not* need to mark their territory."

Ben looked back at her. "Sure, we do. It's how we get the word out."

Holly shook her head. "Hell no. No one's ever gonna pee on my leg to mark their territory," she said with utter disgust at even the thought of it. "And, if someone ever tried, I'd rip off his dick and make him eat it."

Ben let out one of the most genuine deep laughs she had ever heard.

"I like you, Grace."

When she lifted her arm as if to punch him, he held up his hands in surrender. "I mean Holly. You're funny. And, I wasn't saying men have to *pee* on items or people to mark what's theirs. That could be done lots of ways."

"Oh yeah?" she questioned crossing her arms over her chest. "And, what do you suppose that is?"

"Well, for starters, a wedding ring would do a pretty good job, maybe a tattoo declaring their undying love for the other person."

Holly rolled her eyes. "I'd never be foolish enough to get a tattoo of someone's name on me." She wasn't going to admit the idea of having her husband tattoo *her* name on him sent shivers down her spine.

In reality though, she knew if she ever did get a tattoo with her luck the ink wouldn't take or worse... She'd most likely develop some infection and the entire body part she'd tattooed would end up having to be surgically removed. No, thank you. She was not taking that chance. She knew how the cards fell for her.

"Men aren't the only ones that can mark," he continued, ignoring her as the tension in the room shifted. "My favorite marks are scratches down my back."

Heat flooded Holly's cheeks.

Ben stood taking a step closer to her.

What in the world was going on? She fought the urge to look around for the cameras. She had to be on some prank show. "Yeah, well, I'd think a vet would be better equipped to detain his patients so he *wouldn't* be scratched."

As soon as the words were out of her mouth, her face paled. *Oh, God, Holly. Good going. Why are you so awkward! Now, he probably thinks you're into all the handcuffs and other stuff. Why do I have no brain to mouth filter?*

Ben's eyes darkened. "Maybe you're right."

"Nope!" Holly backtracked. "No, I'm not right at all. I am so far from being right; I'm left. Oh, look over there." She pointed behind him. When he turned, she bent and tried to pick Waffles up.

Ben laughed again. "You are something else, Holly." He nodded toward the exam table. "Come on, let's have a look at you."

Holly glanced at the table and then to Ben. Did he really think she'd get up there? The exam table was higher than her hips. She then looked at the one metal pipe holding the table in place. There was no way in hell that thing would hold her weight.

Ben must have read her mind. "It's weighted for four hundred and fifty pounds. I don't just get domestic animals in here. I've been known to perform surgeries on pot belly pigs."

"Did you just call me a pot belly pig?"

His eyebrow rose.

"Okay fine, even if it was weighted with some industrial enforcing secret ninja strength mechanism, how do you suppose I get up there?"

Before she knew it, Ben's hands were on her hips lifting her onto the table. "Well, okay then."

He smirked.

The confidence radiating off Ben sent shock waves through her. His jawline was intense but somehow inviting.

She had the urge to reach out for it. As she felt her arm start to move a growling commotion on the floor snapped her out of whatever spell she was under. *What the hell is wrong with you, Holly Flanagan? Get it together. This insanely hot vet is not flirting with you!*

Shaking the thoughts from her head, she looked to the dogs who were now wrestling.

A chuckle from Ben diverted her attention once again. "Come on, Holly." Ben reached for the extendable light attached to the wall. "Let's take a look at the damage."

Chapter Three

BEN PIVOTED the light so it was directly in front of Holly's mouth.

His heart still slammed against his chest. He didn't know what came over him, but the second she questioned getting onto the exam table he jumped at the chance to assist her. And he was sure as hell glad he did. Her hips molded to his hands perfectly. He had to stop himself from slipping his fingers under her shirt to feel her skin.

Get it together, Ben. Damn.

Okay, she was beautiful but this was unusual behavior for him. There was just something about Holly that ignited every nerve ending he had.

Right now, the only thing he wanted to do was explore all the possible reasons why. Maybe it was her quick wit, her adorable clumsiness, or her insanely delicious curves. Whatever it was, he wanted to drown himself in it.

Taking a deep breath, he commanded his body to control itself. "Close your eyes, Grace. I don't want the light to blind you."

Ben was instantly rewarded with her defiant glare. *Oh, she sure is fun to rile.*

"I will sic Waffles on you in a heartbeat." She gave him another dirty look.

"Do you mean the same Waffles that's licking my leg right now?"

Holly looked at the floor, her eyes narrowing before shooting back at him. "He's faking you out. He's trying to trick you into believing he is as sweet as maple syrup, but as soon as I give the command he'll attack."

"Is that so?"

To make a liar out of her, Waffles rolled onto his back and demanded a belly rub.

He laughed. This woman was something else, and as her death glared hardened even further on him he realized he hadn't had this much fun in months.

"Don't you have a job to do?" she demanded, snapping him from his thoughts.

Oh, he liked this. Ben laughed harder, placing his hand on his stomach. "Yes, your highness, I do. Now close your eyes and let me take a look."

When Holly *finally* listened to him and closed her eyes, he got a better look at her mouth. There was one cut a little under a half of an inch wide on her bottom lip. Carefully he used his fingers to move around the tissue looking for any other damage. He instinctively started caressing the side of her lip that didn't have the cut. And try as he might, he couldn't stop himself from imagining what it would feel like to have his lips pressed against hers.

Quickly, he averted his gaze to the wall. *What the absolute fuck is going on with me?* No one ever enticed these reactions from him before.

Taking a deep breath, he focused. As he examined her upper lip he noticed a smaller laceration. Thankfully, neither cut seemed to need stitches.

Moving into work mode, he pulled out some cotton balls and cleaning solution from the drawer. He then took one of the saturated swabs and started wiping away the dried blood.

"Ouch, you jerk."

"This is the exact reason why I went the animal route instead of the human route," he said, ignoring her as he worked cleaning up the cuts.

"Why, because humans fight back?"

"If you think animals don't fight back you are sorely mistaken," he answered. "Animals don't run their mouth while I'm trying to fix them."

"I wasn't running my mouth. I explained what you were doing hurt."

His heart stopped. He'd hurt her? As he was about to apologize he saw the faint smile on her lips as her eyes danced with glee. That little shit was messing with him. "Sure thing, Grace," he said retaliating.

Instantly her face changed from smug to annoyance. "Jerk."

Ignoring her, he continued. "Open, Grace. Let me take a look at your tooth."

Holly crossed her arms over her chest, but did as he asked.

When she opened her mouth, he was able to see the chipped front tooth clearly. From what he could tell there weren't any cracks. He moved the tooth around to see if it was loose.

When he was done he turned off the light and pushed it back toward the wall. He then removed his gloves with a snap, causing both of the dogs to turn his way. "Well, Grace, your lips will survive to bring enjoyment to unexpecting patrons another day." Her eyes started to twitch again... Maybe he really should have her go to the urgent care in case something was wrong with her brain.

"That's good to know," she grumbled.

"Yup, no stitches. Your tooth on the other hand—"

She threw her hand to her mouth. "Am I gonna die?"

"You're pretty dramatic, anyone ever tell you that?"

"Am I gonna die is a legitimate question for someone that finds herself in certain positions more times than not."

Ben chuckled. "And, what might those positions be?"

When her eyes narrowed, he held up his hands in surrender. "Like I was saying, your tooth has a chip in it, but I don't see any cracks. Which is a good thing. I'm not a human dentist, but no cracks mean your tooth should be fine. I'm sure a dentist can easily add some composite to the chipped part, and you'll be good as new." Ben turned away from her retrieving his phone from his pocket.

"All you see is a chip?"

He didn't look up from his phone as he answered. "Yeah. I also moved your tooth around. There is some looseness, but nothing to be too concerned about. I don't think you'll have any lasting issues with it."

"Do you always ignore your patients?"

He finally looked from his phone he saw she was glaring at him with her arms crossed. "I'm not ignoring you. I'm setting up a dentist appointment for you."

"You're what?" Holly's eyebrows shot to the ceiling.

"That's the next logical step. I'm trying to see if he can get us in today."

Did he just say us? Holly's head spun as she tried to make sense of what was happening. "What do you mean *us?*"

Ben leaned against the counter across from her. He crossed his legs as he furiously typed on his screen. "We'd have to drop the dogs off at my house first, so not them."

"Whoa." Holly threw her hands up. "You need to take a step back. I am not dropping my dog off anywhere that isn't in my apartment. Besides, I am not going to some random crackpot dentist."

That dang smirk appeared on his face again as he looked at her. "I can't wait to tell John you said he was a crackpot. It'll make his day."

"I am not going to your dentist."

"Why not?"

"Because I don't know him. Hell, Ben, I don't even know you."

He put his phone down and opened his arms. "What do you want to know, I'm an open book."

"That's not what I meant." She took a calming breath. "I appreciate what you are trying to do, but I really just need to get out of here." She looked around the room for something to help her get down from the table.

Ben must have read her mind again because his hands were back on her hips before placing her safely on the ground. "John's my best friend. Let me help you here, Holly. I feel horrible that it was my miscalculation with the Frisbee that caused all of this. I want to fix it."

To make matters worse, her betraying dog plopped his big butt next to Ben's foot and whined at her agreeing with him. She narrowed her eyes at the loaf of bread. *Do you not understand,* I'm *the one who feeds you?*

When Waffles sent her a death glare that rivaled her own, her tongue had mindlessly touched her front tooth.

Dang it.

She ran her tongue over her tooth one more time. She knew the chip wasn't that bad, but she also knew she wouldn't be able to stop touching it with her tongue.

She closed her eyes. Could she deal with the possibility of cutting her tongue on the jagged edge? Opening her eyes, she saw a picture-perfect scene. Ben was on his knees with Waffles on his right, and Ripley on his left, all three of them had the puppy dog look on their faces. "Fine, you know what, let's go to your guy, but I swear if he turns out to be some weird dealer on the black market trying to harvest my appendix, tell him it was removed years ago. Oh, and I will murder you."

Ben plucked her dog into his arms who happily ate up the attention. "You mean you'll finally sic Lord Waffles on me?"

She was going to kill them both.

Chapter Four

BEN WATCHED Holly from the corner of his eye as they sat in the waiting room. She bounced her leg nervously as she pretended to be focused on an old magazine in her hands. There was something about Holly he couldn't quite put his finger on. He couldn't help but feel enamored by her.

Everything about Holly screamed adorable. Especially right now, every few seconds she'd shift her weight in the seat trying to relax. Maybe she wasn't a fan of going to the dentist? Or maybe —

Then she did it again.

Fuck me. Ben did his best to bite back his groan. Holly ran her tongue across her plump bottom lip, feeling the laceration. His heart raced as he couldn't stop himself from imagined it being *his* tongue. He'd gladly kiss away the pain. Or better yet, he'd kiss along her jawline being cautious of the tender spots. He'd make it his soul mission to distract her with his hands— *Jesus fucking Christ, Ben. Calm the fuck down.*

He was even starting to scare himself. He needed to get a grip. The poor woman had been through a lot today, and she didn't need him fantasizing about her to add to it. It didn't matter the raw lust he was feeling toward Holly was a new sensation to him. Sure, he'd lusted after beautiful women before, who hadn't? But with Holly, his nerve endings came alive and he had absolutely no idea why. But he sure as hell wanted to find out.

Ben continued to stay focused on her lips. He was soon rewarded for his ogling. Within less than a minute her little pink tongue snuck out of her mouth to touch her lip again.

Did she not understand what that did to him? Right now, his dick pressed so tightly against the front of his jeans, he was about to explode.

"Yo, earth to Ben, can you hear me?"

Jarred out of his thoughts, he looked at her. He felt his cheeks slightly heat. *Get it together, dude.* Clearing his throat, he sat straighter in his seat tugging on the front of his pants, desperately trying to make more room. "Uh, yeah."

Holly raised a brow.

No pulling the wool over her eyes apparently. "You caught me. I honestly have no idea what you were saying."

"Ben, this is serious."

The panic he saw in her eyes acted like a bucket of cold water being thrown on him. He uncrossed his legs moving his body a few inches closer to her. "What's the issue?" He knew no matter what was upsetting her, he'd do anything to fix it. It didn't matter the cost, if it were within his power to fix, he'd fix it. "What can I do?"

"For the love of all things, you weren't even a quarter listening."

"I already said I wasn't, Grace, now tell me what's got your panties in a bunch?" The glare she shot him went straight to his crotch.

Focus, dumbass.

"Do you think Waffles and Ripley will be okay at your house? I've never left him alone with another dog. What if he thinks Ripley is out to steal some scrap of food that was left on the floor and they fight to the death?" She worried her lip between her teeth. "Ouch."

Without questioning his gut reaction, he reached for her lip, pulling it from her mouth. "Careful, Holly. It's stopped bleeding for now, but you can easily break it open again." He used the opportunity to caress the sensitive tissue briefly before pulling away. "Ripley is a well-trained dog, but she's also a huge couch potato when she's at home. I can guarantee you right now she's sleeping on the couch, probably with her legs in the air."

"How can you be sure there isn't a food scuffle going on at this moment?"

His heart warmed. Someone this concerned about her dog was an animal lover, he had no doubts about it. Another point for Holly in the "pro" column. "Ripley is the best vacuum cleaner you will ever find. Every nook and cranny of my house has been well accounted for. I can assure you there will be no food scuffles."

"But aren't you not supposed to leave animals that just met by themselves?"

"Technically, as a DVM I would say yes. However, I was watching the way they interacted. There were zero signs of aggression. Not only that, Ripley is a certified therapy dog. If there is a high-stress situation, she defuses it pretty quickly. Or, if she feels the best course of action is to remove herself from the situation, then she will."

Holly's eyes still showed her concern. "You think they're okay?"

"I can prove it."

Ben pulled out his phone before opening his home security app.

When he looked at the screen he laughed. "See, Grace. Exactly like I told you." He handed her the phone. Ripley laid precisely where he said she would be. On her back with all four paws in the air, sleeping away. Waffles on the other hand, though, was trying with all of his might to jump onto the chair in the corner of the room. Unfortunately, for him his little Corgi legs didn't help.

"My poor baby," Holly cried.

Ben looked at the video feed again. Waffles backed up a few feet then ran with all of his might trying to jump onto the chair. Waffles: Zero. Chair: One, or however many times the poor guy had tried to jump onto the cushion. They watched as once more Waffles went through the motions, however this time, when he jumped his stomach hit the chair causing him to be flipped onto his back.

"Waffles!"

"He's fine." Ben chuckled at the Corgi. "Watch."

Waffles gave up his stance on sitting on the chair and moved to the dog bed by the wall.

"Crisis averted."

"For now," Holly grumbled.

"Let's do something to take your mind off everything," he suggested.

Holly turned all her attention on him. "Okay, like what?"

"Tell me about yourself?"

"There's not much to tell."

"Sure, there is." Ben once again crossed his legs. "Where do you work, what are your hobbies, have you ever been arrested, do you have a boyfriend?"

Holly scrutinized him for a second before throwing her head back in laughter. "You are something else, Benjamin."

His body froze. "Don't call me that. That's what my mother calls me."

She studied him. "Oh, that is definitely something we are going to explore."

"Not on your life."

"Oh, yes, Benjie. Friends talk to each other. Isn't that what you kept insinuating we are... Friends, that is?"

"Well, yeah." However, the last thing he wanted to talk about was his over botoxed, judgmental, bitch of a mother.

He needed to change the subject and fast. "I see you're avoiding the questions, is there something you're hiding, Holly?"

"Nothing to avoid. I work for the public library on Eighth and Johnson, I've been employed there for three years now, and I love it. No boyfriend, unless you count Lord Waffles. I love to read, hence working at the library. It's a dream job for me. I also like to write short stories here and there. I want to try my hands at writing a full novel. I really spend most of my free time taking care of my dad. As for being arrested, I plead the fifth."

So many questions and images were running through Ben's head. *A fucking librarian?* There was no way for her to be more perfect. His heart raced as fantasies of her being the dirty librarian ran through his head. He'd love to see her hair pulled into a tight bun, maybe some dark-rimmed glasses on her face. Her wearing a black tight pencil skirt with a white blouse. This time he didn't hold back his groan.

"You okay?"

Through his haze of lust, her other words dawned on him. "Wait, were you arrested?"

Her face flooded with heat. "Yes and no."

He uncrossed his legs before bringing his elbows to his knees leaning closer. "Explain."

"There isn't really a lot to explain. It was all a misunderstanding. Like today, I was in the wrong place at the wrong time."

"Keep going."

"It's nothing really. One day I decided I wanted to walk a new route home after work. You know, mix things up a bit. Well, I got a little lost and ended up in some back alley. After a few minutes of walking, I saw some guy leaning against a brick wall."

"Holly, please tell me you didn't."

"I thought they could help me get back on the right path. Before I knew it, I was being thrown against the wall and being told I was under arrest for buying drugs."

Ben shifted back into his chair and burst out laughing.

"It wasn't my fault and as soon as everything calmed down, I was released."

"You really are something else." Ben smiled from ear-to-ear. "Okay, so a felon you ain't. You said you take care of your dad during your free time, does he live close?"

Holly's face lit. Clearly, the mention of her dad made her happy. He couldn't help the slight chuckle that escaped him when she smiled showing her teeth. The chipped tooth and all.

"Yes, he only lives a few miles from me. I've been trying to get him to move in with me, though. But he swears he's still able bodied enough to live on his own. I don't agree, but it's like beating a dead horse. Eventually, he'll get the picture."

"Why do you want him to move in with you? If he's able to live on his own, I don't see a problem with it."

Once again, she worried her lip. "No, I understand what you're saying and he's still, for the most part, independent. It's just after he got hurt and couldn't go back to work, things took a turn for the worse. See, it's just him and me. We're all we've got in this world after my mom died when I was five."

Ben blindly reached for her hand, giving it a light squeeze. "I'm sorry to hear that."

"Don't be. We do just fine on our own. Most of my free time I spend helping him do things around the house that he can't do anymore. I always make sure his pantries are stocked, and he has everything he needs until I can get back over to him."

"You sound like a good daughter."

"He's my dad. I'd do anything for him." Pain slashed through Ben's heart. He knew the feeling.

"Now that you know my sad life story, why don't you tell me all about you and why you apparently hate the name Benjamin?" Holly adjusted herself on her seat once again, smiling showing off her chipped tooth. *That little shit!*

As Ben opened his mouth to speak, one of the dental technicians came into the waiting room. "Holly Flanagan."

"Oh, boo." He jutted out his bottom lip. "I guess story time is over."

She gave him a dirty look. "I'll be back."

"I'm looking forward to it."

Over an hour later Holly's tooth was good as new. Well, for the most part. The dentist, or John as he liked to be called, was able to fix the chipped part with a composite. Although, he did warn her she needed to be careful with her tooth from now on. The fact there now was some damage apparently might weaken the tooth and could cause a crack. If that were the case, she might need to get her whole tooth fixed. Thankfully, that wasn't anywhere on the horizon for her.

Holly walked into the reception area and watched Ben stand and make his way toward her. "How'd it go?" he asked.

"Not as bad as I thought it was going to be. Like you said, he didn't see any cracks, and he was able to fix it."

"That's great." Ben's face brightened. "Did he say anything else? John's been known to never shut up. He has his hands in your mouth and he'd asked you questions like you could actually answer him."

A laugh escaped her. That was exactly what John had done. He'd be asking questions about everything and anything, and when she would try and answer, he'd tell her to keep her mouth open while he worked. "Not really, he only said I need to be careful about how I bite."

"Makes sense."

Holly leaned over the receptionist counter. "How much do I owe you?"

The lady behind the desk started typing on her computer. "Let's see." After thirty seconds she looked at Holly. "The total will be $698.98."

Holly blanched. *What the hell?* How could fixing a small chipped tooth cost that much? "Umm, can I ask why it's so expensive? I gave you my dental card when I came in."

The lady looked back at her screen. "Everything done today was considered cosmetic work and your insurance doesn't cover that."

"Oh." Holly heart sank. How was she going to pay for this? As of right now, if she paid this bill she'd have all of five dollars left to her name. How could that last a full two weeks until she got paid again? And, what about her Dad? Every spare dime she had she put toward his medical bills. *Great, why does this crap always happen to me? Why can't I catch a break?*

Holly quickly tried to do some calculations. She went shopping two days ago. If she split all of her meals into three servings, she should be able to make it. Then she remembered her Dad's recent late notices. She'd been trying to work out a payment plan with the medical billing department but they weren't willing to help.

She was toying with the idea of getting an additional part-time job to help pay his bills. Maybe this was the gentle push she needed.

Shoving all those thoughts away, she took a deep breath. She had no other choice here. The work had already been completed on her tooth. She reached into her purse.

"Put it on here." Ben's voice shocked her.

"What are you doing?"

"What does it look like I'm doing?" He was giving his card to the lady. "I'm paying your bill."

"What do you mean you're paying my bill?"

"Exactly that. It was my mistake not watching where the Frisbee was headed. I should be the one to pay for this." Ben tried to hand the receptionist his card again.

"I don't care about that. I can pay my own way."

"I never said you couldn't."

"I'm not letting you pay for this, Ben. Plus, it's far too expensive." Which was true.

"I'm not taking no for an answer."

"What's all this commotion out here?" John, the lovely and sadistic dentist she'd just had the pleasure of meeting asked walking into the room. "Ben, what the hell is going on? You causing trouble?"

"We're having a lover's quarrel on who's gonna pay."

A lover's quarrel? I'll kill him.

John's eyes widened for a brief second, before pure glee clouded his face. "I see, buddy. Ms. Flanagan—"

"Holly," she corrected just as she had every other time he tried calling her Ms. Flanagan.

"Fine, Holly. Trust me when I say this, let Ben fit the bill."

"Exactly," Ben agreed.

"No."

"He can afford it." John winked at Ben.

"Yeah, well so can I," Holly countered. *Well sorta.*

"No, he really can afford it. Plus, he needs to put his money to good use, like my practice." John winked at Ben.

"You know, you could just comp the dental work," Ben remarked.

"And lose out on watching this, what did you call it, a lover's quarrel?"

"No one is comping anything." Holly turned toward the receptionist and handed over her card. "Here."

Ben yanked the card away. "Nope." He shifted his body so he was now completely facing Holly. "I'm paying for this. End of story." He held his hands up. "How about you buy me dinner to make up for it?"

Holly clenched her fists at her sides. This was getting her nowhere. You know what, if he wanted to pay, then fine. When she took him to dinner it would be the most expensive restaurant she could find... well, within her budget of course. "Fine. But, we're getting steaks."

"You know the exact words to make my heart flutter," he said before placing his hand on his head to fake swoon.

Yup, she thought. *I'm gonna find a way to make that steak have poison on it.*

"Told you, Holly, the Richman's *always* get their way," John said.

"And we always will."

"Remind me to tell that to your mother the next time she comes in and starts bitching about how you refuse to give up the silly animal job and work for the family business. She sucks all the good out of everything," John stated matter of fact.

Ben paled.

Before she could ask what was going on, recognition dawned on Holly. *Richman? As in Richman Industries?* She felt her stomach bottom out. *Holy Fuck.*

Holly's eyes widened. "You're a Richman."

Chapter Five

HOLLY WALKED AS FAST as she could along the city street. Right now, her primary goal entailed getting as far away from a *Richman* as possible. Doing her best not to trip on any invisible cracks she quickened her pace.

Universe, why do you hate me?

Tears welled in her eyes. Of all the people she could've made a fool out of herself in front of, it had to be one of the most influential people in the whole state.

Freakin' Richman Industries.

She blanched.

Good going, Holly.

"Grace, why are you running away?"

Because, I'm an idiot.

Ben instantly by her side. "Seriously, what's got you running like your ass is on fire? You do know John wouldn't have charged you right? He only did it 'cause he's my best friend and was messing with me." He laughed. "Plus, I don't think running down the street's a wise move for someone who's so..." He paused for a moment. "Shall I say accident-prone?"

Holly came to an abrupt halt and scowled at him. "It's not nice to make fun of people."

"I'm not making fun of you, Holly, I'm merely stating a fact." He placed one of his hands in the pocket of his jeans. "Now, explain to me why you took off out of the office like a bat out of hell?"

"I did not," she protested, crossing her arms over her chest.

Ben cocked his brow.

"Fine. I felt foolish, okay?" Her eyes fell to the ground as her face flushed.

"Why?"

Holly glanced at him. "Uh, I don't know. Maybe it has something to do with making myself look like a, how did you put it? Oh yeah, an accident-prone loser in front of someone who could be the most powerful man in the whole state?" She huffed. *Great, now you've just word vomited all over the man.*

Ben's face contorted. "I never once called you a loser."

"Semantics."

Ben quirked his head to the side. "No. It's not. I never and would never call you a loser, Holly. Sure, I might joke around with you, but I'd never say anything like that. I don't think you're a loser at all. Actually, I like all your qualities." His eyes darkened. "*A lot.*"

She couldn't help but roll her eyes. "Sure."

"Okaaaaay." Ben grabbed her arms and started moving her from side to side, looking all around her.

"What are you doing, you weirdo?"

"I'm trying to find the same girl I met at the park a few hours ago. Did she get abducted by aliens and you've been sent down to replace her?"

Holly jumped out of his grasp and scrutinized him. "You're strange."

Ben's eyebrows shot to the sky. "Says the one that might have been abducted."

Within that instant all of the tension she was feeling subsided. "You're something else."

"You ain't seen nothing yet." He threw his arm around her shoulder, pulling her into his side. "Now, how about we head to the store, pick up some food and we can cook dinner at my place."

"I don't think—"

"If I recall correctly," he said interrupting her. "You promised me a meal."

She stopped walking and turned toward him. "No, I agreed to take you out."

Ben's face brightened. "Oh, Grace. Did you just ask me on a date?"

She paled. "Wait, what? I never said that."

"No take backs. I accept." Ben pulled her to his side again, coaxing her to walk.

"I don't like being manipulated," she grumbled. Even though every fiber of her being wanted to throw his arm off and run in the opposite direction there was something about Ben that pulled her in.

"I'm not manipulating you, Grace. I'm simply agreeing to your terms," he stated as a matter of fact.

"Anyone ever call you a jerk?"

His eyes brightened. "All the time."

Holly's head still whirled as she sat at the island countertop in Ben's kitchen across from where he was preparing their meal. How did she get herself into these situations? Shaking her head, she looked at the red mark forming on her upper arm. The trip to the grocery store had been by far one of the most eventful experiences of her life. Which was saying something because every day was an experience for her. Maybe it was due to the fact Ben unnerved her or maybe she was still rattled by the events of the day? It seemed as though when she was around Ben, she ended up being even more of a klutz than she usually was.

In aisle eight, when she tried to reach the top shelf to get some of the fried onions, the whole shelf collapsed with all its products cascading onto her. She wasn't hurt other than a few red marks and after Ben got most of his laughs out, he righted her in one swift movement.

Then, when Holly tried to pay for their items, Ben growled at her. Honest to God growled at her. She'd never heard of that happening in real life. Sure, in her romance books she'd read it tons of times. But that wasn't real world stuff, at least that's what she thought.

Holly was only mildly annoyed he refused to let her pay. Even with her argument that she was the one supposed to be treating him to a meal, she bit her tongue and gave in. At that point, he still had her dog.

"Steaks will be done in few minutes," Ben announced, turning away from the food to face her.

Waffles and Ripley both barked in unison with their excitement causing Holly to roll her eyes. They both sat like picture perfect dogs at the edge of the island counter where she sat.

"Who said I'd share?" Holly directed her attention to Waffles who goofily stared back at her, his tongue dangling out of his mouth. He must have thought her words were an invitation because he trotted over to her legs and started licking her jeans. "You're such a weirdo, Waffles." She reached for his fluff burying her hands in his fur giving him a good scratch. "You know mommy will always give you anything you want."

"And that might be why he takes advantage of you," Ben chimed in as he moved the steaks to a plate he'd already prepared.

Holly glared. "Are you going to ignore that your dog barked, too?"

Ben pat Ripley on top of her head. "She knows she'll only get what I give her and not all the time. What kind of vet would I be if I fed her human food?"

Holly sheepishly looked at Waffles, then back to Ben. "Whoops."

Ben chuckled as he got the baked potatoes out of the oven.

As he finished preparing their meals Holly glanced around his kitchen. It was modest. Not at all what she would've pictured a Richman having. Mind you, it was bigger than her apartment, but it wasn't quite what she envisioned for the powerhouse name. Before she could stop herself, the words were out of her mouth. "If you're a Richman and deemed one of the richest families in the state why don't you live in a mansion or something by a lake?" She winced.

After placing the baked potatoes onto their plates, Ben turned toward Holly. "First, I'll never live on a lake. Mosquitoes are a bitch. Second, I'm not rich. My parents' company is rich, my *family* is rich, but I'm not. I live off of the income I make with my practice." He walked toward the island leaning both of his arms on the counter directly across from her. "Is this why you've done a one-eighty after learning I'm a Richman? You think having money is some sort of superpower?"

"Not at all, it's just that—"

"Holly, I want absolutely nothing to do with Richman Industries and as far as I'm concerned the place can burn to the ground."

Holly's eyes widened. "Wow."

"Yeah."

"Okay," she murmured. "I'm sorry I brought it up."

She watched as Ben's body stiffened. "Don't be."

"You don't get along with your parents, then?" she asked before hitting her head with her palm of her hand. "Don't answer that. Along with my clumsiness I seem to win the award of saying the wrong thing at the wrong time."

Ben chuckled. "And yet, I find that extremely adorable."

"Adorable." She rolled her eyes. "Yeah, right."

Ben's eyes darkened before leaning across the counter. His face was only inches from hers. "Oh, Holly, if you only knew what I thought about you."

She swallowed hard. *Abort, abort.* She had to do something. "Waffles has to pee!"

A half-smile appeared on his face. "That so?" He glanced at Waffles who was sitting at his feet looking toward him with pure devotion in his eyes. *I feel ya, Waffles. I'm enamored with the guy as well.*

"Do you have to go outside, boy?" Ben asked.

Waffles flopped over onto his back, giving Ben his belly. *Stupid dog.*

"I think he wants human food."

"Whatever," Holly grumbled. "What's the deal with your family? Do you really hate them?"

Ben scoffed. "It's not that I hate them, it's more of we don't see eye to eye on a lot of things and I don't agree with ninety-eight percent of the shit my mother does."

"What about your father?" Holly questioned before reaching for her drink.

"My dad was amazing. He's the reason I'm here today."

Holly sat straighter on her chair. "You said was. Is he no longer around?"

Ben looked away before speaking. "No, Richman Industries killed him and I blame my mother for that."

Okay, Holly wasn't sure what can of worms she'd opened, but she was desperately looking for some sort of reverse can opener to put it back.

Ben must've seen the panic in her eyes, as he further stated, "He worked himself to the bone to please my mother, but she was never satisfied. Every dollar he earned, she wanted him to earn two more. Every present he bought her, she'd scoff at and demand something else. He worked his ass off and all that got him was a heart attack that led him to an early grave."

"Oh, Ben, I'm so sorry." Holly wasn't sure what else to say. She'd only known Ben a few hours, but for him to speak so personally with her, melted her heart. She fought the urge to run to him and pull him into her arms.

"Don't be sorry it wasn't your fault, it was my mothers."

The pain in his voice crushed her. "Now, I understand why you don't like her."

"Not liking her is an understatement. We don't see eye to eye on anything, and after my dad died, she demanded I take his place as CEO of the company."

"That's not what you wanted, right?" Holly asked.

"Hell no." Ben jerked back. "Whenever there's a reason I have to step into Richman Industries I get the heebie-jeebies." He shuddered. "I fucking hate that place. That's not the life I want. Since I was a kid, I've always been interested in animals. Everything about them fascinated me. From their loyalty to their unique personalities. They gave me unconditional love when no one else was able to. Even my dad was too busy pleasing my mother to be there for me. Animals were always there, though."

Holly's heart went out to Ben as she thought back to her own life. "I completely get it. After my mom died my dad got us a cat. I loved that cat more than anything in the world. I named her Princess Huffle Stuffle and she let me tell her all of my secrets. I loved her more than I ever realized. I was heart-broken when she was diagnosed with renal failure and passed away."

"You and the strange names you pick for your animals." Ben chuckled. He shook his head, before sighing. "Animals bring out a side of us that we didn't know we had. Animals can calm you. They can protect you and be a companion when you think the world is against you. My dad understood that. He never once pushed me to follow in his footsteps. On the contrary, he did everything in his power to help me achieve my dreams of owning my own veterinarian practice," Ben reminisced. "I remember the day I graduated from Veterinary Medicine and he handed me the deed to the building my practice is set up in. He told me he was proud of me and he wished he'd followed his own dreams." He shook his head. "Apparently, that caused a fight between my parents. She didn't understand why my dad wanted me to pursue happiness instead of joining the family business and making as much money as I possibly could."

Ben quickly turned away opening a drawer to retrieve their silverware. "I was never sure of her motives but I knew her pushing for me to be the head of the company is to solely benefit her." After closing the drawer, he handed Holly her plate. "My father wasn't even cold yet when my mother started knocking on my door demanding for me to take his place and make her more money."

"Shit." Holly bit her bottom lip, before remembering the cut. "Ouch. I, uh, don't even know what to say."

"You don't have to say anything. Honestly, I have no idea why I even told you all of this. I never talk about it. Plus, I've lucked out in life. I walk into my practice every day and know I'm following the path that was laid out for me."

Ben had a point. He clearly knew what he wanted out of life, and he wasn't afraid to pursue it. Holly wished she could say the same about herself.

"Now that I know more about you," Holly said, trying to lighten the mood. "I don't feel as creeped out that I'm sitting in your kitchen after only meeting you six hours ago. Eating a steak that might have been poisoned while my dog has decided you're a better human being than I am." She shrugged giving him a side smile.

Ben threw his head back and laughed after taking a bite of his food. "You make me laugh, Holly. I like that about you."

She smiled. "Maybe I should change my day job to be a clown?"

"Nah," he replied. "You're more the sexy librarian type." His eyes sparkled with mischief. "Speaking of that, what about that date you promised me?"

Chapter Six

HOLLY SAT at her desk chewing on a pen cap. Every time she tried to focus on cataloging books, her mind would wander to Ben and their evening together. The events of yesterday still boggled her mind. How had she gone from walking Waffles in the park, to having dinner at the Adonis' house?

She shuddered.

Could she still call Ben her Adonis now that she knew him? A part of her thought it was weird, but then there was another part of her that liked it.

It was rare for someone like Ben to pay attention to someone like her. Okay so he was the reason for her having a chipped tooth and he probably felt guilty. His pity was more than likely the reason for his actions yesterday... Except there was something about Ben that made her want to believe his motives were honest.

Holly idly ran her tongue along her front tooth. Carefully, trying not to irritate her cut, Holly nibbled on her bottom lip, something she did while she was thinking.

When she closed her eyes, she could still feel the gentle touch of Ben's fingertips as he examined her. She couldn't stop herself as she stroked her tongue over the cut. Leave it to her to be hit with a Frisbee, chip a tooth, and then be cared for by one of the hottest men she'd ever seen. Then that same man turned out to be a Richman.

Holly inadvertently cocked her head to the side as she thought. After talking with Ben she couldn't see him as a Richman anymore. Not with the way he loathed Richman Industries.

As Holly sat there at her desk her heart broke for him. It had to be rough living pretty much isolated from your family. She didn't know what it was like to be secluded from her loved ones. Her dad meant the world to her. Then again, Holly's dad was loving and supportive.

After hearing about Ben's mother, she couldn't blame him for distancing himself from her and Richman Industries. Once Ben finished telling her about his mother, all Holly wanted to do was find his mother and punch her in the nose.

Deciding it was best to leave it alone she thought back to Ben. How in the world was a man built to be that good looking?

Over conversation last night, he'd leaned forward on the table showcasing his solid arms. She almost died right then and there. Then there was the way he looked at her. It was unheard of in her book. The intense look in his eyes when he watched her made her heart race.

There was something about him that she couldn't ignore. Lord knows she was trying to. No man like him would ever be interested in a klutzy woman like her. And she knew that.

Sighing, she opened her eyes to get back to work. Might as well forget him. It was better that way.

"You better spill."

Holly jumped at the sound of Mildred her sixty-seven-year-old co-librarian. "What? You almost gave me a heart attack."

"You heard me, missy. There are only two things that can put that type of look on a woman's face. That's a man that knows what he's doing or food. And I don't see any food around you. So, you better start spilling your guts." Mildred pulled the rolling chair from her desk over to where Holly sat. "I've been waiting for the day I can start reliving my life through you. Normally, you've got your head so far up a book, I thought you were a crazy cat lady with a dried, shriveled up hoo-ha. But now, no sirree, Bub. That face right there is a face of a woman who knows she's got a man that can bring her to her knees and vice versa." Mildred waggled her eyebrows.

"Eww. God, Mildred. Do you have to be so crude?" Holly asked before turning away from the nosy woman back to her computer.

"Crude? I wasn't crude. It'd be crude if I asked how long his dong was."

"Mildred!"

"What?" She sat back in her chair crossing her legs. "Can I not ask how your day was yesterday?"

Holly pushed back from her desk turning toward her. "Of course, you can ask how my day was. I did the same thing I do every time I have a half day here. I go home and walk Waffles. That's about it."

Mildred cocked her head to the side. "That it?"

"Yes, that's it." Holly glared at her as laughter gleamed in her eyes. That was one thing she loved about the crazy old coot. She'd be the first one to call you on your bullshit. And, she'd also be the first one to back you up in a fight. She had more fire in her than Holly had seen in anyone.

"Is Waffles the one that's got your cheeks red, and your eyes filled with lust?"

"Mildred, my eyes are not filled with lust!" To her horror, she heard someone clear their throat from behind her. She instantly felt her cheeks heat. *Damn it, Mildred. This better not be old man Robins.*

Doing her best to ignore her embarrassment, Holly turned ready to apologize for shouting and ask the person what she could do for them. As soon as she saw who was standing there, she panicked. "Ben!"

"Is this the young man that's got your panties wet?"

Holly shot her head back to Mildred. "Enough, old woman! Back to your witch's cavern before I sic overdue calls on you." Holly did her best to be firm as her insides were a jumbled mess. Of all the things for Ben to hear, the nonsense out of Mildred's mouth about the state of her panties was not one of them.

Mildred's face lit. "Yup, this must be the man." She held out her hand past Holly. "Name's Mildred. Nice to meet you. I'm glad someone's finally dusted off the ol' cobwebs between Holly's thighs."

Ben roared with laughter as he shook Mildred's hand. "What can I say? I'm very satisfying." He winked.

Mildred turned toward Holly. "You should be lucky I'm not thirty years younger or I'd be jumping on him so fast it'd make both our heads spin."

"You're married," Holly reminded her.

"And?" Mildred winked before departing into the far end of the library.

"Please excuse Mildred, her old age has made her senile. I think we're going to have to look into putting her into a home soon." Holly nervously laughed.

"Huh?" Ben smirked. "That's a shame. I liked her."

"Who doesn't?" Holly sat farther back in her chair before pushing the hair out of her face. "What can I do for you, Ben? What brings you to my neck of the woods?"

Ben's face brightened as he leaned his left hip onto her desk. "I was in the area and I figured I'd stop by and say hi."

She looked at him curiously.

"And, Ripley told me she missed Lord Waffles and wanted a playdate. What do you say to dinner and a movie tonight? Your choice."

"My choice in food or the movie?"

He scrunched his face. "You only get one choice: food or movie. I pick the other."

"How very chivalrous of you."

"I thought so."

"Why are you really here?"

"For the exact reason I just said."

"Your dog wants a playdate?"

"Yeah?"

Holly burst out laughing. "Sure, your pup wants a play-date. You can't even convince yourself."

Ben's face broke out into a ridiculously wide grin. "Well, when you put it that way I want a playdate too."

Holly raised her brow. "Do you want me to get Mildred?"

"Nah, she's undoubtedly too much woman for me."

"You're probably right."

"All joking aside, Grace..." She glared at him. "I had a good time yesterday, apart from hitting you in the face."

"You hit her in the face?" Mildred hollered from behind a bookshelf.

"Get back to work, you old lady!" Holly yelled back.

"You two are no fun."

"If I knew the library was this entertaining I would have spent more time in one rather than on the field." Ben shook his head.

"Of course, because you just had to be a jock, weren't you?"

"You say it like it's a bad thing." At her dirty look, he held his hands in surrender which caused her to narrow her eyes.

Ignoring her, he continued, "Anyway, I had a great time with you yesterday. I can't remember the last time I laughed as much as I did. I figured we could hang out again tonight if you're not doing anything."

"She's not doing anything!"

Holly shot her head to where she heard Mildred's voice.

Low and behold the old coot was peering at them from in between a few books.

"As much as I would like to disagree with Mildred..." Holly turned back toward Ben. "I'm not doing anything. I only planned on working on a short story I'm writing and watching some reruns."

"Perfect." Ben stood bringing his hands together in a clap. "What time do you want to meet?"

Holly leaned over her desk looking at her schedule. "I promised I'd help update our electronic reader catalog tonight. I don't think I'll get out of here until around six thirty. I can run home and get Waffles and meet you at your house at seven fifteen."

"I get off at five today unless there's an emergency. How about I pick up something to eat, grab a movie, and meet you at your house when you get off? That way you won't have to worry about anything else other than going home."

Holly thought about it for a few moments. Did she want Ben to know where she lived? His boyish glee melted her heart. Plus, she hated feeling hurried. Whenever she felt rushed her clumsiness skyrocketed by one thousand percent. It'd be better for Ben to deal with everything, and Holly just show up. "You know what, that sounds pretty good." She took out a piece of paper and wrote down her address. "Here you go. Meet me outside of my apartment building at six forty-five."

"Deal." He reached around Holly grabbing her cell phone that was on her desk. He started fiddling with it before he gave the phone back to her. "My number's in there in case you need to call. I also texted myself, so I have yours as well."

She took her phone putting it in her pocket. "Okay, Ben. I'll see you later."

"Yeah," he said turning away. "I'll see you tonight." He looked over his shoulder and winked. "Maybe then we can talk about how I make your panties wet."

Chapter Seven

BEN SAT OUTSIDE of Holly's apartment building with Ripley by his side. He hadn't known what came over him throughout the day. When it hit lunchtime at the clinic before he knew it, he found himself headed toward the library. No plan in mind, all he knew was he wanted to see Holly.

He was pleasantly surprised when he walked in on the conversation Holly and her coworker were having. He thought he'd hit the jackpot.

Mildred was a hoot. Her foul mouth and crude remarks only made him like her more. It was to his advantage they were talking about him. Plus, how could he go wrong when wet panties were involved?

The mortification on Holly's face amused him beyond measure. You'd have thought she'd been caught with her pants around her ankles with her ass up in the air.

Instantly his lower half stirred to life as he bit back a groan.

Ripley sensing the change in her owner, leaned against his leg placing her head on his lap. Her ice blue eyes looked to him for guidance. "Sorry, girl. Your dad has somehow went and lost his mind."

Ripley whined.

"You're still my number one girl, Rip. Promise." Ripley's response was a tongue flop onto his right knee. Ben scratched her head ruffling her fur. "What would I do without you?"

"You'd probably be sitting out here talking to yourself." Ben looked from Ripley to see Holly making her way down the sidewalk.

Damn, she was beautiful. She wore a fitted long sleeve hunter green top with black pants that hugged her hips. Her hair was pulled on top of her head in a neatly placed bun. From what he could tell, she barely wore any makeup, if any at all. Holly was such a natural beauty and the fact she didn't see herself that way made his desire for her stronger.

Everything about her screamed lust, from her ample hips that begged for his hands to caress, to her incredible chest. Then there was the way she sashayed her hips from side to side as she walked. If he didn't know better, he'd have sworn she was trying to seduce him.

"Were you waiting here long?" she asked, reaching the steps to the lobby door.

"No," he choked out, before clearing his throat. *Get yourself together.*

"Hi, Ripley." Holly bent at her waist to greet his dog giving him a perfect view of her delectable ass. He had to control himself from reaching out and squeezing it. Closing his eyes, he fought the images of her bent over as he took her from behind. He let out a tiny groan.

"You okay?"

His eyes shot open. "Yeah." He shook his head. "Yeah, no, I'm fine."

"You looked a little weird there for a second."

He held up the take-out bag. "It's the food. I brought Chinese and the smell is making my mouth water. I'm starving."

"I didn't know food did it for you," Holly joked.

"Oh, Grace, many things do it for me." He held open the

lobby door for Holly to walk in, once again giving him a perfect view of her ass. He held onto Ripley's leash and the food as they made their way to the elevator.

Once they were inside, Ripley couldn't contain her excitement. She trotted to be right next to Holly. When Holly turned to face him, she hadn't seen the leash which caused her to stumble into Ben's arms. Thankfully, he had quick reflexes.

"And you say Grace isn't the name for you?" he joked while righting Holly.

She brushed her shirt down before looking at him. "It's not." Holly lifted her chin and made her way inside the elevator. Damn, she's adorable when she's stubborn. It only made him like her even more.

"I live on the third floor." She pressed the button. When the doors closed, she descended to her knees to scratch Ripley. There she went again being perfect.

When the elevator door opened, they made their way to her apartment. When she opened the door, Waffles came running toward her. He started wagging his butt as fast as he could, while bark-whining his excitement that his mom was home.

"There's my big boy! Who's mommy's big boy?" she said as she eagerly welcomed Waffles into her arms.

Within seconds of their greeting, Waffles looked around Holly and stared at Ben and Ripley, whom at his command was sitting patiently at his side. Waffles took off in a full speed pursuit toward him and Ripley. Once his little legs made it to Ben, he jumped on him demanding pets.

Holly faced the commotion. "What am I chopped liver now?"

Ben laughed as he greeted Waffles. "What can I say, Waffles is a man's man."

"Whatever," Holly huffed before throwing her bag onto the nearby table. When Waffles turned his attention from him to Ripley, Ben took the time to examine Holly's home.

It was a relatively small apartment. The front door led right into the living room. The walls were a light shade of blue, with inspirational quotes that were framed and scattered all around. There was a decent sized couch in the middle of the room that had seen better days, with a secondhand coffee table in front of it. Everything appeared pretty tame. Which surprised him, Holly seemed anything but tame. Looking toward his right, he noticed a tiny kitchen that only had room for the essentials. Once again there were inspirational quotes on the walls accompanied by odd knickknacks.

Continuing his scan, he made his way into the middle of the living room turning toward the opposite wall. That's where he saw family photos. Well, he assumed they were family photos. In the pictures Holly stood next to an older man who looked remarkably like her. There was also a photo of Holly and the same older gentleman releasing what looked like butterflies into a sunrise.

"That was on what would have been my mother's fiftieth birthday. My dad and I wanted to do something special, so we released butterflies in her honor," Holly remarked, moving to stand right next to him.

"That's a wonderful way to honor someone," he said, thinking about his own father.

"We thought so too." Holly reached to pat Waffles on the head before she quickly turned away from him making her way over to the front door. She then toed off her black flats before slipping her feet into flip-flops that were placed by the door. She removed the elastic from her hair letting it fall naturally. The brief head shake she did to make her hair free rocketed right to his groin. *Oh, fuck!*

"Make yourself at home. I need to take Waffles out." She reached for his leash causing the little guy to jump around with excitement.

"Let me," Ben said before taking the leash from Holly's hand. "How about you set out some plates and put in the movie." Right now, he needed some distance from Holly. Whenever he was around her his body lost its mind and he forgot how to be a rational human being. He desperately needed some fresh air.

"You sure?" she asked, worrying her bottom lip. Yeah, he was sure... He needed to fight the urge to push her against the wall and nibble on that lip.

"You know where everything is and I'm sure us men can handle a little potty break." He bent to Waffles ruffling his neck before hooking his collar. "You gotta go potty, little guy?"

Waffles barked in excitement before jumping in circles causing Ben to laugh. "I'll take that as a yes."

Ben nearly ran Waffles out of the apartment and outside. As soon as the air hit his skin, he took a deep breath filling his lungs with the fresh Holly free air he needed.

The leash pulling on his hands brought him back to reality. He started walking Waffles around the front of the building waiting for him to do his business. "Did you know your mom is something else?" Ben asked, looking at Waffles who was on a mission to find the perfect spot.

"There's something about her that I can't put my finger on, but I can't get enough of it." Waffles ignored him as he found the spot he'd been looking for and started doing his business.

Once Waffles finished, he looked at Ben then back at the grass, then once again to Ben. "Damn. I guess Holly was right. You demand for it to be picked up right away." Ben barked out a quick laugh. "Well shit, you really do think of yourself as a King, now don't you?"

A few minutes later they returned to Holly's apartment. There were two plates set at the coffee table with two glasses of water.

Holly walked out of the kitchen with two dog bowls in her hands. "I saw you had Ripley's food in a little baggie, so I made her dinner too. I hope you don't mind I added chicken broth to it. When I was adding it to Waffles' food, Ripley looked at me like she was starved and started to whine."

Ben rolled his eyes. "Don't let her manipulate you, but yes, it's fine."

"I'm glad." She placed the food bowls at opposite ends of the living room before turning back to Ben. "You never know if there might be an altercation and I am pretty sure Ripley would kick Waffles' ass."

Ben's face brightened as he laughed. "You're probably right, and that's good animal parenting. I wish half of my clients were like you."

Holly smiled at him before she placed the Chinese food containers on the coffee table and sat down. "Everything is ready when you are." She grabbed her plate and started adding bits of food to it.

He sat beside her doing the same. "Did you put the movie in?" he asked, leaning back once his plate was full.

"Heck no!" Her eyebrows shot to the ceiling. "I do *not* do jumpy horror movies. Now serial killer, stabby movies, I'm fine with, but that crap you tried to pull, no way. Nope." She shook her head.

Ben couldn't help but smile. Even if his plan of scaring her into his arms didn't work out, her over-animated personality warmed him.

"Fine scaredy cat. What did you pick instead?" he asked, reaching for the remote.

"Some random comedy." Her eyes screamed with mischief as she placed a forkful of noodles into her mouth.

Ignoring it, he pressed play. A few minutes into the movie he groaned. "Grace, you've got to be kidding me, isn't this the vampire movie where they sparkle or some shit like that?"

Holly burst out laughing before grabbing the remote from Ben. "That's what you get for trying to scare me." Her face beamed as she maneuvered around the streaming program before picking a movie they would both enjoy. She placed the remote on the coffee table and started to eat again.

"You don't use chopsticks?" he asked.

"You've seen how clumsy I am, right? There is no way I'd get through a meal using chopsticks unscathed." She sat back on the sofa pulling her knees under her.

"You're right, Grace." He plopped a dumpling in his mouth with a chopstick smirking.

"Jerk." She jutted her chin toward the screen. "Watch the movie."

As the movie played in the background, Ben found himself inching closer to Holly's side of the couch. In his defense, Waffles and Ripley both joined them on the sofa pushing him closer to Holly.

He wasn't complaining, though. Instead, this gave him a better opportunity to watch her reactions. Holly became completely engrossed in the movie. She was on the edge of the cushion with her full attention on the screen. Her enjoyment in the scenes was contagious. Whenever there was a funny moment, she'd laugh as if she was the only one in the room. She had absolutely zero cares in the world.

His heart skipped.

Holly was genuine and in today's day and age that was a rarity. He focused his attention back to the movie and watched idly as he made sure to pet each of the dogs by his side that kept demanding his attention.

When the movie finally ended, he turned toward Holly. She glowed. The light reflecting from the screen illuminated her face, highlighting her features.

How the fuck was she so beautiful?

"Thank you for coming over," she whispered, staring at him. "It was a lot of fun."

"It was fun," he agreed. As the shadows danced on her lips, he saw the cut.

He watched as her tongue slipped out wetting her bottom lip. He couldn't hold back another second more. He leaned closer to her. When he heard her breath hitch, he whispered, "Holly..."

Her eyes widened as her breath quickened. He couldn't stop himself as he placed his hand behind her neck.

"Wh-what?" she stammered.

Ben looked into her eyes. "I'm going to kiss you."

Chapter Eight

THE AIR in the room thickened as Holly stared at Ben. Their lips only were millimeters apart from each other.

Could she kiss him? Her head felt light as she tried to analyze everything. Men like Ben were not supposed to want to kiss a frumpy, klutzy woman like her. Were they?

No.

Try telling that to Ben, though. Even in the darkness of the room Holly could see his eyes full of lust.

This was her do or die moment. Did she try to make sense why this Adonis wanted her or should she throw caution to the wind and go for it?

Even if he never spoke to her after tonight shouldn't she live her life? Or maybe she should live the life of the women she wanted to write about?

The sensual, sexy, confident women. The type of woman Holly always wanted to be. Plus, who was she to look a gift horse in the mouth?

That's it. She made her decision.

Throwing her arms behind Ben's neck, she launched herself into his arms. The moment her lips connected with his, the tension exploded. Throwing all her reservations aside,

Holly kissed him like she was starved and his lips were her the only food she'd ever get again.

Ben welcomed every second of it as he wrapped his arm around her waist. He effortlessly leaned back onto the couch bringing her body on top of his, keeping her body molded to his.

Whoa Holly nearly choked on the thrill. She'd *never* be caught dead actually being on top of someone, but with Ben it was different. She wanted more.

She needed more. Thank fuck Ben must have read her mind again since his hands moved to her ass, squeezing it. He pulled her hips down as he thrust upward grinding their bodies together.

The friction rocked through her body sending earth-shattering sensations everywhere. She could already feel her slickness as Ben's member pushed against her apex.

"Fuck," he groaned, as he tore his lips from hers. "God damn, Holly." Ben moved toward her neck nibbling and sucking her skin.

"Not yet." Holly's breathy voice echoed through the room as she threw her head back giving him better access. She might not be super experienced in the lovemaking department, but she was well versed in her romance novels. Her mind raced to recall all of the information she'd read over the years that turned her on. And Ben kissing down her neck was one of them.

Ben's hand moved to her hips pushing her down harder onto his dick. "Fuck, I want you, Holly. I want you bad."

"Me too. Me too."

"Off." He grabbed the hem on her shirt pulling it from her body and throwing it behind him. Once she was topless, his hands moved to her lace covered breasts. "I knew you'd overfill my hands," he said more to her chest than her.

Mentally saying 'fuck it', Holly reached behind her unhooking her bra in one fell swoop. She tossed it behind her, doing her best to ignore the telltale sign of two dogs racing to play tug of war.

Ben's groan brought her attention back to him, though. He placed the palms of his hands on her back as he righted himself kissing down her exposed chest.

The moment he took her right nipple into his mouth, her nerve endings came alive. Ben's warm breath and whiskers were almost too much to handle.

"How are you this perfect?" he asked into her skin.

"Less talking, more sucking." She thrust her chest into his face which he gladly accepted. Ben's tongue circled her nipple before dragging it across her skin seeking out the other. He pulled that one into his mouth giving it the same treatment as the other.

Ben trailed his hands from her back to her legs wrapping them around his waist before moving her entirely onto her back. He started peppering hot kisses along her skin before making his way to her lips once more.

At least Holly wasn't the only one hungry.

She moved her hands to the hem of Ben's button-down shirt, letting her fingertips caress against his skin. Feeling his heat invigorated her. She could touch the bottom of his abs.

She wanted more.

She needed to count them. If this was her one shot at being with a Greek God, she might as well go for broke. She quickly thought back to a scene in a dark erotic novel she'd only finished a few days ago. With all the courage she could muster, she grabbed onto the bottom his shirt and pulled with all her might.

Nothing happened.

Not one button popped.

Holly opened her eyes to see Ben's amused face staring back at her.

At first she was mortified, but Ben's gentle kiss on the tip of her nose melted her heart. "Do you need some help, Grace?"

That name. Holly's eyes narrowed at him.

Before she could chastise him, though, he captured her lips with his. As she opened her mouth to say something his tongue slipped inside, making her forget her retort.

After a moment he pulled away and looked down at her. He straightened his back reaching for his shirt. Quickly he ripped his shirt open sending buttons flying across the room. "This is what you wanted, right?" That dang half smile appeared on his face as his eyes danced.

Holly was about to maim him for making fun of her, but the sight of his body made her lose all coherent thought. Was he always hiding such a perfect body under his clothes?

Holly touched his skin with her fingertips. When she caressed down his abs his muscles tightened, causing a hiss to escape from him.

Her index finger followed the dusting of hair that led toward his lower half.

Ben held perfectly still as he let Holly explore his body. Thank God, because right now she wanted to memorize every inch of him.

When Holly reached his belt, she looked into his eyes silently asking for permission.

With a slight nod from him, she brought both her hands to his belt. Taking a deep breath, she undid the buckle and unbuttoned his pants.

Quickly she pushed his pants and boxers down in one hurried move causing Ben's cock to break free nearly hitting her in the face.

"Holy McJeebers. How do you walk around with that thing?" Her eyes widened as she examined him. *This* was the kind of dick she'd only read about in her novels.

She looked at Ben's eyes once again only to see his amusement.

"Very carefully," he replied.

Holly looked back at his member and saw the tiny drop of moisture at the tip.

Could she? Hell yeah, she could. This was her one moment to shine. She quickly stuck out her tongue lapping at the bead.

When she heard him groan, she knew she'd done something right. When she went back to fully take him into her mouth, a hand fisting into her hair stopped her.

"Not this time, Grace. If you so much as look at my dick again I'm gonna explode all over your face."

Holly didn't see anything wrong with that. This was her ultimate fantasy come to life.

"Naughty girl," he remarked with a tsk. "This time I want to be inside of you when I come. We can talk about other options later."

This time?

There wasn't going to be anything other than a *this time*. This was a one-night stand.

Holly knew that. She wasn't stupid.

Ben would make an excuse to leave once they were done and she'd never hear from him again. She'd already resigned herself to accepting that.

She might as well enjoy every ounce of it she could. However, before she could bring him back to her mouth, Ben scooped her into his arms effortlessly.

"Bedroom?"

Ben's skin was on fire and he loved every fucking second of it.

"I'm too heavy, you Neanderthal!" Holly screamed, clinging to his shoulders like she was going to fall.

"Are you calling me weak?" he asked, before nipping at the skin on her neck.

"Ouch. Jerk. No, I'm not calling you weak I'm trying to save your back."

He smacked her ass. "The next time you say it, I'll do it again, sweetheart. Tell me where your bedroom is." The same spot he smacked he then squeezed.

Holly's whole body tightened against him, as he squeezed harder. "The only other room in the apartment."

Ben looked around and saw one door. With his destination acquired he started toward the room. Unfortunately for him, he forgot about the two eager energetic dogs at his feet.

When he was only one foot from the bed, Waffles ran in between his legs.

"Shit!" Since Ben's pants were already half-way down his legs, he wasn't able to counter the obstacle. His only option was to toss Holly onto the bed, and fall down nearly onto of her.

"Hey! Gently. Whoa." Holly pushed her hair from her face.

"Blame Waffles." Ben tried to lift one of his legs onto the bed when he felt a tug.

When he looked he saw Lord Waffles attached to his jeans pulling.

Holly must have seen it too, because she burst out laughing. Waffles, Stop!" The dog didn't flinch. Instead he tugged harder.

Ben looked back at Holly who had tears in her eyes from laughing so hard. He couldn't help but laugh himself as he yanked the material from the dog before pulling them off and tossing them onto the Corgi's head. The little devil fought his jeans for a moment before taking them into the living room as if he'd won a prize.

An ear-to-ear grin appeared on his face as he looked back at Holly. "I knew sex with you would be entertaining."

Another laugh escaped Holly, making her breasts bounce. That had heat running through Ben again.

With his dick at attention, he pumped himself once. Twice. And as he was about to do it again, the room fell silent. As he looked into Holly's eyes, he knew his lust mirrored hers.

Then the devil bit her bottom lip causing a new wave of desire to wash over him. He crawled toward her on the bed. "You've got too many clothes on," he growled.

"Are you going to do something about it?"

Fuck yes, he was going to do something about it.

His eyes scanned her body. Her curves enticed him, and the roundness of her soft stomach made him want to kiss it. He let out a strangled breath as he placed his hands on her black pants and slowly started to bring them down her legs.

Once they were gone, he looked at her. Really looked at her. From her thick thighs all the way to her lust filled eyes.

He wanted her.

He wanted her so bad he could taste it.

Ben hooked his thumbs into her panties and slowly peeled them from her body leaving her completely naked.

Holy shit.

Holly was fucking beautiful.

As he watched her, he saw worry cloud her eyes. The moment she tried to hide herself with her hands, he gently held her arms down. "Shhh, let me show you."

Ben needed to make sure Holly understood how beautiful he thought she was.

Her body tensed as he moved his face toward her apex, inhaling deeply as her scent made his mouth water.

"Ben..." Worry clouded her voice.

"I've got you." Before Holly could protest further he used his shoulders to spread her thighs.

When he took his first taste, her flavor exploded on his tongue. *Fuck him.*

He'd tasted many women in his life but none were as sweet as Holly. He couldn't get enough.

Within seconds Holly's hands were at the back of his head

pushing him deeper into her. There was something about a woman taking charge that drove him wild just as it did when she jumped him on the couch. He kept going until her legs snapped around his head and her body started to shake.

"Yes, oh yes. Don't stop."

Never.

Ben pulled her clit into his mouth lightly biting down. He was instantly rewarded with her moisture flooding his mouth.

That is how you satisfy a woman.

He pulled away from her core as Holly laid limp on the bed her chest rising rapidly as she tried to catch her breath.

He couldn't stop himself from licking his lips.

"Please tell me you have a condom?" Ben braced himself on his knees as he looked down at her.

Without opening her eyes, Holly lazily pointed to her nightstand.

He laughed as he leaned over her body opening the drawer.

Holy shit.

Ben's heart stopped the moment he saw her little collection of toys. Quickly, he made a mental note to remember they were there. They were definitely going to come out and play one day.

But, not today.

Pushing aside the images of Holly using them, he put the condom on and wrapped her legs around his waist. He then brought himself to her entrance.

"Grace, my Grace, are you ready for me?" he asked slowly inching his way inside of her.

There was a hint of fear in Holly's eyes, but there was also desire. She gave him a nod.

Ben looked down at their joining, trying his best to control himself. Her light dusting of brown hair ignited him. He loved she wasn't bare like most women these days. Instead, she was lightly trimmed.

Fucking perfect!

He watched closely as he inched his way inside of her center. Clearly, he was going too slow. When he reached the halfway point, Holly shocked the shit out of him by lifting her hips, helping to accommodate him.

"Fuck, you're huge," she groaned.

Damn that nearly unmanned him. Clenching his teeth, he closed his eyes trying to think of anything else other than the clumsy, outspoken, funny, beautiful woman beneath him.

Once Ben felt himself completely inside her, he stilled letting her adjust. Truth was he needed the few seconds to regroup himself. Her heat coupled with her tightness drove him to the brink.

"I'm ready," she announced, encouraging him to move.

Holy shit. This was perfect. He wanted to burn this imagine into his head for the rest of his life. The way Holly felt, the way she looked. Damn he never wanted to forget this. He'd never seen anyone more beautiful in his life.

He needed to get a grip. He looked at their connection. Slowly he removed himself only leaving the tip, before thrusting fully into her.

Ben's whole body tightened. He wanted to take this slow, build her next release, but she felt too hot, too tight, too perfect.

"Next time. Next time I'll go slow." Ben started thrusting harder and faster. Making sure to reach between them pinching her nub. When Holly began to shake he knew she was on the brink. He deepened his movements as he quickened his assault on her clit.

"Now. Holly. Fuckin' come now!"

He didn't have to wait for an audible response. Holly's walls tightened like a vise grip around him. She shot off the bed, as her second orgasm of the night took hold. He reached for her hips pulling them onto his dick, bringing them as close as possible. Holding her there he stilled, releasing himself.

His own orgasm shook through his body.

His breathing became ragged as sweat marred his body. He'd never felt this good being with someone before. Placing his hands around Holly's waist, he brought her on top of him. He then flipped them over so he was on his back. "Fucking perfect," he said.

Holly laid her head on his chest, her own breathing out of control. "I'd say." She started circling his nipple idly with her fingertip. "When I've read scenes like this in books I'd used to roll my eyes and say the author had an overactive imagination." Holly turned her head to look up at Ben. "Guess I was wrong?"

Chapter Nine

IT'D BEEN a total of three days since Holly heard from Ben. Looking at the clock on her desk she felt the familiar ache she'd grown accustomed to. Seventy-six hours twenty-five minutes and thirty-four seconds, to be more exact.

She shook her head. She didn't know why she cared, it's not like she didn't know this would be the outcome. Ben had been her once in a lifetime chance and she was happy she took it.

Holly pulled out her phone and looked at the screen.

Nothing.

It still hurt, though.

She couldn't quite wrap her head around Ben leaving her high and dry. Especially, after the way he'd treated her throughout the night and the following morning.

This is what you get for dreaming...

After what Holly could only describe as the best sex of her life, he'd held her and softly caressed her skin for hours. Once she'd fallen asleep, he woke her with his expertly skilled head between her thighs. It wasn't just the sex, though.

Ben took care of her in the way you would a serious lover. He'd also surprised her by taking Waffles out, cooking a full-blown breakfast, and his goodbye kiss as he made his way off to work reeked of promises of what was yet to come.

You're such an idiot.

"Why the long face?" Mildred inquired, tearing Holly from her thoughts.

Damn it. Not now.

Holly did her best to keep her tears at bay. She hated feeling this vulnerable. It wasn't like she didn't know he wasn't really into her. She was a convenience for him. A horny man will always go for the easy option and that's what she was.

Nothing more.

Clearing her throat Holly looked at Mildred. "I don't have a long face." She winced when she heard the fakeness in her voice.

"Honey, I may be an old coot, but I can tell when a girl's gotten her heart broken. What did that hunk of burnin' love do? Want me to tear his balls off and make him eat them?"

There was a seriousness in Mildred's tone Holly had never heard before. "Mildred, you are something else." Holly laughed for the first time in days.

"I'm like a fairy godmother or something like that. Why don't you tell me what happened and I'll make it all better? Or if I can't I'll call in a favor and they will." Mildred winked.

"I don't know if I want any of your favors being connected to me in any way." Holly flipped her phone over checking to see if Ben had texted her.

Her shoulders dropped when there were no messages or calls. *Buck up, Holly. You had mind blowing sex with a sex god. Put that checkmark in the, "you are freakin' awesome" column and move on.*

Mildred placed her hand on Holly's arm drawing her attention. "Seriously, Holly, do you want to talk about it?"

Holly should talk about it, as soon as she spilled her guts she'd feel better right?

Screw it. "You know, Mildred, I have no idea what

happened. But I am not going to let it get me down. If Ben wanted a quick roll in the hay, that's okay because I got some earth-shattering orgasms out of it. It doesn't matter to me if I haven't seen hide nor hair of him in three days." She looked at the clock on her desk. "Seventy-six hours thirty-two minutes and ten seconds. It doesn't bother me one bit."

"Sure, it doesn't," Mildred remarked, moving a hair back from Holly's crazy rant. "Men are pigs, honey. And in the end if you had yourself a good time, right on, and more power to you. However, if he physically hurt you or did something malicious let me at him."

"No. It wasn't anything like that. It was more of a, we started a friendship that could possibly turn out to be pretty cool, then we slept together and he left. That's it. Nothing more. Nothing less."

Mildred sat there for a few minutes observing her. "If it was nothing more than why are you bothered?" she asked, gently.

Why was she bothered? That was the million-dollar question. "It's not that I'm particularly bothered," she answered. "It's more of a, I knew this was going to happen, but it still stings, you know?"

Mildred nodded. "Well let's focus on something else." From the pocket of her long skirt Mildred pulled out the pen and pad she always carried with her. "Can you tell me more about the earth-shattering orgasms, please?"

Holly shifted back into her seat more and burst out laughing.

"You *are* something else, Mildred. That's why I love you."

"Aww, you love me?" She placed her hand on her chest. "Be still my heart. But honey, I have to tell you I'm a married woman, so you can't go using me as your rebound."

Holly rolled her eyes. "Damn. Well then, what's a girl to do?"

"If I were you, I'd march my butt to his front door and ask

him what his problem is."

"I would never." Her eyes widened.

"Why not?" Mildred asked. "There is no rule that says a woman can't pursue a man. Even if she didn't want to pursue him, she could damn well ask him what his problem is."

"And have him laugh in my face? I think not."

"So, what if he laughs in your face? You can sock him right in the nose." Mildred threw her fist into the air.

Holly thought about it as Mildred pretended to fight the air. Could she really confront Ben? Would she want to?

"Here's the thing," Mildred continued. "I've known you for a while. I also know you overanalyze until your head explodes. You can either confront him and take the bull by the horns or you can sit here twiddling your thumbs until your mind has come up with a million different scenarios. All of which are probably wrong."

Holly leaned into the back of her chair. Mildred did have a point. If her past relationships or lack thereof told her anything, it would be she'd overanalyze every possible outcome or situation for days. But then again, she knew sleeping with Ben was probably a one-time deal. Why would she keep pushing it?

Mildred stood, putting her notepad and pen back into her pocket. "I think you should do it. Right now. You should get up from that chair and go confront him. His answer might not be one that you want, but in the end, you'll know. You'll be able to walk back in here with your head held high."

She was right.

"And, if it's really bad, I'll spend the next few hours in the Violent Crimes section getting pointers."

Holly couldn't help but laugh. Leave it to Mildred to go to the extreme. Outlandish as Mildred might be, she was right. This was Holly's chance to stand up for herself and all other women who've been wronged.

I am woman, so hear me roar.

Holly grabbed her purse and yelled to Mildred, "I'll be back in a little while. Cover for me."

"Always."

God Damnit!

Ben's nostrils flared as he did his best to rein in his emotions. Right now, he paced the exam room trying to stop himself from pulling out his own fucking hair.

"Benjamin, I don't understand why you refuse to give up this silly dream and work in your rightful place," his mother Barbra asked, crossing her arms over her chest.

"Why are you even here?" Ben stopped pacing and glared at her.

"To get you to do the right thing."

Ben mentally ordered himself to calm down. He'd spent the last two days up to his eyeballs in back to back emergency surgeries. Unfortunately, two dogs had been hit by cars within forty-five minutes of each other. Both operations took over six hours.

Then, when he thought he'd gotten a moment to catch his breath, he'd gotten a call from his buddy, Will, down at the police station. They'd saved a kitten that'd been poisoned by a local troublemaker. Thankfully, the police were able to catch the punk, but the poor kitten was in rough shape. At twelve weeks old, the poor guy's body didn't have the strength or ability to fight.

Ben spent the whole day trying to save the little guy.

As of right now though, because of Ben's quick actions, they were all on the road to recovery. But, he hadn't had a moment to himself. The few hours he'd slept were in the cot he kept in his office when he wanted to stay close to a critical patient. His phone died on day two and now to top off all of his frustrations, his bitch of a mother was here once again demanding that he take his rightful place at the head of Richman Industries.

Rightful place. Fuck off.

"I *am* doing the right thing," he snapped. *Take it easy,* he told himself. His mother thrived on confrontation.

"You think playing with these flea-ridden mangy *creatures* is the correct choice for you?"

Don't get angry. Don't get angry. "Yes, *mother*. This is the right choice for me."

As his mother opened her mouth to respond the exam room door flew open.

"Why have you been ignoring me?!" Holly stormed into the room with his receptionist Stacy, hot on her tail.

"I'm so sorry, Dr. Ben. She came in and refused to wait. When she heard your voice she ran in here," Stacy tried to explain.

"It's fine, Stacy. I'll take it from here." This was the last thing Ben wanted to deal with. Holly meeting his mother was something he wanted to avoid inevitably if he could.

"Who is this..." His mother looked Holly up and down. "Peasant?"

Holly's head shot toward his mother. "Who are you calling a peasant, you old hag?"

Holy shit. The fire coming from Holly made him hot.

"Excuse me, young lady?" His mother's eyebrows shot to the ceiling. "I do believe you did not refer to me as an old hag."

Holly mimicked his mother beautifully as she looked her up and down. "Actually, I did. But right now, this doesn't concern you." Holly turned her attention to Ben. Her eyes showing more fire than he'd ever seen. However, when he really looked at her, he saw pain if even just a small hint of it.

"Ben." He could see the panic and vulnerability in her.

"Young lady, you need to leave right now. I am having a private conversation with my son, and you are *not* invited."

Holly's eyes widened as her faced paled. "Oh, shit."

"Why am I not surprised a woman of your stature would also have a filthy mouth?" his mother remarked.

"Knock it off," Ben demanded, stepping in when he saw Holly physically swallow.

Barbra turned from Holly and stared at him for a moment before her eyes narrowed. "Benjamin, you have got to be kidding me. Have you really stooped so low as to associate yourself with this *woman*?" she asked, shaking her head. "Please tell me she isn't pregnant? I can't tell with all the weight around her middle."

"Knock it the fuck off, Barbra," Ben spat. From the corner of his eye he could see Holly start to slowly back away toward the door.

He pointed at her. "Don't move." Turning back toward his mother, he glared. "Don't ever fucking say shit like that to or about Holly. So help me God, it will not end well for you."

"You admit you're sleeping with her then?" she asked, not even phased by Ben's words.

"We're not," Holly squeaked.

"Oh, thank God. I was worried he'd muddy our family with you." Barbra glanced at Holly.

"Get the fuck out!" Ben ordered. "By the way, I *am* sleeping with her and I will continue sleeping with her. I'll also make sure to come in her so many times she has no choice but to get knocked up."

His mother gasped before placing her hand on her chest. "I did not raise you like this."

"You didn't raise me at all."

"If your father were here he'd be ashamed of you."

Ben's eyes hardened as he clenched his teeth. "Do *not* bring dad into this."

"I'm only speaking the truth. He'd be so disappointed in you. First, you refuse to give up this silly play job and come work for Richman Industries, and now you're sleeping with *her*."

"Stacy," Ben yelled, calling for his receptionist.

She came running into the room a moment later. "Yes?"

"Can you do me a favor and call the police station and ask for Will? I need him to remove my mother from the property." Stacy's eyes widened before shooting to his mother.

"Well of all things," Barbra said, she gathered her belongings in a huff. "I don't know what's gotten into you." She turned her glare from Ben to Holly. "This is not acceptable behavior for a Richman. This is not the last time you'll be seeing me, Benjamin." She walked toward the door stopping in front of Holly. "And this will *not* be the last time I'll be seeing you either."

His mother stormed out of the exam room leaving him, Holly, and Stacy in her wake.

Taking a deep breath, Ben looked at his receptionist. "Can you do me a favor and hold my next appointment for a few minutes? I want to talk to Holly."

"No need to," Holly squeaked. "I'll see myself out."

"Don't move a muscle," he demanded, causing her to plant her feet on the ground.

"Sure thing, Doc." Stacy closed the door behind her leaving Holly and Ben alone.

Holly broke the awkward silence first. "I'm sorry for barging in here."

"Don't," he said, bracing himself on the exam table. The same exam table he'd placed Holly on the day they'd met. "I'm sorry you had the misfortune of meeting my mother."

"She seems wonderful," Holly scoffed.

"Sure, wonderful is a word you can use." He swiped a hand across his face before turning toward Holly. "Before we get into what just happened, I want to say sorry for not calling you."

"Don't worry about it. It hasn't even crossed my mind." Holly worried her bottom lip before straightening her chin.

"Is that so?" The corners of his mouth lifted.

She looked away briefly. "I thought about it once or twice."

"Then you only stormed in here to what?"

"Well, you see..." She looked around the room. "Okay, fine. You caught me. I wanted to know why you disappeared. I mean, I know I'm probably not the best lay." She looked away. "Before we slept together I thought we were, I don't know, starting some weird friendship or something. Plus, Waffles really likes you. I wanted to know what happened, so I can be honest with him when he demands for your presence." She shrugged.

Her vulnerability warmed him. It also made him realize he'd gotten under her skin just as much as she had gotten under his.

In two swift steps, Ben was in front of her. His fingers threaded through her hair as he devoured her mouth. He'd missed her lips the past three days. Once he had his fill, he pulled away from her, resting his forehead on hers. "I'm sorry," he said again. "I planned on calling you tonight and begging you to give me another chance."

When she opened her eyes he saw doubt there which killed him. "I'm serious. The day I left your apartment I had two separate dogs hit by cars."

She gasped.

"Then when I finally got that under control a friend at the police station brought in a kitten that had been poisoned. The only spare moments I had were spent sleeping on the cot in my office."

His eyes closed remembering the events of the last few days. He loved his job, but sometimes it took a toll on him.

"Did they all make it?" she whispered. When Ben opened his eyes, he saw the tears cascading down Holly's cheeks. Right then and there, he knew this was the woman for him. He used the pad of his thumb to wipe away the tears. "Would you like to meet them?"

She nodded.

Ben reached for her hand before pulling her into the back room and made their way over to the kennels. "This is Murphy. He's been a long-time patient of mine. His leg got pretty messed up, but he'll be fine. I'm going to release him to his owners tomorrow."

Holly nodded, keeping silent. Ben could see the tears still in her eyes. "Over here is Red, a Blue Tick Beagle. He didn't fare as well. We had to fix quite a bit of internal bleeding, but he's on the up and up now. I'm going to keep him here a few more days, but I'm positive he will make a full recovery. His owners have been in every day to see him."

"That's wonderful," Holly whispered, never tearing her eyes from Red.

"Would you like to meet the kitten?"

"It made it?" Ben heard the hope in her voice.

"Yes, baby. He made it." Ben gently pulled her to one of the cages by the wall. Pointing to the one in front of them. "This is him. He's improved tenfold, but he still has a little twitch in his head. It's nothing I'm too concerned about. I've done everything I can to flush the poison from his body. His last blood test results showed all the poison is gone. He might have lasting neurological issues, though. I'm waiting to see if the twitch is going to be a permanent side effect or if it will fade in time." He put his fingers through the bars and the little orange and white kitten slowly moved to the bars rubbing them. He'd improved remarkably over the last day, Ben could even hear his purr through all the noise of the clinic.

"He's so friendly," Holly announced. "Can I pet him?"

"Sure thing, baby."

Holly placed her finger through the openings, and the kitten instantly started to play with her. "He's so cute."

Ben nodded. "Not as cute as you," he announced, with a cheesy grin which made Holly laugh.

"I see you've been busy."

"I have. Holly, I'm sorry for not calling you and telling you what was going on. After the first surgery I was going to text you, but I realized my phone died. I don't have my charger here. As soon as I got a free minute, I planned on running home to get it."

Holly relaxed as she played with the kitten. "It's okay, Ben."

"It's not. I don't want you thinking I did a hit and run. It wasn't like that for me." He placed his fingers under her chin making her look at him. "I want to date you."

Holly's breath hitched. She tried to mask it by moving her attention back to the kitten. "What happens to him once he's healed?" she asked.

Ben chuckled at her avoidance. Going back to the kitten himself he touched the bars. "I don't know. If he ends up with the twitch he'll be considered a special needs animal. Shelters won't take him. Then again, I haven't really thought about it. I want to keep him here as long as possible to make sure—"

"I want him," she interrupted. "I mean, I've taken care of cats before. I loved Princess Huffle Stuffle with my whole heart." She wiggled her fingers getting the kitten's attention. "Do you want to come home with me, Twitch?"

Ben's heart nearly exploded in his chest. The tenderness Holly had for animals was astonishing. It then clicked. "Did you just name him Twitch?"

"Yeah," she answered. "It's kinda fitting don't you think?"

Ben looked at her as a sweet smile appeared on his face. "Yeah, I think it is." He took the pen from his pocket and under the line that said owner on the paper hanging on the cage he wrote Holly. Along with Pet's name: Twitch.

He turned back toward Holly, her face beamed with excitement right before her eyes narrowed. "You're going to come in me so many times I have no choice but to get knocked up?"

"Uh, about that."

Chapter Ten

WAFFLES SAT in the back of Holly's car as she drove to her father, Henry's house. She knew bringing Waffles along would lessen the blow of not seeing her dad in a few days. Holly had made a habit of visiting him every three days, minimum, but with the recent events she was ashamed to admit it'd been almost five.

Turning into the driveway she glanced into the rearview mirror. "Waffles, get your nose out of the grocery bags!"

Waffles eyed her for a moment before he continued his quest.

"So help me God, Waffles. I will turn this car around and drop you off at home." Hoping Waffles wouldn't call her bluff, she waited for his response. After a standoff, he removed his head from the bags before plopping onto the seat.

"Good boy." Waffles wagged his butt, showing her he knew he was a good boy.

Holly parked the car in front of the garage as she did every time she saw her dad. She leaned back in her seat, looking at the two-story bungalow that she'd called home for so many years. The wear and tear was now clearly visible on the house. She could recall all the times her father would be on a ladder, installing new and improved windows, painting trim, or even fixing loose shingles.

Her father thrived on tinkering with the house. Every few years, he'd restain their front porch and he'd always let her help. Her father found his happiness working around the house.

That all came to an end one day three years ago.

Holly could still remember the phone call from the hospital. That was before the unknown blood clot in his neck migrated to his brain. It'd been a dark day in the Flanagan household.

After many surgeries and months in rehab, her dad regained some of his motor functions. Paralysis had set in on his left side, though. He only had about fifty-six percent use of his left arm and he was able to walk again.

She wouldn't have known what would happen if her father had been confined to a wheelchair. Even now, she could still see the frustration in his eyes when he'd have to sit or lay down. Going from being on a ladder eighty percent of his free time, to not being able to stand for long periods took a toll on him, as it would anyone. Not to mention, the guilt he still harbored about his bills.

After being released from rehab, the bills started coming in. With her father's new handicaps he wasn't able to go back to work. That left the financial strain on Holly's shoulders. Sure, there were times she'd want to rip her hair out, especially when she'd try and renegotiate interest or a payment and she'd ultimately end up nowhere.

She wouldn't trade it for the world. She had her dad, and that surpassed everything.

And if you were to ask Holly, she'd tell you her dad was still perfect. She loved spending the extra time with him and she never minded helping him around the house or making sure he had meals ready to go, clean laundry in his dresser, and a spick and span house.

It was the least she could do.

Her father gave her everything she ever needed growing up, and after her mother died, he took on that role, too.

Being able to give back a quarter of what her dad gave her was what daughters were there for.

Holly glanced around the outside of the bungalow. It'd seen better days. Right now, the porch had a few loose boards sticking up and there was paint peeling off some of the walls.

She felt that familiar pang in her heart. One day she'd be able to pay off his bills and find enough money to hire a contractor to fix the house. She believed that with her whole heart.

In the meantime she'd spent however many hours it took, searching the internet for tutorials and doing her best to implement them.

"Is that my girl?"

Holly heard the porch door slam. She then saw her dad hobble out of the front door looking in her direction. Happiness erupted through her. Even with his limp and arm plastered to his side, and the left side of his face drooping slightly, he was still the most handsome man around.

Waffles started to whine from the back seat. "Is that your Grampa?" Holly opened the door. Waffles took her cue and scurried over the center console before jumping out of the car. The dog was on a mission.

"How could I forget you, your holiness?" Henry beamed before bending to pet Waffles as the dog started jumping around him in circles. His butt waggled as fast as he could get it.

"Hey Dad." Holly got out of the car. "How've you been?"

Her dad stood. "I've been better," he admitted, which worried her a little. Her dad's go to answer had always been 'never better.'

"That so?"

"Yeah," he replied. "I've been missing my little girl. Where've you been the past week?"

Holly felt guilt rush through her. "I'm sorry, Dad."

"I'm just giving you a hard time, Pumpkin." He held out his arms, the left not as wide as the right. "Come give your old man a hug." She hurried into his arms, squeezing him.

"Missed you, Pumpkin."

"Missed you too, Dad."

"Come on, let's get the bags inside and we can catch up," he said, giving her one last squeeze.

Holly pulled away from him. "Can you do me a favor and go feed Waffles? I'll get the bags while you do that."

His eyes narrowed briefly as he scrutinized her. "I know what you're doing, missy. Just because I'm an old fart doesn't mean you can pull one over on me."

"Whatever do you mean?" Holly batted her eyelashes.

"I'll let you do it this time, but only 'cause I spent most of the morning trying to change the lightbulbs in the den and now my body's screaming."

"You did what?!" She glared at her father.

"Holly Ann Flanagan. The day I can't change my own light bulb is a day you might as well take me out back and shoot me." He crossed his arms over his chest.

"Oh, for the love of all things, Dad. I didn't think you *couldn't* change them. I just want to make sure you aren't putting too much strain on yourself. Next time just wait for me, okay?"

"Whatever," Henry grumbled before turning to open the front door. "Come on, Lord Waffles. I've got some extra pieces of steak I can add to your food."

Waffles hearing his favorite word 'food' ran past both of them and into the house. Holly couldn't see him, but if she knew Waffles, he would already be in the kitchen sitting on his hind legs begging. "Figures." She rolled her eyes.

Once all the bags were brought in and put away, and the laundry was in the wash, Holly sat with her father in the living room and pulled out a book. Waffles sat at her father's side wedged between the side of the recliner and her father's leg. He laid on his back as her dad idly scratched his belly.

"How was your week, Pumpkin?" he asked.

Holly put down her book and looked at her father. Should she tell him about Ben? How could she even try and explain it when she didn't understand it herself? Deciding on the safe route, she blurted, "I'm adopting a kitten."

"Well, I'll be. You are? What made you think to adopt a kitten?" He started to ruffle Waffles' fur. "This little guy not enough for you?"

"Waffles is more than enough. It just kinda fell into place, you know? There was a kitten who'd been poisoned by some jerk troublemaker." Seeing the worry in her father's eyes, she held up her hands. "He's going to be fine. At least I believe so, other than the twitch he now has in his head. No shelter will take him, so I volunteered."

"A twitch?" he asked before scratching his chin. "So, he's a little messed up, just like me."

It felt like a knife stab right through her heart. "You're not messed up, Dad."

Ignoring her, he continued, "How did you find out about the little guy with a twitch?"

"Well, Ben was showing me two dogs he'd operated on after they'd gotten hit by cars and then offered to show me the kitten he'd saved." The words were out of her mouth before she could stop them.

"Right there!" her dad exclaimed. "I knew it'd come out of your mouth sooner or later."

"What are you talking about?" She tried faking innocence.

"I knew there was something a little different about you."

He held up his hands in surrender when she gave him a dirty look. "Not bad, just different. And now, I know it has to do with a boy."

"A boy. Really?" She rolled her eyes. "I'm not in high school anymore, Dad."

"Then it won't be a big deal when I tell you to bring him over this weekend for dinner."

Holly's face paled. She couldn't bring Ben to dinner. No way. They weren't even really dating. At least she didn't think they were. Sure, he said he *wanted* to date her, and they had slept together, but that wasn't *dating*.

The palms of her hands started to sweat. She could invite him to dinner. It's not like she wouldn't see him before Saturday to ask. Ben texted her earlier in the day saying he'd be over later tonight for dinner and a "movie." Plus, how could she invite him to meet her father after the encounter she had meeting his mother?

She shuddered.

Taking a calming breath, she spoke, "Umm, well Dad, see it's still really new." Then before she could stop herself, she word vomited all over her father. "It all started when I bent over to pick up Waffles... you know, when the Frisbee came screaming through the air and hit me right in the face. That's when I met Ben, he was the one playing with his dog, Ripley, when the Frisbee had a mind of its own and honed in on me. It hit me so hard it chipped my tooth." At her dad's worried expression, she quickly continued, "Before I knew it, Ben had me at his best friend's dental practice fixing me right up. He's a nice dentist, Dad. You'd like him. Talks a little too much, but still nice. I'm not sure what happened next, but Ben and I started hanging out. A lot. He's funny, sweet, and he's a veterinarian. I showed up at his practice to talk to him, that's when I found out about the two dogs and the kitten. Everything kinda clicked, you know? He's a great guy, and by far the best sex I've ever—"

"Whoa there." Her dad grimaced.

Holly hit her hand on her forehead. "When will I ever learn to just shut up?" To her dismay Waffles barked in agreement.

"I'm going to pretend I didn't hear that last part, Pumpkin, and we are going to back it up a second." Henry sat straighter in his recliner. "You say, he accidentally hit you with something, but did everything he could to fix your cracked tooth?"

"Chipped," she corrected. "His friend is a dentist. My smile was fixed the same day."

"Well, I'm glad to hear that. You've got a beautiful smile, Pumpkin."

"Thanks, Dad."

"He's a veterinarian, and he saved the kitten you're adopting?"

Holly nodded. "Yeah. It was touch and go there for a while, and Twitch will probably always have the lasting side effects of the poison, but yes, Ben saved his life."

Henry scratched his chin again. "How long have you known him?"

"The kitten? Only a day." At her father's glare, she continued, "A little less than a week." Embarrassment washed over her. *Good going, Holly. Now, you've gone and told your Dad you've slept with a guy you haven't even known a week.*

"He sounds like he's a good man. If he did all you said he did, then he's all right in my book." Her dad readjusted himself in his chair. "He shouldn't have a problem coming over Saturday to meet me. You know, the honorable thing to do after sleeping with my daughter."

At a loss for what to do next, she threw in the towel. "I'll ask him tonight when I see him. Okay?"

"It must be serious if you're seeing him again so soon." Henry studied her.

"Um, well, yeah, Waffles has taken a liking to him."

Her dad threw his head back and laughed. "I guess if he has the Waffles seal of approval then who am I to question?"

"Can we drop it, please?"

"Sure thing, Pumpkin. Although I do expect him to be here with you on Saturday."

"I'll ask him, okay?" she huffed, grabbing her book and throwing it into her bag. *Just wonderful.* Now, she'd need to either come up with an excuse her father would believe about Ben not coming or actually ask him. *Won-der-ful!* That was the last thing she wanted to do.

"Don't go convoluting one of your elaborate plans there, missy. I expect him to be here no later than five o'clock Saturday. I'll pull out the grill and he can help me cook."

"*Really?*" She shot her eyes to the ceiling. *Please give me strength.* Taking a deep breath, she looked at her father. "Okay Dad, we'll be here. I'll probably have him bring his dog along as well."

"The more, the merrier."

"I'm gonna take Waffles and head home, okay? Your clean laundry's been put away, and you've got meals ready. I'll call you tomorrow. Do you need anything before we leave?"

Her dad smiled. "No, Pumpkin. I've got everything I need. I'll see you and your gentleman friend at four-thirty Saturday."

Four-thirty? What happened to five!

"Yes, Dad." She kissed his cheek. "I love you."

"I love you, too." Waffles started to whine. "And, I love you too, Waffles." Her father's words had the little guy running and jumping in circles.

"I'll call you tomorrow, Dad."

Once Holly got into her car with Waffles safely in the back seat, she pulled out her phone and text Ben.

We need to talk.

She received a reply instantly from him.

Is everything okay, Holly?

How could she ask him this, especially over a text? *Bad idea, Holly.* Shaking her head, she drew in as much strength as she could before she hit reply.

Umm, yeah. We'll talk tonight.

His reply sent shivers down her spine.

I'll be at your apartment in twenty minutes.

She gulped.

BEN SAT OUTSIDE of Holly's apartment building. His nerves were shot. Work had been another tough one. It always was when loss was involved. Then, after getting Holly's cryptic text, he couldn't stop himself from freaking out. He knew their relationship was still new, and she'd still had reservations about them.

He couldn't help but think the worst. Was she going to break up with him?

Ripley whined beside him. He scratched her behind the ear. "I know, girl. I'm nervous too." Ripley placed her head on Ben's lap. She always knew when he needed comfort.

Hearing a noise, he looked from Ripley to the sidewalk. That's where he saw Holly walking toward him.

Warmth washed over him in a way he'd grown accustomed to around her. She'd brought a sense of calm to him.

She walked toward her building with Waffles at her side. He could feel the nerves radiating off her. She gave him a small wave. When Waffles realized Ben was waiting there he jerked out of Holly's hand and ran right for him.

"Waffles!" Holly tried to grab for him.

Ben dropped to his knees catching the runaway pup as he

jumped into his arms. "Hey, bud." Waffles plopped onto his back demanding belly rubs. High maintenance was an understatement.

"Bad, Waffles! Don't pull out of my hands."

Ben looked at Holly, her face scrunched as she watched him. His nerves once again got the better of him. "Is everything okay, babe?"

"Uh, yeah. I mean, no yeah. It's fine." She turned away from him.

No, everything was not fine.

Ben stood from the two dogs now playing at his feet. He reached for Holly's shoulders turning her to face him. "What's wrong?"

Holly's eyes held so many emotions. "Let's talk about it once we get inside."

Wanting to talk inside could be considered a good thing. If she wanted to end it she would have done it outside. There was something else really bothering her. He felt his need to protect her kick in. If someone had hurt her or if she was in trouble, he'd do anything to fix it. Seeing her like this, felt like a knife right in his chest. "Okay, babe."

He whistled for Ripley, knowing Waffles would follow suit. Reaching down, Ben picked up both of their leashes before making their way inside.

The elevator ride to Holly's floor by far, was the most intense feeling he'd ever encountered in his life, even though he'd dealt with his mother on multiple occasions. The tension also started to affect the dogs. Waffles paced uneasy, whereas Ripley sat at Holly's legs leaning into her trying to give her comfort.

Ben watched Holly from the corner of his eye. She was unnaturally quiet. She worried her hands while biting her bottom lip. Every time she winced at the pain, he fought the urge to reach out to her.

Ben was at a loss for what to do next. Right now, he hoped

whatever had her mind racing they'd be able to work through it together.

When they finally made it inside of her apartment he turned to her, unable to hold off a moment longer. "Holly, please tell me what's bothering you." He used his hard voice, just as he did when he told her not to move in his office.

His desired effect on her took hold. She snapped around facing him.

Unfortunately for her, though, the quick uncontrolled movements riled the dogs. Waffles ran between her legs causing her to stumble. When she tried to catch herself, Ripley decided she wanted to help. Ripley ended up blocking Holly's attempt at grabbing the nearby wall.

Within seconds she was on the floor.

"Fuck, baby, are you okay?" Ben raced to her side.

Holly sat on her ass, blowing her hair out of her face. "This is just another day in my life," she said, before putting the palms of her hands onto the floor, pushing herself to stand. Ben seeing what she was doing, grabbed onto her hips righting her in seconds.

"How do you always lift me like I weigh nothing?" she asked.

"You do weigh nothing."

"Humph."

His eyes hardened. "Are you making fun of your weight?" he asked. "Any excuse you give me to redden your ass, I'll take."

Holly paled.

Ben's eyes lit as he laughed. "Lighten up, Grace." He leaned over kissing her nose while lightly swatting her butt.

"Hey!"

Ben walked away with a chuckle before sitting on her couch. Patting beside him he signaled both the pups. Once they were by his sides, he leaned back. "Spill."

Holly watched him for a second before breaking eye contact with him.

"I mean it, Grace. Something's got you all freaked out and if I were being honest, I'd say it has me a little worried too. What's got you on edge?"

Holly started pacing. "Fine. You know how I went to see my dad today?"

"Yeah."

Holly continued pacing not looking at him. "I did all the normal things I do for him. Cleaning, doing the laundry, making sure he has meals planned and ready. But, I guess I looked different or something." She stopped pacing and stared at him nervously.

"Okay."

Holly took a deep breath and blurted, "He's demanding to meet you this Saturday for a cookout!" She started pacing again. "You'd be the one to have to cook on the grill, he can't really do that anymore. I told him I'd think about asking you, but he demanded you come. Especially, after I let it slip you were the best sex of my life. He said the manly thing to do would be for you to meet him, because you've already gotten the goods."

Ben's eyes widened for a brief second before he threw his head back in laughter.

"Don't laugh at me!"

Ben shot from his seat and in two steps landed in front of her. "How can I not, baby? You're adorable." He kissed her.

When they finally came up for air, Holly panted. "What was that for? I mean I'm not complaining. I just thought after I told you you'd have to meet my dad, you'd be pissed."

He rested his forehead on hers. "Why would I be pissed, Grace?"

"It's a big step meeting my dad."

"Why?"

"I don't know, isn't it always a big step meeting the parents? We don't even know what we are yet."

He growled. "I know what we are, Holly." He lifted her into the air, wrapping her legs around his waist. "I'm the man that gives you the best sex of your life."

Holly placed her head in the crook of his neck. "You heard that?"

"You damn well better believe I did." He hurried them to her bedroom. Once he made it to the bed, he gently threw her on top of it, following suit. "We can talk about meeting your dad later. Which I have no problem with, by the way. It'll be nice to meet him. Right now, though, I want to expand on the best sex of your life."

Ben gazed down at Holly as she laid on the bed, her hair a ruffled mess. She never looked more attractive. He used his right hand and gently caressed her skin. "You're so beautiful," he murmured before he leaned down to pepper kisses on her neck.

"Enough talking, more doing." She squirmed.

"So feisty, Grace. I love it." Ben reached for the hem of her shirt forcing her to sit up as he removed it. His hands instantly went to her breasts as he started to massage them. "They feel so good," he explained as he tweaked her nipple through her bra.

"What about you?" she asked, reaching for his shirt.

"Anything you want, baby." He reluctantly removed his hands from her breasts before ripping his shirt off and throwing it behind him.

"I still can't get over your abs." Holly reached for them and began to massage them. "Seriously, how is it possible that you look this good?"

"I have to keep up my strength. Do you know how hard it is to control a one hundred and twenty-pound Rottweiler who is nothing but muscle? It's not an easy task, baby."

Moving her hands south she started to unbuckle his jeans.

Letting her right hand migrate a little lower she cupped him causing a hiss to escape from his mouth. "More," he pleaded.

"My pleasure." She used her hands and pushed against his chest causing him to fall backwards on to the bed.

A dominant woman is a wild woman, he thought before letting Holly take control.

His eyes were heavy-lidded with pleasure as he watched her crawl along his body massaging his muscles. "You wouldn't let me do this last time," she stated, leaning over his aching member. "I want to taste you properly."

Ben clenched his teeth as a moan escaped him, causing him to fist his hands at his side as he desperately tried to keep control.

Holly slowly lowered the zipper of his jeans before quickly removing the material from his body.

Ben's dick instantly sprang free glistening at the tip.

"Yes," she hissed. She grabbed onto the base, giving it a slight squeeze. "It amazes me you walk around with this thing. How do you not sit on it?"

He was about to give her a smart aleck reply when she enveloped him in her mouth.

"Oh fuck." Losing control of his hands, he fisted her hair.

Holly started moving up and down his shaft, swallowing once he was entirely inside of her mouth. "Don't do that," he growled.

She released him with a pop. "Why not?" Her eyes held a hint of worry. "Did I not do it right?"

"You did it too right," he growled, trying to keep his control.

"Oh." She smiled. "Okay then." Ignoring his plea, she went back to the task at hand. This time, she let her tongue dance across the head before sucking him in.

"Nope." He pushed her off before collapsing on top of her. "When I come, I want it to be inside of you."

"I was having fun." Her adorable pout made him smirk.

"Believe me, so was I. But I want you, Grace. I need to be inside of you." He moved down her body removing her pants and panties in one motion. "Don't you want that, too?"

She cocked her head to the side. "Well, duh."

"Exactly." With Holly's pants removed he let her legs fall open along either side of him. Looking at her core, her wetness called to him. "Plus, I intend to not make a liar out of you."

"What?" She gasped as he pinched her clit.

"I have to deliver on the best sex of your life."

Her eyes shot to him. "Oh, for the love of... are you ever gonna let me live that down?"

"Not on your life." He thrust himself inside of Holly, her walls instantly tightening around him as her orgasm rocketed her off the bed.

"Holy crappolie."

Ben pulled her into his arms so they were both sitting up. Holly's legs wrapped around him, as she sat in his lap, his dick fully inside of her. "Holy something is right." He used gravity to his advantage as Holly clung to him. His movements were deep and slow. He wanted to build her to another release.

Holly was always so damn responsive, she'd explode at the mere touch of his hand. Not this time, though. No, this time he wanted to build a slow burn inside of her. He wanted to mark her. He wanted her to remember what he felt like sunk deep into her, for days to come.

"Faster," she pleaded, clinging to him.

"No." Ben placed his hands on the small of her back forcing her to stop her bouncing.

"Please."

Grabbing the side of her hips, Ben slowly moved her in circular motions. He knew the friction along her clit would only intensify her pleasure. Holly began to shake as her breathing increased. Before she could come he flipped their position on the bed.

"No," she begged, trying to replace the sensation on her clit. "Please."

Ignoring her, Ben positioned himself behind her on his side. He wanted to feel every part of her skin and he knew the only way to do that was to spoon her. Throwing her leg over his hip, he gently thrust himself into her warm treasure. Using his left hand, he reached around them seeking out her clit.

"Oh God, Ben," she moaned.

He moved inside of her, feeling her walls clench around him. Pushing Holly's hair to one side, he whispered in her ear, "Now." He bit gently on her earlobe causing her to explode.

Holly's body convulsed around him caused his own control to slip. Ben stilled spilling everything he had deep within her walls.

"Holy crap." Holly tucked herself into his arms.

After only a few moments Ben heard Holly's gentle breathing and he knew she'd fallen asleep. He couldn't blame her.

Ben laid there with Holly curled in his arms.

This is how he wanted to spend the rest of his life. A huge smile spread across his face. Even though his body was exhausted, he couldn't fall asleep. His mind was too energized with the woman in his arms.

Ben thought back to their conversation. Her frazzled behavior about telling him her dad wanted to meet him was adorable.

"I have no problem meeting your dad, baby," he whispered making sure not to wake her. Ben kissed her temple before repositioning himself.

That's when he realized his mistake.

"Oh fuck." He looked at his soft dick with no condom on it.

Shit! His stomach bottomed out. How was he going to tell Holly he fucked up? Sure, he joked about knocking her up, and the more he thought about it the more he liked the idea.

But, he would never force her into anything. "Fuck!" he groaned, pulling away from her.

"What?" Holly shifted to face him. "What's wrong?"

Ben jumped from the bed before pacing her small room. *Okay, it was one mistake it's not a big deal. She won't hate you.*

Waffles ran into the room, Ripley right behind him before they started to wrestle.

"Ben, you're kinda freaking me out here."

Ben stopped pacing long enough to throw his boxers out of the room making the dogs chase after them. He shut the door, locking them out before turning back to Holly. "I fucked up."

Holly reached for the comforter to cover her body, alarming him on how his words sounded. He snagged the material yanking it from her hands. "No, that's not what I meant."

Clearly not willing to believe him, Holly used her hands to cover herself. "What's the problem then?"

Ben crawled up the bed before cupping her cheeks in his hands and passionately kissing her. Pulling away he sighed. "There is something about you that carries me away. "

"Okay." She worried her lip.

"I forgot to put on a condom."

Holly's eyes widened before she looked between her legs.

Leave it to Holly to go there. Even in tension, she still found a way to make him laugh.

"Oh, umm, well I guess you're right." She looked at him.

"I'm sorry, babe. I would never willingly put you in danger."

"Do you have something?" Her eyes widened.

"No!" Ben reached for her hand squeezing it. "Hell no, I don't have anything. Shit Holly, before you, I hadn't had sex in almost a year."

"Almost a *year?*"

"Yeah. Don't look at me like that. I devote my time to my practice."

Holly sat on the bed not saying anything for a few minutes. "I'm clean too," she whispered. "The last time I had sex was way over a year ago, more like two."

Ben looked at her. "I know you're still worried about everything, especially, getting pregnant. I promise, Holly, I will be there for you no matter what. I've always wanted children—"

She held up her hands. "Holy crap on a cracker. I won't get pregnant. I'm on the pill, Ben. I have been for years."

Ben felt a weird sense of relief along with disappointment run through him. "Okay, what were you upset about?" He didn't like the idea there was no chance of her getting pregnant.

"I didn't want you to judge me that it's been way longer for me in the sex department."

"I wouldn't judge you," he assured her.

"Well, you make fun of me for other stuff why not this?"

He growled before jumping on her causing Holly to laugh. "I like the idea of knowing you haven't been with a lot of men. Makes me want you more."

"Whatever." She laughed before moving her neck to give Ben better access.

"It drives me wild."

"Well, I'm glad my lack of sexy times does it for you."

"It won't be lacking anymore." He nibbled on her neck.

"Good."

Ben made his way down her chest. He was about to suck her nipple into his mouth when he heard her laugh. He looked at her as she was trying her best to hold in her amusement. "Am I funny now?"

"No." She laughed. "I was just thinking about how you might have had to meet my dad knowing there was a possibility you'd knocked me up."

Chapter Twelve

HOLLY PARKED the car in front of the garage at her father's house, like she did every time she visited. Only this time, the tension in her stomach made her want to throw up. Hoping Ben wasn't a mess like her, she looked out of the corner of her eye.

When she saw Ben sitting in the passenger seat with a stupid smirk on his face her eye started to twitch. *How is it possible he's this calm?*

"If you hold the steering wheel any tighter, you'll lose feeling." Ben laughed, jarring her from her irritation.

Holly quickly removed her hands from the wheel and placed them in her lap wringing them. "I wasn't holding it tight."

"Yes, you were, Grace." He cupped her chin with his left hand moving her head to face him. "It's going to be okay." He kissed her on the tip of her nose before kissing her lips softly.

"I know." Did she, though? This moment felt more real to her than anything she'd ever experienced in her life.

"I want to meet your dad, babe. Anyone that can help produce half of you must be pretty remarkable."

"Eww. Gross, Ben." She blanched before punching his shoulder.

"What'd I say?"

Waffles started to whine from the back seat scratching at the window, breaking up their conversation.

"Do I need to get the hose and cool you two off?"

Holly's head snapped around. Her father had come out of the house and now stood on the front porch staring at them.

"Oh, crap." Holly's eyes widened. Waffles barked doing everything he could to get out of the car and see his grandpa.

Ben laughed before opening his door for the little guy. Waffles jumped over the seat and ran past him, Ripley not far behind.

Ben exited the car and strode right to her father with his hand out. "Nice to meet you, Mr. Flanagan."

"Were you in there foolin' around with my little girl?" Her father nodded his head toward the car.

Oh, shit. Holly wanted the ground to open and swallow her whole.

"Depends on what your definition of foolin' around is?" Ben countered.

Her father analyzed him for a split second before roaring with laughter. "Call me Henry." He clasped his good hand on the back of Ben's shoulder. "I like you." Her dad looked at Holly and pointed at Ben. "We'll keep him."

"Kill me now," she grumbled before opening the car door. She made her way up the front steps trying her best not to die of mortification.

"This is Ben, Dad." She gestured toward him.

Henry leaned in kissing Holly on the cheek. "I figured as much, Pumpkin. I didn't think you'd bring another boy over." He bent at his waist. "And who's this?"

"That's Ripley. She's my Australian Shepherd," Ben replied, reaching his hand down to scratch the pup.

Henry's eyes hardened. "This the one you were playing with when you caused my girl to break her tooth?"

"Chipped, Dad. Chipped."

"Same difference." Henry crossed his arms over his chest the best he could before narrowing his eyes at Ben.

"No, it's not." Mimicking his movements, Holly crossed her arms over her chest. Was her dad trying to be difficult?

"Yes, sir. Unfortunately, the Frisbee had a mind of its own," Ben answered.

"But you got her all fixed up, though?"

"Yes, sir. It was my number one priority."

Her dad looked him up and down, trying to find the lie.

"Not sir. Henry. Sir makes me feel old."

"All right then, Henry. Making sure Holly was okay was all that mattered to me." Ben joined the party by crossing his arms over his chest.

"You sure it wasn't getting into her pants?"

Holly blanched. "Okay, that's enough." Holly pushed past the two opening the front door. "Everyone inside. Time to cook food."

Ben not moving a muscle stared her father in the eyes. "I think your daughter is the most beautiful woman I have ever laid eyes on. I'd be lying if I said I wasn't attracted to her, but no. I did not *only* want to get in her pants. It was *my* rogue dog toy that hit her making it my responsibility to fix whatever needed to be fixed. At that time, getting into her pants was not a priority; her health and safety were."

Her dad straightened. "And now?"

"Now, her health and safety are still my number one priority." Ben turned to face Holly who'd stopped in the doorway to witness the testosterone showdown. "Along with getting into her pants." He winked.

Holly's cheeks heated as she threw her hands in the air. "That's it." She turned away from them darting into the house making sure the door slammed behind her.

Holly heard both of them laugh before following her through the door.

"You've got moxie, and I like that," Henry remarked. "Holly needs someone like you around."

"I'm glad you think so. I plan on sticking around."

Holly hearing enough of their chatter grabbed the bag of charcoal that sat along the wall. "I'm going to start the grill."

"Are you leaving in hopes that we stop talking about you?" her father asked.

"No, I'm leaving because if I stay here any longer I'm liable to kill both of you."

"Feisty," Ben laughed.

"Isn't she?" Henry agreed.

Ignoring both of them, she picked up the bag and headed toward the back door. "Waffles, Ripley. Outside," she hollered over her shoulder.

"Now, she's even taking the pups." Henry pouted.

As Holly turned back to argue with him her foot snagged on the trim under the door. Before she knew it, she was falling to the ground. She braced herself for impact but it never came.

Opening one of her eyes, Holly realized she'd somehow ended up in Ben's arms instead of on the ground. "I can't take you anywhere, Grace."

"Holly, I'm so sorry." Henry ran over to her. "I forgot to mention the door trim started coming up. I meant to get down there and nail it back but I couldn't get a solid grip on the nails," her father pleaded.

"It's okay, Dad," she tried reassuring him. "I'm okay."

"No, Holly, it's not okay. I meant to warn you about it." The disgrace in her dad's voice broke her heart in two.

"No harm, no foul," Ben said righting Holly. "Grace didn't even drop the bag of charcoal."

Her father straightened, before squinting his eyes. "Grace?"

"Holly's other name." Ben took the charcoal bag from Holly's hands placing it on the back porch.

"Is that some weird sex thing?" Henry asked.

"Oh God." Holly briefly closed her eyes.

"No," Ben laughed. "Holly's extremely graceful."

Henry nodded, with his own chuckle. "Ahh, now I understand. She is quite graceful, isn't she?"

"Very." Ben's eyes lit.

Henry turned to Holly. "I am sorry, Pumpkin."

"No worries, Dad. Everything is fine." Holly walked into his harms.

"Love you, Pumpkin."

"Love you too, Dad."

Two hours later, Ben had fixed the door trim and the food had been cooked and served. After their initial pissing war, everything between Ben and Henry seemed right as rain.

Actually, it seemed better than that.

Henry reminded him a lot of his own father. Within a short time, he'd felt the same level of comfort he'd had when his dad was alive. The two freely talked about everything from sports, animals, his condition, and Holly.

Ben loved the way Henry spoke about Holly. Ben could clearly see the love he had for his daughter.

Henry was a down to earth, blue collar man, and he admired that about him.

Ben could feel the pain coming from Henry when he talked about the joy he used to have fixing up the house. One look in his eyes and you'd see Henry thought he was less of a man now.

It broke his heart, even though he'd only met Henry now, he would help him anyway he needed. He would have done the same thing for his father if he'd been alive and in Henry's condition.

As Holly played with Ripley and Waffles in the back yard, Ben sat on the back porch listening to Henry. His eyes couldn't help but follow Holly as she ran through the yard tossing the tennis ball through the air.

For a split second, Ben replaced the dogs with their children.

"You've got it bad."

Henry's voice jolted Ben out of his fantasy. Looking at her dad, he shrugged, why deny it. "I do."

Henry sat back in the rocking chair.

Before Ben knew it, he started spilling his guts. "There is something about Holly that makes me want it all. I know that sounds insane, even more so that we haven't known each other very long, but I can't help it." He focused his attention on Holly.

"It's not insane, son."

Son.

Ben froze. Hearing that word caused a new pang of hurt to rip through him. His dad used to call him son. Doing his best to ignore it, Ben looked at Henry.

"I felt that way about Holly's mother, Helen, when I met her." Henry got a faraway look in his eyes. "She took my breath away. I never could quite put my finger on it, but there was something about her that drew me in. It was like she was my homing beacon. We were married not long after we met."

Ben's eyes went back to Holly playing with the dogs as he listened to Henry.

"She was taken from me too soon."

Ben understood that. He felt the same way about his father. "I'm sorry."

"Don't be. Even though I ache for her every day. I would rather that, then not have had her at all."

"That's pretty deep." He looked back at Henry who was staring him down.

"Love is deep, son."

Ben lowered his head. *Yeah, it is.*

"Holly doesn't remember her mother as much as I'd like her to. I made sure I always brought up stories with her, and pictures to try and help her. She's a lot like her mother. Even acquired the clumsy gene."

Ben chuckled. "So, she does get it from somewhere?"

"Most definitely." Henry eyed him. "Helen was known for her clumsiness. I can't count the number of times I'd be talking to her at eye level and the next minute she was on the floor after stumbling over an invisible rock."

Ben snorted. "Sounds exactly like Grace."

"It was adorable."

Ben sat back watching Holly again. "It is. It makes me want her more."

Both men sat in silence for a few minutes before Henry decided to speak. "You never know how long you're lucky enough to have someone," he whispered. "My only advice I can give to anyone is don't wait around. Take that leap and follow your impulse. We are all living by a time clock and no one knows when that clock stops."

Ben listened to the words and let them sink in. After last night's condom scare, he thought he'd be more on edge, more cautious. Even more reserved about settling down. The exact way he'd always thought when it came to his future.

Instead, he found himself following Holly in the backyard. His mind instantly pictured her swollen with their child. That image ignited something inside of him. Something he'd never realized he wanted.

"Food for thought," Henry remarked.

Ben watched as Ripley jumped onto Holly and stole the ball out of her hands.

"Get back here!" she hollered, running after Ripley.

Waffles with his little legs ran alongside Holly trying to herd her just as Corgi's do, causing her to stumble in her steps.

Ben didn't know if it was too soon or not, but he knew for damn sure he was starting to fall in love with Holly. Hell, he might already be there.

"Go get your girl," Henry mumbled. "Seems as though she needs a little help." He jutted his chin toward Holly in the yard.

Ben jumped from his seat hopping down the steps to help steal back the tennis ball. "I plan on it."

Chapter Thirteen

HOLLY MANEUVERED her way around the endless bookshelves, trying to avoid Mildred's prying eyes. And so far, she'd done a pretty good job of it.

Placing a book in its rightful spot, she turned to her cart ready to grab the next book.

"Holy crap!" Holly held her chest trying to get her breathing under control.

Mildred stood next to the cart with her arms crossed over her chest. "Are you done avoiding me?" she asked, raising her right brow.

"I wasn't avoiding you."

"Liar! Now tell me everything." Mildred took the footstool at Holly's feet and sat.

After a few second standoff, Holly blew out a deep breath. "I don't even know where to begin."

"I'd say Friday night after you left is a good place to start." Mildred took her pad and pen out of her pocket, as she always did when gossip was involved. Crossing her legs, she readied herself to take notes.

"You're something else." The corner of Holly's lip turned up.

"Never said I wasn't."

Forty-five minutes and an inquisition later, Holly was back at her desk cataloging overdue books. Mildred was off in the romance section scouring to find tips. For who? Holly didn't know, but it was best to leave Mildred to her research when she was on one of her kicks.

"It wasn't hard to find you."

Holly looked from her task to see Ben's mother Barbra walking toward her.

Wonderful.

"Hello, Mrs. Richman. Can I help you find anything?" Holly placed a smile on her face and did her best not to scowl at the woman.

Barbra marched toward her like she had a stick up her ass. At this point, Holly wouldn't have expected anything else. "No." Barbra sized her up. "You cannot help me find anything. What I *need* you to do is stay away from my son."

Holly recoiled in shock which instantly melted into anger. Who the hell did this bitch think she was? "I'm sorry, Mrs. Richman, but that's not something I am willing to do." She squared her shoulders.

"It's money you're after, isn't it?" Barbra reached into her purse ignoring Holly's now stunned expression.

Holly's body shook with anger. Crossing her arms over her chest, she raised her brow in challenge. "Excuse me?"

"You heard me, young lady." Barbra closed her purse in a huff, before looking down at Holly. "Are you only with *my* Benjamin because he has money?"

That sealed the deal. Yes, this bitch was crazy. "First off, *old* lady, I am not *only* with your son because he has money. I didn't know he had money when I first met him."

Barbra narrowed her eyes. "Likely story."

"What's your freakin' deal?"

"My deal?" Barbra asked. "I'll tell you what my deal is. I cannot have my Benjamin be seen with the likes of you. You'd only ruin the reputation he's worked so hard to achieve. If word gets out he's with someone like *you*, all my hard work would be for nothing."

Holly shook her head in disbelief. "Wow. Some mother you are."

"I am the *best* mother. I'd do anything I can to protect his name."

"You mean your name."

Opening her bag once again, Barbra removed her checkbook. "I am here to offer you ten thousand dollars to stay away from my son."

Holly's mouth fell open while her eyebrows shot to the ceiling. "Are you kidding me?"

"I do not kid."

"Wow." Holly sat back in utter disbelief. "If you're not joking then you are seriously messed up in the head. You can't buy me, *Barbra*."

"Everyone has their price," she stated matter of fact. "And, I just so happen to know yours."

"Listen here, you crazy whack-a-doo, I will never take a dime from you."

Barbra placed her checkbook back in her bag. "Are you sure about that?" she sneered. "I know your father's medical bills are piling up. I also know if you don't pay his back mortgage by the end of the month, his precious little home will be set for foreclosure."

All of the blood drained from Holly's face. "How did you know that?"

"I own this town, *Holly Flanagan*. I know everything."

Holly stared at her as her heart froze in her chest. Could Ben's mother honestly be this evil? Taking a deep breath, Holly squared her jaw. "I don't appreciate you going through my father's financial records."

Barbra's eyes lit as she chuckled. "Do you think my regard for others got me to where I am now?"

"You mean a coldhearted bitch? No."

"Glad you think so." Barbra turned on her heel before looking over her shoulder. "I wonder if you understand four out of the five members of the library's board of directors are personal friends of mine. I do hope you hadn't had your heart set on working here much longer."

"Excuse me?" Holly's eyes widened.

Barbara turned back. "You heard me, you little whore. Maybe I should say *big* whore. Stay away from Benjamin. You're not what he needs, and you'll never be good enough for him. You're nothing but a poor unfortunate excuse for a human being. Mark my words, Holly Flanagan, if I so much as hear you've been seen with Benjamin..." She stopped talking while a creepy smile spread across her face. "All it takes is one phone call and you can say goodbye to your precious little job. Hmm, I wonder what will happen to your poor disabled father? There's no way you'd be able to pay all his bills." She placed her finger on her chin looking at the ceiling. "Oh, well."

"You wouldn't?"

Barbra laughed. "You don't think I will?" Her expression hardened. "Hear this missy, I will do anything I need to protect my son from the likes of you. I have no problem destroying your life and the life of your poor sad sack of a father if I need to." Without another word she turned on her heel and marched out of the library.

Holly sat there frozen as the implications of Barbra's words swam around her head as her heart raced.

How could there be someone so awful like Barbra? Panic started to creep in. She looked at the picture of her father on her desk.

Her dad meant the world to her. In every way, shape, or form. She'd never do anything that could potentially hurt him in any way.

What if Barbra followed through on her threats? If Holly

lost her job there would be no way she could pay her father's bills and keep him out of a nursing home.

She couldn't fail him.

She wouldn't fail him.

"What a bitch." Mildred walked from behind a bookshelf. "What crawled up her ass?"

Holly couldn't speak not while everything was falling apart.

Even though she still couldn't help having doubts about Ben, she foolishly thought she was on the right path for once. But now, with even the mere thought of her father suffering, caused bile to rise in her throat.

Panic set in. This couldn't be happening.

"Holly, honey, are you okay? You've lost all the color in your face."

Snapping out of her trance, Holly looked at Mildred with tears pooling in her eyes. "She demanded I stop seeing her son and if I don't she'll have me fired." Holly's heart was on the verge of exploding from her chest. "I can't lose my job, Mildred. More than half of my paycheck goes to my dad. If I lose my job, *he'll* lose everything."

Mildred placed her hand on Holly's shoulder. "Calm down, honey. I am sure we can come up with a solution. One where you don't lose your job, and you can still see that sexy man meat."

"What solution? You heard her. She owns this town. She could destroy me and my dad in one phone call." Holly held her hand against her stomach willing the bile to stay down.

"I understand you're panicking right now, and I would be too," Mildred calmly replied. "I think you should call Ben and talk to him."

Holly jerked out of Mildred's grasp. "Call Ben? Did you hear what just happened? I can't call Ben. If she finds out it'll all be over." Holly grabbed her purse and ran toward the door.

Once she made it outside, she looked down the street. Her

first instinct was to run to Ben's clinic and into his arms. As she took her first step her phone rang so she blindly answered. "Hello?"

"Hi, Pumpkin," her father's voice came over the line.

"Dad."

"Holly, I wanted to know if you were coming over tonight? I got a strange call from the bank and wanted to talk to you about it." Holly's heart shattered into a million pieces as she clenched the phone to her ear. She looked down the street toward the direction of the clinic. She knew she had a choice.

She swallowed before closing her eyes, allowing a stray tear to slide down her cheek.

Holly could go to her father, the man who raised her and had been there forever through everything in her life. The father, who'd become her best friend. The father she owed her life to. Or, she could run to the man who she knew she'd already fallen in love with.

As the tears freely cascaded down her cheeks, she already knew the answer.

Chapter Fourteen

BEN PLACED his hammer on the ground before wiping the sweat from his brow. He'd spent the better part of the morning replacing wood on Henry's porch, and the sun's heat made sure to make its presence known.

Henry was a good man. Ben could see why Holly loved him so much.

That's why on Sunday, he personally called all his scheduled clients and rearranged them throughout the week leaving his Monday completely free. Thankfully, his clients were more than happy about the "inconvenience" if it meant they'd get free service when they did come in for their appointment. He did however make it clear if an emergency arose, he'd be at the clinic in a heartbeat.

Ben wasn't quite sure what compelled him to show up at Henry's doorstep at seven in the morning, but he knew after Holly's near accident over the weekend and the look of devastation that ran across Henry's face, he knew he wanted to help.

Glancing around the porch, he felt the corners of his mouth turn upwards. Over the watchful eyes of one Henry Flanagan, the porch was looking ten times better, if he did say so himself.

Ben chuckled when he saw Ripley sprawled out on her back in the shade, doing her best to keep herself cool.

"I brought you some water," Henry announced, handing the glass to Ben with his good hand.

Thankful for the gesture Ben gladly took the glass. "Thanks." Taking a huge swig, he let the cold water slide down his throat.

"I still don't fully understand why you're here, but I'm grateful for the help." Henry plopped onto the front step. "It still drives me batshit crazy I can't fix these things myself anymore."

Ben understood that. How could he not? Sitting back onto his ankles, he placed the glass on the ground.

Henry stared at the porch. "After Holly's near fall, I knew something needed to give. I planned on coming up with a course of action this week."

"I guess it worked out that I was free today." Ben smiled. "I'm here to help and you seem to be enjoying bossing me around with the *right* way to do things." Ben chuckled, hoping to lighten the mood.

"Son." Henry looked at him. "There is a right way and a wrong way to do things. In this household, we always did things the right way. Even if that took more time." He puffed out his chest.

Ben's smile grew wider as he held up his glass. "I couldn't agree more."

They were both silent for a few moments while Henry leaned his back onto the handrail and watched as Ben worked to remove a rotted piece of wood. "Thank you, Ben."

"It's really no problem."

Looking away, Henry focused on a nearby tree. "I know I should start looking into a nursing home. That'd be the right thing to do. Especially now that Holly has you. I don't want her feeling obligated to be here all the time or help fix broken crap around the house."

Ben raised his brow. "Holly doesn't seem the one to fix items around the house without injuring herself."

"Oh, I didn't say she went about it unscathed, but she does do anything she can." Henry's eyes lit. "I think she's been saving some money to hire someone."

"I'm glad I came around, then. Neither of you will need to worry about fixing up this place or hiring some whack job to do it. Once we get the porch done we'll make a list of all the things you'd like to fix up and improve around the house. We'll tackle everything one step at a time. And, with you overseeing everything, this place will be good as new."

Henry scrutinized him. "Why are you so eager to help me fix up a house that's seen better days?"

He knew this was coming, it was only a matter of time. "I like you, Henry, and I know if the roles were reversed, you'd do the same for me."

"Are you sure that's your only reason for helping?" Henry asked.

"I am." He didn't mention he wanted any obstacle in Holly's way eliminated. He knew the old man tried to do right by his daughter, but with his predicament the house wasn't as safe as it could be for one accident prone walking disaster.

His mind quickly took a path it'd recently grown accustomed to. What if Holly had been pregnant when she fell out of the door? His whole body shuddered.

When she did get pregnant, he was wrapping her in bubble wrap from head to toe.

"You're right," Henry admitted. "If the tables were turned, I'd help out a decrepit old man get his house back in order."

"I wouldn't say decrepit," Ben laughed.

"But you would say old."

"You said it, not me."

Henry chuckled. "Does Holly know you're here?"

Ben sat back on his ankles once again. "Actually, she doesn't."

"Are you keeping it from her?" Henry's brow rose in question. Ben had to bite back his laugh. No one could ever question Henry's love for his daughter. He'd go head to head with anyone in a heartbeat.

"No, sir, I'm not."

"What did I tell you about calling me, sir? It makes me feel old."

Ben's face lit, before smirking. "Sure thing, sir. Won't happen again, sir."

"What does my little girl even see in you?" Henry laughed along with Ben.

"Hopefully a long future."

Henry's face hardened. "You love her, don't you?"

Before Ben could answer him, the phone rang. "Oh hell," Henry mumbled. "Hold that thought. I'll be right back." Henry slowly righted himself before rushing into the house to get the phone.

Ripley, who'd been watching them, made her way over and plopped herself in front of Ben demanding scratches. "You know, young lady, I think you've been hanging around Lord Waffles too much. You never used to be so demanding." Ripley in response rolled onto her back giving Ben her belly. "Yes, your highness. I didn't know I had two divas on my hands now." He started ruffling her belly making her kick her legs out. "I can't wait to blame Holly for your newly found bossiness."

Ripley quickly turned away from Ben, ignoring his comment while moving back to the area in the shade. "I'm only good for a few measly scratches before you retreat back to your spot?" Ben narrowed his eyes at her before he let out a laugh. "I'm blaming Waffles."

Holly threw her car into park once she made it to her father's house. She quickly removed her seatbelt and exited the vehicle ready to find her dad.

Once she looked toward the house, she came to a complete halt seeing Ben. He was on his hands and knees with a toolbox to his right.

She was momentarily taken aback by his appearance. She couldn't help but stare at him. He wore dark jeans, that clearly had seen better days. Even with most of his lower half blocked by his position on the porch, she could see the jeans were ripped and well-worn. He also had on a light blue tee-shirt, that stretched across his chest. It had dark patches where his sweat had seeped through. The sleeves on his arms were taut as his muscles threatened to rip through the material.

When he flexed his upper arm, her breath hitched.

Ben looked like someone she'd read about in a blue-collar romance novel that dripped with sexy men. The only thing he was missing was a utility belt around his waist.

"Pumpkin, aren't you supposed to still be at work?" Her dad's voice broke her trance.

She looked from her father back to Ben, who now stood and was giving her a grin that could melt ice.

Holly stared at her father ignoring Ben. "After your phone call, I knew I needed to get here right away." She moved toward the porch. "Why are you here, Ben?"

Ben's face brightened. "I wanted to help your dad around the house." He wiped his hands on his jeans.

For the first time in her life, Holly felt honest to God real heartbreak. Here in front of her stood the man that made her feel like she'd never felt before. His gaze held a passion she knew she'd never come close to seeing in another man's eyes again.

Knowing she was about to let go of that made her heart break that much more. She knew she had a choice. A choice to save her father from going to a nursing home and after the text message she'd received not long after she hung up with her dad, she knew she had no other option.

Closing her eyes, her heart shattered the impossible bit more as she recalled the message.

Just so we are clear. Unfortunately, I would hate for Ben's clients to find out he's lost his license. The Board of Veterinary Medicine has been so busy lately. I know how paperwork can easily be misplaced. I would hate for him to have to close up shop.

Looking at Ben, Holly realized she'd never jeopardize his career or happiness. No matter what her feelings were.

She looked between both men as he did her best to harden her heart. To her left, stood Ben. The man she felt completed her like no other would or could. To her right, stood her father. The man who raised her and was always there for her.

In her heart she knew her next actions would hurt them both. She just hoped in time they'd grow to forgive her and she could forgive herself.

With any luck a day many years from now, when she so happened to run into Ben, probably with his wife and family by his side, the heartbreak would have faded. Even if only a little.

Holly took a deep breath preparing for her next words. "You need to leave, Ben."

At her unexpected words, Ben jumped up and quickly descended the stairs to stand in front of her. The worry on his face was almost too much for her to handle. "What's wrong, Holly?"

Make him hate you. Give him no other choice but to leave.

"The only thing that's wrong is you thinking you can come over to *my* father's house and shove the fact he can't fix anything in his face. Just because your dad's dead doesn't mean you can hone in on mine." She wanted to vomit.

"Excuse me?" Ben took a step back as if her words slapped him.

"Young lady," her father scolded.

"I mean it, Ben, get your shit and leave. You're not welcome here." Ben took another step back this time holding his gut like he'd been punched.

"Holly Flanagan, what has gotten into you?" Her dad started making his way down the porch steps.

Holly's eyes burned with unshed tears. *Put the nail in the coffin.* She tore her eyes from Ben and looked at her father. "Go inside, I'll be there in a second, and we can discuss the issues. But first, I need to make sure Ben takes his mutt of a dog and leaves."

"Holly!"

"Get inside now, Dad!"

Henry looked from his daughter to Ben. Her gut clenched when he looked as though he'd still been sucker punched.

Holly's world was falling apart. Everything she felt inside of her, broke. Now he'd hate her and although that's exactly what she wanted from him, seeing the pain in his eyes would haunt her for the rest of her life.

"I'm only going inside because this is not how you normally act, Holly. I'm disappointed in you. I'm gonna let you two talk but listen here, little girl. I'm not sure about the honing in on your father part, but the only one who shoved my disability and inadequacy in my face, is *you.*" He turned on his heel and stormed inside.

Holly closed her eyes as the hurt washed over her. Hearing she's now a disappointment to her father broke her beyond repair.

This is why you don't fall in love. It only leads to heartbreak and destruction for all.

"Holly?" Ben whispered.

She couldn't open her eyes. She knew if she did, the pain in Ben's eyes would take the last bit of control she held.

The tears fell down her cheeks with no stop in sight.

Ben placed his hand under her chin forcing her to look at him. "Open your eyes, baby."

She wouldn't.

She couldn't.

"I can fix whatever is going on," he pleaded with her. "Let me fix it. Please, Holly."

How could he still want to help her? How could he still be standing here trying to fix *her*?

Holly's control snapped. Her eyes shot open as her fists pounded into his chest pushing him backwards. "You can't fix this. You can't fix any of this. It's all your fault to begin with. Before you I had a normal life. I never had to worry about anyone other than my dad and now you've come in here and screwed up everything! I wish I never went to that dumb dog park that day. I wish I never met you." The realness of the situation was too much for her. She crumbled to the ground, her body shaking with sobs.

Ben instantly followed, holding her in his arms while she openly sobbed. Her shoulders shook as she let the events of the morning finally took its toll on her.

Ben pulled her into his lap encasing her in his arms, as he used his body to shield her from the outside world. "It's okay, baby, I'm here. Everything is going to be okay." He rocked her gently.

Holly wanted to pull away. She wanted to stand strong, but as she tried to grab at the courage she found herself clinging to Ben's shirt, pulling him closer instead.

How could being in Ben's arms make her feel safe? And why was he still willing to hold her, especially after what she'd said?

Pushing those thoughts away she cried.

She cried for her father and pain she'd caused him.

She cried for Ben and all of the hurtful things she'd said.

She cried for the love she knew she'd lost.

She cried for all of the pain she put everyone through.

She cried for her one real chance of happiness being ripped away.

BEN ROCKED Holly in his arms as he tried to wrap his head around the last few minutes. From the shocked look on Henry's face, which he was sure mirrored his own, to the pain in Holly's eyes as she spoke.

He knew something was very wrong. Although her comments about his father stung, he knew every word out of her mouth was not really her.

Even as Holly's words echoed through his head, he knew he couldn't believe them.

He wouldn't.

Ripley sat beside them looking from Holly to him. Even she was at a loss for what to do. Squeezing Holly tighter Ben waited for her gut-wrenching sobs start to slowly subside.

Once he knew they were under a manageable control, he lifted her chin so he could look at her. "Talk to me, Holly, Please."

She shook her head as he saw more tears pool in her eyes.

"Please, Holly." He rested his forehead on hers. "Let me know what's going on. I can't fix it unless you tell me what the problem is."

She pulled back from his embrace to stare at him. The sadness in her eyes felt like a knife right through his chest.

"I-I..." Her voice hitched. "Ben, I don't know what to do!"

He placed his hand behind her head and brought her onto his chest as another sob escaped her. "Shh, it's okay, baby, we can work through anything."

She kept her head on his chest as she spoke, "When my dad couldn't go back to work, I took on all his bills."

As she spoke, the pain and concern in her voice broke him.

"Then all of a sudden his medical bills started coming in. I realized I couldn't do it all no matter how hard I tried or how much money I brought in. Before I knew it the bills started falling behind. I never wanted to burden my dad about it, so I never told him how bad it really is. I planned on getting a second job so I could at least get his mortgage up-to-date. When I met you, I guess I got distracted and it slipped my mind. Then today when I was at work I received a wake-up call."

Ben rubbed her back. If it was a money issue, he'd gladly take care of whatever she needed. Even if that meant tapping into the money his father left him. "Baby, if you're worried about money I can help you."

She shook her head pulling away from him. "It's not about the money or you helping. Besides, I'd never allow you to help with that. It's everything else, including the behind payments."

Ignoring her brush off of his offered financial help, he gently spoke, "Okay, explain it to me, Holly. Explain what 'everything' is. What was this wake-up call? What happened?"

She looked away from him.

"Holly. Talk."

"I can't lose my job, okay! It's the only income I have to help my dad. He means the world to me, and if that means I have to let you go in the process than I have to. No matter how much it hurts me I have to take care of him."

Ben's eyebrows knitted together. "I don't understand." Why would being with him make her lose his job?

She looked toward the trees in the yard. Her shoulders slumped as she took a deep breath. "Your mother has more pull than I ever thought possible."

What the fuck? His mother had something to do with this? There was a small part of him that wasn't all that surprised, though. His mother would find anything that made him happy and would try and destroy it. Holly included.

Knowing his mother was behind Holly's distress had every muscle in his body tighten. He needed to know more. He was only a few seconds from snapping. "Explain," he demanded.

Holly's body tensed at his hard words at first but she then firmed her jaw and looked him in the eyes. The determination he admired about her was back. "She showed up at the library this morning and told me if I wanted to keep my job I had to stop seeing you."

"What?!" *This had to be a fucking joke.*

Holly sat in his lap a little straighter as she continued. "She tried to pay me knowing I'm so far behind on my dad's bills. This house..." She gestured behind him. "...is about to be foreclosed on. I've been trying to work out a payment plan with the medical companies, so I can rearrange more money to the mortgage, but no one wants to budge." Tears pooled in her eyes once more with defeat. "She thought she could give me money to fix my problems, but I'd have to stop seeing you. No one bosses me around, Ben. No one. When she offered me the money I told her to shove it. When I thought she finally got the picture, she casually mentioned she knows four of the five library board members and she'd have me fired in one phone call. I thought she might be bluffing, but I still panicked. Obviously, her threats have merit. Not five minutes later my dad called asking when I'm coming over next because the bank called him." Her whole body slumped. "She said I had a choice. Pick my father and I wouldn't lose my job or pick you and I lose everything." She pulled out her phone and shoved it in his face. "And, so will you."

Ben read the screen as he did his best to digest everything Holly had said. His anger toward his mother was at an all-time high. Once the words on her phone registered, he saw red. "That fucking bitch," he growled.

He took Holly's phone and swiped through the message. Sure enough, it came from his mother's business phone. The same phone that *used* to belong to his father. "I'll fucking end her."

"You can't!" Holly pleaded. "She'll destroy you. She has the means to do it. She made it clear she owns this town."

He quickly pulled Holly into his arms. "She can't do anything."

"She already has."

In his mind, his mother was as good as dead at this point. She'd crossed one too many lines this time. "Do you trust me?"

When he looked into her eyes, he saw her trust in him. With her quick nod, he kissed her forehead.

"Good. First, let's take care of this one step at a time. I want you to go inside with your dad and call the bank. Find out how much is owed on the house. Then round up his medical bills. I'll take care of it."

"No!" Holly yelled. "I would never let you do that."

She tried to pull out of his embrace, but he wouldn't allow it. "You're not *letting* me do anything."

"You don't get it, Ben. Even if I won enough money in some lottery and paid everything off, if we stay together *you* lose everything. If she can easily manipulate the board of direc-tors for the library or even a bank official, she could definitely follow through on her threats. I can't do that to you. I can't be the cause of you losing everything you've worked so hard for."

The concern for him and his happiness, overwhelmed

him. "Holly, I promise you she can't do anything to my career."

"Yes, she can." He heard the desperation in her voice, causing him to reach out and hold her chin. "No baby, she can't. Even if she went to the state's veterinarian board and demanded my license be removed, she'd get nowhere."

"How can you be so sure?"

He smiled at her. "Seeing as I'm personal friends with half of the members and one of my dad's oldest friends is on the board, I'm safe."

"What does that even mean?"

"I can say we're not the only ones that aren't fond of Barbra Richman. She wouldn't have a leg to stand on."

"Fine, so you know the board, that doesn't mean she can't file complaints, or like she said make paperwork disappear. If she can ruin me, a measly librarian, with no sweat if she put in a little effort she'd destroy you."

"Baby, don't you think if she had the power to revoke my license, she would've already done it? She's been trying to force me to work at Richman Industries since my dad died."

Holly stared at him blankly.

"The woman that birthed me is a manipulative bitch. She stops at nothing to get what she wants. If she had any chance of taking away my license she would have done so already. She can't do anything to jeopardize my practice. I promise."

Holly's face fell. "I don't understand why she'd go through all this trouble."

"I wish I could tell you, Holly, I really wish I could." He kissed the top of her head. "Now, I want you to go inside and talk to your dad. Call the bank and get all his bills in order."

When she opened her mouth to object, he stopped her. "Now. Holly."

She crossed her arms over her chest, her stubbornness back in full force. "And what makes you think I'll listen to you?"

Ben raised his brow. "Go inside, Holly." He lifted her off

his lap. "By the time I get back, I want to know everything that's owed."

She narrowed her eyes at him. "And where the hell do you think you're going?" she asked.

"I'm going to see my mother."

Chapter Sixteen

HOLLY MADE her way into the house. However, when she rounded the corner to the kitchen the look on her father's face stopped her dead in her tracks. The confusion and hurt in his eyes caused her stomach to bottom out.

"Are you going to explain to me what happened out there?" her father's harsh tone echoed through the room.

"I'm sorry." She resigned herself. What more could she say?

"You're sorry?" His right brow rose.

"It's been a terrible morning."

"That is no excuse, young lady." He stood from the kitchen table then made his way over to her. He pulled her into his arms. "Hearing those cries broke me in two, sweetheart. I never want to hear that pain come from you again."

Holly pulled herself deeper into her father's embrace. How did she end up so lucky to have both the men in her life care so deeply about her? Sure, her father might be disappointed in the situation, but he'd never turn his back on her. Instead, he pulled her closer rubbing a small circle on her back letting her know everything would be okay. "I'm sorry, Dad," she whispered.

Giving her shoulder a quick squeeze, he motioned to the table. "Come, sit. Let's go over what happened."

"Okay." Blindly, Holly reached down to her side and pat Ripley on the head who had followed her inside. She hoped the dog would give her strength. "I don't really know where to start other than this morning."

"That sounds like a good place."

Holly tried to smile, but the gesture fell flat. "First, we need to get some things out of the way."

Henry looked at her slightly confused. "Okay."

"I haven't been honest with you." She took a deep breath.

"What do you mean?" He cocked his head to the side, studying her.

"The bills haven't been as up-to-date as I would like."

Both of his brows shot to the ceiling, one slightly higher than the other.

"I've fallen behind on everything." Holly's head fell in defeat. "I know I should have done better. I've disappointed you as a daughter. I should have tried harder."

Henry pulled her into his arms as tight as he could. "Holly, Pumpkin. Don't say that. Why didn't you tell me things weren't going well?"

"I didn't want to burden you. You've taken care of me your whole life. It's my turn to take care of you."

"We're family, Holly. Family sticks together and when one of us is struggling, all of us are struggling." He kissed the top of her head.

Pulling back, she did her best to look at her father through her watery gaze. "I realize I should have told you and I'm sorry for keeping everything a secret." She placed her palm on the side of his face that drooped. "After seeing you struggle after the blood clot and how hard it was for you to give up something you loved, I couldn't put you through anything that would hurt you again. I couldn't see that look of devastation on your face one more time."

Henry watched her with the pain in his eyes burrowing into her. "So, you took on everything so your old man wouldn't feel sorry for himself?"

Doing her best to lighten the mood she shrugged, before saying, "Well, when you put it that way, it sounds silly."

Henry kissed her head. "It is silly, Pumpkin."

"I promise to be more honest with you."

"That's all I ask for. That's all any father asks for."

She pulled herself from her father's arms. "You might want to sit down, Dad."

He looked at her quizzically.

"If honesty is what you want, I'm going to tell you everything."

Her father moved to the kitchen table before sitting. "I'm ready."

Ben stormed into Richman Industries ready to murder.

The moment he made it through the lobby, the cold dread he felt anytime he entered the building started to seep in. He did his best to avoid this place. Nothing good ever came from being inside of here.

Making his way past the receptionist, he headed toward the elevator. Stepping inside, he hit the top floor. He knew the layout all too well. As a child, he spent countless days playing at the foot of his father's feet. This whole building had been his personal playground.

He used to love the days his father took him to work.

Now the thought of stepping one foot inside of Richman Industries made him sick to his stomach.

When he reached the top floor the elevator doors opened. With a determination he didn't know he had he headed toward his father's old office.

"Mr. Richman, it's so nice to see you again," his mother's assistant greeted.

Ben took a controlled breath. He wasn't angry with her assistant and he refused to take it out on her. "Is Barbra in her office?"

"Yes, your mother is in there." She beamed at him doing her best to stick out her chest and entice him, which caused him to roll his eyes.

"She's no mother of mine." He blazed past her and threw open the office door.

There in front of him sat his mother. She had absolutely no right to sit where he sat. She was a fucking fraud. Always had been, and always will be.

Hearing the door open, Barbra looked from what he assumed was a fashion magazine and eyed him. The smug smile that spread across her face sent new waves of anger to course through his body.

"Benjamin, it's so nice of you to have stopped by," she sneered while sitting back in the chair.

"Cut the crap, Barbra."

She should win an award for the fake look of hurt and confusion that swept across her face. "Whatever do you mean?"

Ben walked toward her. "You've got to be fucking kidding me, *mother*. I knew you were a slithering bitch, but I never thought you'd stoop so low."

His mother straightened, her fake act dropped. "Oh son, haven't you figured it out by now? I will do *whatever* I need to in order to get what I want." She smirked at him.

Ben fisted his hands at his sides trying to control his rage. "You're a fucking piece of work. How dare you go to Holly and threaten her and her father? Do you really think you have this much pull? Newsflash, *Barbra*, you're nothing around here."

Her eyes hardened. "I'm everything in this town."

Ben took a step closer to his mother. "You're a fucking joke. No one can stand you. They only tolerate you because you're unfortunately the head of Richman Industries."

"Oh, Benjamin." Her hurt act made its appearance once again. "Don't you understand? I only want to help you. I'm doing this all *for* you. Your words hurt me." She had the gall to place her hand over her heart.

"You are not doing this for me. You've never done a damn thing for me in my life."

She sat back in her seat. "How could you say that? I'm your mother. The only mother you'll ever have."

"Not anymore." He turned, ready to start his plans to take her down once and for all.

Barbra's features darkened. "You've always been an ungrateful bastard. Now that you have that cow in your life you think you're better than the rest of us," she spat.

Ben spun around, his eyes narrowed as he glared at her. "What did you just say?"

"You heard me, you ungrateful nuisance. As a mother, I've done everything I could to help you succeed. You were supposed to take the head of Richman Industries when your father died. I've groomed you for this moment, but you know what you did instead? You took everything I've ever done for you and threw it in the trash. Not only that, you think spending each day with mangy flea infested creatures makes you better than everyone else. Your silly clinic ruined you."

"*You* ruined me."

"I did no such thing. I tried to help you. Even your father tried to help you."

Ben's blood boiled at the surface of his skin as his lips flattened. "Don't fucking bring him into this. He'd still be here if it weren't for you."

Barbra crossed her arms over her chest as she smirked at him. "You're so naïve."

"Fuck off."

"Seriously Benjamin, do you really think your father would approve of you mingling with disgusting creatures all day? Not to mention, you are now associating with that... can you even call her a *woman?*"

Ben's control snapped. He leaned over the desk entering her personal space. "Listen here, bitch. Get your story straight. Dad paid for my practice. He *never* wanted me to follow in his footsteps. He wanted me happy and so help me God, if you so much as look in the direction of Holly or her father again I will end you."

Barbra laughed. "Oh really, *son.* Do you really believe *you* of all people have enough pull in this town to do anything to me?"

For the first time since entering the room, Ben smiled. "Why yes, Barbra, I do."

She stared at him a few moments, trying to call his bluff. When she got nowhere she reached for the phone. "I guess you leave me no choice." She picked up the receiver. "I do hope your *plaything* has another job lined up. Oh wait..." She smiled at him. "I know she doesn't."

Ben snatched the phone out of her hands slamming it onto the desk. "Fucking Christ. You're seriously messed up in the head."

"Is it messed up in the head to want what's good for you?"

He threw his hands up in disbelief. "In your eyes what's good for me is to destroy the woman I'm in love with?"

"You do not love that dreadful woman."

"Yes, I do love her. She makes me whole. I've never in my life wanted someone more than I want Holly." He placed his hands on her desk leaning even closer into her space. "And I will destroy anyone that thinks they can hurt her."

"Please, you can't do anything."

"Watch me."

"It sure is a shame, Benjamin. I wonder how her father will feel about losing his home." She opened the magazine on the desk and started thumbing through it dismissing him.

Ben saw red.

He might have lost his own father to his crazy mother's demanding ways, but he'd be damned if he lost Henry too. No one could ever replace his father, but when Henry came into his life, much like when Holly did, the void he'd felt for years slowly started to disappear.

God he hated her. He hated everything about her. It was time to bring out the big guns. The pieces of information he'd had in his possession for years that he let stew in case he ever needed them.

Ben's blood rushed with adrenaline. It was time. He knew his mother thrived on confrontation. If he wanted to end her, he knew the perfect way to do it.

Ben straightened before popping his left hip on the side of the desk. Casually, he pulled out his phone and started thumbing through it. "I didn't know you cared so much about me," he remarked, looking at her through his peripheral vision.

Barbra's posture switched to one of a champion. "Of course I care, Benjamin. You're my son."

"I see that now." He nodded.

"I'm so glad you're finally coming to your senses." Barbra excitedly opened the desk drawer taking out a calendar. "Now that you realize where you belong, I've got a list of events for you to attend." She looked at him. "You know, schmooze the investors so we can get to their checkbooks. I know quite a few of them have daughters your age, some a little younger."

He felt the bile rise in this throat.

"Oh, the Jackson's have hinted recently how they want to see their daughter married to someone who aligned with their views. Howard Jackson owns a textile company a few cities over." Barbra clasped her hands together. "Could you imagine the income we can acquire if we merged with them?"

Ben's gut clenched. "You mean, you'll sweep in for a hostile takeover?"

The evil gleamed in his mother's eyes. "Of course."

"And you think it would be best if I marry someone like the Jackson's daughter?"

"She'd be perfect on your arm. Everyone will be in complete envy of her and of you."

Ben continued to swipe through his phone looking at pictures he'd sneakily taken of Holly throughout their time together. "And envious of you, no doubt."

Barbra's smile widened. "Precisely."

He looked at her face. "I have a question for you, *mother*?"

She nodded.

"Have you ever heard of a person that goes by *Douglas*?"

Her eyebrows knitted together. "I cannot say that I have."

"Huh?" Ben put his phone back into his pocket. "Before Dad died, he let me in on a little secret."

Barbra's mouth thinned. "What secret is that?"

"Toward the end, Dad stopped trusting you. He had a feeling you were up to no good, but he couldn't quite put his finger on it."

"What are you saying, *Benjamin?*"

Ben looked her dead in the eyes. "Did you know private investigators can find out *anything?* Including insider trading, threats, transferring funds from the company to an offshore account in the Bahamas that just so happens to have a monthly transfer that matches the exact amount deposited into your separate account each month?"

Barbra paled.

"Interesting how those funds have somehow always avoided the tax man. Speaking of the tax man..." Ben tapped his finger on his chin. "I wonder what the going rate for tax evasion is right now?"

"You wouldn't. I'm your mother."

Ben lifted a brow as he smiled at her. "You've taught me so

well over the years. I know I can ruin you in, how do you like to say it? Oh, yeah, one phone call."

Barbra's face hardened, her lips thinning. "I'll destroy you first."

"I dare you to try." He pulled out his phone.

"What do you want?"

This time when Ben looked at her, he saw nothing but pure hatred. This should have been the woman to protect him from the world. This should have been the woman that wanted him to be happy and follow his dreams. This should have been the woman who was beyond excited that he'd found the person he wanted to spend the rest of his life with. Instead, she was the woman that killed his father with her greedy ways. She stole from the company his father worked himself to the bone to make successful. And worst of all, this was the woman that threatened the happiness of Holly and her dad, who he'd now loved like his own father. "For you to fucking disappear. Give this company to the board and leave."

Her eyes narrowed.

"And listen clearly, Barbra, if you ever fucking threaten my family again I won't hesitate to make the call."

"I'm your only family," she sneered.

"You've never been my family."

She sat straighter in her chair. "You'll have no one."

"You're wrong." Ben chuckled. "Holly and her dad are the *only* family I need."

Chapter Seventeen

AFTER TELLING HENRY EVERYTHING, including Barbra and her threats, he wanted to explode. He demanded Holly drive him to Richman Industries so he could give her a piece of his mind. Holly couldn't blame him, she felt the same way.

After talking him down a little bit, she knew he needed time to digest everything. Especially the financial situation. He wasn't too happy about taking Ben's offered help, but at this point, neither one of them had much of a choice.

Once she gathered the documents Ben requested and gave her dad another kiss on the cheek, she contemplated on where to go.

Before the shitstorm of the morning, their original plan was to have dinner at Ben's house. He'd given her his extra key and told her to bring Waffles over after work.

Could she still follow through with those plans?

There was a part of her that wanted to abandon them and cocoon herself in her apartment. However, there was a bigger part of her that wanted to be surrounded by Ben's stuff.

When the hell did I get so weird and needy?

Shaking herself from the thoughts Holly knew after a day like today there was only one choice.

Ben.

Always Ben.

Not to mention she was sure whatever hell Ben encountered with his mother, he would need her as much as she needed him.

Not being able to help it, she worried her bottom lip. *What if Ben decides his mother is right? Or what if he decides this whole thing is too much work and gives up?*

Instantly, her heart tightened.

No, that wouldn't be the case. She trusted Ben. Relationships like this didn't happen every day, and Holly knew that. She had to let go of the fear.

Ripley barked from the back seat clearly agreeing with her.

"Are you a mind reader now?" Holly looked in the rearview mirror at the dog.

Ripley barked again.

"You're right, Rip. Let's go get your comrade." Shaking her head at Ripley jumping around the back seat, Holly turned onto her street ready to retrieve Waffles from her apartment and head *home*.

Sitting in Ben's living room, Holly's nerves started to get the better of her. At this point, she didn't *think* anything else could go wrong, but based on her track record she knew it could.

Ripley and Waffles were playing in the kitchen, hopefully not developing a master plan to jump on one of their backs, using the extra boost to reach the treats on the counter. She honestly wouldn't put it past them. Ever since bringing them together, they've done a bang-up job of hatching elaborate plans.

She smiled to herself thankful for the distraction.

From the corner of her eye she saw Twitch make his way

out of the other room. She couldn't help but smile at the kitten. Ben brought him to his house on Friday.

When Holly had asked why he didn't bring him to her apartment, his excuse consisted of, "I'm the trained professional, and I want Twitch to be close by just in case something happens."

What a complete load of crap that was.

Other than the twitch he still had, the kitten was in perfect health.

Holly knew the reason Ben wanted Twitch at his place. He wanted a reason for them to end up at his house rather than her tiny apartment. She was sure it had something to do with his king-size bed versus her full.

Chuckling to herself, Holly couldn't entirely blame him. Two people, two dogs, and now a cat...

"Hey, Twitchy," Holly cooed as the groggy kitty who'd apparently been sleeping, made his way further into the room. Once Twitch heard her voice, his ears perked. He ran toward Holly jumping onto the couch to be next to her.

Maybe there will be an animal in this house that will listen to me.

Twitch settled in next to her, his little twitch knocking into her every now and then. Even though most people would consider it an unwanted side effect, it made her heart melt and only made her love him more.

Holly scratched behind his ear, enjoying the purr that erupted from him.

That's when she heard the front door open.

Holly braced herself as she waited for whatever form of Ben was going to come through the door.

Ripley and Waffles came flying into the living room as soon as the door opening registered in their little minds.

Typical. Neither one of them cared she was dying on the couch just a measly few feet from them. They only wanted Ben.

As Ben entered the room he smiled at her before dropping to his knees to greet the pups. "Hey guys," he cooed. He did his best to keep himself upright from the onslaught of kisses.

Holly watched as he scratched both dogs who simultaneously plopped onto their backs demanding belly rubs. Knowing once the ceremonial greeting of the dogs was over, he'd look at her. She bit her bottom lip knowing that moment would come any second.

"What havoc did you two cause while I was away?" he asked.

Ripley replied in a deep bark followed by Waffles whining when Ben pulled this hand away.

"Sounds wonderful," Ben laughed before righting himself. When he finally looked at Holly the smile on his face made her stomach bottom out.

What does a smile mean?

Throwing his key on the nearby coffee table, Ben made his way to her. "I see Twitch is right at home in your arms."

Holly looked at the sleepy cat who'd made himself quite comfortable on his back.

As she looked at the sleeping baby, Holly's vision blurred with tears. She didn't know when her life had gotten so intertwined with Ben's, but she knew this conversation could go one of two ways. He'd either tell her he took care of his mother and her job and father were safe or he'd changed his mind.

Wait a second.

What if he murdered her and he now needed me to help him hide the body? Holly couldn't be an accessory to murder. Sure, she loved the guy but she had a demanding dog and now a kitty to take care of. Not to mention, her father. Plus, she would never look good in a jumpsuit. No one ever did.

Feeling her emotions about to snap she shot her head to Ben. "What happened? Tell me."

"Tell you what?" he asked, smugly.

"Jerk."

"Oh." He leaned over her lap kissing her forehead before standing. "Are you referring to what happened when I saw my mother?"

She narrowed her eyes. Never mind her being the accessory to murder, she was about to be the person committing the crime. "Don't make me throw something at you."

"All you have in your lap right now is Twitch and I know you'd never throw him."

Well damn, he had her figured out. "You're right, I'd never throw him but I will take off my shoe and aim right for your head."

"So violent." He cocked his brow.

Holly's left eye twitched.

"Have you ever realized when you're annoyed your eye starts to twitch?" He pat the kitten behind the ear, waking him. "I guess you two are perfect for each other with the twitching and all."

Ben reached around the cat plucking him from her lap. After giving him a chaste kiss on his head, he placed Twitch on the other end of the couch where he promptly fell right back asleep.

All of a sudden, Holly was yanked off the couch and into Ben's arms. Not giving her any time to protest, he kissed her like a starving man.

After a few seconds she remembered she needed answers and him playing around was going to get him in an early grave. Placing her palms on his chest, she pushed him away. "Ben, so help me God I will hurt you. What the hell happened with Barbra? Do I need to find a new job? Oh crap, that's it right?" She started pacing. "I need to find a new job. One that will pay enough for my bills *plus* my dad's." She snapped her head to Ben. "Do you think the bank will still foreclose on the house if I plead with them?" She didn't let him answer as she continued her pacing. Unfortunately, in her hasty movements, she misjudged the coffee table's edge and smacked her shin.

Before she knew it, she started toppling over headed directly for the floor. She held out her hands ready for impact. However, like every other time Ben was around during one of her mishaps, she found herself in his arms rather than on the floor.

"Jesus, Grace." He laughed, pulling her into his arms. "I might need to wrap you in bubble wrap now, not just when you're pregnant."

Holly jumped out of his arms. "What?"

Ignoring her question Ben leaned forward kissing the tip of her nose. He then moved to the couch and plopped down next to Twitch.

Holly's eyes started to twitch again. *He wants me to kill him, doesn't he?*

Taking a deep breath, she decided to face one obstacle at a time. But, mark her words the whole pregnant talk will be discussed later. Bubble wrap, who did he think he was? "Ben, if you don't tell me what the hell happened between you and your mother so help me God, I will take Ripley, Waffles, and Twitch and leave." She glared at him. "And you *won't* be able to follow us."

Ben's eyes danced as his right brow quirked. "You gonna steal my dog?"

"She likes me better." She pointed to the dogs. Waffles now used Ripley as his own personal pillow. "Plus, I can't break up the dynamic duo."

"And, what makes you think I wouldn't be able to follow you?" He crossed his arms over his chest.

"You can't follow me when you're rolling around on the floor searching for your balls after I kick them so hard they find a new home deep inside your other organs."

Ben cupped between his legs making Holly raise her chin in triumph.

After a few minutes, she placed her hands on her hips,

waiting for Ben to stop his dramatics. Once she realized he wasn't going to stop, her eyes narrowed. "Talk," she growled.

"Oh, I like it when you get all dominant." He laughed before pulling her onto his lap. Within seconds he had her positioned with both of her legs on either side of his.

"No, Grace..." He gave her a chaste kiss on the lips. "You do not need to find yourself a new job. You do not need to worry about your father or his finances. No, you are not taking our babies and leaving town. You are staying right here, beside me, forever. Got it?"

Holly's brows shot to the ceiling. Was he seriously going to play with her? Okay, great, she didn't need to worry about her job or father, but she needed to know what happened between him and Barbra. *Was she dead?* "Freakin' tell me what happened, Ben, or I will pinch you!"

Ben's belly laugh echoed throughout the room as he kissed her forehead. "Now I can't have the dreaded pinch pirate come after me, can I?"

When Holly made the move to pinch him, he held out his hands in surrender. "Okay, jeez I went to Richman Industries and explained to Barbra if she ever threatened someone I love again she'd lose everything."

Someone I love... Holly froze. *He loves me?*

"My father was a smart man, Grace. He knew something wasn't right. He might have loved her at one point, but somewhere along the line he realized something wasn't quite as innocent as he wanted to believe when it came to Barbra Richman."

Pain flashed in Ben's eyes as he talked about his dad.

"All of the information his private investigator found on her was handed to me after his death. I never planned on using it against her. She's still my mother and as much as I despised her for her role in my father's death, she was the woman that gave me life."

"What?" Her mouth fell open.

"I know this doesn't make sense. Hell, it doesn't make sense to me. I should've outed her right after my dad died. But I didn't. Maybe there was a part of me that still looked at her as family. I don't really know." He rubbed Holly's arm in slow circles. "After what you said this morning and what she did, I had a choice. Do you want to know what choice I had?"

Holly nodded, biting her bottom lip.

"Given a choice between her and you, I will always choose you. I knew what I had to do, baby." Ben placed his hand on her chin making Holly face him.

He looked deeply into her eyes. The passion in his gaze made her breath hitch.

"I love you, Holly Flanagan."

"You love me?"

"Yes baby, I love you. I love everything about you. From your sense of humor to your mouth watering body and the way you stumble through life tripping and falling into everything." The corner of his mouth turned up as love poured out of him.

"Hey!"

"I don't call you Grace for nothing."

Holly looked into Ben's eyes and saw the love he had for her. Everything melted away from them. It was just them, two people that loved each other. A few hours ago she thought she'd lost everything: her father, her job, and the love of her life. But here in front of her, Ben wanted to give her all of those and more back. He wanted to give her what she'd always craved and never thought she'd be lucky enough to feel.

Holly captured her lips with his, as she poured all her emotions into their embrace. She loved him. She loved him more anything in this world.

When she pulled away, Holly rested her head on his forehead. "You came into my life and it felt like I was thrown onto a roller coaster. It's been nonstop since the day at the park. Somewhere along the way, though, you made me fall in love with you, Ben. I don't know how, and I don't know why, but I love you."

Ben smiled a sexy crooked smile at her. "It was Lord Waffles. We've been in cahoots this whole time trying to get you to love me."

"Really? Is that so?"

"Yep. We developed this master plan the day at the park. We knew all we needed to do was get you to stand in the right spot at the right moment and you'd be so enamored with my charm you couldn't help but fall in love with me."

"That's what happened?"

"One hundred percent." Ben kissed her lips. "That's my story and I'm sticking to it."

Holly chuckled as she shook her head. "What am I going to do with you?"

"Love me."

Chapter Eighteen

BEN CUPPED Holly's cheeks in his hands as he pulled her into a kiss. Both their emotions were raw from the events of the morning, but as long as Holly was in his arms, he knew everything would be okay.

Hell, it would be better than okay.

He had Holly.

Ben nipped at her bottom lip causing a groan to escape from her.

Holly moved her hips, grinding against his lower half igniting every one of his nerve endings on fire. He growled as his dick threatened to break through his jeans.

The moment Ben felt the heat from her core, his eyes rolled back in his head. *God damn, she was perfect.* Ben placed his hands on her hips helping her grind against him.

Fuck he loved this woman.

Love.

He did love her. Ben loved everything about her. From her stubborn sass all the way to her diva dog. When Holly came into his life, he finally felt what he'd been missing all along.

Holly was the woman he planned on spending the rest of his life with.

And he couldn't wait.

As Holly continued to grind her hips against this dick trying to get more friction a hiss escaped him. She knew exactly what she wanted and would do whatever it took to get it.

Ben's thoughts were cut off the moment Holly reached between them to cup his dick through the material. A deep growl escaped him as he arched into her, giving her everything she wanted.

When he looked at her, he almost lost it. Her cheeks were red, her eyes clouded with passion.

Fuck she was perfect.

As her body rocked against him, he could feel the love that poured out of her.

Ben's body pushed against hers as the tension in the room thickened. He moved closer, kissing her neck before lightly nipping at her skin.

He needed more. He needed to taste her.

In one quick movement, he removed her hand from his dick and flipped them. He secured both of her wrists in his left hand above her head. Returning his head to the crook of her neck he inhaled deeply. "How the fuck do you always smell so good?"

"I shower daily," Holly remarked which made Ben laugh before shaking his head. *Only, Grace.*

He licked her neck once more. "It makes me want to taste every inch of you." He felt her pulse along his lips as he sucked gently on her skin.

"More," she begged, moving her neck to the side giving him better access.

Oh, he was going to give her more. He was sure of it.

Ben repositioned himself so he was cradled snuggly between her legs. Grinding against her center, she moaned.

Music to my ears.

That sound was something he planned on hearing many more times tonight.

Letting go of her wrists, Holly straightened as Ben reached behind him and pulled his shirt from his body. Tossing it to the side he reached for Holly's top and ripped it from her body causing a tearing sound to echo through the room.

"I'll kill you!"

"No, you won't." He laughed at the annoyed face Holly shot his way. Ignoring her, he cupped both of her breasts in his hands. Her hardened nipples peaked through the lace material of her bra. Flicking his thumbs over them, her body arched toward his touch, which only encouraged him more.

How did he end up this lucky to have someone so damn responsive?

A huge smile spread across his face. God, he loved this woman.

In his same skilled movement, he'd done with her shirt, Ben took the two cups of Holly's bra and ripped them apart. The lace gave way in seconds.

"Bras cost a million dollars!" She punched his chest.

He was going to have to invest stock in woman's lingerie, because he planned on ripping every scrap of underwear from her body for the rest of their lives. "I'll buy you another one."

"Hell no!" She glared at him. "You'd probably come out of the store with the most unsupportive scrap of nothing." She held up her breasts and his mouth watered. She looked like a goddess, offering her succulent desserts at his altar. "These big girls need support. I won't have you buying me garbage that makes these babies dangle down to my knees."

Diving his head between her chest he ignored every word out of her mouth as he took what she offered and worshiped them. Plus, as soon as he hit up the store he would buy exactly that. Less material meant less barrier.

Ben pulled her nipple into his mouth causing her to let

out another moan. He sucked and tongued her peak as he used his other hand to tweak its twin.

Releasing her with a wet pop, he started working himself down her body kissing every inch of her as he went. When he reached her belly button, he dipped his tongue in while locking eyes with her.

The passion that stared back at him had his heart skip.

He kissed right below her belly button before he straightened himself. Quickly he removed her belt and with a few skilled movements, he had her naked beneath him.

"Why am I always the one that's naked while you've got most of your clothes on? This never makes any sense to me."

"I'm not as nice to look at as you are."

"The heck you say." Her brow quirked.

"It's true." Ben brought his head to her center. "I fucking love looking at you. You're perfect." Kissing the top of her mound, he looked at her. Holly's lower lip drew between her teeth.

"Yeah, but you're just as gorgeous to look at."

"Not to me." He kissed her mound again this time letting his tongue slip out. When he swirled it around her sensitive skin, she moaned, nearly making him snap.

Ben grabbed onto her hips pushing her back further to the arm of the sofa almost making her sit up straight. Placing one of his legs on the floor, he spread Holly's legs.

Taking a moment to lean back he gazed at her wanting to burn this image into his mind forever. Holly spread wide for him, her legs bent and her chest rising and falling as she stared at him with nothing but love in her eyes.

His eyes moved back other core, the wetness he saw drove him to the brink. He had one goal right now, and that was making Holly come as many times as he could before the sun came up.

Slowly, Ben trailed his fringe across her stomach down to

her center. He gently spread her lower lips as be brought his mouth to her ready to finally feast on the woman he loved.

As Ben's expertly skilled tongue worked her core, Holly thought she'd somehow died and gone to heaven. She pulled Ben's hair as he used his fingers to seek out her spot.

Whoa!

Holly could get used to this.

When Ben lightly grazed her clit with his teeth, her orgasm overtook her. Ben held her down as her hips tried to rocket off the couch.

"Holy shit," she panted as she felt every muscle in her body explode. After her body released, she opened her eyes to see Ben's smug face staring back at her.

She couldn't help the smile that spread across her own face. Yep, she could one hundred percent get used to this.

"You're breathtaking when you come." Ben kissed the inside of her thigh.

"Not as breathtaking as your dick." In one quick movement, Holly pushed Ben onto his back.

"Shit!" He stopped Holly's assault before he sat upward looking behind him.

Oh, no did she hurt him?

Ben reached behind him grabbing Twitch.

"Is Twitch okay?" How could she have forgotten? Poor kitten, he'd already been through so much, now he had to deal with almost being mushed to death by his parents.

The kitten looked at her and Ben with disgrace and demanded to be placed on the floor. Once he was on solid ground, he took off running but not before looking back at them one more time in shame.

Okay cool, now her kitten thinks she's some sex starved woman, and judge the crap out of her. At least he was okay.

"Did you see the look on his face?" Ben barked out a laugh.

"He's gonna hold this over us. I can feel it now." Holly smiled at Ben shrugging.

"Never a dull moment, is there?"

"Never." Holly stood holding out her hand for Ben to take it. With confidence in her stride, Holly led him to the bedroom. As she walked through the hallway, she couldn't help the feeling that spread through her. Before Ben she would have never dared to be openly naked in front of a man. Especially, a man that looked like Ben.

Glancing over her shoulder, she saw him blindly following her as he refused to take his eyes off her ass. Seeing where his attention was, Holly did the only thing she could do. She gave her ass a little shake. She wasn't instantly rewarded when a deep growl came from behind her.

The way Ben worshipped and loved her body sent another wave of confidence through Holly. If she'd known a sex god was all it took to skyrocket her self-esteem, she would have signed up for one years ago.

Holly shook her ass once more, causing a deeper noise to escape from Ben.

God, she loved him. With everything inside of her, she loved this man.

Once they made it to the bedroom, Ben pulled on her hand making her swing back toward him. He effortlessly caught her in his arms. Ben grabbed her hips lifting her into the air making Holly wrap her legs around his waist.

Don't mind if I do.

He pushed himself into her center. "Fuck, I can feel how hot you are through my jeans."

"Imagine how hot I'd feel if you took them off."

Tossing her onto the bed, Ben quickly removed his clothes. Within seconds he was on top of her, kissing his way up her body.

When he reached her face, he cupped her cheeks in his hands. "I love you, Holly."

"I love you too, Ben." And, she really did. She couldn't see herself without him in her life.

With one thrust, Ben pushed himself inside of her causing Holly's eyes to roll to the back of her head as she felt every movement. She was so full, she'd never get used to this feeling.

Ben's movements increased as he reached between them and sought out her clit. When he found it, he pinched. The electricity flowing through her body was enough to throw her over the edge one more time. "Oh man, oh man. I'm—"

Ben brought his lips to hers, cutting her off. He pushed his tongue past her lips seeking out her taste. He kissed her with such passion, she thought she would drown in it.

Tearing his mouth from hers Ben rested his head in the crook of her neck as his movements became more erratic. "I can't hold on."

"Don't." She could feel herself teetering on the edge once again.

Ben moved harder and deeper as her body reached its peak. With one last pinch to her clit, the stars behind her eyes erupted.

"Fuck!" Ben's face contorted as she felt him empty himself deep inside of her.

He then collapsed on top of her, his breathing heavy. "Holy shit, Holly. You're gonna kill me one of these days." He wrapped his right arm around her waist as he laid his head on her chest.

"Right back at cha."

Her world sure as hell had become a whirlwind since Ben ran into her life. There was no doubt of that. But as she laid there with Ben she never wanted this to end.

Holly's smile widened as she realized Ben started tracing idle circles on her stomach. A stomach she desperately tried to hide so many times in the past. But with Ben, she finally felt free enough to not be ashamed.

This was her, take it or leave it, and if you didn't like her or her size you could see yourself out.

Why? Because, she had Ben and that's all she would ever need.

As Ben placed his hand on her stomach she couldn't help but imagine him doing the same thing as their baby grew inside of her.

Wait a second!

A baby? Their baby. She didn't know whether to laugh or cry. She never thought about having kids before, but now... She closed her eyes as she thought about it.

Hold on...

He'd wrap me in bubble wrap?

Holly smacked Ben's hand off her belly.

"Why'd you do that?" he asked, annoyed.

"You will *not* wrap me in bubble wrap."

Ben's brow rose as the challenge swam in his features. "Wanna bet?"

"Yeah, I wanna bet." She tried pushing him off her body to no avail.

"Oh, Grace, how I love your feistiness." His smug look made her eye twitch.

"My feistiness is gonna punch you in the teeth."

"Nope," he announced so sure of himself. "Your feistiness gets me hard." He pounced on top of her going between her legs.

How was he hard again so soon? Holly didn't have time to ask since he pushed himself inside of her. Their talk of babies and bubble wrap was going to have to wait until another time.

Chapter Nineteen

BEN WOKE with Holly nestled on his chest. Ripley and Twitch slept at the foot of the bed, Lord Waffles was on his back with his legs in the air. He had wedged his way between Ben's legs, snoring.

He huffed out a chuckle at the crazy dog.

Ben couldn't help the feeling of warmth that rushed through him. He wanted every morning to be exactly like this.

Removing his eyes from the occupants of the bed, he looked around his room. Before he met Holly, he thought his house was enough. His bedroom used to be his sanctuary, but now, he realized it felt barren and cold.

His eyes focused on the dresser where Holly's overnight bag sat.

Glancing around his room again, he had the urge to go to her bag and remove her belongings and place them around his room.

The thought made adrenaline rush through his body, as his heart rate sped.

That's exactly what he needed in his house. He needed Holly, and her belongings here on a permanent basis. She would make his house a home.

"What's got your heart racing?" Holly's groggy voice sounded from his chest.

"Morning, sleepy head." Ben kissed the top of her head.

"If your heart is racing 'cause you've got a stiffy, I'm gonna need to take a rain check. You wore me out last night."

Ben barked out a laugh as he placed his hand under her chin, pulling it upwards so he could kiss her lips.

"Eww morning breath." Holly pulled away.

"Are you saying I have morning breath?" He lifted his brow.

"No. I'm saying *I* probably have morning breath and I do not want to subject you to it. That shit is not all roses like they say in the movies or books."

"Noted." Deciding to ignore her, though, he pulled her into a deep kiss. When he pulled away from her lips, he winked. "That's what I think about your morning breath prejudice."

Rolling her eyes, she settled back into Ben's side. "This is nice."

He couldn't have agreed more. He kissed the top of her head once again. "Waffles sure thinks so." The dog's tongue hung out of his mouth as he snored away.

"That's my boy." Holly smiled. "Tongue out for days."

"That so?" Ben's eyes lit with mischief causing Holly to punch him lightly on the chest.

"You've got a one-track mind, mister."

"With you. *Always.*"

She laughed, nodding her head. "Me too."

"Do you have work today?" he asked, looking at his alarm clock. He didn't have to be at the clinic until nine forty-five, and right now, the clock only read six-fifteen.

"Yes, I work the morning shift from eight-thirty until three." She started scooting away from him. "That reminds me, I'm gonna need to get a move on if I plan on walking

Waffles, having a shower, and actually eating breakfast before I head to work."

"I have a backyard, Grace," Ben announced. "I'll let Waffles out, and you can hop in the shower while I make us some breakfast."

"Don't call me Grace." She gave him a dirty look. "That all sounds fine and dandy, but I have to head to my apartment first. I forgot to grab work clothes with all of the stress of everything that happened yesterday."

Ben didn't like her response. Holly deserved every free moment she got. She shouldn't have to worry about heading home to get clothes to be at work on time.

He tilted his head to the side as he started to ponder her situation. The library was closer to her apartment and she did walk to and from work most days. But... fuck it. "Move in with me."

"Excuse me?" She tripped, falling over as she got out of bed.

"You heard me, Holly. Move in with me." He gestured with his hand around the room. "Look how empty everything is."

She glared at him as her lips diminished into a thin line. "You want me to move in with you so your house doesn't look as sad?"

"No, I mean yes," he backpedaled. "No...damnit."

"Go shopping and buy knickknacks to fill the space."

"That's not what I want." He swiped his hand over his face. *Use your adult words, Ben. Don't fuck this up.* Taking a deep breath, he started again, "I want *your* items in the empty spaces. I want to wake up every morning the same way I did today. I want Waffles pushing me out of bed every night demanding himself more room." Ben looked into her eyes. "I want you."

"So, it's not just my stuff you want?" Holly cocked her head to the side.

The corner of Ben's eyes crinkled as he smirked. "Why are you so stubborn?"

"Most people don't ask someone to move in with them by saying they need more stuff to fill the empty spaces."

He laughed at her upturned nose. "You have a point."

"I have a good point."

"What's your answer?"

Holly bit her bottom lip as she shrugged. "I don't know, Ben. Don't you think this is all going a little too fast? One moment you're hitting me in the face with a Frisbee and the next you're asking me to move in with you."

Ben rolled his eyes. "I am not even going to dignify that with a response." His words must not have registered because she continued, "And, what do you expect I do about work? I walk there every day. It's the only exercise I get."

Ben lifted his brow. "I'm pretty sure our horizontal tango counts as exercise."

"It does not!"

"It's pretty physical."

"You're such a man."

"And you love it." He pulled the sheets from his body causing Waffles to growl at being covered.

Ignoring the dog, he reached for his hardening dick, palming it. He winked. "You love it all."

Holly barked out a deep laugh before crawling onto the bed. "I don't know if it makes me crazy or not, but I have some strange voice in the back of my head telling me to say yes."

"Listen to it," he said, reaching for her.

"What do I get out of it?"

"Other than this?" He held the base of his hard on.

"You're impossible."

Letting go of himself he maneuvered on the bed to be right next to her. "Say yes. You know you want to. Your apartment is tiny, and here we have a backyard for the dogs to play in. Twitch is already accustomed to his new home and well... I want you here. *All the time.*"

Holly sat on her knees before tapping her finger on her chin. "I don't know."

"Grace," he warned, which caused her to glare at him again.

"I'll never move in with a bossy pants."

"Holly Flanagan, do not make me bend you over and spank your ass," he said sharply.

Quick as lightning Holly moved in to give him a quick kiss before pulling away. "Fine. I'll move in."

After hearing the words and registering her trying to get away he pounced. He grabbed onto her waist flipping her under him. Straddling her legs, he started to kiss his way down her body. It was time to celebrate.

Holly sat at her desk with a huge smile on her face. After she agreed to move in with Ben, he'd thrown her onto her back and made her explode more times than she could count. She hoped living with him would mean many repeat performances exactly like this morning.

Wow, I am really going to do it. I'm going to move in with Ben. Her mouth formed into a lopsided grin. *Holy Crapolie.*

"That is a look of a very satisfied woman," Mildred announced, coming from around the corner, which made Holly smirk.

"I'm not all that surprised, though."

"What makes you say that?" Holly asked.

"Do you really think that hunk of man meat would let you go? I knew once you told him about what happened he'd figure out what to do." She pointed to Holly's face. "He obviously did."

Holly nodded.

"Here you are sitting at the job you'd thought you'd lose, after that wretched woman yesterday. I'd say Ben took care of everything."

"She was a bitch, wasn't she?" Holly agreed.

"That she was. I may or may not have looked up how to place a Voodoo curse on her after you ran out of here."

Holly shook her head. "Only you, Mildred."

"Of course, only me. Who else is going to take care of my chickadee?"

"I'm your chickadee?" Holly asked.

"You're like the daughter I never had."

Holly's heart warmed. "That's sweet, Mildred. I didn't think you did sweet, more feisty and nosy." She smirked. "But, I can honestly say, you've been like a mother figure to me too."

"Are you sure you don't mean to say sister? Can't you throw this old lady a bone and make me sound younger."

Holly laughed. "Sure."

"That's what I like to hear."

"Glad I can be of service to you."

"That's why I keep you around. Now, let me guess what put that smile on your face."

Holly shook her head with a laugh. "Have at it."

"After you bolted out of here like a bat out of hell, you smartly took my advice and ran right into your man's arms, spilled your guts and then he informed you he'd take care of it and then nailed you on the closest wall."

"Does your husband know you talk like this?"

"Where do you think I got it from?"

"Mildred," she said as her eyes gleamed. "I can truthfully say you're wrong. I didn't run into Ben's arms. I went to my dad's and Ben just so happened to be there. Get this? He was fixing the porch. Anyway, after a few crappy words on my part, he did say he would take care of it. He went right to his mother and gave her an ultimatum, but I must say you are correct on one part. Once he came home, he did nail me. More than once."

"Get it girl!" Mildred threw her fist in the air.

"And once again after he asked me to move in with him this morning."

"You better have said yes, missy. So help me God, if you didn't, I might be old but I *will* kick your butt from here all the way to Timbuktu."

Holly roared with laughter. "I said yes, you crazy old lady."

Mildred placed her hand over her heart. "Oh, thank God. I really didn't want to have to hurt you."

"There you are!"

Holly and Mildred snapped their heads to the front door.

Holly's stomach bottomed out when one angry Barbra Richman started charging right toward them.

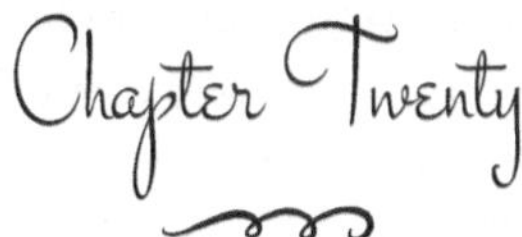

Chapter Twenty

ALL THE COLOR left Holly's face as her heart raced and her palms began to sweat. Quickly she glanced around the lobby as she tried to make sense of the situation. Why in the hell was Barbra here?

The Universe strikes again!

Swallowing hard, Holly pulled her eyes back to Barbra. The look that stared back at her held nothing but pure hatred.

Holly gulped as Barbra stormed toward them, her movements fast and precise.

Before Barbra made it to them, though, Mildred took a step forward. "What do we owe the pleasure of seeing the devil so early?" Mildred remarked. "I didn't think you came out during the day." She tapped her chin looking to the side. "Oh wait, that's vampires."

"This doesn't concern you, old woman," Barbra sneered which caused Mildred's eyebrow to skyrocket.

"The heck you say." Mildred shook her head. "What if you really are a vampire? I mean it would make sense you seem to have a fondness for sucking the life out of people. I understand the vampire realm is on a need to know basis kind of thing, but if you really are a blood-sucking creature, I want to know." She took out her pen and paper.

Barbra spun to face her. "Keep talking, you old crone and watch what I can do to you."

Mildred crossed her arms over her chest, daring Barbra to do anything. "Sounds like a vampire to me."

Although Mildred always found a way to make any situation entertaining, Holly knew it was better to cut this off at the pass. Plus, Holly was absolutely done with Barbra and her antics. Time to finally put this psycho in her place. Holly stood with her hands on her hips, jutting her chin toward her target. "You can't *do* anything, Barbra. You and I both know you can't do shit. Why are you even here? After what Ben told you I thought you'd be long gone by now." She shrugged. "Guess your freedom doesn't mean much to you."

Barbra's glare turned to Holly as her nostrils flared and her lips thinned. "This is all your fault. If it weren't for you and your meddling in my son's life he wouldn't have questioned me. It's because of *you* everything is falling apart."

"I wasn't the one that stole from the company." Holly marched closer pointing her finger at Barbra's chest. "You did all of this by yourself. Everything is falling apart because *you're* a piece of shit human being. You can't blame your actions on me." Holly turned away moving back toward Mildred.

"Keep your voice down, little girl," Barbra sneered toward Holly.

"Have you met me?" Holly pointed at herself. "I don't keep my voice down. It's not in my DNA."

"Just like having any sort of class isn't in your DNA."

"Get off your high horse, Barbs. Your insanity is showing." Holly rolled her eyes at the woman.

"Can you not handle the truth?" Barbra smiled, as she straightened.

Holly's brow shot to the ceiling. The smug look on Barbra's face made her skin crawl. Why in the hell would

Barbra act proper all of a sudden? This woman really did have a few loose screws.

Shaking her head, Holly stated, "You're seriously not making any sense, you crazy halfwit."

Barbra chuckled before placing her hand on her upper chest, smiling.

Holly's eyes went round as she instinctively took a step back. Clearly, Ben's mother had snapped. If the insane look in her eyes wasn't telling enough, the bipolar behavior was the nail in the coffin.

"You think I am the one that's crazy?" Barbra's mouth twisted into a smile. "Do you really think someone like my Benjamin, who is so far above your class, would ever truly want to be with someone like *you?*" She laughed a little higher pitched than before. "You're nothing but an experiment, my dear *Holly.*"

The holier than thou demeanor coming from Barbra made Holly's eye start to twitch.

"I guess every man should slum it with a cow before he marries someone closer to his status. You understand, right? Get it out of his system."

Holly bit her bottom lip. Sure, she didn't believe the words out of Barbra's mouth, but that didn't stop the pang of not being good enough that coursed through her body. Holly whole-heartily believed in Ben. He made his feelings toward her clear, but when she'd spent her whole life being looked down upon or being the clumsy one that is there for comic relief, those negative feelings had become ingrained in her. Even if she knew they weren't true, words like that still hit her where they can hurt the most.

"See, you already know the truth." Barbra popped her hip with glee. "You don't think someone like my Benjamin would really be with anyone who looked or acted like you. That's right, he'd never muddy our family tree by adding *you* and your degenerate DNA into it." Her eyes brightened. "I must say, though, I am quite surprised, you're lucky he even remotely pitied you."

The smug look on her face made Holly's blood boil. Sure, there were times she couldn't help but wonder why an Adonis like Ben wanted her, but in the end especially after last night, she knew he was her one. Somewhere along the pages written for them it was spelled out they were meant to be together. Who was Holly to question what the Universe decided?

Holly's fists clenched.

She wasn't, and she was damn sure going to make sure Barbra took her judgmental, bitch of a self and hightailed it out of there.

Clearing her throat, Holly looked Barbra firmly in the eyes. With the tightest smile she could muster, she began, "Funny you should mention that, Barbra. Did you know your son asked me to move in with him this morning?"

"Suck on them apples!" Mildred yelled.

Holding up her hands to stop Barbra from speaking Holly continued, "Not only did I say yes..." Holly took a step closer to the seething woman. "Ben has already *muddied your family line*. Do you want to know how? By consummating our new living arrangements by *nutting* inside me so many goddamn times and might I add without protection. If he didn't knock my *cow* self up there is something seriously wrong."

Barbra's mouth fell opened with disgust, before snapping shut. Her eyes honed in on Holly. "If he did, then you're both fools. No one will ever take him seriously as a Richman if he's ever lumped together with *you*. I hope for your sake and his, you're not as your degenerate self likes to put it, knocked up."

Holly hardened her stance about to tell Barbra Richman off once and for all when an angry voice cut her off.

"I thought I told you to stay away from Holly!" Ben's baritone voice bellowed through the library's entrance.

Holly's eyes snapped to Ben, after hearing his voice. The anger radiated from him. His jaw was firm as his eyes burrowed into his mother's face. If he had been a cartoon, she would've sworn there would have been smoke coming out of his ears.

Huh. That could be funny. Stop it, Holly, this is serious.

She swallowed hard before she focused on Ben's eyes. The hatred she saw there made her stomach bottom out. She'd never seen him this angry, hell she'd never see anyone this angry before.

"Benjamin, what a pleasant surprise," Barbra cooed. Holly didn't miss the slight back step Barbra took away from Ben, though.

Ben held up a paper bag before turning to Holly. "I realized Holly didn't bring lunch today and I wouldn't be able to get away from the clinic later. I needed to make sure she had something to eat." His words were harsh, but the gesture of caring for her well-being melted Holly's heart. How had she end up so lucky to have a man like Ben?

"Question is," Ben continued. "Why are *you* here? I didn't think you'd actually be stupid enough to not believe me. I thought you were smart. I guess the ivy league diploma is all for show then, huh?" He took a step toward his mother, his body now towered over her.

If Holly didn't already know Ben wouldn't physically hurt another human being she'd be scared for Barbra's life. "She was just leaving," Holly announced, trying to defuse the situation.

"No, she wasn't!" Mildred made her way toward Ben. "This crazy buffoon showed her face here whining about how everything falling apart is Holly's fault and how you were only with her out of pity."

Holly's eyes shot daggers toward Mildred. Didn't the old coot understand it was best to defuse these types of situations rather than add lighter fluid on it? Mentally hitting herself on the head, Holly rolled her eyes.

Of course not.

This was Mildred after all. The old bat lived on drama like this.

Ben's eyes snapped to Holly. When he saw the acknowledgment that she didn't believe Barbra's bullshit, he physically relaxed. He'd never been more thankful in his life than he was at this moment. If he hadn't decided to bring Holly lunch, he would have never walked in on this situation. And, by the stance Holly made he walked in at just the right moment.

Plus, he knew Holly didn't like confrontation and how she'd rather handle everything on her own. Case in point, how she tried to break up with him rather than telling him his bitch of a mother threatened her.

He knew beyond a shadow of a doubt if he'd never shown up at the library, he wouldn't have heard about his mother making an appearance.

Ben's eyes narrowed on Holly.

As soon as this situation was dealt with, he was having a talk with her.

He knew Holly could handle her own, but being in a serious relationship meant not having to handle everything alone. And, he damn well was going to remind her of that.

Images of Holly bent over her desk with her ass in the air, as he made her promise to always talk to him rushed into his mind. Her ass would color nicely.

Not the time.

Pushing the thoughts into the back of his head, he turned his focus on to his mother. Right now, he had bigger things to deal with.

Ben finally understood exactly what he needed to do. It no longer mattered they shared the same bloodline.

Moving to stand in Barbra's personal space Ben's eyes

hardened. "I never thought you would be this stupid. I guess, I was wrong. Coming after someone who had nothing to do with your mistakes is fucking ridiculous. Threatening her job, her father, and even her man." He pointed at himself, before shaking his head. "Deep down I always knew you were fucking trash."

"Do not speak to me that way, Benjamin. I'm your mother."

"No. Like I told you yesterday, you aren't." He held out the bag of food. "Take this, Holly."

Holly grabbed it only to throw it in Mildred's outreached arms.

"Free lunch? Don't mind if I do." Mildred snatched the bag from the air.

Ben reached for his phone in his back pocket. "You screwed up, *Barbra*." Using all his control, he took a step away from her. He knew at this point it was best to call Douglas and let him take care of the next steps.

"You fucking bitch!" Holly's words made Ben to snap around only to see his stubborn girlfriend jump for Barbra as his mother lunged for him. "Don't you touch him!" Holly screamed.

"Fuck!" Ben dropped his phone as he ran to where Holly had his mother pinned to the ground.

"I'll have you arrested!" Barbra bellowed at the top of her lungs.

"Not if I kill you. Mildred, help me!"

"I've been waiting for this!" Mildred gleefully rejoiced.

"No." Ben grabbed Holly by the waist pulling her off his mother. Which only resulted in Holly flailing around in his arms, kicking and punching the air. "Let me go, Ben!"

"*No.*" He did his best to hide his laugh as Holly's narrowed eyes directed at him after he placed her on the floor. When Holly's eyes snapped behind his shoulder, he turned his head to see his mother staring at them.

"Yes," Holly demanded. "If this piece of shit is already going to press charges, at least let me get one good hit in." Holly's eyes swam with something he'd never seen before.

Holy shit. In his whole life, no one, other than John had ever shown they'd cared enough to protect him the way Holly was doing right now.

Realization dawned on him.

Holly would risk going to jail in order to protect him. Her father, Waffles, her job, were all thrown out the window the moment he could have potentially been in danger.

Damn, that was hot.

But, also stupid as hell.

Even if she'd tried to jump on him, his mother never stood a chance. What's the most she could have done, pull him to the ground? And then what? He'd wrestled Great Danes that weighed more than his mother on more than one occasion.

"Let me go, now!" She pushed at his chest.

Damn she wanted nothing more than to protect what was hers. He fought his chuckle. "I'm not letting you hit her."

Holly started bouncing around him like a cage fighter without taking her eyes off of her target.

God, he was lucky.

"Why not?" Holly held up her fists.

"Yeah, why not?" Mildred chimed in.

How had these two not gotten into more trouble? He saw Mildred from the corner of his eye trying to egg Holly on.

"I'm pressing charges." Barbra stood, before fixing her skirt.

"No, you're not," Ben growled.

"Why, yes I am." With her words, Barbra smoothed her hair before pulling out her phone.

"I will kill you where you stand!" Holly's voice echoed through the lobby as she swung her fist in the air. She must have had a little too much oomph behind it since Holly ended up spinning in a circle.

"I'll hold her down!" Mildred happily offered to help.

For Christ's sake!

In fear of letting Holly free, he decided he needed to end this once and for all. Quickly turning to face his mother, while he kept Holly securely behind him, Ben spoke, "I'll only say this once, Barbra. You have twenty-four hours to leave. Leave this town and everything you know behind. I'll see to Richmond Industries being handed over to the board. You've got one chance to make it out of here without ending up in a jumpsuit. One phone call and everything gets sent to the proper people."

Barbra's eyes hardened.

"And to make myself clear one final time, I can and *will* destroy you."

For the first time since battling his mother, Ben saw the resignation in her eyes. This time she knew he wouldn't hesitate in putting an end to her.

"Fine." She moved closer to him. "You want me gone, you've got it. I'm gone. Listen to me, little boy, the moment you allow someone like *her* into your life, *you* lose everything."

"The only person losing everything here is you."

Barbra sneered.

"You have twenty-four hours."

With a huff, Barbra turned on her heel ready to exit. When she made it to the door, she turned to Holly. "I hope you're happy knowing you're destroying a family."

Ben moved into Barbra's line of sight. "No, Barbra, she's *made* a family."

His mother's lips curled as she growled. She looked him up and down once more before hastily leaving the building.

Once the door shut behind her, Ben finally let his body relax.

"Well damn, who needs coffee when you get a show like that?" Mildred plopped another chip in her mouth.

Seeing Holly's lunch almost gone, Ben made a mental note

to have a pizza delivered at noon for Holly. These two are going to be the death of him. Moving to his discarded phone, he picked it up before he started thumbing through it.

"Umm, uhh, thank you for the lunch, or what's left of it." Holly bit her bottom lip. The uncertainty in her eyes broke him.

"Come here, Grace." Instead of her normal protest at the name she willingly walked into his arms. Ben kissed the top of her head as he rubbed her back. "I love you, baby."

"Didn't I say you make my life a freakin' roller coaster?" Holly asked, resting her head on his chest.

"I think you might've mentioned it."

"In case you didn't realize what I was referring to..." She gestured to the doors which made Ben laugh.

"I know, baby, but guess what?" He kissed the top of her head. "Sometimes a roller coaster can be fun, and the best part, from now on, we'll get to ride these roller coasters together."

"Until your crazy mother shows up again." Ben saw the hint of panic in her eyes. "I don't want to keep dealing with her. What if she tries going after my dad?"

"Won't happen."

"What makes you so sure about that?"

Ben held his phone to Holly. "I might have lied on the twenty-four hour part. I may or may not have contacted the private investigator this morning to get the ball rolling."

"My kind of man!" Mildred threw one of her fists in the air as she took a bite of Holly's sandwich with the other.

"Mine too." Holly stood on her tiptoes bringing her lips to his.

Chapter Twenty-One

TWO MONTHS LATER

BEN SAT BACK on his knees on the newly finished porch watching as Holly played with the dogs in the backyard. When he heard the screen door shut, he knew Henry had made his way out to them. Over the past couple of weeks, it'd become a routine.

Ben would work around the house repairing what needed to be fixed while Henry guided him through every step. Holly would take care of the chores before feeding the dogs and packing meals for the week. She'd order them dinner, or Ben would help Henry cook on the grill.

After they ate, Holly would always insist on going out to the backyard to play with Ripley and Waffles, while Ben finished whatever project he had at hand. Somewhere along the evening, Henry would come out to the porch and sit next to Ben. Sometimes, they sat in silence, other times Henry told stories of his past.

The stories were always Ben's favorite. He'd quietly work as Henry retold stories of his wife, his years working, and of Holly.

The ones about Holly Ben liked the most. He couldn't help but picture a round faced Holly as she ran throughout the backyard causing havoc as she tripped and stumbled on invisible objects.

From his spot on the porch Ben glanced at the woman that had captured his heart. Currently, she sat on the ground while Lord Waffles ran around her in circles while Ripley sat directly in front of her waiting patiently for Holly to throw the tennis ball.

A chuckle escaped his lips as he shook his head at their antics.

This was perfection.

"One day, I come out here and you'll be in the yard with Holly playing with your children," Henry stated.

Henry smiled wide as he watched Holly playing with the dogs.

"One day," Ben agreed. That was another thing he'd grown accustomed to. Henry's not so subtle hints that he wanted to see both of them married and with children. He couldn't blame him, as the days went on, Ben wanted the same things.

Every night when he came home from the clinic to Holly in their kitchen trying not to burn the place down, or if she was curled up on the couch with Twitch at her side, made him feel whole.

Not the her burning their dinner, but her being there. In their *home*.

Ben laughed to himself thinking back to the nights he'd come home to find Holly in the kitchen. He found out early on she was *not* a cook.

Hell, Holly couldn't cook even if her life depended on it. Oh man, when they were moving her into his house, as a gesture to everyone that helped, Holly decided to sneak away and make everyone lunch. John and Ben, along with Henry's supervision, had worked the whole day getting her stuff in so she wanted to do something nice for them.

Three hours later a used fire extinguisher, and burnt

chicken tenders was the outcome Ben realized how dangerous Holly was in the kitchen. So he made a deal with her. Ben would handle anything that involved any sort of cooking appliance or fire and she could do everything else.

He *thought* it was a foolproof compromise. How could she hurt herself or the house making a sandwich or cutting vegetables, right?

One emergency trip to his clinic later where he stitched up her sliced finger, told him otherwise.

Laughing at the memory, he shrugged his shoulders. Not everyone needed to know how to cook, and he could say for sure, whenever she tried, he found himself on some whirlwind ride. But, he wouldn't change any of it.

"There she goes again," Henry spoke, as Holly threw the tennis ball in the air. When Holly ran after it along with the dogs, she tripped. Thankfully, she caught herself, though. "She's definitely gotten good over the years at catching herself."

"I've witnessed it," Ben agreed. "Remember when she brought the box of dishes from her apartment to the house? She tripped up the steps. Instead of falling and breaking everything in the box, she did some weird ninja move where she spun around. She then ended up with her back on the side of the railing her and the box unharmed." Ben laughed at the memory. He still didn't know how she managed it, but she did.

A red hue appeared on his cheeks as he images of last night poured into his mind. After coming, as Holly tried to dismount from his dick, her whole body shifted weird and she toppled off the bed. On the way down, though, she somehow grabbed every sheet to cushion her fall.

He panicked at first that she'd hurt herself, but when he looked over the side of the bed, she laid there tangled in blankets, her hair a mess, and her face red.

Nope. She wasn't hurt. Instead, she had the biggest smile

on her face that he'd ever seen. She took pride in knowing she was fast on her feet. When it came to her as she liked to put it, her 'clumsy award.'

Yep, living with Holly had shown Ben just how resourceful *and* clumsy she truly was.

Waffles bark snapped him out of his thoughts. He sat back on his heels as he watched Holly throw the ball.

Life was perfect.

"Ben, I want to talk to you about something," Henry remarked.

"Shoot."

"I know you paid off the mortgage on the house along with taking care of my medical bills. But, I wanted to make a deal of some sort." Henry sat on the rocking chair as Ben worked on replacing a rotted piece of wood on the railing.

"How many times are we going to have this conversation? You don't need to pay me back."

"I know you keep saying that, but it doesn't sit well with me that you paid all that money out of your own pocket."

Ben wanted to roll his eyes. It was almost the same exact conversation each time they'd end up alone. "I'm not taking any money from you."

"Why not?"

Ben resigned himself before turning entirely to Henry. "You don't take money from family. That's why. When I lost my dad, I never thought I'd have a father figure or any type of parent in my life again. We all know how shitty Barbra was." He shook his head. "When my dad died, I thought I was pretty much an orphan in a weird sort of way. I had no one to go to. My dad was the one who supported me. He did everything in his power to help me achieve my goals of owning my own veterinary practice. He was the one I turned to when I had trouble or when I needed advice. He was always there for me... until he wasn't. I know you aren't my actual father, and I'm freakin' grateful for that or me sleeping with Holly would open up a whole new can of worms. But, in a weird way, you've stepped into that father role that I was missing."

Henry's eyes widened. "Ben, I didn't know."

"How could you? I've never said anything. Here's the thing, Henry, you're a good man. One of the best I have ever known. You've got integrity and a good heart. You care for everyone."

"Not your bitch of a mother."

Ben huffed out a laugh. "Point taken. Regardless, you're my family. You, Holly, all the animals, and whoever else comes along. From here on out we have each other's backs. Family takes care of family."

Henry's eyes lit. "When you came into Holly's life I knew you were the one for her. You made her happy and you took care of her. Since you've shown up she hasn't stopped smiling. The first day I met you I knew you'd be good for her. That's also the day I first saw you as a son, Ben."

Well, shit.

Ben didn't know what to say. Feelings and emotions were never his strong suit. But then again, words weren't needed.

Ben turned back to his task of fixing the railing as they settled into silence. It felt good to have a "dad" again. Especially, one that reminded him so much of his own.

Another five minutes passed until, Henry finally spoke, "I might not be okay with the fact you paid so much money, but I'll stop bringing it up."

"You can keep bringing it up if you want, but you'll always get the same answer." Ben laughed.

Scratching his fingers along his chin, Henry squinted his eyes. "Maybe I can make it up with an exchange. Whenever you and Holly want some free time, I want the pups."

A ridiculously broad smile appeared on Ben's face. "Sounds like a deal to me."

"Good." Henry sat back in his chair and watched as Holly played with the dogs.

Hopefully, now they'd come to an agreement.

Ben went back to work as Henry stared into the backyard watching Holly.

A few minutes went by before Henry cleared his throat getting Ben's attention. "I'm not going to be around forever, son," he spoke softly. "Lord knows after everything I've been through I shouldn't be here now... but, I know there is a reason why I am."

Ben focused his full attention on Henry as he cocked his head to the side. "And what do you think that reason is?"

Henry watched Holly as she moved through the backyard before he turned to Ben. That's when Ben saw his eyes glossy with unshed tears. "To walk my little girl down the aisle to you."

Holly tossed the ball again for Ripley and Waffles. She couldn't help but laugh when Waffles fell over himself running after the ball.

Like mother, like son.

After making sure Waffles didn't hurt himself, she looked behind her. Ben and her father sat on the porch and talked much like they did every time they came over.

The first couple of evenings she'd sat with them as Ben worked on whatever project he was commissioned on for the time being. However, her idea of a good time did not include her father nitpicking everything Ben touched. Nor did it involve the dogs getting underfoot and constantly worrying about them. Instead she made it a point to take the dogs into the yard and give them all some much needed exercise.

Holly watched as her father pointed to something Ben was fixing. Ben liked the guidance from Henry. He never once complained. Instead, he soaked up the knowledge and was grateful for it.

The pride Holly saw on Ben's face once a project was completed made her heart skip. He'd always wait for her father's approval of his work. Once he got the, "job well done, son," he'd beam. Seeing Ben's expression matched a child getting approval from a father. It only made her love him more.

When a wet nose hit her leg, she looked down to see Ripley drop the ball at her feet. "You want me to throw it again, Pretty Girl?"

Ripley barked while jumping around in circles, which made Waffles do the same. "Will you let your brother actually get the ball this time?"

"You know she won't."

Holly turned to see her father making his way over to them.

"What are you doing out here?" she asked, before tossing the ball.

"I wanted to come see you. I told Ben to finish up the handrail."

Holly looked at him sideways. "And you didn't want to be there to guide him?"

Henry screeched his chin. "I may have also left him with his thoughts."

"And what thoughts are those?"

"None of your concern, Pumpkin. Now, why don't you drop the third degree and tell me how you are?" He gave her his lopsided smile.

This time she really did look skeptical of her father. "What's going on, Dad? You already know how I am."

"I know, Pumpkin. I just wanted to check on you. You've been living with that big oaf a while now. I wanted to make sure everything was to your standards. Do I need to threaten Ben with my "I know people in the mafia" speech?"

Holly lightly pushed her father's shoulder. "No, you don't." She laughed shaking her head no.

"I could. You don't know who I know."

Holly cocked her brow. "Seriously Dad, what's this all about?"

Henry smiled. "I'm happy for you, Pumpkin."

"I'm happy too, Dad." Her smile matched his.

Holly picked up the ball Ripley had placed at her feet and threw it before jogging with the dogs to get it.

"Good. Now, when can I get some grandbabies?"

Holly instantly tripped over an invisible rock before finding herself face first on the ground. She rolled onto her back before she pushed herself into the sitting position. That's when she saw Ben sprinting toward her while her father doubled over in laughter.

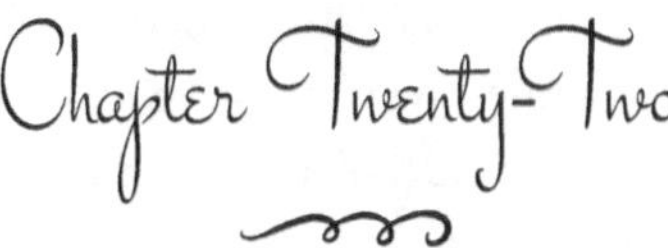

Chapter Twenty-Two

HOLLY PARKED her car in the driveway of her and Ben's home. Even though it had been over two months, she still couldn't believe she lived with him. In a house, nonetheless.

Once his mother was out of the picture, everything fell into place. The move was easy, minus a situation with burnt chicken tenders that was blown way out of proportion, if you asked her.

All of her belongings felt right amongst Ben's. It was like they were always meant to be. Also Holly started writing again. She didn't quite know if she felt confident enough to actually publish a story, but she was having a good time writing.

Walking toward the path to the front door, she noticed what looked like brown dog treats laying on the ground. Bending over she picked one up.

"Why's this here?"

Looking ahead, she noticed more dog treats in a line leading up the front steps. "What the hell?"

Instead of picking them up, she decided to follow the path curious as to what was going on. When she reached the front door, she opened it. The treats continued on a path into the living room. Throwing her belongings on the table by the door, she moved through the room to follow them.

Holly froze when she reached the living room.

In front of her on the floor was a massive heart made out of dog treats. In the middle, stood Ben. At his side, Ripley waited patiently, while Waffles on the other hand, was munching on the right side of the heart. Slowly making his way around to all the treats.

"Waffles," Ben growled. "Get back into formation. We've practiced this for days!"

Waffles reluctantly looked at Ben and then the treats. After one last longing look toward his goodies, he slowly padded next to Ben and plopped onto his butt with a huff.

"Why are you such a piece of work?" Ben asked before scratching the little guy between the ears.

Twitch not wanting to be left out, made his way to stand between Ben's legs, his head twitching every few seconds.

Holly's hand flew to her mouth at the sight in front of her.

Her family.

From the corner of her eye, she saw lit candles and roses scattered throughout the entire room. She looked at Ben, who presented her with a lopsided grin.

"Hey, baby." Ben winked.

"Ben?"

As Holly took a step forward, he held out his hands. "Stay right there."

"What's going on?"

Ben cocked his head to the side as a chuckle escaped his lips. "Now, Grace, you and I both know what's going on."

Holly's mouth fell open as her eyes widened.

Ignoring her reaction, Ben lowered himself to his knee.

Is this really happening?

Ben pulled out a tiny box from his pocket.

Yep, this was happening.

When Ben opened it, she saw the ring.

"Oh shit."

"Only you, Grace." He laughed before he cleared his throat. "Holly Flanagan, you came into my life like a tornado. One moment you were standing, the next you were on the ground with blood all over your face."

"Your fault," she was quick to interject.

"Yes, technically it was my fault but don't forget I *did* yell watch out." He smirked. "Who knew your klutziness and quick wit would turn me on?"

"Really? Can you not be serious even at a time like this?" She placed her hands on her hips.

"I am being serious. When I had you on the exam table looking at your tooth, I almost lost my shit. I wanted you then just as bad as I want you now."

"Ben," she warned.

"Fine. I won't mention how you get me harder than I've ever been in my life." Her glare made him laugh. "But, it's your love for animals that really sealed the deal. When you found out about Twitch, you were more concerned about the kitten than my ditching you."

"You didn't ditch me, you were saving lives."

"And that right there is another reason I fell in love with you. Grace, you complete me. After my dad died, I never was whole again. I walked around aimlessly just going through the motions, but when you brought hurricane Holly into the picture, I finally felt whole again. I felt right. *You* make me feel right." He gestured around him. "We now live together in this home with our four-legged children. Holly, I hate to break this to you but I think it's about time we made it official. Waffles keeps telling all the other dogs his mommy and daddy only live together but aren't married."

Holly raised her brow. "And what's wrong with that? People can live together and not be married. There is absolutely nothing wrong with that."

"I agree there isn't a thing wrong with it." Ben laughed.

"But, Waffles also let it slip he wanted to see his mommy in a beautiful white dress and him in a tuxedo. In reality though, I think he's only pushing for us to get hitched so that he can strut his stuff in a tux."

Holly looked at Waffles who'd sneakily made his way back to the edge of the heart where he started eating the dog treats again. "I wouldn't put that past him."

"And Ripley wants to put on a doggie dress to match her momma."

She nodded. "And what do you want?"

"I want to spend the rest of my life with you. I want to fill this house with animals and kids. I want you to be my wife, the mother of my children, and my partner for the rest of our lives."

Holly crossed her arms over her chest, with a smile. "And what do I get out of it?"

"Me."

Holly ran into his open arms making him fall onto his back. "Watch out for Twitch!" He pulled their cat from behind him and placed Twitch out of harm's way.

The look of annoyance on Twitch's face had Holly biting back a laugh. Thankfully, Twitch had seen the danger coming toward him and moved out of the way on his own. That didn't stop his judgmental glare shot their way though.

Once Holly saw Twitch make his way out of the room, she turned back to the only man that would ever own her heart. "I love you, Ben."

"Is that a yes?" he asked, his eyes hopeful as he stared at her.

"You haven't asked me anything yet," she joked, while kissing the side of his cheek.

"So picky. Fine. Holly Flanagan, will you marry me? Will you put me and Waffles out of our misery and do me the honor of becoming my wife?"

Holly tapped her index finger on her chin. "I'll think about it."

Ben growled, before he rolled her onto her back as she laughed. "I'll give you something to think about." He started tickling her showing zero mercy. When Holly started flailing around on the ground, the dogs started to bark and play, running around them in circles.

"Yes, Ben, yes!" She held her sides, trying to get him to stop tickling her. "I'll marry you!"

"I never had any doubt." He finally stopped his ambush before he leaned in and kissed her.

After a few seconds, Holly pulled away from Ben's lips. She glanced at what remained of the dog treats on the floor. Waffles was on his belly crawling from treat to treat as he went around the heart eating. "Why the dog treats?" she asked, with a laugh as she saw Ripley doing the same on the other side.

"I thought it was a perfect choice. We did after all, meet in the dog park." He kissed her neck.

"Where you hit me in the face with a Frisbee." Ben glared at her. "What? Don't glare at me. You did!"

Ben placed his hand behind her neck before bringing his lips to hers. "And I wouldn't have it any other way."

"Damn straight."

They laid on the floor laughing while the dogs cleaned up the treats. Holly looked around the room and smiled. This was exactly where she wanted to be.

Holly moved herself onto her elbows, when she saw something that grabbed her attention. "Ben, why is there a baby gate around the cat tree?"

Ben glared at Waffles, before answering, "Talk to your son."

"What do you mean talk to my son?"

"I got tired of coming in here after hearing him whine." Holly cocked her brow.

"He'd somehow managed to get himself stuck on the top

of the cat tree. He thinks if he can reach the cat treats, that means they are his for the taking. I only placed them that high for Twitch *thinking* they'd be safe." Ben shook his head. "He climbed up there and ate them fine, but Lord Waffles has no idea how to get back down."

Holly burst out laughing before she called Waffles into her lap. "That so, little guy? Is your daddy tired of you stealing all the cat treats?"

"No," Ben answered. "I'm tired of having to put his ass back on the floor."

"It's not his fault he has short legs." Holly scratched Waffles' belly.

"He gets up onto the tree fine, doesn't he?"

"We all have our talents."

"And his revolves around food."

Holly placed her hands over Waffles ears to shield him. "Hey, be nice!"

"I am being nice. I didn't say I didn't love him."

Holly's mouth broke into a smile as she laughed. "What a crazy family we are."

"And we wouldn't have it any other way." Ben plucked Holly from her spot on the floor and placed her into his lap. "Now, let's celebrate." He didn't give her a chance to say anything before he kissed her lips.

Chapter Twenty-Three

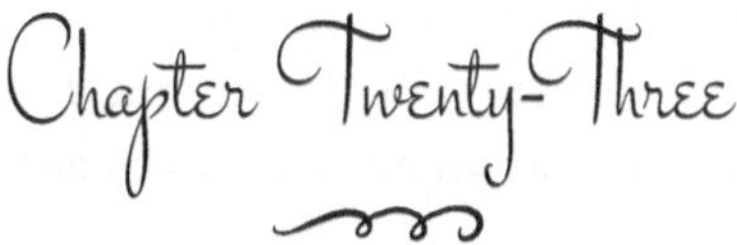

ONE MONTH LATER

HOLLY PACED AROUND the living room of her father's house trying her best to remain calm. As she let her mind wander, she realized how much work Ben had accomplished. The house looked just as it did when she was younger. If not better.

Ben with her father's watchful eye, really did a great job of restoring the bungalow.

Pay attention!

She had bigger things to focus her attention on.

In less than ten minutes, she was supposed to walk out of the back door and down the porch steps into Ben's arms.... to become his wife.

His wife.

Holy shit, Holly Flanagan was about to become someone's wife.

Ben's wife to be more exact.

Holly never thought she'd be here. But, here she was, about to marry the man of her dreams.

"You okay, Pumpkin?" Henry asked, as he walked into the living room.

Whoa.

Holly was momentarily taken aback by her father's appearance. She'd forgotten how handsome he cleaned up. Henry stood before her with bright eyes and a lopsided grin in a perfectly tailored tux.

Holly looked down at her dress. If her father looked this good, Ben would look ten times better. She'd never be able to compare. Biting her bottom lip, she looked at her dad. "Do I look okay?"

"More breathtaking than your mother on our wedding day," he answered, tears in his eyes. "But, Pumpkin, if the hole on the floor from your pacing is any indication of your state of being, I would say something is wrong." He moved to sit on the couch, before focusing his attention on her. "What's got you all up in arms?"

Before she knew it, Holly started pacing again. "This is really happening, Dad."

"It is."

"I'm about to marry the love of my life."

"That is a good thing, Pumpkin. If you are going to marry someone, you want them to be the love of your life."

At his words, she stopped pacing and glared at him. How could he not comprehend her dilemma here? Didn't he understand what was going on? Holly crossed her arms over her chest. "What if I make a fool of myself?"

When Henry bite back his smile, her eye started to twitch.

With a small shake of his head Henry stood. "How so?"

Absentmindedly Holly started pacing again. "I don't know. What if I'm at some veterinarian function with Ben and I do something stupid like spill red sauce down the front of my dress? Or, what if I try to make chicken tenders again and I burn down our house?"

"That's a simple fix. Don't make chicken tenders anymore.
"

"Dad..." she warned.

Before she could say anything else, he continued, "And as

for you spilling something on your dress, do you really think Ben would care about something like that?"

"No." She shook her head. "He wouldn't. If he knew it bothered me, he would probably spill something on his shirt to match."

"Exactly." Henry clapped his hands together. "So, then what's the problem?"

Holly bit her bottom lip.

"Tell me, Holly. What's got you freaking out?"

She lifted the bottom of her wedding dress. "What if I fall? I have no idea why I thought it would be a good idea for me to get married in heels and in the backyard at that. I'm gonna break my neck before I ever say I do!"

Henry threw his head back as he barked out a deep laugh. "Well, damn."

Holly glared at him. He might be her father, but no one laughs at a bride on their wedding day. She calculated how fast she could get Mildred to speak to one of her contacts.

"Put those daggers away, little girl. I'm only laughing because I now owe Ben ten bucks."

Holly's eye started to twitch. "What do you mean you owe him ten dollars?"

Henry walked over to a spare bag on the floor. "Ben bet me ten dollars you'd freak out about your choice of footwear. Something about your stubborn ways and demanding you wear heels like every other bride." Henry pulled out a pair of Holly's favorite work flats. "He packed these for you."

A part of Holly wanted to yell at him for not believing she could walk in the heels, but a bigger part of her sighed in relief.

See, this just proved how perfect Ben truly was for her. Not only did he know she would freak out but he brought her an option to change into. She was one hundred percent marrying the right man. However, she still planned on giving him shit for it regardless. A small smile appeared on her face. She knew a way he could make it up to her.

"Put these on, and let's get this party started," her father remarked while handing the shoes to her. "I'm gonna make sure Waffles is in place."

After Henry left the room, Holly sat on the couch smiling as she slipped on her favorite pair of work flats. Righting herself once she was done, she fixed her dress before making her way to the back door.

This was it.

Today she married the love of her life.

The moment Holly stepped outside, Henry held out his good arm so she could hook her arm with his.

"Better?" he asked, before kissing her on the cheek.

"Much." Holly took a deep breath as she turned away from him and started down their makeshift aisle.

That's when she finally saw Ben. Instantly everything felt right in world.

Ben stood under the archway he'd built only a few weekends ago. He took her breath away. He looked every bit of the Adonis as she thought he was the first day they'd met. Pure happiness rush through her body as Ripley sat by his side in a pink dress. John stood behind Ripley, as Ben's *human* best man.

Holly smiled when she saw Ripley had a thin leash in her mouth that attached to one sleeping Twitch at her feet.

Oh, did he? Holly looked back to Ben who winked her way.

Leave it to him to somehow include the whole family.

Perfect.

It was a small wedding. Only a few people were in attendance. In the chairs on either side of the pathway sat some of the board members for Richman Industries that Ben had become good friends with as he helped with the transition. On the opposite side sat Mildred and her husband.

Holly had to laugh at Mildred's outfit. She wore one of the

biggest hats she'd ever seen. Her poor husband kept getting hit in the head with the thing.

Typical Mildred.

Then sitting only a few feet in front of Holly in the middle of the aisle was Lord Waffles. He looked so handsome in his doggie tux as his tongue flopped out of the side of his mouth. She had to fight the urge to run for her phone to take a picture of him. Her heart skipped when she realized he even had on a black bow tie.

"You ready to marry that man waitin' over there?" Henry's voice brought her back to reality.

Holly's eyes once again went straight to Ben. His grin spoke volumes as he watched her from afar. The love that poured from him made her feel like everything was going to be okay. Always. She had to stop herself from running into his arms.

Holly couldn't wait another second to be by his side. "Let's do this."

Henry squeezed her hand before he signaled for Waffles to start walking. Once he was a few steps ahead of them, they followed suit.

Through the entire time the music played, Holly couldn't take her eyes off Ben.

Who said real life wasn't like romance novels? Her life was a romance novel come to life.

Score one for the big girls!

They stopped a few feet from Ben where her father leaned over and kissed her cheek. "Go get your man, Pumpkin."

Holly smiled brightly. "I plan to." Stepping out of her father's embrace, she started moving toward Ben, her full focus on him.

Unfortunately for her, though, she didn't noticed Waffles had stopped walking. Before she knew it, Holly found herself stumbling through the air. She placed her hands out in front of her, trying her best to cushion her impact.

Closing her eyes, she cursed her clumsiness, ready for the hit.

The impact never came though.

Instead, Holly found herself in Ben's arms before she hit the ground. When she opened her eyes, she was neatly tucked in Ben's embrace.

Ben shook his head as he chuckled before he kissed her. "What am I going to do with you, Grace?" His face glowed with happiness as he smoothed some of her hair behind her ear.

Holly gave him a half smile, as she watched his eyes filled with love that she was sure matched her own. "Always catch me."

Stumbling Into Forever

STUMBLING THROUGH LIFE BOOK TWO

Chapter One

"Drop that donut right now, Waffles, or so help me I'm gonna murder you *and* enjoy it!"

Ben Richman heard his wife, Holly, yelling from their kitchen. With a chuckle and a shake of his head, he removed their cat Twitch from his lap and made his way through the house to investigate.

What has she gotten herself into now? A smirk spread across his face.

"Don't you run away from me, Waffles! That's mine and you know it!" The growl Ben heard coming from Holly had him laughing. Leave it to her to argue with a dog. Then again, this was Lord Waffles they were talking about. Arguing with him was a must, as Ben had come to find out since meeting Holly and her overly opinionated, high and mighty Corgi.

As Ben rounded the corner, he saw his oh so graceful wife running around the kitchen island chasing after their dog.

The same dog that just so happened to have Holly's last donut in his mouth.

As Waffles ran past the spot where Ben stood, the dog had the gall to eye him, almost begging to get the crazy lady to stop chasing him.

Figures.

Ben rolled his eyes. He'd be lying if he didn't say there was a part of him that wanted to watch the catastrophe he was sure was about to happen. Everyone knew whatever Waffles wanted, Waffles got, and if that meant destroying everything in his wake, or taking his mother's last donut, even though he knew he'd be staring death in the eyes, he'd do it. Everyone was beneath Waffles, and that dog made sure they knew it. Including his mother, who clearly wanted that last donut bad enough, she'd fight for it.

Ben shook his head with a sigh. As much as he'd like to watch the explosion there was another part of him, a bigger part, that wanted to make sure no one ended up on the floor in a pile of blood because they banged their head against the countertop.

And by no one, he meant Holly.

Better get this over with. "Grace, stop chasing him before you end up on your ass." Ben laughed as he stepped into the kitchen.

Ben had learned a thing or two after being married to Holly for the better part of a year and there was no doubt in his mind what was coming next.

Prepared, Ben strategically placed his hands out in front of him.

Within seconds, Holly came barreling into his arms at full speed. Although Ben was ready, he somehow lost his footing causing them both to cascade onto the floor with a loud oomph.

"Ahh!" Holly screamed as they landed.

The moment they were on the floor she tried to jump off him. You know that fight-or-flight instinct? Ben wasn't having any of it though. He held onto her hips keeping her locked in place on top of him.

"What on earth am I going to do with you, Grace?" Ben

chuckled, as he helped Holly straighten herself so she was now straddling his waist.

"Where in the world did you freakin' come from?" Holly huffed while she pushed her auburn hair out of her face. She didn't wait for an answer as she scanned the room for any sign of his holiness.

As if on cue, Lord Waffles walked past them with the donut in his mouth and an extra pep in his step.

Holly growled as she narrowed her eyes at the betraying bastard. The moment Waffles shot her a wink, Ben had to stop her from lunging.

Ben's brows shot to the ceiling when Waffles winked at him too.

Waffles freaking *winked* at him.

No matter how many times he'd seen Waffles demand his peasants listen to him, Ben still couldn't believe it. For a dog, he sure did have a lot of quirks. In the name of veterinary medicine, maybe he should study him, possibly resea–

"You knew that was mine!" Holly made a second lunge for Waffles as he happily chomped on his treasure taunting her.

Thank God Ben's reflexes were sharp, that's what happens after spending years wrestling Rottweilers. And clearly, Holly couldn't be trusted not to strangle their dog right now.

In one swift movement, Ben grabbed onto Holly's hips flipping her onto her back and under him with ease. "It's too late now, Grace. You wouldn't want it after he's slobbered all over it anyway."

"Says you!" Holly glared at him. "That was my last peanut butter and glazed donut. I've been saving it until I reached my word count. He knew that! We talked about it in great detail when I was struggling to hit my next two thousand words. He did this on purpose." Holly's eyes snapped to Waffles who was swallowing the last bite before licking his lips. "I'm gonna remember this the next time you need something." She glared at him before she threw her head back onto the floor in defeat. "That was my donut."

The pout that spread across Holly's mouth had Ben laughing.

And he wondered where Waffles got his flair for the dramatics?

"I'll buy you more." He laughed kissing Holly lightly on the lips. As Ben looked down at his wife, a smile ran across his face. He still couldn't believe how lucky he was to have found Holly. He still couldn't believe how lucky he was to have found Holly. Even though that meeting involved her getting hit in the face with a rogue Frisbee, which now knowing Holly wasn't all that surprising. She was, after all, a master at tripping on thin air, falling over, and if you looked up the word klutz in the dictionary, you'd see a picture of her, with the title walking disaster under it. But to him, she was absolutely perfect in every way. From her lush hips down to the deep hunter green of her eyes.

Holly was made for him.

"It won't be the same," Holly groaned as she pushed the palm of her hand to his chest and gave a nudge. "And stop calling me Grace! You jumped in front of me. It was *your* fault I ended up crashing into you. Not mine. What was I supposed to do? You came out of freakin' nowhere!"

Ben threw his head back and burst out laughing, causing Holly to let out a growl. That only made him laugh harder. "I don't know, Grace. How about stop?"

"As if I could stop. Once this load starts a-movin' nothing is stopping it."

"Excuse me?" Ben's brows shot to the ceiling.

Panic flashed through Holly's eyes.

Good. After all this time you should know better than to say shit like that.

Before Ben could say anything more, Ripley came bouncing into the kitchen, with Twitch right on her tail.

"Oh, oh, Ripley, baby girl, come save your momma," Holly cooed at their other dog, Ripley, their Australian shepherd.

Ripley quickly made her way over to Holly's face and started licking. "That's not saving me!" Holly squirmed as she did her best to avoid the onslaught of kisses coming from Ripley.

That's when Ben felt something nudge his arm. He looked down to see Twitch — rightly named so because of the slight twitch he has in his head from some punk kid poisoning him when he was a kitten.

Twitch jumped onto Holly's chest trying to lick her face just as Ripley was, making Ben laugh again.

Somewhere along the lines, Twitch had taken to Ripley like she was his own mother and converted himself into being a dog.

Where Ripley went. Twitch went.

Whatever Ripley did. Twitch did.

Ben's heart warmed at the memories of Ripley and Waffles play fighting and Twitch trying to jump in and hold his own. The play fighting only lasted a few seconds before Ripley would grab Twitch in her mouth and take him away from the fight.

Go figure. Protective. Just like Holly.

Although right now, Holly looked more like she wanted to throttle Waffles rather than protect him.

Twitch looked at Ripley before assessing they were still kissing their mother. So, he dove back in.

At this point, Ben was positive all their animals were certifiably insane. And with their ringmaster, Lord Waffles, with plans of world domination, calling most of the shots he'd given up trying to make any sense of it.

And he wouldn't have it any other way.

Life was always an adventure between their pets and Holly.

Oh, and Ben couldn't forget Mildred. Holly's completely inappropriate older coworker at the local library. Whenever Mildred was around, things *always* got interesting.

Ben pushed himself off Holly before grabbing onto her arms yanking her to her feet. "Up you go, Grace."

"I'm gonna put arsenic in your dinner tonight."

"That'd be a welcomed taste with your cooking." At Holly's narrowed eyes he barked out a laugh. "Come on. You know it's true. Sexy, talented, outspoken, kindhearted, feisty, best writer in the world you are, a chef you ain't. Or do you want me to bring up the time you almost burnt the house down when you tried to make chicken tenders?"

Another growl came from Holly. "That wasn't my fault!"

"Yes, my bad, that's right it was the chicken's fault."

"Damn right it was! Plus, I was only trying to be nice and feed you and John 'cause you guys were working hard moving my crap in."

"Oh, we got a break from moving your shit in when we had to call the fire department." Ben smirked at her narrowed eyes and thinned lips.

"Am I ever going to live that down?"

"No." Ben's eyes twinkled with amusement. "Hey, at least I'm not as bad as John."

Annoyed Holly jerked herself away from him and grabbed her bag. "You and John can kiss my ass."

When she started for the front door Ben hollered after her, "Where do you think you're going?"

From over her shoulder, Holly shot him an evil look. "Out to get more donuts."

At the word "donut" Waffles ran to Holly's side and started jumping. Well, if you can consider whatever Waffles does with his tiny little legs jumping.

"Not for you!" Holly sidestepped Waffles shooting her glare from Ben to their dog.

Holly almost made it all the way to the front door without an incident.

Almost.

As she moved through the hallway, she tripped over an invisible crack and stumbled. Without looking back at Ben, she quickly righted herself before blowing her hair out of her face.

Ben did a quick assessment of her to make sure she was okay. When he realized she was fine, he let out a laugh.

As Ben opened his mouth to tell her to bring him back some donuts too, Holly did what she was known for. She tripped over the entranceway and nearly fell right out of the door.

Ben had to bite back his joy, as his smile spread from ear to ear. *Never a dull moment.*

Holly straightened herself with a huff as she hiked her bag higher onto her shoulder. Once she was composed, she turned to face him with narrowed eyes. "Not. A. Word."

Ben held his hands up in surrender as he bit his lip, trying and failing to keep from laughing.

The second Holly turned from him and stomped out of the door, he shouted, "And you wonder why I'll never stop calling you Grace!"

# Chapter Two

HOLLY PLOPPED the box of donuts onto her desk as she threw herself into her chair with a sigh.

Universe, if you love me at all, please let today be an easy day.

"What did ya bring me?" Mildred, Holly's coworker, made her way toward Holly with her eyes honed in on the box.

Holly had to do a double take. Seriously, like where in the hell had Mildred come from? For an old woman, she sure was fast.

Before Holly could even register Mildred had her sights on Holly's delectable goodies, the old hag had one of the donuts shoved into her mouth.

"Damn, this is good," Mildred mumbled around the food.

Holly's eyes widened for a brief second trying to stop her brain from short-circuiting. Wasn't it a known rule older woman needed to watch their sugar intake? Holly watched as Mildred chomped on the donut.

Clearly not.

Holly rolled her eyes before opening the box to grab a peanut butter and glazed donut. "I know. That's why I bought them."

"Mine!" Mildred snatched the donut from Holly's hand bringing it to her mouth before taking a big bite. "You don't need any sweets when you got that hunk of burning man meat to satisfy all your cravings." Mildred took another bite of the donut as Holly watched in horror.

I'll kill her! No one would blame me!

"Cat got your tongue there, missy?" Mildred winked. "Or, should I say dog got your tongue?" She licked the remainder of the peanut butter glaze off her fingers with a pop. "You get it? 'Cause you have dogs."

Do not kill your coworker. Do not kill your coworker. Holly narrowed her eyes at her. "I also have a cat. You know, Mildred, you are so unbelievably lucky I already ate one on the way here. If I hadn't, you'd be a dead woman." Holly opened the box and blindly grabbed for a tasty treat making sure not to break eye contact with the old hag.

"Are you trying to intimidate me?" Mildred placed one of her hands on her hips.

"Is it working?"

"Not on your life, little miss. Where do you think that stare came from?" She pointed at herself. "I've perfected it over the years."

Giving up, Holly moved her eyes to the donut she'd grabbed. *Why the hell didn't I just buy a dozen of the peanut butter ones?* Holly rolled her eyes. *That's what I get for trying to be more health conscious.*

"What are you doing here so early, anyway?" Mildred asked, plopping herself onto the corner of the desk. "Ole' Benny boy not performing as he should? Did you know they make this pill that—"

"Oh, for the love of all things."

"That's what I'm saying. If Mr. Hotness has a problem in the love department, I know a guy."

"Eww." Holly threw her fingers in her ears as she shook her head. "I don't want to hear that."

Mildred held up her hands in surrender. "Fine. I'll call Ben myself and tell him." She picked up the phone, but Holly snatched it back.

"How do you go from zero to ten thousand in the span of two seconds?" Holly placed the phone back onto the receiver.

"It's a gift." Mildred eyed the donut box. "Ask my husband."

"I'll be sure to mention to him how you need to be placed in a home under intense supervision."

Mildred shrugged before reaching for another treat.

I should have known better than to bring them here.

"If Benny isn't the problem then what's got you all in a huff?"

"I'm stuck."

Mildred arched her brow. "To the chair? Do I need to call the fire department? Remember the last time we had to call them when you tried to heat up leftovers. Oh God, they were mouthwatering."

Holly could see drool form in the corner of Mildred's mouth as a faraway look washed over her eyes. "Geeze, Mildred, how does your husband handle you?"

"With rough hands, if I'm lucky."

"For the love of —" Holly stopped before taking a deep breath to calm herself. "Mildred, I'm stuck in my story. I've been going back and forth for weeks trying to get it right but everything I do is a disaster. I don't know which way to turn."

The old bat scrutinized her for a few seconds. "Are you sure it's not Ben and his dong?"

Holly jumped from her seat. "Why do I even bother talking to you?"

"You love me, and you know I can help."

Holly started making her way to the book return ignoring Mildred. You think she would have known better than to believe walking away from her would have stopped the conversation.

"You're unsettled," Mildred remarked.

Holly spun to face her. "What?"

"Missy, do not *what* me like that." Mildred placed her hands on her hips. "I'm telling you, I can see it in your eyes. You're unsettled. Something is missing from your life."

"My life is perfect," Holly protested. "Well, other than the missing words. I couldn't ask for anything more."

"Liar." Mildred turned on her heel and started making her way back to the desk.

"I am not!" Ignoring the fact Mildred was chomping on one of the donuts Holly turned back to her task. "I am not a liar. My life *is* perfect," she mumbled.

And it was.

She had Ben by her side. He was the love of her life. She still hadn't quite figured out why a hunk like him was interested in a world champion klutz machine like her, but at this point, she learned to accept it. Their home was filled with love. Even if Lord Waffles felt he owned the place and only *allowed* the rest of them live there, she loved it. She had Twitch, Ripley, and Ben there.

Stupid old woman. Holly looked back toward the desk and noticed Mildred was gone. "I bet she ate the last of my donuts too."

Would it be crazy if I got a lockbox and put donuts in it? She pondered the idea for a moment before dismissing it. Man, this writer's block is making me crazy. I doubt other aspiring authors argue with themselves over donuts. Who does that? Oh yeah, me. I do that.

Holly felt her phone vibrate in her pocket.

She sighed.

For some reason her agitation was in full swing. *Maybe I'm PMSing.*

With a quick glance at the screen, she answered. "Hey, Dad."

"Pumpkin, how are you?"

"I'm doing good, Dad. What's up?" Holly took a cleansing breath. Whatever was bugging her was her problem, not her father's. She wasn't going to take it out on Henry.

"*Oh, nothing. Why does something have to be up for me to call my daughter? Can't an old man just want to say hi?*"

The guilt rushed through her. "Yes, Dad, of course. I didn't mean to imply anything." Holly grabbed one of the books and placed it on the shelf. *Great, now I feel like a jerk.* "What are you doing?"

"*I'm talking to you of course.*"

"Dad..."

"*Okay, fine. I wanted to see if you and Ben were free to come over for dinner tonight?*"

Holly felt the start of a headache coming. "I planned on coming over after work tonight you know that," she reminded him.

"*Yes, I know you were planning on coming over. But, I want to extend the invitation to Ben and the pups.*"

Holly eyed the phone suspiciously. "Okay fine, I'll call Ben on my lunch break. He took Ripley and Waffles to work today."

"*Good, good.*"

"You sure you're okay?" It had only been two days since she saw her father last, but with his disabilities, anything could have happened in her absence. Her worry started to rise. What if something happened? What if he was trying to fix something in the house and fell and hurt himself? What if he was calling from the floor with a broken hip? What if he needed more food? What if-

"*Of course, I am...*" Holly could swear she heard him growl. "*Now, I'm going to hang up and let you get back to work.*"

Holly's brows knitted together. "Sorry, Dad. I guess I'm in a mood or something." She sighed. "We'll be over later. I know Ben will want to come."

"Perfect. Oh, and Pumpkin?"

Just like that Holly's eye began to twitch. "Yeah, Dad?"

"Do you think Ben would be able to make his spicy chicken tonight?"

Oh, for the love of all things! She knew her father better than to just have a quick "how you doing" phone call in the middle of the day. *First Waffles eats my donut, then Mildred eats my replacements, and now my dad wants nothing to do with me, but wants Ben to make him his favorite food.* She bit back a growl. Holly shook her head as she tapped her finger on one of the books. "Yeah, Dad. I'll tell him that's what you're requesting. Is there anything else?"

"Wonderful! Oh, and Holly, please don't make anything. Leave the cooking up to Ben. See you tonight, Pumpkin!"

Holly squeezed her phone a little tighter after the call ended. She took another cleansing breath trying to ease her annoyance.

Holly had absolutely no idea why everything was getting to her today.

It's all Mildred's fault. Her lips thinned.

Holly quickly sent a text message to Ben letting him know they'd be going to her Dad's for dinner and if he wouldn't mind making his spicy chicken.

She knew Ben would be all for it. He loved hanging out with Henry.

Holly put her phone in her back pocket and picked up the last return book before placing it onto the shelf.

Unfortunately for her, the frustration she'd been feeling reared its ugly head in her movements. She slammed the book onto the shelf harder than she needed to.

Within seconds the shelf collapsed causing all the books to cascade onto the floor. "You have got to be freakin' kidding me!" Holly threw her hands over her head before she walked away.

Today was not her day.

She walked back to the desk with Mildred's "You're a liar" ringing through her head. When Holly reached for her box of donuts she noticed a book placed on top of them.

When she saw the title, it was like a sucker punch to the gut.

Chapter Three

"TELL ME, how are the newlyweds doing?" Henry, Holly's father asked, as they sat down for dinner that evening with Lord Waffles sitting at his feet begging for any scrap grandpa would send his way.

"Are you going to ask us that every day, Dad?" Holly asked, sitting in the spot across from her father.

"Probably." Henry took a bite of his chicken. "Ben this is outstanding, thank you. It gets better and better each time you make it."

A whine came from under the table. When Ben leaned over to see who it was, he saw Waffles at Henry's feet with big round eyes staring back at him.

"You know you're not supposed to have table food," Ben remarked, looking at the pup. "Plus, you wouldn't like it, anyway. It's spicy." Ben popped a piece of food in his mouth winking at their dog.

Waffles gave him the most judgmental side-eye he could muster before turning his nose up. "Jesus, dog, you act like we don't feed you." Ben shook his head.

Waffles answered with a huff before moving his attention to Henry.

You've got to be kidding me.

Ben watched as Waffles placed one of his paws on Henry's left foot. The little shit then had the gall to look up at Holly's dad giving him *sad* eyes.

"Come off it, dude. You're not getting any chicken." Ben looked at his father-in-law. "Don't feed him any. Besides, he's in trouble anyway."

Henry placed his fork back on his plate before moving his good arm down to scratch Waffles behind the ear. "Waffles in trouble? Why he could never be a bad boy," Henry cooed. "Ain't that right, little man?"

"Don't enable him."

Waffles, the jerk that he was, ate up the attention. He even fell onto his back, giving Henry better access for belly rubs.

The second Ben groaned his annoyance, Waffles sent him another evil glare.

Ben shook his head before placing another piece of food in his mouth. "Why can't you be more like your sister? Ripley is at least waiting in the corner."

How has my life come to this?

"Because he's too smart for that," Henry remarked. "He knows where his bread is buttered and that's with Grandpa."

Ben darted his eyes to Holly where all she did was shrug her shoulders. "I've had to deal with this since I got him. *Grandpa* takes his role very seriously." Holly smirked before taking a bite of her own food.

"Yeah, but we can't reward him, especially when he's been an ass. That little shit decided to intimidate a Great Dane today at work. Do you know how hard it is to control one of those massive things?" Ben glared at their Corgi who in return scoffed before turning back to Henry.

"Oh, I'm sure it wasn't Waffles' fault," Henry responded as he continued to scratch the Corgi.

"It was most certainly his fault." Ben narrowed his eyes at the menace. "The client brought her dog in and *Waffles* decided he *needed* to remind everyone who was in charge. As the owner pulled Bruce, who might I add was terrified, into the waiting room, Waffles decided to run from behind the reception area and make himself known. When Bruce noticed him, do you want to know what he did?"

Henry bent shielding Waffles with his arms to coddle him, the best he could with his physical disabilities. "Did the dog attack, Waffles?" Henry asked with concern. Waffles being the ham he was, had the audacity to cry out as if to tell Henry that's exactly what happened.

"No." Ben rolled his eyes. "On the contrary, Bruce took off running the other way, nearly pulling his owner's arm out of her socket. Then Waffles *chased* him. He freaking chased him all through the waiting room causing chaos to erupt."

"So, you're saying a Great Dane — those big old dogs, was afraid of this little guy?" Ben could see Henry trying to hide his smile.

"That's exactly what I am saying. Who knew a massive guy like that would be terrified to death of a puffed out loaf of bread? I know Bruce has had some issues in the past, but damn."

"Do not call our son a loaf of bread!" Holly exclaimed before glaring at Ben. "He is not a loaf of bread."

"My apologies, babe." Ben held his hands in surrender. "I meant to say an oversized potato."

A mischievous smile appeared on Holly's face. "Damn right. And that's Mr. Potato to you." She pointed her finger at him while she absolutely failed to control her amusement.

A loud huff came from Waffles causing Ben to turn the attention back to him. That's when he saw their Corgi shooting death glares directed right for him and Holly.

"Who's a good Mr. Potato?" Ben mocked, his eyes full of joy.

"You all need to stop being so mean to my grandbaby." Henry took a piece of broccoli off his plate and handed it to the dog. The second Waffles realized it wasn't chicken he promptly spit the offending food out before turning his glare to Henry.

With a dramatic huff and a rise of his snout, Waffles turned and made his way out of the kitchen. When he got to the start of the hallway, Waffles turned back to glare at all three of them.

With one last huff to inform everyone of his disdain of how he'd been treated he waddled away.

The room fell silent only for a moment before they all erupted in laughter.

"Aww, poor little guy. Should one of us go out and comfort him?" Henry asked as he picked up his fork to start eating.

"Not it," Holly and Ben said at the exact same time with smiles on their faces, which caused more laughter to burst throughout the room.

Ben doing his best to control his amusement of the situation looked at Ripley who was sitting patiently at the entrance to the kitchen watching the show.

As she cocked her head to the side waiting for Ben's command, she realized what he was asking. With her own drawn-out sigh, Ripley slowly made her way out of the kitchen in search of her brother. She only looked back once, which caused Ben to give a small nod of encouragement. Ripley then did something Ben never thought she would do.

Ripley dropped to the floor in a full-on tantrum.

What the hell? I mean I know she's picked up a few things from Waffles, but damn!

Not sure what was happening Ben pushed himself from the table. That's when Ripley stood before sighing loud enough for everyone to hear before disappearing out of sight.

Holly's mouth fell open, and Henry's eyes were so wide, Ben thought they were going to pop out of his head.

He was also positive his expression mirrored both of theirs.

"Uh, Ben," Holly finally broke the silence, clearly trying to get her bearings. "Did she just throw a hissy fit like a teenager that was just asked to clean up their bedroom?"

Still in disbelief, Ben nodded. "I think she did."

"Not her too!" Holly cried, throwing her hands into the air. "You have got to be kidding me."

"Ripley was never a diva until Waffles showed up." Ben narrowed his eyes at his wife.

"Are you saying this is my fault?" Holly glared back.

"No. I'm saying it's Waffles." Ben darted his eyes to the spot Ripley had just vacated. "That's it. We are separating those two from now on."

Holly nodded. "Agreed."

When did my life become a reality TV show?

Ben pulled his seat back to the table to finish his meal. *Out of sight, out of mind.* As he picked up his fork he saw Ripley accompanied by Waffles make their way back into the kitchen.

They both simultaneously plopped onto the kitchen floor right next to the entrance.

Ben didn't miss the evil eye still coming from Waffles, though.

He shook his head. Ben was determined to ignore the insanity his life had become.

Holly picked up a forkful of chicken and shoved it in her mouth. Secretly she was glad her father wanted this for dinner. It was one of her favorite meals. And after a day like today, she needed the pick me up.

Had she mentioned the same bookshelf fell three more times during her shift? Or how Mildred kept leaving her little surprise books everywhere she turned?

She worried her bottom lip. Leave it to Mildred to throw her world completely upside down.

Holly kept stealing glances at her husband, trying to pick apart what he was thinking. She knew they had talked about having children before but nothing solid.

But now that was all Holly could think about.

The idea of growing a little Richman inside of her made her feel things she never thought were possible.

Now, if she could only get a few seconds to talk to Ben about it.

She pushed around a piece of broccoli on her plate, as she continued worrying her bottom lip. When she looked at Ben again, she noticed him staring at her.

Her heart soared. There was so much love in his eyes, it was almost too much to take.

A warm smile spread across his face the moment their eyes met. Holly was positive it matched her own.

She loved him.

And she was ready.

Ben would be the best dad there could be, other than her own of course. Look at the way Ben handled their fur-babies.

As she stared at him, she couldn't help but imagine a little blue-eyed boy that looked exactly like his daddy on Ben's lap.

She quickly looked away. If she didn't, she probably would have pulled a Holly and blurted it out in front of everyone.

That was not something she wanted to discuss with her father around.

When Ben arched a brow at her, she decided she needed to change gears.

Stay cool. No need to embarrass yourself during dinner. We've got a whole car ride home to talk about it. Think about something else.

Holly turned her attention to her father.

There'd been so many years they'd sat across from each

other at this exact same table sharing a meal together. Back then, however, his eyes always held torment and pain.

Now his eyes held a lightness and joy. She wasn't exactly sure what changed in him, but she was grateful for it. Seeing her dad happy filled her heart. She was sure some of it had to do with the fact his bills were no longer hanging over his head, but it was more than that. She liked this new look on him.

Whenever she looked his way now, he'd have his lopsided grin fully on display.

Holly's life had morphed into something she'd never thought she'd be privileged to. Ben, her dad, their animals. All of it. This type of fulfillment was never in the cards for her, but now that she had it, she couldn't help but fantasize about the one thing she knew would make her heart feel one hundred percent full.

I want a baby.

The sucker punch feeling she had earlier in the day returned with a new force. She knew she couldn't wait another moment. It was do or die.

Unfortunately, the second Holly opened her mouth Ben's phone rang.

Dang it!

"This is Ben."

Within seconds Holly watched as Ben's face paled. All thoughts of their future disappeared as a gut-wrenching feeling of wrong swept through her.

Oh no!

Ben's face contorted as he continued with the call. "Are you serious, is everything all right? How about the animals?" Ben asked.

Holly was nearly in a full-blown panic. She shot out of her seat knocking her chair onto the floor behind her.

Ben jumped from his seat and started heading to the front door. "I'll be there in a few minutes," Ben said before shoving the phone into the back pocket of his jeans.

"What's going on?" Holly asked running after him.

"Yeah, son, is everything okay?"

Ben turned back to them, an expression of panic on his face which caused Holly's stomach to sink. She'd never seen this type of dread on Ben before, not even when they were dealing with his psychotic mother.

"Someone broke into the clinic."

Chapter Four

WHEN THE CLINIC appeared in Ben's sights, he realized it was surrounded by police cars causing his stomach to completely churn.

Oh God.

As he heard dogs barking in the background a new wave of dread washed through him.

At least let the animals be okay. The other stuff I can deal with, just please let them be okay.

He pulled into the parking lot and jumped out of the car. From the corner of his eye, he saw Holly was right behind him.

When Ben spotted an officer standing outside of the building, he took off in a run. "Can you tell me what's going on?" he asked. Since the officer didn't immediately say anything Ben added, "Can you tell me if a Detective William Bower is here? He's a friend of mine."

The officer nonchalantly turned toward Ben. "And you might be?"

"I'm Benjamin Richman. I own this clinic." All the officer did was nod in return.

Jesus fucking Christ. What do I do?

By the look of this guy, this was clearly someone you did

not want to piss off. He had a certain presence about him. Maybe it was the muscles upon muscles, or maybe it was his hardened face? He wasn't quite sure. One thing he did know was he should probably go and ask someone else. However, the second he took a step away from the officer in search of someone else he heard Holly.

"That's all you've got, a freaking nod?" Holly stomped toward them. "You tell us exactly what's going on you big lug. And right now!"

The officer's right brow shot to the sky. "And *you* might be?"

"Are those the only words you know how to say?" Holly spat. "You'd think to be an officer of the law you'd have better communication skills. You tell my husband right now what the hell is going on or I'll—"

"You'll what?" The officer turned his body fully in Holly's direction before crossing his arms over his chest.

Fucking A!

Ben pulled Holly to his side away from the officer that looked like he was about to break something in half, and he was pretty sure that something in half was going to be Holly. Or, you know, he might've been constipated. Either way, he wasn't taking a chance. "Let's try not to piss off Officer..." Ben looked at the officer's badge. "Jones. I don't want to have to bail you out of jail while trying to deal with all of this."

Holly jumped out of Ben's arms, disbelief written all over her face. "Bail *me* out of jail?"

Ben didn't know if it was his adrenaline or whatnot, but the audacity on Holly's face nearly sent him into hysterics.

He bit back his reaction as he took a deep breath. Not the time nor the place.

Leave it to Holly to find a way to calm him and bring him back to reality. And right now, while she practically had her dukes up ready for battle - a battle she would not win against a two hundred plus pound man that would snap her in two - she grounded him. "Relax, Cujo. Let me take care of this."

"You wanna see Cujo, I'll show you Cujo." Holly narrowed her eyes at him as her nostrils flared causing him to hold his hands in surrender, before he turned back to Officer Jones.

"I apologize. We both are a little riled up. Let's start over. Would you be willing to give us some information or at least point me in the direction of someone that can?"

Officer Jones gave him the once-over before nodding.

"Is that all this guy can do?" Holly growled as she pointed her finger at the officer. Ben darted his eyes to her in warning. *Do not get us killed, or arrested.*

"What?" Holly arched her brow.

Please give me strength. Any strength. I would take anything at this moment. The universe must've answered him since Officer Jones started walking toward the front door of the clinic. Ben looked back at Holly who shrugged.

Following his cue, they walked behind the officer. When they made it inside of the clinic his gut twisted into a knot.

It was a disaster.

Chairs from the waiting room where thrown all around, there was glass from the smashed in window everywhere. It was horrifying.

"Bower, the owner's here."

As soon as Ben saw his old friend, relief washed through him. Will turned to face him, a sad expression marring his features. "Ben."

"Will." Ben reached out to shake his hand.

"I know we said we wanted to catch up soon but this was not what I had in mind," Will remarked as he scratched his chin. He then turned to Holly. "You must be Ben's wife. Ben mentioned he was getting married the last time we talked."

"Yes." Ben pulled Holly to his side. "This is Holly. You never got to officially meet her."

"It was my fault," Will remarked. "You know when my little girl got sick it took all my time." Will sheepishly looked away. He didn't have to though. Once Will's daughter was diagnosed with cancer he and his wife had spent all their time with her. The day of Ben and Holly's wedding Will and his wife Martha were taking their girl in for treatment. There was no fault in that.

"How is she doing?" Ben asked, hoping for the best.

"Better." Will's face lit. "She's in full remission now. The day we got the last results was by far the happiest day of my life." A smile spread across the detective's face. "You know, Ben, I'm sure Martha would love to see you, maybe one day we can have you and your little lady over for dinner one night."

"We'd like that," Ben answered.

"It's nice to finally meet you." Will placed his hand in front of Holly's. "I do wish it was under better circumstances, though."

"You and me both." Holly took his outreached hand and shook it.

"Can you tell us what happened?" Ben asked, while he looked around the room again.

"To be honest, we don't know much. The station got the call when the alarm went off. When officers first arrived on scene, they noticed the window smashed in. Since veterinarian clinics often get broken into because of the controlled substances they carry, the arriving officers called it in right away."

A cold sweat broke out on the back of Ben's neck. "This was a robbery?"

"It doesn't look that way." Detective Bower scratched his chin again. "From our initial search of the premises, we didn't find any locked cabinets tampered with. Nor did we find any evidence of a robbery. It doesn't seem to appear as any money is missing. Although, you will need to confirm that for us."

"So, someone just did this to do it?" Holly asked. "Oh God, what about all the animals in the back?" Holly pushed herself through the officers as she finagled her way to the back of the clinic where the boarded animals were along with the ones recovering from recent surgeries.

"Mrs. Richman this is an active crime scene. You can't go anywhere," Will yelled after her.

Holly clearly didn't care if it was an active investigation or not. She ignored his words as she tore through the clinic.

Screw it!

Ben took off after her. He had the same concerns she did. Especially, since he could still hear the dogs barking.

Ben heard Will mumble something under his breath before he followed after them.

Once they all made their way into the back, Ben saw Holly crouched in front of one of the cages that housed a dog who had recently gone through surgery.

"Grace." Ben started walking toward her.

"I know. I know, I just needed to make sure none of them were hurt. Okay?" Quickly she jumped from where she was to the next cage checking on one of their dogs that was being boarded.

Ben watched as she bounced from cage to cage confirming all the animals were unharmed.

God, he loved her. At this moment his heart soared for his wife. All she cared about was making sure the animals were safe. Ben followed suit checking on his patients as he went.

"Grace? I thought you said her name was Holly," Will questioned.

As if on cue, Holly pushed over a step stool to check on a cat in one of the top cages. In her frantic movements, she missed her footing and started tumbling over.

Ben was at her side in an instant as he caught her in his arms just as he'd done time and time again.

He turned back to Will, with Holly cradled in his arms. "Grace is short for her gracefulness."

Will looked at them quizzically, but nodded with a smirk.

"Ben, the cameras!" Holly exclaimed as she jumped out of his arms and ran toward his office.

"Do you have surveillance cameras set up?" Will asked.

"We do." Ben followed behind Holly as she made her way into his office.

"I'll have to ask if you could please provide us with a copy of the footage so we can conduct our investigation."

"Of course, Will, anything you need."

"I can't remember what program it is." Holly was bent over the back of Ben's office chair typing away at his computer. Any other time he would have laughed at her *Holliness*.

Instead, Ben strolled behind her before picking her up into the air and moving her out of his way. "Let me get it open and we'll hand it over to the detective. Right now, we're only in their way."

"I'm never in the way." Holly placed her hand over her heart like she'd been shot.

Holly then darted her eyes to Will whose brow was cocked.

"Okay, fine." She threw her hands up before storming out of the office leaving a concerned Ben behind. "I know when I'm not wanted."

Ben rolled his eyes. He loved her but he was one hundred percent going to remind her of this the next time she complained about Waffles and his dramatics.

He couldn't blame her. Hell, if he wasn't as in control as he was, he'd be acting the same way Holly was. Ben turned back to the detective. "Man, Will, it's great to see you again but this is definitely not the way I wanted to reconnect." He rubbed his forehead. "Something like this has never happened to either of us. Why would anyone want to break in here, Will?" Ben shook his head still in disbelief. *How and why did this happen?* "Whatever you need from us we can provide, you know that."

"It's understandable, Ben." He nodded. "This isn't something anyone is prepared for. I'm just glad I was working tonight." He jutted his chin out to the computer. "I'll have my men take it from here, okay?"

"Thank you."

"I know it's going to be a long night getting everything back in order. How about you come to the station tomorrow morning and we can fill out all the paperwork then? Since this is a clinic that has controlled substances, the reports are a tad more tedious. There's no need in you having to deal with it tonight, though."

"I appreciate that, Will. I'll be there first thing." Ben looked around his office. Nothing seemed to be out of place, but he would do a more thorough check once he was allowed to clean up. "Do you have any idea why you think the clinic was targeted?"

Will shook his head before crossing his arms. "At this point, I don't. I can speculate, but that won't do either of us any good. The next step is for my guys to review the footage and go from there. Hopefully, by the time you come into the station, we'll have more information for you."

"Thank you." Ben sighed, still trying to make sense of everything that had happened.

"Do you have any plywood that we can board the window up with?"

Ben hadn't thought of that. Maybe at home sure, but here, no. He wouldn't have anything.

"I'm gonna call a friend to see if he'll be able to bring some by." He pulled out his phone.

Will uncrossed his arms with a nod. "I'm going to step outside while you make the call. I want to inform my team about the footage. Try not to touch anything on your way out, at least until the crime scene analysts are done.”

“Can I take care of the animals?”

“If they can wait another hour or so I’d leave them in the cages. If anyone of them needs attention by all means, though. Once my team is done you’re free to do whatever it is you need to do.”

This was freaking wonderful. Ben’s head started to pound as he watched Will stand in front of his office door.

First things first.

Ben quickly called John.

“The only reason you should be calling me right now is ’cause you broke a tooth and are bleeding so much out of your mouth it looks like you got into a cage fight—”

“Did anyone ever tell you that you’re charming?”

“All the time. What’s got you calling me this late at night? Wait, did Holly try to cook?”

Ben rubbed his hand on his forehead trying to ward off his headache. “No, the house isn’t on fire.” He had to chuckle. It was their favorite joke between the two of them now. Holly didn’t like it, but hell, it gave them a good laugh. He took a deep breath. “If only it were that easy. John, someone broke into the clinic tonight.”

“Holy shit. You’re kidding?”

Ben heard John rustling around. “I wish I was.” He closed his eyes trying to take a calming breath. “I need your help, can you do me a favor? I don’t know if you’d have any at your house, but we need some plywood to board up the smashed front window until I can get a hold of the insurance company and figure out what we need to do. If you don’t have any can you swing by my house? I’ve got some in the garage.” Ben thought back to the large window up front. “we’re gonna need a few pieces.”

“Of course, man. I’m on my way.”

"Thanks." Ben placed his phone in his back pocket before making his way out to the lobby of the clinic.

That's when he saw Holly standing in the middle of the room in handcuffs with Officer Jones holding onto one of her arms.

The second Holly spotted him, her eyes widened. "It's not what it looks like!"

Chapter Five

By the time everything at the clinic was back in order and there was a board over the broken window, it was well into the morning. Ben wasn't surprised at how long it took, he was just thankful it was done.

Ben scratched his head as he tried to make sense of the events that had transpired. He still couldn't wrap his mind around the clinic being broken into, especially since nothing ended up missing. All the medicines were accounted for, and even their petty cash was still there.

So then why would someone break in? It made no sense.

He looked around the room and spotted John moving one of the tables to its proper place. He'd never been more thankful for John than he was right now. Without even a question, John arrived at the clinic and got to work. With John's help, everything was looking back to normal, minus the window.

Ben moved his attention toward the back room. While he and John worked on the cleanup, Holly stayed in the back making sure the animals were okay. That was a task on its own. The animals had no idea what was going on and to them, the world was ending. Holly definitely had her hands full. And when you throw in all the loud noises from him and John, it was a recipe for disaster.

There was one thing that Ben knew for certain, though. He knew Holly had it covered. Her love for animals outweighed everything. There was no doubt in his mind Holly was able to take charge of the back while he and John did what they needed to do.

Although... Ben smiled. There was one mishap with a cocker spaniel that wanted out of the cage somewhere between one and two in the morning.

Holly might have had it handled, but there was never a moment *something* didn't go awry.

Thankfully, John was quick to grab the escaped convict as he came bouncing from the back room with a crazed Holly chasing after him.

Ben didn't know what was more entertaining: the dog purposely running back and forth in front of Holly taunting her, or Holly tripping on everything while cursing as she chased him.

It had definitely been a night.

"Thanks for helping," Ben remarked, looking at his best friend. "I owe you."

"Damn right you do." John looked over his shoulder at him as he moved the last chair in the waiting room into its proper place. "Are you going to call the insurance company and then get someone out here to fix the window?"

"That's the plan." Ben looked at his watch. It was six-forty-five. "They won't open for another hour, though."

"Good." John straightened before placing his hand on top of his stomach. He then puffed it out. "You have time to take me out for breakfast."

Ben's brow arched.

"What's with the pot belly?" Holly asked, coming from the back staring at John sidewise. Her scrunched face caused John to huff out a laugh causing his stomach to go back to normal. "Oh, that's more like it. Show those abs who's boss, big guy."

"Holly Richman," Ben growled at his wife while giving her a pointed look.

"What?" Holly stared back at him. Her eyes sparkled with mischief. "He's got a nice tummy."

"And why are you looking at his *tummy?*" Ben asked tilting his head to the side.

"Hey, if you guys want to play your sports games without your shirts on, that's not my fault." Holly shrugged.

That little shit. He saw her bite her bottom lip to stop from laughing. *Oh, I'll give you something to laugh about. Just wait until tonight.*

Ben turned back to John narrowing his eyes in warning. "From now on, you're wearing a shirt. End of story."

"Hey, don't go all asshole on me. It's not my fault your lady has good taste." John puffed out his chest. "I got the goods everyone wants a piece of." John started circling his hips.

"Eww!" Holly shuddered, throwing her hands over her eyes. "Don't ever do that again. I can't unsee it."

"Hey, you were all for my goods a few seconds ago." John pouted.

"No. I said you have a nice tummy." Holly moved in front of Ben before placing her hand on his abs. "But not as nice as his."

With a chuckle at John's flabbergasted expression, Ben bent and kissed the top of Holly's head. "Thank you, baby. But don't think I'll forget what you said."

"What? What did I say?"

Ben swatted her ass causing Holly to jump. "If I ever catch you *staring* at John's goodies, there will be more of that to come."

"You can try, but you'd have to catch me first."

As Holly took a step away from him ready to run, Ben growled. *Oh, it's on.*

"For fuck's sake." John threw his hands in the air effectively distracting Ben from chasing his wife. "I'm right here. Can you all wait to do your kinky shit when I'm *not* around? Besides, let's get back to my *tummy* and feeding it." John pointed at Ben while looking at Holly. "Your husband just promised to take me out for a big breakfast. One that's going to make him question everything he knows with the amount of food I plan to consume."

"You have been known to pack it away. Where it goes, I have no idea. If I ate the way you do, I'd be as big as this room," Holly grumbled.

Ben sent a warning growl in her direction. *Oh, tonight is gonna be fun.*

Holly threw her hands up at his glare. "How about I stay here and start rescheduling patients? I'll call the clients that have animals here and tell them what happened. Sound good?"

Ben decided to drop the conversation about her talking bad about herself for later.... And there would be a later. "Sure. Do you have to go to work today?"

"Yes, but I'll call Mildred and let her know what's going on. She can cover for me until Stacy comes into the clinic. Actually..." Holly placed her finger on her chin. "When Stacy comes in she can help me rearrange the appointments. Maybe I should tell Mildred I can't make it in. No wait, yes I can. It won't take long to do all this. If I remember correctly, you had a light day." She looked up at him. "Right, or am I making that up? Friday's are normally your off day. Maybe I'm losing my mind. Am I losing my mind?"

Ben couldn't help but laugh at her rambling. "Yes, babe. Fridays are normally my light day, and no you are not losing your mind. You just need some sleep." He leaned over and kissed her cheek.

"Sounds like she's got it under control," John chimed in. "Now, feed me."

"You're a pain in the ass." Ben looked at his best friend.

John straightened while he smirked. "'Tis true."

"Fine." Ben rolled his eyes. *Is it too late to get a new best friend?* "But we're stopping at the station to file the report."

John's whole face brightened as a lopsided grin appeared. "You mean we're gonna do the walk of shame in and *out* of the police station?"

"Wait, what?" Holly asked.

"Yeah, what?" Ben mimicked.

"You know, only people with *stories* get to stroll out of the station doing the walk of shame." He pointed at his clothes before he placed both of his hands in his golden-brown hair and started disheveling it.

Holly and Ben both watched him in awe. "You're strange, you know that right?"

"This is coming from the woman with a dog that thinks it's a human and that he's *your* master."

"Hey, you can't blame me for how my dog acts," Holly defended, as she placed her hands on her hips. "Have you ever tried to reason with him? It doesn't work. Plus, you can't say anything when *you're* the one trying to make yourself look like a crazy person so people will notice you and think you have some epic story to tell. And you say *me* having a human dog is strange."

"You enable him," John countered.

"Enabling him is safer. When Waffles eventually takes over the world I hope to get one of the better jobs." She pointed at John. "You, on the other hand, will probably get pooper scooper duty."

"And, Ben will be imprisoned since he's a vet." John tsked at him. "No dogs like the vet."

Holly shrugged and looked at Ben. "He has a point."

"You know what? Both of you are strange." Ben scratched

his chin. *But that does remind me to give Waffles a few extra treats when we get him from Henry's.*

John moved his hands through his hair one more time causing Ben to roll his eyes.

"Let John do whatever the hell John's brain thinks is a good idea, Ben." Holly placed her hands in her pockets looking away from him. "Plus, it's best you take him with you to the station anyway. I don't think it'd be wise for me to show my face there." Not looking at him, Holly started moving toward the reception desk causing him to quirk his brow.

John burst into laughter. "What are you scared you'll run into Officer Jones?"

"He started it." Holly snapped her head toward John as her eyes narrowed on him.

"Holly." Ben gave her the eye.

"Do not Holly me, Ben! Jonsie boy had it out for me from the second we arrived." She crossed her arms over her chest. "He's a jerk face McJerkerson."

"You threatened him." Ben's brows shot to the ceiling.

"Is that why she was in cuffs when I got here?" John asked.

"No." Ben shook his head. "She was in cuffs because he ran her name and saw she'd been arrested before. Add in her threats and he said he did it for *safety* reasons."

John darted his eye's to Holly. "No shit. You've been arrested before?"

"It was a misunderstanding!"

"Just like last night was a misunderstanding? A misunderstanding that ended with you in handcuffs and me having to promise to keep you away from Officer Jones for the foreseeable future?"

"It's not my fault he can't handle me."

"He looked like he was handling you just fine. You were after all the one in cuffs. He was just standing there eating a donut." John laughed which caused Holly to punch her fist in the air.

"That's another thing! He was taunting me with those donuts. Where the hell did they even come from?" she growled, narrowing her eyes at John. "You want a piece of me, Bub? Just say the word."

"Down girl." John held his hands up. "You're liable to trip on your way over here and break an arm anyway."

Ben saw it coming from a mile away. You know that thing cats do right before they pounce? Apparently, Holly was part cat. He saw her take a small step back then shake her ass before she leaped into the air, her sights set on the man who was now hunched over uncontrollably laughing.

Thankfully, Ben caught her in mid-flight before cradling her in his arms. He kissed the top of her head. "Have I ever told you that you're sexy when you get all protective and domineering?"

John gagged. "Eww, not again."

Holly's face glowed as her eyes brightened. "Love you, Ben."

"Love you too, Grace." Ben placed a stray piece of Holly's hair behind her ear after setting her down. "I'll call you as soon as I'm done at the police station. See if Mildred wouldn't mind covering your whole shift so you can go home and get some sleep."

"What about you?"

"What about me?"

Holly looked at him. "You've been up as long as I have." The love and caring that radiated off Holly filled Ben with warmth. Her concern for everyone else was one of the biggest reasons why he loved her. Ben bent before kissing her lightly on the cheek. "Don't you worry about me. I'll be home before you know it and we can both take a nap."

"Does anyone care about me?" John whined. "I've been here just as long as you two. Don't I get a nap?"

Ben laughed before shaking his head at his friend. "You are pretty cranky."

"And hungry." John lifted his chin.

"Whoa." Holly looked at John. "You clearly *do* need a nap. You're on the brink of a temper tantrum like a two-year-old." Holly then turned and winked at Ben. "But that's someone else's problem, not mine."

Ben groaned at the realization.

"Right through the heart." John held his hand to his chest like he'd been shot. "And all this time I thought we had something going, Holly. I'm heartbroken."

Holly shrugged, before walking to the reception desk leaving Ben to deal with John. "You'll get over it."

Chapter Six

AFTER SPENDING the morning rearranging all of Ben's appointments for the day, Holly was downright exhausted. Once Stacy, Ben's receptionist, made it in which was a chore on its own since Stacy nearly had a full-on meltdown once Holly told her what happened, they worked nonstop.

Thankfully, all of the clients had been very understanding, and there weren't any emergencies.

Holly closed her eyes the moment she pulled into her driveway.

Universe, when I asked for something interesting to happen for book material this was not *what I meant.* She finally let the events of the last twenty-four hours really sink in. *Holy freakin' crap on a cracker!*

No matter how hard she tried, she couldn't fathom any reason why someone would want to break into the clinic. Not only that, but *nothing* was taken.

It was like they only did it just to be a jerk.

Holly placed her hands on her forehead trying to ward off the headache she had.

Wonderful. As if today couldn't get any worse. She glared up at the roof of her car. *Now you're gonna give me a headache?*

Holly placed her head on the steering wheel. Well, it could have been worse. At least she didn't have to go to work.

Once Holly called Mildred and told her what happened, she was more than happy to cover for her.

Although Holly got the feeling if it were up to Mildred, she would have stormed into the police station demanding answers herself. Holly had to listen to Mildred for twenty minutes as she detailed what she'd do to the person that dared to hurt her *Mr. Hotness.* She was so up in arms, she was about five seconds from interrogating everyone she came across. Young or old she didn't care.

Holly shuddered.

Calm and collected Mildred was a freaking tornado. Angry and determined Mildred was someone the freaking devil feared himself.

Me too, Holly thought as she smiled at Mildred's nonsense words as she started naming off her contacts and who she could call to *take care of it.*

Holly wouldn't be surprised if Mildred was at the library right now scouring through investigation books and crime dramas.

With a shake of her head Holly pushed the thoughts of Mildred out of her mind, she reached for her phone. She hadn't heard anything from Ben. She really wasn't all that surprised though. She'd seen the way John ate before. If Ben were lucky, he would have gotten John out of the diner with only two meals instead of four. That man could eat everything in a buffet and *still* ask for more. Worst part was, he never gained a pound. He was still built like a damn cover model no matter what he stuffed in his large mouth.

Bastard.

They were probably just now getting to the station. Plus, once they were at the police station, there was no telling how long they'd be there. The one and only time she had been arrested she was there forever and a year.

She just hoped once this was all said and done, they'd never have to deal with it again.

Holly turned off her car and grabbed her bag. In slow movements, she dragged herself to the front door. Something was missing though. Once she made it up the last step, she realized it was quiet. Too quiet.

It was weird walking up to their house and not hearing barking.

Extremely weird.

She didn't like it.

Right before Holly left the clinic, she'd called her dad to give him the full rundown of the events that had transpired. After getting an earful from him too, Holly couldn't tell who was more pissed, her dad or Mildred.

Thankfully her dad agreed to watch the pups while Ben and her dealt with the situation.

It was a win-win. Henry always loved having the dogs around. He always spouted stuff about how the dogs made him young again and if we were only going to give him dogs and no grandbabies, then he'd take every moment he got with them.

Speaking of that...

Right now, she was too tired to really think about it. All she wanted was to crawl into their bed, and never get back out again.

That wasn't too much to ask for, right? She didn't think so.

Holly opened the front door. When she looked down the hall she saw Twitch running with all his might straight toward her. Her smile spread from ear to ear. *What a way to come home.* "Hey, little guy. Did you miss your momma?"

Twitch jumped on her legs trying to get Holly to pick him up. She couldn't help but laugh as she reached down and scooped him into her arms. "You'd think I'd be used to you acting like a dog when we come home, don't cha think?" She kissed his head. "But, I'm not."

When Ripley and Waffles were at the door ready to greet whoever was coming in, Twitch was always there too.

While Holly pat his head, she felt his little twitch, and her heart warmed. It wasn't as strong as it was when he was first poisoned but it was still there. She suspected it would always be there. Especially, since he'd grown out of his kitten phase and there was no sign of the twitch going away. But that was okay. It gave him character.

It made her love him all the more.

Holly scratched between his ears as she cooed at him. "How could anyone try to hurt you? You're nothing but a big lump of love."

Holly was just glad the kid that poisoned him had gotten in trouble. She still however wanted to punch him whenever she thought about it, though.

But no, two wrongs don't make a right. And there was that whole being an adult thing, and never punching a child. But still, anyone that hurts an animal and —

She stopped herself. Whenever she started going down that path it was never a good thing. And right now, she didn't have the energy.

She gave Twitch another squeeze. "Love you, Twitchy." She was rewarded when he started to rub against her chin while he purred.

Holly placed him onto the floor before making her way toward their couch. With a dramatic sigh, that could rival Lord Waffles, she plopped down.

Twitch was having none of it though. How dare his mom get onto the couch without him? He jumped onto her lap demanding more attention.

"My bad, sorry little one." Holly scratched under his chin before Twitch crawled into a ball.

A broad smile spread across Holly's face.

Ignoring her kitty, she reached into her pocket before pulling out her phone once again.

Nothing.

Holly let her eyes fall closed. What a day it had been.

But even with everything that had happened, she still had one thing in the back of her head.

Holly knew there was no way she'd be able to bring up the conversation with Ben now. She'd been seconds from letting Ben know at dinner last night, but now it didn't seem the time nor place to bring it up. At least not today. Not while everything was still happening.

A longing ran through her body as her heart squeezed.

Soon.

Holly opened her eyes and looked around their home. "One day. One day it will happen." She let out a drawn-out sigh as she looked down at her lap. In an instant, she scooped Twitch into her arms before rolling onto her side. She brought her fur-baby up to her chin and carefully placed him in the crook of her neck. *This will have to do for now.*

Twitch opened one of his eyes briefly before stretching and making himself more comfortable.

"Glad to see I wasn't an inconvenience for you there, little mister."

Twitch yawned before shutting his eyes completely ignoring Holly.

I can't tell if he missed me or he was just upset he was home alone this whole time and away from Ripley? She decided she would leave well enough alone. Ignorance is bliss as they say. At least he didn't talk back to her like Waffles did.

Yet.

Holy shit John can eat a lot.

Ben stared at his best friend in awe. *And how the hell was he able to run up these damn steps?*

"What's that look for?" John asked, as he took the steps two by two up to the front of the station.

"I'm trying to figure out how you're not over in the bushes spewing your breakfast. How the hell can you run after all the shit you just ate."

John's face morphed into a boyish grin as he patted his stomach. "It's truly a gift."

"I can see that." Ben shook his head before also taking the steps two by two getting to the front of the station. *If John can do it. I can do it too. Hell, I'll take them three at a time.* "Promise me you won't do anything stupid."

"Like what?" John pushed his hair one more time.

Like that.

Ben strode past him rolling his eyes. When he got to the front of the station he opened the door. To his surprise he saw one of his clients, Bruce's owner, sitting at the reception desk.

"Doctor Richman," she announced as she stood throwing her hand out to shake his. "It's good to see you out of the clinic."

"Likewise," he replied a little taken aback to see her.

"When I came in this morning I heard some of the officers talking about it. I was going to call to see if you needed anything."

"That's very sweet of you..." Ben was at a loss for what to call her. Normally, he had a chart in front of him. Plus, he always categorized his clients by their pet's names.

"Please, call me Emma."

Ben gave her a small smile. "Thanks, Emma. How's Bruce?"

"He's fine. He's a big lug like usual."

Ben chuckled. That was right, other than Waffles tormenting him, Bruce was this giant teddy bear.

"Who's Bruce?" John asked as he made his way next to Ben.

"Oh, I didn't see you there." Emma turned toward John as her cheeks slightly colored.

John looked around the *empty* reception area and then back to them. "What do you mean you didn't see me? It's just us here."

Emma's face completely colored before she looked down at her hands in embarrassment. "Sorry," she whispered.

"Jackass." Ben punched John in the arm. *Idiot.*

"What? It was a valid question."

Emma looked at him with panic in her eyes. "I didn't mean anything by it. It's just when I saw Doctor Richman I kinda lost track of everything else. I've been in a panic about the break-in. It's such a wonderful establishment. I've gone to three other veterinarians before I found Doctor Richman and every other one looked at Bruce and wanted nothing to do with a scaredy dog that had issues. Or they wanted to put him on weird meds and I never wanted that. Doctor Richman saw Bruce as he is. Perfect. Just a little broken. But that's okay because I'm a little broken too and that makes us perfect." Ben saw Emma's eyes widen in horror as she realized she'd just word vomited, as Holly liked to call it, all over them.

Thankfully, he'd been used to Holly word vomiting most of the time, so he never changed his expression at Emma's confession. However, from the corner of his eye, he saw John take a step back.

If he says anything, I swear to everything I'll murder him. Police station or no police station.

After a few seconds, John broke the silence. "It's okay, Ben does take up half the room."

"Are you jealous I have more muscles than you?" Ben narrowed his eyes at John as his lips thinned. His attention fully turned on him.

"You've got nothing compared to me. Who could be

jealous of you?" John crossed his arms over his chest as he did his best to make himself look bigger.

"Obviously, you."

"Yeah right. How could I be jealous of you when I have this?" He pulled up his shirt showing his abs.

"Jesus Christ no one wants to see that, you dimwit." Ben faked a gag.

However, when he heard a small laugh come from Emma he understood what John was doing. When Ben looked back at her he could physically see her relief.

"I'm telling Holly." John glared at him

"And what exactly are you going to tell my wife?" Ben arched his brow.

"I'm going to inform her *you* called *me* a name." John lifted his chin.

"What are you five?"

"No, I'm thirty-five. That's thirty more than five."

"I'm so glad you can count." Ben folded his arms across his chest. "Now if we can only get you to practice your manners, we'd be all set. Maybe we can move you out of pre-school."

"Now I'm telling her you said I had no manners." John's face morphed into shock.

"Emma," Ben turned to her ignoring John, "can you put me out of my misery and tell me where Detective Will Bower's office is?" He looked back at John. "The sooner I can get this over with, the sooner I can get rid of him."

"I'm your ride!"

"Don't remind me."

Emma shyly took another glance at John before looking back at Ben. "Is he always this dramatic?"

"Pretty much. I can never tell who's worse, him or Waffles."

"Oh." Emma's face brightened. "That little Corgi?"

"I don't know about *little*," John grumbled.

Ben shot his eyes back to John. "I'm telling Holly you said that."

"You wouldn't." John's eyes widened in horror.

"Try me."

Before John could retaliate Emma chimed in. "Detective Bower is down the hall on the left. You can't miss him. I'll send him a quick message to let him know you're coming."

"Thank you." Ben gave her a small nod before walking around the reception desk leaving John behind.

"Hey wait up, dickwad."

Ben sighed. *Give me strength.*

"Who was that?" John asked as he ran to catch up to Ben.

"She's a client. Couldn't you tell?"

"I figured as much." John looked over his shoulder back at the reception desk once more. "She's pretty. Kinda reminds me of Holly."

Ben stopped before pivoting to look at John. "What, can I not say Holly's pretty? Is that against the bro code? It's not like I said she's fuckable or something. I mean she is, but all I said was she's pretty."

Ben cocked his brow. "Excuse me?"

John bounced his head back and forth. "You know what I'm saying. Holly's fuckable. I mean obviously you thought so." At Ben's deep growl John raised his hands. "Whoa, there, killer. Not that I ever thought anything of it. She's got a wack-a-doo dog and can't seem to figure out how to walk in a straight line without tripping. No one wants that kind of baggage. Plus, it's a compliment. One you are clearly not seeing."

"Explain to me why you saying my *wife* is fuckable is a compliment."

"It is," John protested. "I mean you do her, so obviously you agree. Or you wouldn't have married her."

"You know if we weren't surrounded by police officers I'd kill you where you stand, right?"

"You couldn't hurt a fly." John looked around the room, clearly glad they *were* surrounded by people in uniform. "Anyway, I was complimenting your client. She's pretty."

"So you said." *Pick your battles,* as his dad used to say.

Ben decided the best course of action was to ignore John. If he didn't, he most likely would be thrown in jail.

Turning back, he looked down the hall. That's when he spotted Officer Jones. "Hey, it's good to see you again," Ben announced as he made his way toward him. "Arrest anyone interesting?"

"Other than your wife?" John said, coming up from behind him.

"He didn't arrest her," Ben spat, glaring at his dimwitted best friend. "He only detained her for a few minutes."

"Oh yes, the curvy woman with a loud mouth." Officer Jones took a drink from the mug he was carrying.

"That would be her." Ben nodded with a smirk.

Officer Jones looked behind them. "Is she by chance with you?"

Ben watched as the officer's left hand went to the handcuffs on his belt.

"No," he said, looking back at John with wide eyes.

"Pity."

"Jones, stop being an ass." Will made his way out of a nearby office. "Ignore him, please. He finds it *fun* to intimidate people. Your wife turned out to be the perfect person for Jones to, excuse my lack of a better term, but *fuck* with."

Jones shrugged not denying it. Ben could see the hint of a smile on Jones's face. That's when Ben's body relaxed. "She is a fun one to rile, isn't she?"

A ridiculously wide smile spread across Officer Jones' face before walking away.

"What just happened?" John asked.

"I think he likes to mess with people and Holly just became his prime target."

"And how do you feel about that?"

Ben shrugged. "It might be fun to watch."

John's face brightened in pure amusement as he gave that all-knowing look. "Can I watch too?"

Ben tried but failed to hide his smile as he brought his attention back to Will. As long as Officer Jones didn't actually do anything to harm or scare Holly he'd be all for a little harmless prank or two. Maybe he could talk to Officer Jones on the way out.

Plus, being able to rescue Holly out of the situation last night sent a wave of *white knight* through Ben.

Yeah, I'm definitely going to talk to Officer Jones before we leave.

"Let's go into my office so we can get this paperwork finished," Will announced before leading Ben and John into his office.

Chapter Seven

Ben walked into the house to see Holly curled up with Twitch on the couch. At the sight, he warmed. They looked picture perfect together.

Even after the craziness of the last twenty-four hours, Holly still looked downright beautiful. Her hair was all over the place and her mouth was just the tiniest bit open as she slept.

She was fucking breathtaking and he knew it. His eyes traced along the curve of her body as he took her in.

He was a lucky bastard and he knew it.

He had to bite back his groan as his dick pressed against the front of his pants. It took all of his willpower to control himself.

She looked so peaceful as she slept. Plus, Ben knew she needed it. So did he. And if that meant a case of blue balls then so be it.

Her body did look inviting though. As he scanned her sleeping form one more time his eyes focused on Twitch. He was curled tightly under Holly's chin. As if the little guy could sense Ben staring at him, he opened one of his eyes. He gave

Ben a quick once-over before closing his eyes promptly dismissing him.

Good to know who you like better there, Bub. Ben could swear he saw Twitch open his eyes and then roll them. *I'll remember this come shot time.*

He was definitely going to have to start separating Waffles from the rest of the gang every once in a while.

Looking back at Holly he decided to sneak in behind her and curling up was a much better plan than going into their bed alone.

As quietly as he could, he removed his shoes and socks along with his shirt. He eyed his delectable wife, one of his favorite things was to cradle her to his body as they slept. Although, halfway through the night, it never failed. Holly would threaten him with death if he didn't move over and give her some space. She'd mumble how between him, Waffles, Ripley, and now Twitch she'd end up dying of heat stroke.

Only Holly.

He knew if he was careful, he'd be able to finagle his way behind Holly and nap with her in his arms.

And that was exactly what he was going to do.

Ben tiptoed over to the couch before placing his left leg behind Holly's knees. Before he made his next move, he glanced at her to make sure he hadn't woken her.

Okay, now what?

Seeing as she was still asleep, he started maneuvering himself behind Holly. When he was halfway in place, he saw Twitch turn his head to stare at him like he was crazy.

Ben narrowed his eyes right back at him. *You know, instead of judging me you could help.*

Twitch closed both of his eyes before stretching out getting more comfortable.

Figures.

Ben carefully bent his knee placing his full weight onto the back of the couch.

See this wasn't so hard. Alright, now just wedge yourself between the couch and Holly.

He was making damn good progress if you asked him. He was nearly fully wedged where he wanted to be when he heard a tiny laugh escape from his wife.

"You're awake, aren't you?"

"I plead the fifth."

Ben growled before bumping Holly with his hips giving him the room he needed. "You could have just moved over, you know?"

"And miss out on this acrobatic feat? No way." She turned her upper body to face him with a huge grin.

That little shit.

"You think you're funny, don't you?" He tried his best to give her a stern look, but failed miserably.

"Maaayyybbbeee," she cooed before scooting to the front of the couch giving him all the room he needed.

"You're gonna get it, Grace."

"You keep telling yourself that, honey." Holly patted his side.

"Oh, Mrs. Holly Richman," he growled in her ear. "I think you know damn well what I can do to you." He pushed his hips forward causing his dick to rub against her ass.

Holly let out a tiny gasp before she wiggled her hips back into his groin. "Oh, do tell. I'm always in the mood to be enlightened."

Ben pushed her hair from her neck before nibbling on the exposed skin. "I thought you were tired."

"Not anymore." She turned to face him giving complete access to her mouth, which he gladly took.

Fuck yes.

He ground his hips into her as he devoured her mouth. With his free hand, he reached around her body and grabbed onto her breast, enticing a moan from her.

Fuck he loved his wife. He loved every fucking inch of her.

Without removing his lips from hers, he inched his hands lower. Once he found the hem of her shirt he snaked his hand under it. Her skin was so heated it sent his blood racing. Right now, his dick was pressed so forcefully to his pants he was sure there'd be a permanent zipper mark.

He didn't give a shit though. His hand moved up her belly seeking out her taut peaks.

"Ben," Holly whispered, pulling her mouth from his.

Ignoring her cries, he sought out her mouth again.

He was instantly rewarded when her hand moved between their bodies and started to palm his member through his jeans. "Fuck," he growled, as shivers moved down his spine.

"What do you think I'm trying to do?" Her words ignited him. Quickly he moved his hand to his belt undoing it with ease. As soon as there was room, Holly shoved her hand inside his pants seeking out his dick. The second she reached the base, he couldn't stop himself from thrusting his hips forward.

"You're awful happy to see me." Holly smirked at him as her hand stroked up and down his dick.

"I'm always happy to see you." Ben didn't know if it was all the excitement of the recent events or that this was just how crazy his wife normally made him, but he *had* to be inside of her. If he didn't, he'd die.

There was something about Holly's warm body next to his that fucking sent him into hyperdrive.

As Holly worked him, he reached around her waist once again cupping her sex. The heat he felt through her leggings almost fucking unmanned him.

He moved his hand to her waistband. Thank fucking God she had on leggings. He easily pushed his hand past the material.

The moment his fingers brushed against her lower lips, Holly gasped throwing her head back.

Fuck he loved this.

He let his fingers slide against her slowly, teasing her,

causing Holly to start to thrash around. "No teasing more doing!"

At her words, he bit down onto her neck. He placed his index and middle finger at her entrance. "Please," she begged.

He pushed his fingers deep inside her. She shot her hips off the couch.

He fucking loved watching her like this.

Holly, the equal opportunist she was, used her hot little hand and grabbed onto his dick before giving a squeeze. "More," she panted.

If Holly wanted more, well he was damn well going to give it to her. He hoped like hell these were not her favorite leggings.

Fuck it, I'll buy her more.

He sat up pulling his hand from her center.

"No!"

He ignored Holly's cry as he flipped her over onto her stomach. He then grabbed a hold of her leggings at her ass and ripped them in half exposing her perfect bottom.

"I'm gonna murder you for that." She looked over her shoulder at him. *Ehh, it was worth it.* Plus, he would have been more concerned if he didn't see lust staring back at him. Not to mention the fact she kept pushing her ass into the air.

"I'll remind you to murder me later. Right now, I'm busy." He bent kissing her exposed flesh before biting it.

Holly pushed her ass back at him. It was a sight to worship.

He palmed her ass before seeking out her core with his tongue. He took one long lick as he moaned. Fuck, even after all this time she still tasted like pure fucking honey. He could eat her all day and still not tire.

That's it, he had to be inside her. The thing about relationships was, sometimes you needed slow-burning sex. Other times you needed to fuck. Smart men knew the difference.

Holly moaned as he worked her. Ben pulled back before he grabbed onto her leggings and ripped them near in half now.

"I'm gonna kill you!" she shouted, looking over her shoulder at him. When she saw his smirk she sent him a dirty look.

"They were already ruined, Grace." He ignored her as he moved his hands to his pants. He grabbed a hold of his dick finally freeing it. He looked down at her pussy, and his mouth watered. Her lush lips were swollen and coated in her cream. He couldn't help but palm himself at the site.

When she shook her ass he lost all control.

He lined up and entered her in one quick move.

God Holly loved it when Ben got like this, and right now this was exactly what they needed. Especially after all the stress of the break-in.

The moment he was fully inside of her everything felt right again.

Then she felt it. "Ouch."

Ben stopped his movements. That's when it happened again. "Owie."

"What's going on?" Holly heard the concern in Ben's voice, before she could say anything she felt it again. When she looked over her shoulder, she saw Twitch's orange and white head bobbing up and down. *What the hell?*

Twitch then did what Twitch did best. He reared back and jumped to the side of her leg, his claws out for attack.

Ben barked out a deep laugh. "Holy shit, he's playing with your ripped leggings."

Holly felt a pull on the material and sure enough, Twitch had a piece of it in his mouth and was pulling with all his might.

"Stop it." Holly reached for the torn piece only to have her hand swatted away by Twitch's paw. When she tried to grab it again Twitch growled at her. A full-on angry cat, this is my prize, kind of growl.

She glanced back at Ben who was in full hysterics at his point. "Help me!"

Ben held onto his stomach as he laughed. "I'm trying."

"No, you're not!" Holly reached for the fabric again but was once again warded off. "Ouch. Twitch you don't do that to your momma! You're going in time out!" Holly pushed onto her forearms. *I swear to all things, if it's not one animal it's the next.*

"Don't you dare move," Ben demanded.

Amongst his laughter he grabbed onto the part of her leggings and ripped it clean off. "Ben!"

"What?" He cocked his brow at her. Ben took the ruined fabric and chucked it across the room, which had a crazed Twitch run full speed after it.

"That'll take care of him." He bent to her back ready to kiss it. Unfortunately, Twitch had other ideas. With his prize in his mouth he came back running to Ben.

Twitch dropped it at his foot.

"You have got to be fucking kidding me," Ben growled. "Does he want me to play fetch with him?"

Holly watched the scene in astonishment. When Twitch picked up the piece of fabric and then dropped it at Ben's foot again she lost it. "Holy crap, he's doing what Ripley does when you play fetch with her."

When Holly pushed herself back, her core brush against Ben, causing a shiver to run through her. Oh man, she was so torn. Should she deal with her crazy cat or continue what they were doing?

Damn it.

"Twitchy." Ben did his best to handle the situation. He picked up the piece of fabric and balled it into his hands. "Hey little guy, you want this?" Twitch jumped and eyed the material. "Nope. How about I throw this and you go find Ripley. Go show her what you found. You know she'll love it."

Ben tossed the fabric in the middle of the floor. Holly's mouth fell open the moment Twitch ran after it and then pranced out of the room with the legging piece in his mouth.

"Holy hell, is he really going to look for her?" Her eyes widened.

"Fuck, if I know." Ben laughed, before turning his attention back to her. "That just means we have no time to lose." Ben placed his fingers at her core and started massaging her again. Instantly, a new wave of heat flowed through her.

God, how can he do that so fast? She looked over her shoulder at him, he was once again stroking himself. Her insides clenched. Watching him touch himself always sent her over the edge.

"You ready for me, Grace?"

She pushed her hips back answering him. "Put it in me," she demanded. "And you better hurry before Twitch remembers Ripley isn't here." Holly wiggled her hips demanding for him to move. Ben grabbed onto her hips and slowly entered her again.

Ben pulled out, only leaving the tip.

She snapped her head over her shoulder to give him a warning look. *Not today, Bub. I know what I want.* She slammed her hips back causing him to enter her. "Fuck me," he growled. Ben tightened his grip on her hips as he started to move inside of her.

As they found their frantic rhythm, Holly could feel herself building.

"Harder." Holly pushed herself onto her hands before bouncing back onto him with force.

Something must have snapped in Ben. He placed both of his hands onto her shoulders pushing himself harder inside of her.

"Yes!" Holly screamed as she started to feel her body quiver.

Ben grabbed her middle lifting her as he fell onto his side. He then placed her right leg over his hip as he continued his thrust.

Holly could feel every one of her nerve endings. She loved this position. Ben snaked his hand around her body seeking out her clit. Once he found it he started rubbing in circles.

"Oh, I'm gonna - I'm gonna," Holly panted as she met him thrust for thrust. She was right there. When Ben pinched her clit, she exploded. Through her ecstasy Ben grab onto her hip and started moving faster, then with a loud groan, he bit down onto her neck as he came deep inside of her walls.

Holy crap on all the crackers.

They both laid there panting as they tried to get their breathing back under control.

Ben slowly kissed along her neck before he pushed himself onto his elbow to kiss her lips.

"Well, if I knew you were gonna do that when you got home I would have never taken a nap."

Ben huffed out a laugh as he placed the palm of her hand onto her belly. "Like you didn't know this was gonna happen? You planned it." He gave her a pointed look. "I came home and there you were, sexy as hell spread out on the couch. You knew what you were doing." He sent her a quick wink before kissing her neck.

"So, you're saying I'm just so sexy all I have to do to get you turned on is drool and snore a little?"

"Oh, Grace, that's the shit that gets me hard for days," he laughed, gently biting down on her earlobe. "Those snores." She heard a growl escape from him.

Holly started to laugh but then quickly stopped. "Hey, hey, no more groping for you. I'm mad at you." She narrowed her eyes. "As soon as I regain some strength I'm kicking your ass for destroying my favorite pair of leggings."

Ben's face morphed into a lazy grin. "If I didn't destroy them would I have been able to do this?" He slowly pushed himself inside of her again.

"Mmhmm." Holly's eyes started to roll back in her head before she snapped them open. "No. Stop trying to distract me. You didn't have to go all Neanderthal on them, you could've just pulled them down. And now a piece of them is a freaking chew toy for Twitch."

"Could of, would of, should of." He shrugged.

Holly's face broke into a smile. "Do you think we lose points for us still being pretty much dressed?"

"Mistakes were made." Ben's grin spread from ear to ear. "Love you, Grace."

"Love you too, Ben." Holly's eyes started to close. That's when she felt something land on her. When she opened her eyes, she was greeted by an evil glare coming from Twitch. "I wasn't the one that lied to you."

Ben moved his hand to scratch Twitch behind the ears. "Your mommy's a mean old liar, isn't she?"

Holly snapped her eyes to Ben with a glare. "I'm the liar?"

"Shh." Ben ignored her. "Can't you tell Twitch wants to take a nap?" He pulled Holly into his arms.

"I'm going to remember this. Both of you!"

"Sleep." Ben chuckled as he made himself comfortable.

Holly crossed her arms over her chest pushing Twitch to lay on Ben. "Don't tell me what to do!"

Chapter Eight

It had been a total of three weeks since the break-in. Three freaking weeks and they were still no closer to getting any answers than they were on day one. Holly didn't know whether to pull her hair out or cry.

And poor Ben.

Her heart broke for him. He'd been so stressed about the whole situation. And add in the insurance company dragging their feet, having no idea if they'd be broken into again, and what you got was Ben as a full-blown mess.

Which in turn made her a mess.

Try as she might, Holly still hadn't been able to bring up the conversation about having a baby. Which added another weight to her shoulders.

There'd only been one time she thought she could broach the subject, and she really was seconds from doing just that.

Then to her utter shock, the moment she was ready to spill her guts, Ben started talking about how he wanted to add extra security to the clinic. But that wasn't the big, *what* moment. No, that came when he pulled out blueprints to add on a pseudo clinic onto the house so he could bring home all the animals that were left at the clinic overnight.

That was a shock.

Sure, she got where he was coming from. Ben would cut off his own arm if it meant keeping his animals out of harm's way. That was one of the many reasons she loved him. Ben's heart was huge and completely full of love.

So was hers.

But the idea of having a revolving door of boarded or sick patients at the house sounded like it would do more harm than good.

Talk about added stress.

She couldn't deny his heart was in the right place, though, but with everything going on he also wasn't thinking clearly. It wouldn't be smart to keep moving animals that were recovering back and forth every night.

Not to mention, Waffles would lose his shit.

Or worse...

He'd probably convert every single one of Ben's patients to overthrow the government and rule the world with him as their new leader.

Nobody needed that in their life. Plus, it was bad enough Ripley had picked up ninety-five percent of Waffles' traits by being around him. Holly didn't need Ben's clients calling her complaining about how their pets now acted.

Besides, could you imagine a whole hoard of *Lord Waffles* running around?

Holly shuddered.

Nope, a pseudo clinic on the house was not the answer.

Ben knew that, and so did she.

Regardless, that didn't stop Ben from constantly worrying about what could happen next.

Maybe they were just overreacting.

Holly was sure once everything was straightened out, all would go back to normal. Well, at least she sure as hell hoped it would.

Especially for her.

Holly had been irritable and moody since everything happened. She kept chalking it up to a crappy sleep schedule, and the fact she hadn't found the time to talk to Ben, but still, her constant mood swings were starting to drive her up the wall.

Oh, and let's not forget her godforsaken heartburn. Shit, it was like her heart was a freaking volcano and every hour it had to erupt. Maybe it was the unhealthy amount of donuts she'd been consuming, or maybe it was all the stress.

Regardless of what the root cause was, she was sucking down antacids like they were her new favorite candy.

Speaking of which...

Holly opened her bottom desk drawer to retrieve her antacids. Her heartburn was in full swing this morning. At this point, she was about three seconds from deciding if she wanted to grind down the whole bottle of antacids and make a smoothie or fall into the fetal position and pray for sweet death.

She'd be lying if she didn't say she was leaning toward the latter.

"Do I need to call our Benny Boy and tell him he's lacking in the sack again?" Mildred asked as she walked into the room with a stack of books in her hands. She plopped them onto the papers Holly was going over.

Holly's eye started to twitch.

Universe, give me strength. Taking a deep breath, she arched her brow at the old coot. "Please tell me you do not call my husband and say crazy shit like that?" Holly stared at the person who, now that she thought about it, was probably the cause for her ungodly amount of heartburn and stress.

"Me and Benny have conversations all the time," Mildred nonchalantly answered plopping her hip onto the desk. "Sadly, he refuses to tell me about his man meat though." Her brows knitted together as she pouted.

"You're joking, right? Please tell me you're joking?"

"Do I ever joke about man sticks? I think not, missy. You do not joke about such things." The appalled expression on Mildred's face had Holly paling.

Universe, how is this my life? Am I your favorite sitcom to watch? That must be it. I'm primetime entertainment for you. That's the only *reason this conversation is happening right now.*

Mildred sighed. "Benny Boy normally thinks I'm joking. Pity." Mildred looked at Holly with a hurt expression. "What am I doing wrong?"

Oh, for the love of all things... Holly rolled her eyes. "I don't know, maybe it's the fact you're asking my husband about his... how did you put it, oh yes, *man stick*?" Holly threw her hands in the air with resignation. "You know what, I'm going to pretend we didn't have this conversation."

Although, as soon as she got home she was damn well going to ask Ben some questions. And he better have some answers.

"Fine, suit yourself." Mildred started foraging through the papers on Holly's desk. "Now, back to you. Why do you look like someone kicked your dog?"

Instead of answering her, Holly zoned in on Mildred rummaging through her stuff. "What are you doing?"

"Looking for donuts." She gave Holly a 'duh' look. "You have donuts on your desk every day."

"Maybe I don't have any today." Mildred's brows went to the ceiling. "Fine." Holly opened up her drawer and placed a box on the top of the desk. Holly threw her hand on top of the box glaring at Mildred stopping her. "Only one!"

"Yay." Mildred's grabby hands pushed Holly's out of the way before opening the box. "You must have one of those newfangled reward cards with the donut shop with how many times you go in there. You must be in the frequent flyers section by now."

"Don't remind me." Holly groaned. "I've already put on about eight pounds." She reached for the donuts. "I can't seem to stop. There is something about these things that I crave. If I don't have it, I feel like I'm going to die."

"That's not a healthy way to live there."

"Trust me, I know. But with everything going on, I can't seem to say no." Holly shrugged throwing another piece in her mouth.

"As long as you keep bringing them in, I don't really care. Now, where were we? That's right, you were about to spill your guts about the attitude you got going on." Mildred made a weird moan as she took a bite of her donut. "Momma needs some good gossip to bring back to my knitting club."

"You don't knit."

"Neither do they. We just sit around and gossip for a few hours each week." Mildred shoved the rest of the food into her mouth chomping happily on it. "You should have heard the stuff they were spouting when we were talking about Ben's nutty mother last year. Oh boy, you think *I'm* bad. You should have heard some of those ladies."

Holly shuddered as the thought tingled down her spine. "It's good to know my life is a constant source of entertainment to you and your *knitting* friends."

"You do keep it lively." Mildred smirked at her. "Now spill."

Holly slumped into her chair with a heavy sigh. "I don't know, Mildred. It's everything. Ben's worried about the clinic. Now he's talking about building a room onto the house to keep the animals overnight. The insurance company is a freaking joke. We haven't heard anything about the investigation. I can't write. At all..." Holly sent a death glare to Mildred when she reached into the box again. "And *you* keep eating my donuts."

Mildred shrugged before pulling out the last donut taking a bite. "So, you're saying life is hard and you're having a pity party?"

"Have I ever told you I want to murder you?"

"About once a day. If you didn't, I'd worry you don't love me anymore." Mildred straightened. "Now, let's work on this one step at a time. Ben wants to bring his patients home at night because he's afraid someone else might break into the clinic?"

"Yes, he's got it into this head it wasn't just a prank and it was someone after him or something. I kinda agree with him, though. Remember right after we got married Ben found out about all that stuff at Richman Industries after his mother left and the new board took over?"

"Oh yeah, the embezzlement. The ladies and I at knitting went to town on that one." Mildred nodded. "But I thought all of that had been handled and the new board of directors was doing well?"

"They are." Holly closed her eyes for a second. "Ben said something about one of the employees that were fired going after him. Especially, since he was the one that forced his mother to leave effectively destroying their coverups. So, he's now constantly worried about what is going to happen next."

"That doesn't sound like our Ben one bit." Mildred crossed her arms over her chest.

"Then for some reason the insurance company is being an asshat. Since nothing was taken, per the police report they're saying crap like they have to do their own *investigation*." Holly looked at her. "Can you believe they think we did it on purpose to file a claim? Have they lost their damn minds? Ben has enough money to fix a million windows. But no, we did it all just to get a few lousy dollars." She rolled her eyes. "Leave it to the insurance company to be a jackass."

"It'll get worked out. It always does."

Now that Holly had started, though, there was no stopping her. "You'd somehow think with Will being Ben's friend we would've heard something by now about the investigation, but no. Nothing. What's the use in having friends working on the case, if they can't even help you?"

Mildred nodded. "I told you. One phone call and I can have all of your problems taken care of. You don't get to live this long without meeting some *interesting* people."

Holly laughed. "Thanks, but no thanks. I don't think your type of help will keep us out of jail."

Mildred shrugged. "Suit yourself." Her lips scrunched together. "What I should really do is march my butt into the station and teach those officers about how to do their jobs."

Holly cocked her head to the side "Oh, I'm begging you, *please* enlighten me about why you think you could do a better job than them, or how you're qualified to?"

"Since the break-in I've spent night and day reading up on crime dramas. I'm pretty sure I could walk into that station and teach them all a thing or two. Hell, I bet if I started right now I could figure out exactly what happened and in *less* time." Mildred pulled out the pad and pen she kept in her skirt apron.

"What are you doing?"

"Writing down my evidence. Duh. What do you take me for, some rookie cop?"

"You're not a cop."

"The people I'm interrogating don't need to know that." She started scribbling stuff down.

"Mildred, please don't go around interrogating people. That's only going to add to my stress level and right now I don't think I can take that."

Mildred eyed her. "You do look a little flushed."

"Yeah, well that's probably 'cause you give me anxiety *and* this morning I woke up feeling like shit."

Mildred stared at her before nodding once.

"Really, that's all you've got for me? A nod. Normally, you'd be demanding I tell you all my symptoms. And then you'd be off in the medical section looking up my disease."

Mildred placed her pen at her mouth thinking. "Cop or doctor? Decisions, decisions."

Holly shook her head. "How about librarian?"

"Nah, that's boring."

"Yet it's what you've done your whole career."

"Exactly, so I need some more excitement in my life."

"No, no one needs you to have more excitement in your life. You're good."

Mildred sent her a look which Holly decided it was best to ignore her.

After a few uncomfortable minutes of Mildred staring her down, she sighed. "I'll stick with cop for the day."

"Glad you've made your decision."

"Besides, I don't need to play doctor I already know what's wrong with you."

Holly sat straighter in her chair lifting her right brow at the crazy old lady. "Oh, don't keep me in suspense. Please inform me what the oh so mighty Doctor Mildred has surmised by only creepily staring at me."

"Missy, I wouldn't be so quick to discount me." She reached for the donut Holly had been munching on, before she placed it on the stack of papers in front of her. The moment Holly saw what she was doing she lunged for it. "Mine."

Unfortunately for her, Mildred was pretty quick for an old lady.

"And right there proved it." Mildred shoved the last piece into her mouth causing Holly's heartburn to come back in full force as she pictured all the ways she could murder her coworker.

"How is my trying to stop your grabby old hands from stealing my food proof of whatever the hell it is you think I have?"

Mildred shrugged again, which was sure as hell getting annoying.

Mildred pointed at her. "You're moody. Has anyone ever told you you're rude when you're moody? Little old ladies like me need all the food we can get. Especially, if I'm gonna be the detective that breaks the case. It's a stereotype of eating all the donuts. And, I *must* uphold it."

Give me strength, please universe I know you're sitting there laughing your ass off but please give me strength not to murder her. "So, I guess we're back to you being a cop?"

"I never stopped." She pulled out her pad and pen in her lap. "Now, let me ask you a question."

"I can't stop you." Holly sat back staring at her.

"That's right. You can't. You say you're stressed, right? You have bad heartburn all the time. Don't give me that look, there, young lady. I see you sucking down those antacids like they are going out of style. And you can't stop with these majestic goodies." She pointed to the donut box. "Although I cannot blame you on the last one."

"If I play along with your craziness, will you leave me alone to work on this paperwork?"

"I'd be lying if I said I would, but I'll make a deal with you."

"I'm all ears."

"I'm going to put away my Detective Mildred hat and put on my Doctor Mildred hat and ask you one question. If you can answer me with honesty, I will walk away for the rest of the shift and leave you to pout on your own."

Holly narrowed her eyes at her, while her lips thinned. "And who's to say I wouldn't answer you with honesty?"

"I'll know."

"Fine." Holly crossed her arms over her chest. "Lay it on me, Doctor Mildred. What's my diagnosis?"

"If you are going to huff at me, I'll take my expert knowledge and leave."

"Is that all I've ever had to do to get you to leave me alone?" Her brows shot to the ceiling.

"I take it back. I'll sit here all day and ask you about how Ben uses his ding-dong."

"Can we not," Holly groaned.

"Sure. The choice is yours. Now, answer me this, are you sure you don't already have a bun baking?"

"I don't cook. You know that."

Mildred rolled her eyes before she sighed. "You're a lost cause. I'm going to the true crime section. Holler if you need anything." With that Mildred hopped off the desk with her pen and pad in hand and started making her way to the crime section.

Crazy old woman. Why does she always have to talk in riddles and nonsense? Why can't she just come out and say whatever the hell she is trying to say?

Holly grabbed one of the books on her desk Mildred left and pulled out the inventory paper she'd been working on. "Stupid hag. Everyone knows I can't cook. And baking." She huffed. "The one and only time I tried it, I nearly set the kitchen on fire. With baking you have to be all precise and stuff, that's annoying. No one has time to read *every* step," she mumbled. "And to make bread... that sounds like hell. Plus, I wouldn't know the first thing about baking buns I would—"

She froze.

Are you sure you don't already have a bun baking?

Holly sat there in shock as Mildred's words finally took hold. *Oh my God!* She tried to think about the last time she had her period.

"Oh shit."

Holly jumped from her seat and started making her way toward the front door. When she walked passed the crime section she hollered. "I've got to go, cover for me."

All Holly heard as she walked through the door was a giddy Mildred screaming, "Congratulations!"

Chapter Nine

BEN PLOPPED onto the couch with a heavy sigh. No matter how much he tried to work things out with the insurance company, nothing he did seemed to work. Today he'd decided to take a half-day and come home early.

He wanted to look over his plans of possibly adding a room onto their house anyway. Sure, Holly didn't seem to be one hundred percent thrilled about the idea, but at this point what other choice did they have?

Other than Holly, Henry, and their own pets, his patients were his priority. And if that meant housing them at night then so be it. Plus, there was that sinking feeling he had about the break-in. Something wasn't right.

If it were just a prank, he'd know. This. This was different.

Ben didn't know *why* he felt that way, but he did.

And it was getting to him. Over the last few weeks, Ben found himself driving over to the clinic after he'd closed up for the night to make sure everything was fine.

It always was, but there was still an unsettled feeling inside of him.

What if it really was some of the fired employees of Richman Industries had it out for him? Sure, some of them were sent to jail but the ones they couldn't prove beyond a reasonable doubt, were just fired. What if they now blamed him for their downfall. And taking it out on the clinic would be where it would hurt him most. Well, not the most. If anyone ever laid a finger on Holly, they'd be dead before they knew what was coming to them. Hell, he bet before he could do anything Mildred would have called in her goons to take care of them.

He sighed closing his eyes.

Maybe it was payback. Or, maybe it was just a prank.

He needed a vacation.

A real vacation.

Ben brought his hand to his forehead and started rubbing away his headache.

After he and Holly were married, they only went on a four-day honeymoon to a little cabin in the woods.

Shit, those were the best four days of his life. If it were up to him they would have *never* left. He didn't think they wore clothes the entire time they were there, which was fine by him. And if you ignored the time Holly fell out of the bed, hitting the nightstand with her knee and sending it crashing to smithereens onto the floor, there were no mishaps.

It was just him, his fucking gorgeous wife, and no clothes.

Perfection.

Unfortunately, reality had set in far too soon. Although he would have loved to stay there forever, he needed to get back to his patients and then there was Henry. They had made sure he'd have enough food and everything was in order, Holly nor Ben liked leaving him alone for too long.

Especially when he was watching the dogs. Originally John had agreed to watch them, even if that meant having to deal with Waffles and his judgmental side-eye. Henry was having none of that. And the second Henry took a page straight out of Waffles' book and gave Holly the sad puppy eyes, she couldn't say no.

At least he got John to take care of Twitch. Then again, keeping Twitch away from Ripley caused some issues for John. He still motions to the spot on his arm where Twitch scratched him.

Ehh, it was John. He needed a little defiance in his life.

Ben let his head fall back onto the couch.

Damn, he needed a vacation.

Something nudged at his leg. When he opened his eyes he saw Waffles. "What can I do for you, your holiness?"

Waffles barked before looking toward the kitchen. "It's not dinnertime."

Waffles barked again causing Ben to arch his brow. "Does your mother feed you extra meals when's she's home?"

Waffles *and* Ripley barked in unison this time.

"She does now? Well, I'm gonna have to have a little talk with her." Ben slowly moved off the couch before trekking into the kitchen. "One treat. That's it. I'd say don't tell your mother I'm spoiling you two, but seeing as she feeds you extra meals, I'm pretty sure I still have the upper hand."

Ripley and Waffles both sat perfectly as they waited for their snacks. Ben tossed them each one before leaning against the counter.

Speaking of Holly...

Ben placed his chin in the palm of his hand. Something was off with her. He could sense it. He'd been meaning to talk to her about it, but with everything going on it never seemed like the right time. Plus, whenever they finally got a few minutes that weren't dedicated to something else... He jumped her. Ehh, what could he say? His wife was sexy. There was no shame in that.

Regardless though, something was off.

His brows drew together as he scratched the scruff on his chin. She'd been a little snippy the past few weeks. Then this morning, before she left for work she'd mentioned how she wasn't feeling well. Her face did look flushed, and she now had antacids on every table in their house.

Maybe he should make her an appointment at the doctor? Yeah, that's exactly what he was going to do. Ben reached into his back pocket retrieving his phone. As he was about to make the call, though, he heard someone speed into their driveway.

He glanced at the time on his phone. There was no way Holly would be home already.

He made his way toward the front door to investigate with a barking Waffles and Ripley at his feet. The moment the door came into view he saw Holly throw open the door. She tripped over the frame landing on her hands and knees flinging the bag she was carrying in her hands across the room.

Instantly he ran to her side picking her up. "Grace, are you okay?"

Holly must not have registered that it was him since she jumped out of his arms and screamed before holding up her fists ready to fight.

It took everything in him not to burst into laughter.

Once she realized it was him, she held her hand to her chest as she tried to regain her breath. "Where in the hell did you come from?"

"The kitchen," he answered. "Are you okay, did you hurt yourself?"

Holly bent dusting off her pants. "Yeah, yeah I'm fine. Don't worry about me. Why are you home?" she asked in a panic.

When Ben really looked at her, he saw an urgency in her eyes he hadn't seen before, causing his brows to knit together. "I took a half day, Grace."

"Oh, okay good, good." Holly pushed her hair out of her face in panicked movements. "Wonderful. I mean yeah that's great that you are taking a half day. Half days are good. You know we all need them sometimes."

"Holly?" Okay, now he was really concerned.

"I love when I work half days. It's like a nice reprieve from Mildred. So it's almost like a vacation." She started to bounce on her feet.

"Holly, you're rambling."

"I am?" Her eyes widened. "I didn't realize. Are you sure? Maybe it's you that's rambling. I'm fine. I'm calm as a cucumber that's not about to be cut up and thrown into a salad for someone to eat."

That's it, he was calling the doctor. He gave her the once-over, assessing she was physically okay. Mentally on the other hand...

He shook his head as he walked over to the bag that was flung across the room.

"Stop!"

At Holly's scream, Ben froze. He slowly turned back to face her. That's when he saw the terror in her eyes. "Holly?"

"Don't look in there!"

"In where..." Ben reached for the bag. "Here?" Ignoring her protest, he looked at whatever was making his somewhat sane wife hysterical.

That's when his heart stopped.

Oh God, oh God, oh God. What do I do?

Ben wasn't supposed to be home yet. The dogs were barking like they were being murdered. Her heartburn was back in full force, she was positive she was about to vomit. Her knees hurt. And now Ben looked like he'd short-circuited.

Seriously, right now Ben looked like he'd left his body and was replaced with a robot.

Holly's whole body started to go into hyperdrive. *Universe, can you not give me a freakin' break? Ever?*

Ben pulled the box from the bag. "Holly, what is this?"

"It's not what it looks like!" she screamed.

He arched his brow at her. "Really, because this looks exactly like a pregnancy test to me. Or is this how they're packaging candy nowadays?"

Holly looked at him in absolute horror, then she did what she did best. Holly word vomited. And she word vomited hard. "Okay yeah, so here's the thing, over the past two months I've been feeling weird, and kinda off and stuff and I couldn't write and whatever, no matter how hard I tried. I just couldn't do it. One day I was talking to Mildred and she was all," Holly mimicked Mildred, "you're unsettled and shit like that and I was all, no you're a crazy old woman." Holly started to pace. "Then Mildred left this book on my desk that had a baby on it and I was like holy shit I want a baby. I mean doesn't it sound perfect? Can you imagine a little blue-eyed baby running around here that looked exactly like you? I can." She stopped moving.

"Oh, but man, I really hope they don't get my klutz gene." Deciding not to look at him she continued with her pacing. "I was going to bring it up after we left my dad's that night, but then the break-in happened and I just never got to it. Fast forward to today and Mildred is all blah blah blah, you are already baking a bun, and at first, I didn't realize what that meant but then I got it and thought back to when I had my last period and I freaked. I left work and ran to the store and fell through the front door just now." She was entirely out of breath by the time she finished.

She stopped pacing long enough to brave a chance and look at Ben.

Yep. She broke him.

"Ben?" He stared back at her with an unreadable expression. "Uhh, Ben, you're starting to freak me out here."

"You're pregnant?" He finally mustered up some words.

As they stared at each other something shifted in the room. Quietly she answered him. "I don't know. Maybe."

Before Holly could register it, Ben was throwing her over his shoulder in a fireman's pose. "Hey, what the hell?"

"Bathroom," he stated.

Ben then ran them both to the bathroom before depositing Holly onto the toilet. He then ripped open the box and shoved the stick at her. "Pee."

"Do not demand for me to pee." She glared at him. "I'm not a dog. I don't go on demand. Neither does Waffles, but you get what I'm saying."

"Holly, this is the moment we might find out if we are having a baby. Now pee."

"Not while you're in here!"

"I've seen all you got. Now, pee. Don't make me tell you again."

"Benjamin Richman, you leave this bathroom right now! If I'm gonna pee on a stick and it's gonna tell me if our lives are gonna be changed forever, then I am not doing that with you in here."

Ben glared at her. "The door stays open." He sidestepped out of the bathroom.

"*The door stays open,*" she mocked glaring at the spot Ben vacated.

She took a deep breath. *Oh my God.* Was she really about to do this?

Was Ben's reaction a good or bad thing? Did he want to know if she was pregnant so he could figure out what he needed to do with his life? What if he didn't want children right now?

What if she *was* pregnant?

Oh God, I might be pregnant.

I might be having a baby.

A real-life baby.

"I don't hear you peeing," Ben yelled from the other side of the wall.

"I can't pee under pressure!"

"Fine, I'm going to the kitchen."

Holly heard him stomp his feet. "I wasn't born yesterday. All you did was march in place."

"Holly just pee on the damn stick already so we can celebrate."

Celebrate?

At that exact moment, all of Holly's worries disappeared. Ben wanted to celebrate. He wanted a baby.

Holly took the stick in her hand and gave it a quick squeeze. *Here goes nothing.*

However, *nothing* ever went smoothly for her. She should have known better. As she hovered over the toilet, something nudged her leg.

Then it nudged harder.

When she focused, she saw Waffles at her feet. He then huffed before he jumped up onto her leg. Unfortunately, for her, Holly was already unbalanced, but with Waffles sneak attack and her hand already being occupied she saw or rather felt it coming.

Timmmbbeeerrrr, she shouted in her head as she found herself falling through the air. In an attempt to catch herself, she grabbed onto the shower curtain, which effectively fell on top of her. Before she knew it, she was in the bathtub tangled in the curtain with her pants around her ankles.

Ben was instantly in the room. "Holy fuck, are you okay?" he asked, jumping into the shower to help her.

"Why does this stuff always happen to me?" She looked at him before darting her eyes to Waffles who had his two front paws on the side of the tub staring at her with his tongue hanging out of the side of his mouth.

"It's because you're Holly." Ben barked out a laugh.

"That's not a good enough reason."

He kissed her forehead. "It's all the reason you need. Are you hurt?"

"My ego, yes."

He raised his brows at her. "And?"

"And what?"

His gaze darted to the stick still in her hand. "Oh yeah." She was too afraid to really look at it. "I think I got enough on it but the box said we had to wait."

"Fine. Now, we wait." Ben pulled Holly out of the tub before unwrapping her from the shower curtain. "Finish up in here and then we'll read it together."

"Okay." Her mind was going a million miles an hour. And yet, she was still surprised her pants were down around her ankles.

Ben left the bathroom while Holly cleaned herself up.

Only me.

When she made it out of the bathroom, Ben had Ripley, Waffles, and Twitch all at his feet.

"What's with the party?" she asked, as she worried her bottom lip. It was like an intervention.

"If we are about to grow by one, I thought it was only fitting if everyone in the family was present."

"We don't know if I'm pregnant," she stated.

"True." He stared at her. "But if you are, everyone is here."

Holly nodded as her heart pounded. She took a deep breath before she held out her hand with the stick face up for both of them to read.

Chapter Ten

"WE'RE PREGNANT."

Ben stood there in awe as he watched an array of emotions run across Holly's face as she stared at the stick.

The stick that just changed their lives.

He must have been living in a dream world. It was as if everything stopped around them and all that was there was him and Holly.

The soon to be mother of his child.

His child.

Knocking him from his thoughts, Ben heard a whine come from his left. When he looked at his feet, he saw Ripley putting her paw in the air with her head tilted to the side trying to understand what was going on. He bent at his knee coming to eye level with all their pets who soon jumped into his arms nearly tackling him backward. "You guys ready to be big brothers and sisters?" he asked, making sure to scratch every one of them.

This was it. This was the moment he'd been waiting for his whole life.

With a yip from Waffles and Ripley, and a nudge on his

knee from Twitch, Ben's face broke into a ridiculously wide smile.

He was going to be a dad.

And not just to animals.

Ben looked up at his wife. She glowed, and the warm smile she sent back at him made his heart slam against his chest.

They were going to be parents.

This was the start of a new chapter for them.

Ben stood before he took a step closer to Holly cradling her face in his hands. He brought his lips to hers. He licked along her bottom lip demanding for her to open as he deepened their kiss.

Words wouldn't work at this moment.

Not when he was getting everything he ever wanted.

A baby.

They were going to have a baby.

He pulled back from their kiss to rest his forehead against Holly's. "We're going to be parents, Grace."

"We are." She smiled at him as tears formed in her eyes. When he saw a tear fall down her cheek, he used the pad of his thumb to gently wipe it away. "I love you, Holly Richman."

"I love you too, Ben." She stepped into his arms allowing him to enclose her in his embrace completely. Ben reached down grabbing her bottom forcing her to jump. Holly instinctually wrapped her legs around him.

The moment she was secured, he started making his way to their bedroom. Once he made it inside he kicked the door shut.

Sorry guys, but I'm on a mission and being interrupted is not in the plan.

Not this time.

Ben gently placed Holly on her back before moving down to her stomach. He then lifted her shirt before getting onto his knees straddling her legs. Every so gently he placed the palm of his hand on her exposed skin.

My child is growing in here.

Ben was at a loss for words. He vowed at that moment he would do whatever it took to be the best father he could be. Just like his dad was to him, or how Henry was to Holly.

He would stop at nothing to make them proud.

Ben bent kissing Holly's stomach. *I will always protect you.*

"Uh, Ben?" Holly looked down at him. "You're kinda freaking me out here."

"Hush your face, can't you see I'm imagining you rounded with my child? Or children?" He winked at her.

"Take a step back there, mister. Child. Let's go with child as in singular."

"I want a whole sports team full," he said.

"Not out of my hoo-ha."

Ben laughed before kissing her stomach again. "We'll discuss it later. Have I told you today that I love you?"

"You tell me every day, but it's always nice to hear," she answered, looking at him with such love, he could feel it surrounding him.

His face brightened as he looked back at her. "I want to have many babies with you, Holly."

Holly's face softened with contentment as a twinkle in her eye appeared. "Good. 'Cause, Ben, I want to have many babies with you too."

A wicked smirk appeared on his face. "How do you think Waffles will handle it?"

Holly's eyes widened in shock. "I have no idea. Let's just hope for the best. The last thing we need is for him is to recruit our child as his minion in world domination."

"He'll probably try." Ben crawled up the bed to reach Holly. He then pulled her into another deep kiss. "I love you, baby." He moved from her lips as he peppered kisses along her jawline. "You've made me the happiest I've ever been."

"Ditto." A wicked grin appeared on her face. "Less talking, more celebrating."

"Oh, we are. Make no mistake of that." He growled.

Ben started to kiss along her exposed neck causing her to tilt her head back. Once he reached the collar of her shirt he sat up. "Off," he ordered as he pulled her shirt over her head forcing her to sit up.

"You're very demanding."

"Again, hush your face."

You know what? This is taking too long. He reached for the cups of her bra and ripped them in two. Holly then pushed at his chest. "Can you not destroy my clothes, please? I'm getting real tired of that."

He shrugged nonchalantly. "You took too long."

"You didn't even give me a chance!"

"Still took too long." He leaned over kissing her swollen chest. "How did I not notice these had grown?"

"I don't know. I mean I just thought I ate too many donuts." Holly's eyes rolled back into her head. "Donuts. Man, I would kill for a peanut butter glazed donut right now."

"Focus woman." Ben growled at her.

"But donuts."

He sat back on his heels. "You know it all makes sense now. You almost killed Waffles when he took one." He reached his hand out before pinching her nipple causing a slight moan to escape from her.

"I change my mind," she remarked. "No donuts, I want more suckie." She pushed her chest into the air.

"What momma wants, momma gets." Ben huffed out a laugh before he brought her peak into his mouth.

Man, he was so fucking lucky.

After a few seconds, he released her with a pop before moving to her other breast. He could do this for days. He let his tongue slide against her nipple before pulling away and blowing on it.

"Ben, please," Holly moaned.

"Patience," he said after releasing her. He then slid down

her body before reaching her pants. In one quick movement, he pulled them, along with her panties from her body, throwing them behind him.

"At least you didn't rip them this time."

He cocked his brow at her. "Did you want me to?"

"Hell no!" Holly laughed as she let her legs fall open exposing her core to Ben.

Fuck, she was so beautiful.

Lightly he traced her lower lips with his fingertips feeling her wetness.

"Mhhmm." Holly threw her head back the moment Ben reached her clit. Bending over he brought it into his mouth causing Holly to shoot her hips to his face. Instantly she buried her hands in his hair as she rocked against his mouth.

"Ben," she cried.

He bit down onto her clit before sucking it into his mouth

"Ben!" she screamed out. "Fuck me!"

"I plan on it." He used his fingers and pushed inside of her slowly. As her hips started to thrash around he knew she was close.

With one last lick of her core, he pulled back.

"Do you have a death wish?"

"Not today." He yanked his shirt over his head before undoing his belt buckle. He jumped from the bed discarding his pants.

Within seconds he was on top of her. "Is this what you want?" he growled as he positioned himself. Once he lined himself at her core, he slowly circled her entrance.

Holly narrowed her eyes at him. "Duh."

"Oh, you're feisty today, aren't you? You know I love it when you're feisty."

"No," she answered. "I'm horny and I believe since I'm now carrying your child and it wants me to eat nothing but peanut butter donuts, you better fuck me into burning off those calories."

He stopped what he was doing and arched his brow. "What?"

"For the love of all things. Cut me some slack." She bounced her head back and forth. "I can't think straight, right now."

"I'll let it slide this time," he said before inching his way inside of her. Honestly, he didn't have any other choice *but* to let it go. Seeing Holly so wanton, fucking unmanned him. And the fact inside of her was their child sent him over the edge.

Ben started slowly pushing his way inside of her as she clung to him. He gently grabbed onto her hips before flipping them so she'd be on top. After getting her situated he growled, "Ride me."

Without even a question Holly started moving her hips. Fuck he loved that she'd grown so comfortable with him to do so. He remembered when she used to try and hide herself from him.

Holly leaned back bracing her hands on his lower legs as she worked him up and down. Ben had to clench his teeth to keep control. With her legs spread wide, it gave him the perfect vantage point of their joining.

He couldn't stop himself even if he wanted to. He reached his left hand out opening her lower lips to expose her clit to his view. That's when Holly started to work herself harder as she moved around him.

"Oh God," she screamed. Ben started to feel her shake. He was right there with her though. He could feel himself at his breaking point.

With one hand he pinched her clit while the other went to her hip helping with her movements.

He pounded himself into her as he felt Holly start to explode. Abandoning her clit, he lost all control as he slammed himself deep into her walls before bringing her hips down to his, and freezing. He groaned loudly as he emptied himself within her.

"Holy guacamole," Holly blurted out as she laid on top of him.

His sentiments exactly.

He did his best to calm his panting as he came down from his high. After a few minutes, Holly righted herself before looking down at him with a smile on her face that he was sure matched his own. He then let his gaze travel down to her stomach. He placed the palm of his hand on top of it. "I love you, Holly."

"I love you too, Ben."

Just then Ben's eyes widened. "Oh shit."

"What, what is it?" Holly asked as Ben rolled forcing her to fall off of him and onto her side.

Ben jumped from the bed and ran to his pants, grabbing his phone from the pocket. "Shit. There is so much to do."

"What's going on?" Holly pushed herself onto her elbows. "Are you okay? You're kinda freakin' me out here."

He snapped his attention to her at her worried voice. "Me. Yeah, I'm fine. It just hit me. Do you know how much shit you trip on and fall over every day? We're gonna have to Holly proof this house and pronto."

Ben looked back at his phone and started frantically typing. *There has got to be a place I can get a lot of it,* he thought.

"What are you doing?" Holly's brows were knitted together when Ben looked up.

"I'm searching the internet for bubble wrap. There's got to be a place where I can buy it in bulk." He gave her a 'duh' look. This was the most logical solution. Didn't she understand with her track record he was going to have to start *now* in Holly proofing the house?

"You are not covering this place in bubble wrap."

"Who said I was going to cover the place? That would be a waste of time." He looked her up and down cocking his brow.

"Oh no. No, you don't Benjamin. You are *not* wrapping me in bubble wrap. No freakin' way!"

"How else do you suppose I keep you safe?"

Holly jumped from the bed. As she made her way toward him, she banged her shin on the bedpost. "Owwie."

"See." He threw his phone onto the bed before moving over to her and dropping to his knees. "Let me see."

"No." She refused to move her hand from her shin.

"Let me see, Holly."

"No. It's your fault I hit the dang thing anyway. We find out we're pregnant and then you go all crazy. So, no. I'm not moving my hand." She glared at him.

Ben rolled his eyes before he pushed her hand away himself. Thankfully there was only a small red mark. "It doesn't look like you cut it."

"Of course, I didn't cut it," she growled. "Let's get back to where you think it's a good idea for me to be wrapped up like some sort of lunch meat then—"

"You don't wrap lunch meat in bubble wrap."

"Can I use bubble wrap to clean up the mess I make once I strangle you to death?" Her lips thinned as she threw her hands on her hips angrily.

Ben sat back on his feet as he observed her. Damn, she was fucking beautiful. Her hair was all over the place, her face red with annoyance.

And, she was going to be the mother of his children.

He was never going to forget this moment.

Ben pulled her body to his as he rested his head on her stomach. After a few seconds, Holly's hand moved to his hair. Once he realized she wasn't trying to rip out his hair, he smiled. Plus, she didn't need to know he already ordered the bubble wrap.

Ben picked her up at her waist and tossed her back onto the bed.

Round two.

"No manhandling." She glared at him. "How many times do I have to tell you?"

"I'm gonna manhandle you all right." However, as he reached for her hips his phone started to ring. "Shit."

"Answer it," Holly said. "It might be the insurance company."

Fuck. The last thing he wanted to do right now was to be pulled away from his wife. Especially when he registered Holly had lifted one of her breasts before toying with her nipple.

Fuck me.

Ben growled as he answered the phone. "Richman."

"Ben, it's Will."

Chapter Eleven

RIGHT AS HOLLY and Ben started their walk up the police station steps, they saw John burst through the door.

What the... Why the hell is he here? Holly's face scrunched at the sight. *Please don't tell me he was up to no good.* Holly gave him the once-over. Who was she kidding, this was John. Of course, he was up to no good.

The moment John recognized her and Ben his whole face lit up in a boyish grin. Instantly, he ran down the steps in their direction. Once John was right in front of them, she noticed Ben's brows shoot to the sky as he looked at his best friend. "What are you doing here?"

"I can ask the same thing about you two?" John crossed his arms over his chest surprising Holly.

Defensive much?

Holly watched amazed as Ben and John did this weird speaking thing but without actually speaking.

Okay, Twilight Zone, here I am.

Ben broke the silence first. "Will asked if we could come down to the station. I guess he has some information." Ben shrugged. "He didn't go into detail over the phone."

"Hopefully, he's got good news." John lifted his chin.

That's when Holly started to notice something was off. As she took a closer look at John she realized he was fidgeting.

Hold up. Holly looked John up and down. He was nervous, there was no disputing that, but more importantly, he looked... normal. Hell, he even looked like he brushed his hair. And was that... Holy crap that was cologne. "John," she started a little taken aback. "You look like a normal human being, your hair is brushed, your clothes look good... I'm in shock." Holly's mouth curved into a smile. "I'm gonna go out on a limb here and say you weren't at the station trying to... how did you put it before? Oh, yeah, make it look like you had an exciting story or something insane like that." Holly's smile widened from ear to ear as she teased him.

"Hey," he protested. "It worked last time." John lifted his chin as he glared at her.

"Oh, Ben, I think little Johnny here is defensive."

"Settle down children." Ben gave them both a look. "John, if you're not here for some insane logic that only *you* have, then why are you here? I'm pretty positive people don't hang out at the police station just for shits and giggles."

John sighed loudly as he looked behind him at the front door. When he looked back at her and Ben he shook his head. There was this overwhelming sense of disappointment coming from him. "I had to take care of something."

"Do I need to worry?" Ben asked, looking him up and down.

In an instant, John's demeanor changed and his signature boyish grin appeared back on his face. He then took off past them only looking back to shout, "Not yet. See ya later." He waved.

What the hell?

Everything happened so fast, it almost gave Holly whiplash. They stood there in shock as John disappeared from sight. "Ben, what just happened?"

"I have absolutely no idea," he answered. "I have a feeling we'll find out soon."

"Why is he strange?" Holly scrutinized her husband. "Better yet, why do *you* attract the strange ones? There's me, you know, crazy dog, walking disaster, cannot tie my own shoes without falling over... And then there's John? I don't even have words to describe him. You must have this homing beacon for the weird ones."

Ben's eyes twinkled with amusement as he smirked at her. "I wish I had an answer for you, Grace. I stopped trying to make sense of it and decided I'd just roll with the punches. It's safer that way."

"Safer for who?"

"My sanity." A ridiculously wide smile appeared on his face.

"Ehh, you're probably right," she agreed. "It's probably better that way." Holly looked back at the police station and her gut twisted. She took a deep breath trying to shake the feeling that something terrible was going to happen. Or, you know, that might have just been her heartburn coming back.

Right now, it was a crapshoot.

At least she now knew what was causing her constant indigestion.

Whoa. The thought hit her. *I'm pregnant. Holy freakin' crap on a cracker.*

Ben squeezed her hand drawing her attention to him. "You okay, babe?" he asked, his brows knitted together in concern.

Even though inside she felt like she was a jumbled mess, knowing that Ben would be there through everything made her feel better. No matter what happened, they had each other.

She smiled warmly at him as she squeezed his hand. "Yeah, I think I'm just a little nervous. No one wants to come to a police station. Unless you're John or something." Then a new thought hit her sending a wave of ice down her back. "Oh, shit sticks." Holly took a step back as her face paled. "What if Officer Jones is in there?"

Ben's hand went to his stomach as he barked out a deep laugh. "What am I going to do with you?" He shook his head as he took a step pushing her toward the front door. I'm sure you'll be fine. Just don't speak to him and I think you'll avoid him throwing you in handcuffs again."

Holly pointed at her mouth as her eyes narrowed. "I can't stop what comes out of here. You know that."

"Try." Ben leaned forward and kissed the top of her head. "You're gonna have to start to learn to curb your word vomits anyway or our little peanut will pick them up."

Peanut. She liked that. She placed the palm of her hand on her stomach. "Let's hope Peanut doesn't get any of my traits."

Before Holly could register what was going on, Ben pulled her to face him. He brought his lips down to her in a possessive kiss taking her breath away. "Don't say that," he growled. "I want Peanut to have all the best parts of you."

She loved this man more than anything. A half-smile appeared on Holly's face. "Just not the falling over part, right?"

"We might not be able to avoid it." Ben playfully winked at her. "According to Henry, your mother was just like you."

"True. If peanut gets my stumbling gene, you're gonna have to ask my dad for some tips on how he dealt with two walking catastrophes." Her eyes went round, as the thought hit her. "We need to tell my dad!" Holly started fumbling through her bag looking for her phone.

Ben grabbed her hand bringing it to his lips. "Let's work on one thing at a time. What if Will's gonna inform us everything is done and we can go on with our lives?"

"That would be nice."

"It would, now let's go find out." Ben started walking up the stairs holding Holly's hand.

The moment Ben opened the door, Holly saw one of the clinic's regular clients. "You're Bruce's mom!" Holly exclaimed, pulling out of Ben's grasp. "It's good to see you again." Holly turned back to Ben. "Why didn't you tell me she worked here?"

"Please, Mrs. Richman call me Emma." Emma gave Holly a welcoming smile, which Holly returned.

"And you call me Holly." She smiled brightly at her, however after a few seconds, Holly noticed Emma kept looking behind them.

To make sure she wasn't missing anything Holly did the same. When she didn't see anyone she turned back to Emma who was now looking at Ben.

"Is he with you again?" Emma asked as she looked behind them one more time.

"Is who with us?" Holly once again turned and saw no one.

Emma sent Ben a strained look as she worried her bottom lip.

"Wait, do you mean John?" Ben quirked a single brow at her.

Emma's pale face colored as her gaze dropped. "Uh, yeah." She then started fidgeting with her fingers. "I mean he just left, but when I saw you two come in I figured he might have snuck back in."

Holly's mouth fell open. "John was kicked out of here?"

Emma looked back at her desk as she shyly placed a piece of her honey brown hair behind her ear. "Well, technically no. He wasn't kicked out per se. I mean I'm sure if I did call one of the officers I could have gotten them to fill out the paperwork, but he doesn't need to know I didn't really call them. I only fake called them."

"Is John bothering you?" Ben asked.

"Not really, well kinda." Emma snapped her attention to the computer screen in front of her. "Umm, hey, you know what? No need for us to talk about that. What can I do for both of you? I'm sure you two are here for something other than to talk about me."

Uhh, say what? Holly looked around the room to see if she was missing something.

"Detective Bower called us not long ago and asked us to come see him," Ben remarked, distracting Holly from her search.

So, we are ignoring this? She looked at him.

"Oh, good good, that's a good thing." Emma looked back at Ben. "He must have more information on the case." Then Emma started to ramble. "I still can't believe someone would ever do that to Richman Veterinarian Hospital. I mean seriously you are the best vet in town, why would anyone want to do anything to you? And the poor animals. I'm just glad all of them turned out okay. If someone had done anything to even one of them, there would have been hell to pay." Her face hardened as her nostrils flared. "Can you believe the audacity of some people? A poor defenseless animal has no chance when it comes to stupid assholes. I mean sometimes humans can't defend themselves either but we can try. I guess animals can try too, but sometimes bad things happen to good people and it takes a long time, if ever, to get put back together again." She took a deep breath. "And then, what if, when you're trying to be put back together you end up with a dog that's got all the same issues as you? I guess it's funny how the Universe works that way, right? You get a big dog to help make you feel safe, but it turns out he's just like you so you both end up jumping at all the same things." Emma's eyes widened in shock.

"Emma?" Ben's face softened.

Holly darted her eyes to Ben trying to make any sense of the situation. *What is going on?* Holly looked back at Emma who now looked like she'd seen a ghost. At seeing the shame buried in her eyes, Holly's heart twisted. Call it her newly found motherly instincts or whatnot, but all Holly wanted to do was pull Emma into her arms and tell her everything was going to be okay.

Ben glanced at Holly, his eyes telling her to leave it be and they'll talk about it later.

She looked back at Emma and her heart broke.

"Detective Bower." Emma interrupted Holly's thought. "Yes, you are here to see him. Let me send him a quick message and let him know you're on your way back." She looked at Ben with the mask slipped over her face. "Do you remember where it is?"

Ben nodded. "I believe so, it's down the hall, right?"

"Yep." Emma turned back to her computer. However, Holly noticed Emma sunk deeper into her chair as if to make herself appear smaller.

Holly couldn't take it anymore.

Ben must have known what she needed because he gave her a subtle nod and walked toward the back leaving her at the reception desk. "You okay, Emma?"

"Of course, I'm fine." Emma forced a fake smile on her lips. "Sorry about that, it's been a little bit of a difficult morning."

"Is John bothering you, Emma?" Holly tried her best to sound comforting without pity. "He's a pain in the ass but he's a good guy." Deciding to lighten the mood Holly winked at her. "If he's done anything to upset you, I've got a friend that has connections. You say the word, and I'll make him go away."

Emma's face paled. "What? Oh, God no. John's fine. You don't have to do anything."

"Good." Holly let out a dramatic breath. "To tell you the truth, she scares me, and even though I'm not one hundred percent certain if she really does have connections or not. I really don't want to find out. Then there's the fact, John is

Ben's best friend. He might be a pain in the ass but I don't think Ben wants to break in someone else."

Emma stared at her for a second before a smile spread across her face. "Oh, I get it, you're joking with me." Emma sat back in her chair. "You had me going there for a minute."

"Sure, we'll say it as a joke." Holly smiled. No need to scare the poor girl any further and tell her about Mildred. Yet.

"Besides, I think this was all a little misunderstanding," Emma remarked. "John is a nice guy, and he's not really bothering me per se. He's just uhh, I don't really have the right word for it."

"I think what you are looking for is, 'much'. John's a little much."

Emma threw her pointer finger in the air. "Yes, that's a perfect way to describe it. Let's go with much."

Holly watched Emma relax.

There was something about Emma that Holly really liked. She'd always thought that. Anytime her and Bruce had come into the clinic while Holly was there, she'd always gotten a good feeling about her, even if she was standoffish. "How's Bruce?"

Emma's whole face brightened at the mention of her dog. "He's good. He's Bruce, that's all I can really say about him. How's your Corgi?"

Holly shrugged. "Ehh, he's still plotting his world domination."

"He does have that kind of aura about him, doesn't he?"

"That's an understatement, Emma," Holly laughed. She liked Emma. A lot. Without thinking Holly reached over the side of the desk and grabbed a pen from a cup, she then grabbed the notepad that was lying on top. She scribbled her phone number down before handing it back to Emma. "Here, take this. Maybe we can do lunch or something?"

"Oh, well, I—"

Holly cut her off. "We can spend the time gossiping about how insane John is. I've got lots of stories."

A sad smile appeared on Emma's face. "That's very kind of you, but I don't need to know anything about John. I'm sure in a couple of weeks he'll forget all about me and trying to ask me on a date."

"That's why John was here!" Holly squealed, causing Emma to jump.

"No, no, I said that wrong. I mean to say he was-"

"No takie backie," Holly laughed. "Ben and I were trying to figure out why he was here. Now we *have* to have lunch."

"I don't think that's a good idea."

"Why not?" Holly arched her brow. "You've got the perfect inside scoop right here." She pointed at herself. "What's better than having the wife of his best friend at your disposal?"

Emma held up her hands. "Whoa, umm let's take a step back here."

"Plus," Holly continued ignoring Emma's worried expression. "I'm gonna need girl talk. Real honest to God girl talk. I spent most of my time taking care of my dad, so all I've got is this two-hundred-year-old woman that makes overly inappropriate comments all the time. Sure, I love her but I need someone my age to help me through all of this." She pointed at her belly.

"All of what, do you have a stomachache?" Emma's face scrunched.

"We just found out I'm pregnant." She placed her hand on her stomach before snapping her eyes back to Emma. "Whoa, now you have to have lunch with me. You're the first person I've told."

"I am?" Emma's brows shot up in shock before she recovered. "Congratulations!" She jumped from her seat causing the chair to hit the wall. Emma then ran around the desk pulling Holly into her arms. "A baby is amazing news. I've always wanted one."

Emma jumped back from their embrace. "I'm sorry that was inappropriate of me."

"No, it wasn't." Holly pulled her back into a hug.

That was it, Emma might not have known it yet, but she just sealed her fate in joining their *weird club*. She'd fit in perfectly, though, she had a dog that was *different* add that in with Holly's pets and it was like a friendship made in heaven.

"Congratulations again," Emma said, pulling out of Holly's arms.

"Thank you, it's still kinda unreal. We only just found out before Will called." A daze washed over Holly's face before remembering why they were there. "Oh crap. Ben's probably waiting for me."

"You're right." Emma stepped behind the front desk. "It's right down the hall on the left."

Holly smiled at her before she started walking toward the back. However, Emma stopped her, holding out a piece of paper. "Uhh, here's my number. I'd really like to have lunch one day."

Holly took it with a wide smile. "Consider it done." She placed the paper into her back pocket and with an extra pep in her step, she started walking down the hall. She could see her and Emma forming a friendship. Plus, it'd be fun to hear more about this whole John thing.

However, the moment Holly turned the corner she paled. There right in front of her was Officer Jones.

Oh shit.

BEN SAT in Will's office as they waited for Holly. This had been the second time Emma had rambled on about her past. Even though Ben could only speculate, he had a pretty good idea what was going on. Maybe Emma needed someone to talk to? And taking one look at his wife, he knew Holly was on the same page as him.

Ben's brows drew together as he thought about it. On second thought, maybe leaving her with Emma was a bad thing. Holly did tend to get a little overprotective at times.

Yeah, this was a bad idea.

The moment he was about to go look for her, Holly came charging into the room. Her face pale and her eyes were wide. So wide you'd have thought she'd seen a ghost.

"You okay, babe?" Ben jumped up from his seat. Maybe something was wrong with her or the baby. *Did she fall? Run into a wall?* They were two solid possibilities.

"Yeah, yeah." Holly brushed her shirt down avoiding eye contact with him. "I'm fine. Just ran into someone I was hoping to avoid," she answered as she pushed her hair out of her face giving him a forced smile. "But I'm here now."

Holly walked right past Ben refusing to look at him before taking a seat in front of Will's desk.

Ben cocked his brow. *Well, okay then, at least she didn't hurt herself. That I know of...*

"It's good to see you again, Holly," Will remarked, standing to shake her hand. "Ben was telling me you two have been quite worried about the break-in."

Holly's eyebrows shot to the ceiling in surprise. "Did he also tell you he wants to add on a room to the house and bring home his patients at night?"

"No, he left that out." Will's eyes studied Ben.

"I was only contemplating it. I didn't say it was a done deal." Ben snapped his attention to his wife. *I'll remember this.* When all she did was shrug, Ben's eyes narrowed. *Oh, feisty again today I see.*

"Nope, I don't think that's quite right," Holly stated, with that mischievous look she always got when she wanted to rile him. Why she was doing it, he had no idea. But he was going to use it to his advantage later. "Ben, you were drawing up blueprints."

"Hey." Ben shrugged. "Can you blame me?"

Ben moved to the seat next to her where Holly placed her hand in his. "Never. It's actually quite endearing you care so much about your patients. I'm just giving you a hard time. I'm nervous, so I'm rambling."

Ben leaned over and kissed her cheek. "This just means instead of one room I get to build two now."

One point for Ben.

Holly's lips thinned.

Zero for Holly.

Will sat back in his chair scrutinizing both of them. "Truthfully, I'm not all that surprised you're considering other alternatives. We've seen this before. Especially, when the break-in had no rhyme or reason. You feel like you need a new sense of security. It's very common."

"It doesn't make any sense. If someone broke in to steal something as fucked up as it sounds, I would at least feel more at ease," Ben replied, shrugging at Holly's swat to his arm at his language. It clearly didn't faze him since he continued, "You know, when someone gets their house broken into, it's usually for somebody to steal their stuff. This is a mystery even after weeks, we still can't find anything missing."

Will scratched his chin as his brows pulled together in thought. "I'll be honest here. It was extremely odd there was nothing tampered with or missing. That's why I've asked you both to come in today. We believe we now know the motive and have a suspect in mind." Will placed two still photos captured from the surveillance camera outside of the clinic in front of Holly and Ben. "Over the past few weeks we've been going over the information, and the footage my men retrieved."

Ben took one of the photos in his hand, but he couldn't make out the quality well enough to see anything.

"It was hard to recognize the suspect at first, but there was something familiar about him." Will turned his computer monitor toward Ben and Holly and hit play. That's when Ben saw a child maybe fifteen or sixteen take something and smash it through the clinic's front window.

"Oh God," Holly whispered from beside him.

The feed then showed the kid jump through the smashed window as he disappeared into the clinic. Then, seemingly out of nowhere, another child this one much younger than the first, maybe seven came into view. Instead of following the older one into the clinic he bounced around on his feet and worried his hands together.

As Ben watched the screen, he couldn't help the feeling there was something off about this younger child. He looked scared. But not in the way they might get caught scared, it was more than that.

Then the young child looked directly at the camera.

Ben's gut tightened. He was right, there was so much more in his eyes. There was an underlying of pain, mixed in with terror.

Before Ben could study him more, the footage morphed to the inside of the clinic. The older one that had smashed in the window was tearing the place apart. He was flipping tables over, throwing pamphlets around, you name it, he was doing it. He even spit onto the floor of the waiting room.

Then, the boy jumped back through the window plowing into the younger kid making him fall onto the ground. The first boy jumped up not caring to help the younger one, turned back to the clinic, gave it the finger and then took off running, leaving the younger boy on the ground holding his elbow in pain.

After thirty seconds, the younger one slowly got to his feet before looking all around.

Ben watched as the boy looked back at the camera with an almost pleading face before limping away in the opposite direction as the first kid.

"Holy crap." Holly grabbed onto Ben's hand and squeezed.

"At first, before we looked at the footage, we were under the assumption this might have been a neighborhood prank. Then once my guys went frame by frame, we pulled out this." Will took one of the papers on his desk and turned it over.

Ben and Holly both leaned forward to get a better look at what Will had uncovered.

"That's the kid that poisoned Twitch!" Holly jumped from her chair causing it to flip backward.

"You're right." Ben picked up the photo taking a better look at it. He never saw the kid in person, other than the news coverage. During the trial, they used his findings and toxicology reports to seal their investigation.

The only reason the case got media attention to begin with was because of Ben's mother leaving Richman Industries without any notice. Since the news put together Ben and the poisoned kitten, they did everything they could to get some inside scoop about what was really going on.

Ben had spent his whole life trying to avoid anything with Richman Industries, and leave it to the media outlets to do absolutely anything to connect stories, even where there was zero a connection.

"You're correct," Will agreed. "I've had to deal with him quite a few times in the past."

"You'd mentioned something like that when you dropped Twitch off." Ben sat back in his chair.

"So why did he do it?" Holly asked as she righted her seat.

With a heavy sigh, Will began, "Apparently, he blames you for all his troubles now."

"Me? All I did was confirm what he'd done to Twitch."

"Yes, but with the stuff that went down at Richman Industries, the news was all over 'the kid who poisoned the wealthiest man in the city's cat, just to see what would happen'. He holds you personally responsible for him being sentenced to the Juvenile Detention Center."

"I didn't ask for the news to follow the story. Hell, we weren't even aware of it until we saw it one night scrolling through the channels." Ben scrunched his face.

"Yeah, so now in his twisted brain he wants revenge on Ben and the clinic?" Holly asked.

"That appears to be the motive." Will sat back in his chair.

"Okay, so now what?" Ben still couldn't wrap his head around the fact this kid was the one that broke into the clinic and more importantly he did it to get back at him.

"That's the thing. We were able to locate the other boy in the video, but not the one that poisoned Twitch. We don't know if this one incident was his payback or if he has more planned," Will answered. "Since nothing has happened since the break-in this might have been just a one time occurrence but I wanted you both to be aware of the situation at hand right now."

"Do you think he's dangerous?"

"I don't, but I do think he feels wronged. That combination, with his unfortunate track record, does raise some concerns." Will looked at them. "Do I think he will come after you to cause harm? No. Is there always that possibility? Yes. Unfortunately, that's the way it is with these situations."

"I don't get it. So, you brought us in here to tell us it was the kid who poisoned our cat, but we don't need to worry, but then we also do until you find him?" Holly rushed out. "Why can't you find him? You're a detective, that's your job. You *detect* things such as this child who now has a vendetta against my husband because of the news making him the center of attention." Holly snapped her gaze to Ben. "What if this kid decides he needs more revenge and comes after you or me. I mean he's just a child but he *poisoned* Twitch. He tried to kill him. Kill. Him. Ben! We can't go around worrying about what else he might do." Tears formed in Holly's eyes. "What if he does something to me or the baby?"

"You're pregnant?" Will interrupted Holly's tirade.

Ben wrapped his arms around Holly's shoulders bringing her to him. He then looked at Will. "Yes. We only found out a few hours ago."

"Congratulations."

"Thanks." Ben cradled Holly in his arms. "Holly does make a good point though. Are you still looking for him? What is it that we need to do?"

"We have a hunch of where he's been hiding out."

"Then why haven't you arrested him yet?" Holly glared at him as her nostrils flared.

Ben moved his attention to Holly. *I guess these are the pregnancy mood swings I've always heard about.*

"That's where we have a little problem."

"What problem?"

"Do you remember that other child in the footage?" Will handed Ben the other photo.

"Yeah."

"I have concerns about him. We were able to easily locate him in our system. He was placed in the city's foster care system two years ago when both of his parents were killed in a motor vehicle accident. He apparently had no other living relatives."

No wonder he looked downright terrified.

He suddenly had the urge to vomit. Ben was much older when he lost his father, but that had gutted him. He couldn't imagine how he would feel if at such a young age it would have been to lose his father.

"He lost both of his parents?" Holly placed her hand on Ben's knee squeezing it.

"Yes." Will's expression changed to sorrow. "He's been bounced from foster home to foster home every few months."

"Why are you telling us this?" Ben asked as he heard a sniffle come from Holly.

"Yeah, and why are you concerned about him?" Holly asked, wiping away the tear from her eyes. "Sorry, I normally don't cry this easily."

"Martha cried at everything when she was pregnant, then in a split second she'd be throwing something at my head."

"That sounds like something fun to look forward to," Ben mumbled.

"I got pretty good at dodging," Will chuckled before going serious. "Jimmy, the young boy in foster care might be in jeopardy of the other boy lashing out at him."

"Why?"

"Unfortunately, the suspect needs someone to blame in his life and I fear he might turn his anger onto Jimmy."

"Then get the city to move him somewhere else?"

"It doesn't quite work that way, Mrs. Richman." Will sat straighter in his chair.

"Well, that's dumb." Holly crossed her arms over her chest.

"I agree, but my hands are tied. I reached out to his social worker to see what we can do. But in the meantime, we're monitoring this situation closely. As soon as we can safely move forward, I wanted to at least give you both the heads up."

Ben stood reaching his hand out to Will. "I appreciate you taking the time to inform us."

"Yes, thank you." Holly stood. She worried her bottom lip. "Jimmy, you said his name was, right?"

"Yes."

"He looked like he got hurt. Was he okay?"

"Other than a few scrapes and cuts, he seemed fine."

Holly nodded but Ben could see she still had questions. "Why was he with the other boy to begin with?"

Ben had that same question.

Will sighed. "According to the recent reports from Jimmy's social worker, he's lost. After losing his parents, he's done anything he can to feel like he belongs somewhere. Which isn't uncommon for children in the system. He sadly just met the wrong kid."

Ben let the words register as he felt Holly's whole body slump. "Thank you," she said.

"Try not to worry. We will get it all worked out." Will gave Holly a sweet smile. "And congratulations again on the baby. Having a child was the most rewarding thing I've ever done in my life. I wouldn't change it for the world. Even with all the complications that arose."

"Thank you," Ben replied. "Keep us posted, okay?"

"You'll be the first I contact."

Chapter Thirteen

BEN SAT in his office trying to fill out his reports for the day but was ending up nowhere. No matter how hard he tried he couldn't focus.

He sat back in his chair with a groan as he closed his eyes. Especially after a day like today. As soon as he arrived in the office, he was greeted with a hit and run.

Those were the cases that always twisted him. But at the same time, knowing him and his team were the ones that could help save an animal is what he thrived on.

Plus, when you add in the fact a human could hit an animal and then just drive off with no remorse had him seeing red. Call him out of the ordinary, but he didn't get it. Maybe it was his love of animals or whatever? But it pissed him off. Hell, if it were up to Ben, the people that did commit hit and runs on animals *or* humans they deserved the highest form of punishment.

He opened his eyes. *You know, I could lobby for that.*

Then again... he scratched the scruff on his chin. That would take away from what he loved to do, and being there to help save the animals that were hurt was more important.

He looked back at his screen seeing the files on the Basset Hound that had been hit.

He couldn't deny he loved the rush that came from cases like this, though. That quick action, think on your feet and do everything you could to save a life, was the kind of high he liked.

And lucky for him, he had the best team at his side when things got intense.

Sadly, they'd gotten a lot of practice over the years when it came to animals getting hit by cars. Just in the last six months, they'd had about five cases. People had gotten so careless while driving, completely engrossed in their phones, posting social media updates, texting, taking photos, you name it. And when you focused more on the tiny device in your hand rather than the two-ton vehicle you were in control of, it was a recipe for disaster.

In many ways.

Thankfully, as Ben skimmed through his document, he was able to smile at the outcome. The Bassett Hound had survived, with only a few injuries and was right now, in one of the cages in the back recovering.

Today was a good day, though.

Sometimes these cases didn't have happy endings.

Having to tell the owners their family member didn't make it never got easier.

Thankfully today that wasn't the case. Instead, Ben was able to walk out into the waiting room, where the dog's owners, a man and woman in their mid-thirties along with their young son refused to go home and tell them 'Bob the Dog,' was going to make it.

Days like today were the days he knew he made a difference.

He sat back in his chair with a smile on his face. Plus, today was going to end with a bang.

Tonight, Holly and Ben had decided on telling Henry about the baby.

At first, Ben wanted to wait until after their doctor's appointment, but Holly didn't. Maybe it was the medical professional in him or whatever, but he wanted solid proof that everything was okay and as it should be.

Sure, peeing on a stick was helpful, but it didn't give all the answers he wanted or needed.

As he relaxed in his chair he couldn't help but laugh. Their compromise was one for the books if you asked him.

"You have got to be kidding me, Benjamin Richman." Holly glared at him as he ushered her into the lobby of the clinic.

"Do you think I'd joke about something like this?"

"That's what worries me," she admitted. "First there is this. Then who knows what else your brain is gonna come up with."

Ben did have to admit he was overreacting a tad, but after everything that went down at the police station, he had this unsettled and worried feeling running through him. No matter what he did, he couldn't escape it. Maybe, it was all the adrenaline of the situation and the information revealed, but he hoped in doing this he'd get some sort of relief. "Shirt up, pants down, and up you go."

"Déjà vu," Holly remarked, narrowing her eyes at him.

"I don't recall me telling you to undress when you busted your lip and chipped your tooth."

"You mean when you busted my lip."

"The frisbee did, not me."

"You were the one that threw it."

"And you were the one that didn't get out of the way when I yelled watch out." He cocked his left brow at her. "Grace, we can do this all night if you want."

"If only you said those words to me the first time."

"I was thinking it, trust me," he growled, looking at his wife.

Holly threw her top over her head tossing it to the seat in the room leaving her in her bra. She then pushed down her pants exposing her lower abdomen.

"Good." Holly looked at him with lust in her eyes. "Me too."

"Don't play with fire, Grace."

"Or what, I'll get burned?"

"Don't you know it." Ben helped her onto the exam table before leaving the room to retrieve the portable ultrasound device he had in the clinic. Once he made it back he saw Holly sitting on the edge of the table with her hand on her stomach.

It was a surreal feeling.

And to think this was all where it started.

She looked at him with the right side of her mouth curved upward. "Once you do whatever the hell it is you need to do, you think we can tell my dad? He'll be super excited. I think he's been waiting for this moment since I hit puberty."

Ben huffed out a laugh as a smile spread across his face. "I'm not the least bit surprised." He walked over to her motioning for her to lean backward. When she did he placed the gel on to her stomach.

"Fuck me, that's cold. Could you have warmed it up?"

"Oops."

"Don't oops me, mister. Drop your pants and let me squirt that shit on your balls. I bet you'll never forget to warm it up again."

As he opened his mouth she stopped him. "And don't tell me you only use this on animals. They feel the cold just like we do."

"Yes, dear." He had to bite his lip to keep from smiling.

Within a few seconds of searching with the wand, everything froze around him as his heart melted. There in front of him, was indeed a baby.

His baby growing inside of his wife.

He looked back at Holly tears forming in his eyes.

"What, what's wrong? Oh God, is something not okay? Does it have horns? I mean if it did that's okay, I would still love it just the same. But I'm kinda freaking out here."

Only Holly.

Ben placed the portable device in front of her. "No, Grace, no horns or extra limbs."

The room fell silent as Holly focused on the screen in front of her. This was it, this was their baby. This was the start of their new li—

"I don't know what I'm looking at!" Holly cried, interrupting his thoughts.

"You're looking at our baby."

"No, I'm looking at black and white lines on a screen the size of a tiny computer." She looked at him, tears escaping from her eyes. "I'm such a bad mom already. Waffles walks all over me. Ripley only listens to you. Twitch thinks I'm only his food source, and now I can't see my own child. I'm the worst mom ever!"

Ben let go of the wand bringing Holly into his arms as he did his absolute best not to laugh, but was failing miserably.

"Are you laughing at me?" She cried harder.

"Baby...shh." He kissed the top of her head as he comforted her. "You are not a bad mom. Not to our pets and not to this one right here." He picked up the wand finding their baby again. "Do you see that round thing right there in the middle of the screen?"

"Yeah." She sniffled.

"That's our baby."

"Really?" Holly looked at it closer. "Well, I saw that!"

"See you did see our baby." Ben kissed her forehead.

"I did, didn't I." Holly straightened as she puffed out her chest. "I'm a good mom."

"Yes, baby. The best."

Ben laughed at the memory. Leave it to Holly to make everything a chaotic adventure.

Everything.

Between her and Waffles he never knew which end was up.

As he settled back into his paperwork for the night, that feeling of unease or whatever it was came back. Actually, it never went away. Instead over the last few days it had only gotten stronger.

Sure, seeing their baby had helped some, but it was something else. Something he couldn't put his fingers on.

Ben looked around his office once more. He couldn't stop himself from going back to the night of the break-in. And now knowing who had committed it, didn't sit well with him.

The *whole* thing didn't sit well with him. What if this kid wanted to cause him more problems? Now that Holly was pregnant, things changed.

Then his mind drifted to what Will had said about the other boy that was there.

The feeling he had came back in full force, like a punch to the gut.

Seeing that child stare into the camera with so much pain and sorrow in his eyes, did something to Ben.

Then there was the terror.

The little boy who had already gone through so much in his life.

Then seemingly out of nowhere a picture popped into his head making him choke.

Ben's head pounded as his palms started to sweat.

Holy shit. Holy fucking shit. Ben's breathing increased.

The picture in his mind was plain as day. It was of him and Holly carrying their baby in her arms, Waffles, Ripley and Twitch at their feet, but what really sent Ben sputtering all around was seeing that little boy by their side.

Jimmy.

Ben blinked a few times trying to get his brain to work, but every time he closed his eyes, he saw it again.

"That's it." Ben pushed out of his seat before closing down his computer. "No more coffee this late at night."

What the absolute hell was that? Ben could feel his heart still racing. And even though he felt like he'd just completed a triathlon, for the first time since leaving the police station that feeling he had slowly started to dissipate.

He took a deep breath trying to calm himself.

You need to leave this office. Right now.

Ben did his best to push all of his thoughts away. He glanced down at his watch. Maybe he was delirious, he needed to leave anyway. Besides tonight was going to be a celebration. That's what he needed to focus on, and since he was already late, he was sure Holly was crawling out of her skin holding in their news.

Yes, focus on telling Henry. That's what you're going to do.

Quickly he locked everything up and set the alarm. Once he made it out of the back door, he closed his eyes still trying to calm himself.

That's when he saw the image again in his mind.

Shaking his head, he jogged over to his SUV and quickly got onto the road. Maybe putting some distance between him and the clinic would help.

Pulling around the corner he saw Holly's favorite donut shop. *That's what I'll do.* He decided to stop and pick up a half dozen donuts in hopes that focusing on getting Holly her most craved food, his brain would settle.

Unfortunately for him, he never once stopped thinking about Jimmy.

Chapter Fourteen

LASAGNA.

Holly held the store-bought lasagna in her hand as she walked up the steps to her father's house with Ripley and Waffles trotting along next to her.

Maybe after eating this, my brain will go back to normal?

All day Holly had been out of sorts. At first, she thought she was nervous about telling her father they were expecting, but it seemed to be more than that. She just couldn't put her finger on it.

Then, as she pictured their future conversation while eating dinner, she got the strongest craving for lasagna she'd ever had.

So here she was carrying the thing hoping that once she had some, her brain would stop being a jumbled mess.

A mess that consisted of her having a child, being a mother, the break-in, Emma, her normal worry about her father, and now... now it screamed lasagna.

"Pumpkin!" Henry opened the door. "Whatcha got for me?"

Without registering it, Holly pulled the box to her chest with a growl. "Mine."

"Well, it looks like someone woke up on the wrong side of the bed." Henry gave her a look.

"Sorry, Dad. It's been a crazy few days."

"Come on in and tell me all about it." Waffles and Ripley zoomed past Henry as they made their way into the house. "At least they aren't grumpy."

"I'm not grumpy," she protested. Holly walked past her father only stopping to give him a kiss on the cheek before heading straight to the kitchen. "Just hungry."

Sure, she might not be able to cook, but she could damn well preheat an oven and throw in a frozen lasagna.

Well, there was that one time... No. This she could do. And even if she couldn't, so help the person that stopped her from grabbing a fork and going to town on the lasagna, frozen or not.

Once the food was in the oven, Holly turned. Unfortunately, for her, she didn't see that Waffles and Ripley were playing tug of war across the kitchen. She took one step before tripping over them both. "Oh, for the love of all things!" Holly caught herself on the nearby table.

"I'd like to say that was a record, but you've tripped coming up the stairs before."

"Very funny, Dad."

"I thought so."

She rolled her eyes. "Ben had to work late on paperwork, but he should be here by the time the food is done." Holly moved past her father and into the living room.

The more room between her and the lasagna... the better.

Holly's excitement about telling her dad about the baby came back in full swing. She wished Ben was here. She was nearly crawling out of her skin with anticipation. It took everything inside of her not to blurt out she was now the host for a small human creature.

If it were up to her, she would have told her dad the second she got here, but no... something about a special moment and togetherness, and if she told her dad without Ben there... and blah blah blah, she stopped listening the moment Ben threatened to take away her donuts.

The gall of him.

Jerk.

But she got it. She didn't have to like it, but she got it. She placed her hand on her stomach as she watched her father slowly move into the room before carefully getting into his chair.

"Is he still worried about the clinic being broken into again?" Henry asked, making himself comfortable.

"Yes and no. He had some paperwork to finish, but the other day the detective overseeing the case called us into the station with information."

Henry's brows shot to the ceiling, the best his left side could. "And you're only telling me this now?"

Oh crap.

"I'm sorry, Dad," she pleaded with him. "It's been such a busy few days."

You know finding out I'm having a child. Then there's the who in the break-in. Not to mention that poor little boy that-

"So busy you couldn't pick up the phone and tell your old man?" he interrupted her thoughts.

"Do you remember the reason I got Twitch was 'cause some kid poisoned him?"

"Yeah."

"Well, I guess it turns out, that same kid was the one that broke into the clinic."

"You're kidding?" Henry sat back in his chair staring at her.

"I'm not. He blames Ben for everything that happened. With all the stuff happening at Richman Industries the news wanted more of a story. Remember that? You know anything that could connect to the wealthiest man in the city or some crap like that."

"So, you're saying this young man, who I assume has been released from the detention center now is seeking revenge?"

"It seems that way."

"Well, I'll be damned."

As her father sat back onto his chair, Holly's brain zoned back to Will's office. The same way it had done anytime she thought of the break-in. She didn't know why, but the image of the young boy looking up at the camera was forever ingrained in her brain.

Hell, it even haunted her dreams at night. There was this feeling about it she couldn't seem to put her finger on.

Doing what she'd done over the last few days she pushed it aside as she watched Waffles and Ripley play.

"Holly?"

She turned to her father only to see a concerned look on his face. "Yeah, Dad?"

"Have you listened to one word I've said?"

He was speaking?

"I've been talking to you for twenty minutes."

"You have?"

"Yes, you were nodding your head and agreeing about my thoughts on the situation."

Holly looked around the room. Had she really zoned out that much? "I'm sorry, Dad. What did you say?"

"Ehh, it's too much to go over it again." Henry tossed the tennis ball Waffles had laid at his feet across the room. "How about you tell me what's got you all distracted?"

"I'm not distracted."

Henry gave her the look. "Okay fine, I'm distracted."

"How about you throw your old man a bone here."

Waffles must have thought he meant he had bones because he ran to Henry jumping and barking.

"You sure are driven by food," Henry laughed, scratching Waffles behind the ears.

"He's just like his momma," Holly said looking back into

the kitchen. Thank God she'd gotten a smaller lasagna and it should be done any moment now.

"I'm gonna tell Ben you said tha—"

"Sorry I'm late," Ben announced walking into the living room. "It's been one of those days."

Henry's face brightened seeing Ben. He then as carefully as he could stood from his seat. "No worries, son."

"Dad, sit." Holly glared at her father before jumping from her seat to help him once she realized he wasn't going to listen to her.

She was rewarded with a glare of his own, directed at her. "Who is the parent here, young lady?"

At her father's attitude —which Holly knew was warranted when it came to his pain and disabilities — she couldn't stop her agitation. She only wanted him to take it easy. Before she could register what she was doing, she blurted, "Technically all of us." She placed one of her hands on her stomach and the other on her hip in defiance.

Henry froze with his eyes widened in shock. "Come again?"

"That's one way to tell him," Ben remarked, walking fully into the living room shaking his head. "That's why we wanted to have dinner with you tonight, Henry." Ben darted his eyes to Holly. "Although, we wanted to tell you in a more thought out way."

"Hey, he asked a question and I answered it." Holly moved the hand on her stomach to her other hip narrowing her eyes at Ben.

You wanna fight, Bub. We'll fight.

"Pumpkin?"

Henry's voice brought her attention back to her dad. When she noticed his unsureness, her heart softened. She took a few steps over to him before she wrapped her arms around his waist being mindful of his left side. "You're no longer going to be a grandpa just to the animals."

"You two are having a baby?" he choked out.

Henry squeezed her the best he could before she pulled out of his arms and walked over to Ben's side. She placed her hand on her stomach. "Yes, Dad, we're having a baby."

"We just found out," Ben quietly said into the room as he gave Holly a kiss on her temple before turning his attention back to Henry. "You're finally gonna be a grandpa to human children."

"It's true. Ben took me to the clinic to use his ultrasound thingy and there weren't any horns or anything weird growing," Holly stated.

Henry stared at them not moving.

Then he did what Holly could only assume was a jig, well maybe. He stomped his right foot, and slapped his thigh with his working arm, while a giant lopsided smile appeared on his face. "Hot damn! It's about time!" He started limping their way before bringing them into a hug. "This is wonderful news. No wonder you've been so busy."

Waffles started crying at their feet demanding for him to be the center of attention.

Henry bent at the waist before scratching Waffles behind the ear. "None of that young man. You're gonna be a big brother now. You and your sister are gonna have to protect this little one like your life depended on it. That's your job now."

Waffles cocked his head to the side watching him. "Okay, fine. Like getting a piece of steak depended on it."

Waffles must have registered that since he yipped before his tongue fell out of his mouth.

Holly was pretty sure in Waffles' brain he only heard the word steak and assumed that's what he was getting for dinner. But hey, there was no harm in pretending Waffles realized his new role in the family and showed his excitement.

A mother could only hope, right?

However, the second Waffles looked toward the kitchen

and barked, Holly rolled her eyes. *Nope, he thinks he's getting steak.*

"Congratulations, you two!" Henry pulled them in for another hug.

"Love you, Dad."

"Love you too, Pumpkin." Henry started walking toward the kitchen with a pep in his step. "Now, let's eat."

Waffles and Ripley were right behind him.

A chuckle emanated from Ben as he squeezed her into his side. "That was one way to tell him."

Holly shrugged as she pulled out of his arms following her father to the kitchen. They could talk about it later. Right now, it was lasagna time.

As soon as the smell of it hit her nose her mouth watered. Which still blew her mind, before today she wasn't a big fan of it. Now, though, if someone dared to get in between her and the lasagna, she'd murder them with zero remorse.

Holly ran to the food grabbing a fork out of the nearby drawer. She waited impatiently bouncing on her feet as Ben placed the lasagna on top of the stove. As soon as he let go, Holly pushed him out of the way taking a forkful and throwing it into her mouth.

She must have forgotten food that came out of the oven needed to cool. "Hot. Hot. Hot." She did that whole breathing in and out thing, trying to gasp air like she was dying.

"Get used to it, son," Henry said from behind them. "Helen did that exact same thing when she was pregnant."

Ben burst out into a deep laugh as he reached for three plates. He then lightly pushed Holly out of the way with a bump of his hip causing an angry growl to escape from her. *My food.*

"Down, Grace." Ben handed her the first plate.

Seeing the steaming food sent a new wave of cravings through her. It didn't matter she'd burned all her taste buds. It was as if the room faded away and all she saw was the lasagna. She happily took the delicious food as she walked to the kitchen table and plopped down before digging in.

It was like everything faded around her.

She didn't know if it had been three seconds or an hour, but by the time she looked back up, Henry and Ben were lightly chatting about the baby with empty plates in front of them.

"You've finally decided to join the land of the living again there, Pumpkin?" Henry asked with his lopsided grin fully on display.

What just happened?

"Yeah," Ben remarked. "When I asked if you wanted seconds, and went to grab your plate you tried to bite me." Ben's eyes danced with amusement. "I decided it was safer to dump my portion on yours."

Holly sat back in awe. "I have no idea what you're talking about."

"It must be in the genes," Henry laughed.

"I remember when Helen was about four months pregnant, she had an overwhelming craving for peanut butter cake. I had to have the bakery specially make it for her. When I went to pick it up, Helen demanded to come along for the ride. All I can say is that cake never made it home."

"Wait!" Holly threw her arms at her side with a pout. "Now, I want a peanut butter glazed donut."

"Then I'm glad I picked some up before I got here." Ben retrieved the bag he brought into the house. As he handed them to Holly, her heart filled with happiness.

What a perfect man.

Holly looked down at her belly as she retrieved her first donut. *You, little peanut, are gonna have to chill on this blackout eating thing. No one wants a million-pound momma.*

As Holly munched on her food, she idly listened to Ben and her father's chat.

The moment Ben brought up the break-in, however, the image of Jimmy once again flooded her mind.

There was something about that little boy that called to her. She had no idea what it was, but it was there. And it was getting stronger.

The second Holly placed her hand on her stomach, a new image hit her so hard she thought she might vomit.

Jimmy. It was unmistakable. Jimmy with them. All of them, her, Ben, Henry, all their animals. Everyone.

Holly closed her eyes trying and failing to control her breathing as her heart pounded in her chest.

Oh. My. God.

Before she knew what she was doing, she looked up at Ben, her eyes filled with tears. "I want Jimmy."

Chapter Fifteen

WHAT DID SHE SAY?

Ben froze as soon as the words were out of Holly's mouth. It was like in an instant the world had stopped around him. Taking a chance, he looked at his wife.

Her eyes were large, and her mouth open.

Ben's heart started to race as his breathing picked up.

"Did I say that out loud?" Holly rushed out in a panic. "I guess I must have because I'm hearing myself, like for real for real, and not just that voice thing in my head. Right?" Holly started to blink rapidly as she nibbled on her bottom lip like she was working out a problem in her head. "Am I crazy?"

As much as Ben wanted to speak he couldn't. He was still trying to piece together what was going on, so his mouth just opened and closed.

"I feel like I sound crazy," Holly continued. "But now that I said it out loud I can't stop thinking about it. The Universe works in all those weird ways and stuff. What if all this happened just so we could meet Jimmy?" Her eyes pleaded with him, as her words registered to his ears. "See, I am crazy. I don't even know what I'm talking about." Holly placed her head in her hands defeated. "Who thinks like this? And why can't I get his face out of my mind? I don't know what it is, but I have this overwhelming feeling about him being with us."

Holly moved her gaze to Ben. That's when he saw the tears in her eyes. He felt the same, he just didn't know it was possible for Holly to feel it too.

"Ben, I don't know what's wrong with me."

"Nothing." Ben grabbed onto Holly's hand squeezing it. "Nothing is wrong with you." He looked into her eyes. "I can't explain it either, but I feel the same thing. I haven't stopped thinking about it. I don't know where it came from, it just appeared."

"Can we back up here a moment?" Henry asked, drawing Ben's attention back to him. "Who is Jimmy?"

Where do we even begin?

"Remember I was telling you about the break-in and the information the detective gave us?" Holly answered.

"Yes, the boy who hurt Twitch."

Ben gave Holly's hand another squeeze before he spoke, "There was another boy there."

Henry's face scrunched like he was trying to figure out a problem.

"Will, the detective," Ben continued. "Showed us the surveillance video from that night. Outside of the clinic there was another child, however this one just stood there."

"I— I," Holly blurted. "I can't stop thinking about him."

Ben darted his eyes to Holly. Her panicked face as she worried her bottom lip, had him in awe. He couldn't quite believe that somehow, they were thinking the same thing. If that wasn't the universe at work then what was? He turned back to Henry. "The detective told us the little boy's name was Jimmy. Right now, he currently resides in the foster care system after both of his parents were killed in a car accident."

Henry tilted his head to the side as he stared at them.

"Dad, if you saw the look on his face, you'd understand. There was so much pain, worry, and on top of all that. He was scared."

"And you know all of this, how?"

"Will," Ben stated. "The detective assigned to the case also happens to be a friend of mine. He was probably giving us a little more information than we deserved, but he was telling us why they hadn't moved along with the case."

Ben shot his attention back to Holly. This *did* sound insane when he said it out loud.

Right now, they should be focusing their full attention on the baby they were about to bring into this world. That's what they *should* be doing. That's what any expecting parent would be doing. He knew that.

But then...

"Now hold on here," Henry remarked. "Let me see if I've got this straight. A few days ago, you were introduced to a troubled young boy who helped an older boy break into your veterinarian clinic to *seek revenge*, right?"

"Uhh, yeah."

"Somehow through all this chaos, you both had the same overwhelming feeling about this other youngster. Even with Holly now having a baby. Mind you, a baby you all just found out about."

"Well, when you put it that way..." Holly slumped into her chair.

"I wasn't finished, young lady." Henry gave her a pointed look before turning his attention to Ben. "Now, I can't quite say what is going on in either of your minds. Honestly, I gave up trying to figure Holly out years ago."

"Hey!"

"But, like I've told you in the past, Ben. You don't question yourself or your instincts. You never know what tomorrow will bring. Son, do you remember the conversation we had on the porch the night I met you, about Holly?"

"What conversation? Why am I only hearing about this now?" Holly sat straighter in her seat glaring at her father and Ben.

Ben ignored Holly, as the words Henry had said ran through his mind. "Take that leap and follow your impulse."

"That's right. You said you knew the moment you met Holly she was the one for you. I felt the same way about Helen. People said we were crazy getting married so soon after meeting. People said I was making the biggest mistake in my life. But they were wrong. Even though the years I had with her were cut short, they were the best years of my life." He looked Ben in the eyes. "Sometimes the world works in strange ways. How else could you explain the chance meeting you had here with my little girl?"

"Yeah, still kinda angry about the hit to the face," Holly chimed in causing Henry to chuckle.

"And yet, without that you wouldn't be here right now at my kitchen table talking about a poor child that's lost everything."

Ben sat back trying to digest the words Henry said. He was right, look at how he met Holly. That was a once in a lifetime chance encounter. Ben was just lucky enough that everything aligned correctly and over a year later here he was, with Holly as his wife, who also happened to be carrying his child.

"Maybe my brain is all wonky since finding out about Peanut and I somehow made Ben's brain wonky too." Holly started to worry her hands in defeat.

"No, wait." Ben grabbed Holly's attention. More than ever before Henry's words registered with him. "Let's talk this out. We are having a baby, right?"

"Yes." Holly cocked her brow. "That's been established. Did you see how much food I just ate?"

Ben sent her a warning growl.

"You can't get all growly at me when I state a fact, mister."

Give me strength. Ben took a deep breath ignoring her. "We're both excited about having this baby, right?"

"Again, yes."

When it came to Holly, things were never simple. With a quick roll of his eyes, Ben focused all his attention on his wife. "Holly, without even knowing it, we *both* had this feeling about Jimmy. Something resonated in us when he looked into the camera."

"Well, yeah."

"That has to mean something. You're not crazy. I'm not crazy. And there is one thing I know for sure. Your dad's right, we never know what tomorrow will bring."

"What about Peanut?" Holly placed her hand on her stomach.

"What *about* Peanut?" Ben countered. "We can't deny there is enough love in both of us to give. From day one nothing has ever been normal for us, Grace. Why would we expect this to be any different? What's the harm in figuring out if we would even be suitable for Jimmy?"

The idea of fostering him with the potential of adoption later on, sounded better and better to Ben as the moments ticked on.

I refuse to live my life with regrets. I wouldn't when it came to Holly and I won't now.

Holly slumped back into her chair before placing both of her hands onto her stomach in a dramatic show. "Great, now I've got heartburn again."

"That might have to do with what you stuffed into your mouth," Henry laughed, nodding his head to her plate which still housed the last piece of her donut.

Ben bit back his laugh at Holly's glare.

"No," Holly countered. "I'm blaming it on Peanut. This little thing in here is gonna drive me bonkers."

"Why do you keep calling it peanut?" Henry asked.

"That's 'cause Holly can't stop eating peanut butter glazed donuts, so we figured peanut was fitting."

Henry laughed. "That sounds like logic to me."

"Can we stop making fun of me?" Holly pushed out her bottom lip.

"But what would we do with our time, then?" Henry's eyes sparkled as he riled his daughter.

Henry always knew how to lighten the mood.

"Your dad does have a point." Ben sent Holly a wink causing her to growl.

"Whatever." Holly popped the last piece of donut into her mouth.

"Like I said before, you're gonna need to get used to this, son. If Holly is anything like her mother was when she was pregnant with her, you've got a whirlwind ahead of you."

Ben's face brightened as he beamed at his wife. "I'm looking forward to it."

"I'm not going to forget this." Holly glared at them.

After a small chuckle, the room fell into silence as everyone contemplated their discussion. Ben looked back at Holly who was once again worrying her bottom lip.

If anyone could do this, it would be them. He knew that in his heart. And just because they were even thinking about looking into the next steps with Jimmy, didn't mean they would love peanut any less. On the contrary, they both had so much love to give. He planned on having as many children as she'd let him have. He knew this was meant for them.

"What do we do now?" Holly asked, breaking the silence.

"If you want my opinion," Henry started. "I'm going to suggest taking the next few days to really think about this. I don't know much about this process, but I do believe there is a great deal — from fostering to social workers and everything in between. You two are going through a lot of life changes at this exact moment and you want to make the right choices for your growing family."

"You're right," Ben agreed.

"Raising a child is one of the most rewarding things anyone can do. I didn't know what real love was until Holly was born." He looked at both of them. "I would have given anything to have had more children."

Ben sat back staring at Henry as he continued. "Mine or through adoption."

Chapter Sixteen

IT HAD BEEN a total of two weeks since the evening at Henry's house and during that time Holly's feelings about Jimmy had only grown stronger. After that night, Ben and Holly had a serious conversation. One that lasted two days about what they were thinking. There were many back-and-forths, but in the end, they always ended on one conclusion.

They would regret it if they didn't at least try.

The next day Ben called Will.

At first, Will thought they were absolutely insane, but after explaining everything, he soon gave in and got in touch with Jimmy's social worker on their behalf.

Ben had worked tirelessly with his lawyers on the next steps they needed to take.

Holly was still blown away at the fact, if you had money to throw at it, anything could be done. Anyone that said differently was dead wrong.

Not that Ben ever used his money to his advantage, on the contrary, most of the time he gave his share from Richman Industries to local charities around the city, plus, Holly lost track of the number of dog parks around the city that were donated in Ben's name.

And as it turned out, if you had the funds, you could have all the paperwork sent up the chain of command in no time.

That lead us all to this exact moment.

This was going to be their first time meeting Jimmy.

After much deliberation, they decided on going to the dog park. The exact one where Holly and Ben met.

Seemed kind of fitting, if you asked them.

As Ben and Holly sat on the park bench waiting for Jimmy and his social worker to arrive, Holly pulled out the ultrasound photo she carried in her purse from her recent doctor's visit. As she looked down at their peanut, her heart did this flippy thing.

This was her child.

Her and Ben's child.

She didn't know it was possible to love someone before you meet them, but here she was. She was madly in love with Peanut.

Ben put his arm around her shoulders bringing her closer to him. "I still can't believe we are having a baby," he whispered.

"Me too." She kept looking at the photo. "No matter what happens here today, this is our little peanut."

Ben kissed the top of her forehead. "You're right, no matter what happens this is our little one." They both looked at the photo in silence.

"Do you think we're doing a disservice to the baby?" Holly asked. What if bringing Jimmy into their family wasn't right? What if Peanut resented it? Holly knew she had enough love inside of her to love both, but it was insane to be pregnant and also look into fostering another child.

"We've gone over this, Grace." He pulled her closer into his arms. "Don't second-guess yourself now. Remember, we are going to take this one step at a time."

"You're right," she sighed, leaning into his body.

"First things first. We meet Jimmy and see where it goes from there."

Holly looked at the ultrasound photo once more.

I love you, Peanut. I promise no matter what happens today, that doesn't change. She bit her bottom lip. *I'll do everything I can to make you proud and make the best possible choices I can.*

"They're here," Ben announced, distracting Holly from her thoughts. She looked up to see Jimmy and his social worker making their way toward them.

This was it.

Ben held onto Waffles and Ripley at his side tightly, as they both stood.

Holly stared at the little brown-haired boy, with the pale skin and expressive eyes, as he came closer to them. She couldn't help that her heart started to flutter.

"Good afternoon," Jimmy's social worker remarked. "I'm Carol, it's nice to finally meet you in person."

"Likewise." Holly reached out her hand to shake Carol's. "I'm Holly."

"And I'm Ben." Ben shook her hand as well, before dropping to his knee in front of Jimmy making them eye level. "Hey, there little guy. I'm Ben."

Jimmy stepped back hiding behind Carol.

"Would you like to meet our dogs?" Ben looked to Carol who nodded.

"This is Ripley," he introduced her, before bringing Waffles to his side. "And this loaf of bread is Lord Waffles."

Jimmy laughed and emerged from behind Carol. "That's a weird name."

"I agree." Ben smiled at him. "He thinks he's the ruler of the world, it's why we call him Lord."

"What about Waffles?"

"I love waffles." Holly rubbed her hand on her stomach. "Yum."

"Really?" Jimmy's face brightened. "Me too!"

"I make some amazing waffles," Ben added.

"You do?" Jimmy's eyes widened as he looked at Ben. "My mom used to make really good waffles."

"I bet they were delicious." The left side of Ben's mouth turned up as he looked at the child as Jimmy moved his attention to Holly. "Do you make waffles?"

"You don't want her waffles, kiddo." Ben looked at Holly with a smirk. "Unless you want burnt, tasteless, rock hard waffles that is."

Jimmy giggled causing Holly's heart to flip again.

"Hey, I did just fine before you." Holly turned her attention to Ben as she glared at him.

"Yes, throwing pre-made waffles in the microwave is the only way to eat them."

"Eww." Jimmy scrunched his nose.

"I agree, kid."

Jimmy looked at Ben and scrutinized the way he was on his left knee. To Holly's surprise, Jimmy then mimicked him. "Can I pet them?" Jimmy asked, checking once again to make sure he looked just like Ben did.

My heart.

"Of course, you can." Ben didn't have to encourage the dogs to go to Jimmy at all. The moment Waffles heard the word 'pet' he was rolling onto his back demanding scratches.

"He's funny."

"You ain't seen nothing yet." Ben looked Jimmy in the eyes. "Would you be okay if I remove their leashes? Then you can run around and play in the park with them."

"Really?" Jimmy's face glowed with childlike excitement.

"Absolutely, squirt." Ben unhooked their collars. In an instant Ripley took off into the field. Then Waffles flipped onto his feet and nudged Jimmy at his ankles trying to get him to run after Ripley. Jimmy must have understood. Without even a second thought, all three of them were all running around in circles.

Ben stood beside Holly after placing the leashes in his back pocket.

For a few moments everyone watched the sight before them. Holly's heart once again did that thing.

A huge smile appeared on Holly's face as the picture morphed in front of her. However, this time, it had little Peanut playing along with them too.

"I have to say, this is extremely unconventional," Carol remarked, drawing Ben's attention away from Jimmy and the dogs playing.

"We've never been conventional."

"If it weren't for Detective Bower's insistence on this meeting, I wouldn't have allowed it." Carol turned to Ben. "He swore on his career you two were meant for this."

Ben didn't know what to say. He was glad Will stuck his neck out for them, he'd never be able to repay him.

"We appreciate you taking a chance on us," Holly said, saving him from answering.

"Jimmy was afraid to come here today."

"Why?"

"He thought you wanted to punish him since he was there during the break-in."

"We would never," Holly answered appalled.

"Nonetheless, I reassured him you two only wanted to meet him. He only agreed after I told him we were meeting at a dog park."

Thank God we chose this place.

"I've looked into both of your backgrounds, Mr. and Mrs. Richman. I have to say, I was looking for something that would stop this meeting," she was honest. "I don't believe in someone swooping in. These are very young children, impressionable children. Children that sometimes have had their world as they know it ripped from them in an instant. However, there was nothing concerning on either one of you. On the contrary, you both have done so much for the community. I couldn't help but wonder. Especially, you Doctor Richman."

"Please call me Ben."

"Fine, Ben. You donate to local charities every month, you make sure your family's business is being run properly, and you clearly have the funds to sustain fostering a child." Carol looked out to the field. "You need to understand I take my job very seriously. Sometimes I'm all these kids have."

"I'm glad you do."

"Today's meeting is about compatibility," she continued.

Holly bounced on her feet as she looked at the social worker. "Uhh, we want to be honest with you. I'm three months pregnant."

Carol smiled warmly at her. "I was hoping you'd tell me."

"You already knew?"

"Of course, I did. Like I said, I take my job very seriously. I called Detective Bower as soon as I found out to see if this would be something you could handle along with the trials and tribulations of raising a newborn."

"We were made for this," Holly announced proudly.

"That's what Detective Bower said."

They all fell silent as they watched the little boy and dogs play.

"Jimmy's had a hard life," Carol spoke. "No one at his age should have to experience the kind of loss he has. However, to try and cope with his feelings he started turning down the wrong path. His current foster parents don't know what to do with him. That night at the clinic wasn't the first time he'd snuck out of his room."

"He's lost," Ben answered. Even though Ben was much older than Jimmy when his father passed away, he felt the same way. There would be no telling what Ben would have done if it had happened when he was Jimmy's age.

"He is. It's why we're here. At first, I was apprehensive about this, but the more and more I looked into you both I knew he needed to meet you. Call it a weird hunch."

"It's the Universe. It works in weird ways." Holly smiled brightly as she placed her hand on her stomach.

"That it does." Carol turned her attention to Ben. "Mr. Richman, I know your lawyers have been working to file the paperwork, along with that, I will need to check your home and have a few more supervised meetings with the three of you. Do you have any problems with that?"

"Not at all," Holly chimed in. "Our house is pretty much accident proof. It has to be with me around."

"I beg your pardon?"

"What Holly's trying to say is she's the world's champion of tripping over thin air."

Carol laughed. "Huh, I have a daughter like that."

"Then you understand," Ben chuckled. "Our house is as accident proof as it's ever going to get."

Carol nodded.

"It's true." Holly rolled her eyes. "After we found out we were having a baby he bought an industrial size roll of bubble wrap."

"To do what with?"

"Wrap me in it."

Carol laughed at Holly's glare at him.

Ben was sure Holly was remembering when it arrived. It wasn't his fault Holly wasn't a fan of being wrapped head to toe in bubble wrap. It was a necessity in his eyes. But after a few minutes of wrestling her into the bubble wrap and her then demanding she had to pee he ended up cutting her out of it.

It was definitely a sight to see.

Ben scratched his chin. He was still contemplating a way

for her to be wrapped in it when he wasn't around to keep her safe. And he'd figure out a way. He just needed time.

"You seem like a fun pair."

"We're all right," Ben responded with a laugh.

They all idly talked for the next twenty minutes as they watched Jimmy play with the dogs.

However, the moment Holly started ruffling with her bag, Waffles' ears perked up. As if he were in a high-speed chase, Waffles ran to Holly plopping onto his butt in front of her.

"Okay fine, you've been good, so you get a treat. But, listen here, Bub, just 'cause you hear me go in my bag does not mean treat time."

Jimmy laughed as Waffles caught the treat in his mouth. Ripley then barked signaling her treat was needed as well.

"You too, missy." Holly tossed Ripley a treat which she gladly chomped down on.

"When can I play with Waffles again?" Jimmy asked, scratching Waffles' back as his tongue hung out of the side of his mouth. "I really like him. I've always wanted a dog. Mom and Dad said when I was older, they would think about it." Jimmy looked back at Waffles. "I'm older now."

Ripley sensing Jimmy's discomfort nudged her head under his hand, pushing Waffles out of the way. "I like this one too," Jimmy announced, moving to scratch Ripley instead.

Waffles being offended at his scratches being cut in half jumped onto his feet and barked at Ripley. Ripley then turned her back effectively blocking his way to Jimmy.

A smile appeared on Ben's face. He guessed their dogs were now going to fight for Jimmy's attention. "Looks like they both like you too," Ben remarked.

Out of nowhere he could sense Holly was only a few seconds from crying, whether it was the overwhelming feeling of the situation at hand or maybe it had to do with Peanut, he wasn't one hundred percent sure. Regardless, he wrapped his arm around Holly's shoulders pulling her in close.

Then as if Waffles knew they needed the tension to be broken, or he just needed to be the center of attention again... probably the latter. He took a step back then ran full speed at Jimmy knocking him backward onto the grass and started giving him tons of kisses. Ripley not to be outdone started doing the same.

Jimmy's laugh erupted around them.

Waffles nudged at Ripley trying to get her to move out of his way. Ripley then ran toward the open field with Waffles right on her tail.

Surprisingly enough, Jimmy jumped up and ran right after them as his laughter filled the air.

"Looks like they'll be tired out tonight," Ben joked.

"Good. Plus, Waffles needs the exercise," Holly said with a gleam in her eye.

"I must say," Carol interrupted them. "I've been with Jimmy since he was first placed into the system. I've never seen him smile. Not once. Even his foster parents mentioned his lack of joy when doing routine evaluations. All he's done here is smile."

Holly turned to Ben. Her face glowed as her smile spread from ear to ear. "It's Waffles. He does that to everyone."

Carol returned her smile as she wrote something on her clipboard. She then looked at her watch. "Unfortunately, our time here has to come to an end." Carol looked toward the field. "Jimmy, it's time to go!"

Jimmy stopped running after the dogs as a sad expression replaced the smile he had moments ago. He slowly started walking their way with Waffles and Ripley running around him in circles trying to get him to play. When Jimmy made it back to them, he looked up at Ben and Holly, the exact same pain they saw in the video was back in his eyes.

Holly did exactly what Ben had the urge to do. She pulled Jimmy into her arms squeezing him like her life depended on it. "This isn't goodbye, Jimmy."

"It isn't?"

Holly pulled out of their hug but kept her hands on Jimmy's shoulders. "No, buddy, this is a, 'we'll see you real soon.'"

Jimmy then looked to Ben, his eyes wide and hopeful. "Do you promise?"

At that exact moment, Ben's heart soared. He didn't care what he needed to do, or who he needed to get in contact with, but he was damn sure they would keep their promise to Jimmy. Their encounter today only proved what he knew in his heart all along.

Jimmy was made to be in their family.

"I promise."

A wide smile appeared on Jimmy's face as Carol took over and ushered him away. Once he got a few feet from them, he turned back and waved.

Holly and Ben both stood there in silence as they watched Jimmy and Carol leave. When the two were fully out of sight Holly turned to Ben. "He's ours."

Ben agreed.

He kissed the top of her head. Words wouldn't work right now, not even if he tried.

He'd only felt this overwhelming feeling of rightness once in his life before, and that's when he met Holly.

Chapter Seventeen

THE PAST FEW days had been a whirlwind for Ben and Holly. Since meeting Jimmy, they knew they wanted to continue with whatever they needed to do to have him in their lives. Even with Peanut coming they never felt more right about anything.

Ben and Holly walked up the steps to their house with massive grins on their faces. They'd just left his lawyer's office where he signed the last few forms to get the ball rolling to start the process.

"I cannot believe we're doing this," Holly said as they walked through the front door.

"I can," he answered.

Ben followed Holly into the living room where Twitch ran from the back room to greet them. "Hey, little guy."

Twitch started purring as Ben scratched behind his ears. Feeling Twitch's head movement in the palm of his hand reminded him of what they were still dealing with.

Even though they were beyond thrilled with what had started to transpire with Jimmy, they needed to remember there was still a possible threat.

Ben hadn't heard anything from Will since the meeting in his office about the case.

Thankfully, there hadn't been any more occurrences. Ben was hoping everything had died down, and the kid had given up or at least felt he got his revenge. And after talking with Carol the other night there hadn't been any threats to Jimmy.

Which was a good thing.

A wave of protectiveness rushed through Ben. He would stop at nothing to protect Jimmy. He wasn't surprised at that feeling, though. Since meeting Jimmy, in Ben's mind he was already theirs. Right now, they were just crossing all the T's and dotting all the I's as far as he was concerned.

As Ben placed Twitch onto the floor his phone rang. Quickly he retrieved it. "Speak of the devil. Hey, Will, how's it going?"

"Great," he answered. *"I have good news."*

Ben looked at Holly who was staring at him with her brow arched. "Oh, yeah. What's that?"

"Four days ago, we located and detained the suspect. He's since confessed. It didn't take long for him to admit everything. You don't need to worry anymore, this time he's being sent to a rehab facility in hopes to get him the help he needs."

There was a wave of relief that washed through Ben. "You're kidding me?"

Holly started mouthing 'what' as she flung her arms around trying to get Ben's attention.

"I'm not. I would have called sooner but with everything happening, I couldn't."

"Seriously, this is great news, Will. And, don't worry about it. We've been kind of busy ourselves."

Holly picked up a pen from the coffee table and threw it at him. When he ducked out of the way she narrowed her eyes.

"I can imagine with the baby coming and then the meeting with Jimmy and his social worker. How did that go?"

A bright smile appeared on Ben's face. "Really well. Actually, better than well. It was amazing."

"*I'm glad to hear that.*" Ben could hear papers being shuffled around. "*Okay, well, I got to go. Paperwork won't fill out itself, you know? You'll have to call me in a few days so we can catch up on how the meeting went. Martha is dying to have you and Holly over.*"

"Of course." Ben smiled at Holly who was now threatening to throw a book at him. "Hey, Will, wait a second."

"*Yeah.*"

There was something inside of Ben that told him he needed to do more. He avoided the book Holly tossed perfectly at his head, as he spoke, "Can you send the info of the rehab facility to my lawyers?"

"*Why?*"

"What in the hell is going on?" Holly growled at Ben, which had him holding up his hand to her.

"I'd like to offer some financial assistance." Ben watched as Holly's eyes widened. "What?" she whispered.

The other line of the phone was silent. "Will, you there?"

"*Yeah, yeah, I'm here,*" he answered. "*I'm a little in shock. I guess I just forgot how truly good of a guy you are.*"

"Everyone deserves a second chance in life. And if going to rehab can help this kid then I want to be a part of it. It's what my dad would have done." That's exactly what his dad would have done, Ben knew that. He always told him, desperate people make desperate choices. You never know what a second chance could give them.

"*I'll take care of it.*"

"Thanks, Will. I'll call you in a few days." Ben ended the call smiling at his wife. Things were looking up.

"What's going on?"

"They arrested the kid that broke into the clinic."

"They did?" Holly's eyes widened.

"Yeah, he's being sent to a rehabilitation center. I want to offer some financial assistance to him."

"Whoa."

Ben shrugged at Holly's shocked expression.

"I really did marry the best guy ever." Holly smiled brightly. "After what he did to Twitch I would have told them to throw away the key."

"You did." Ben pulled her into his arms kissing the top of her head. He ignored her other statement. He got it, Holly loved Twitch with everything inside of her. But he knew he needed to do this.

"I really did, though." Holly wrapped her arms around him. "After having lunch with Emma yesterday, I've realized more and more what a jackpot I got in you hitting me in the face."

"I didn't hit you in the face."

"The Frisbee *you* threw hit me in the face." She shrugged. "Same difference."

"I told you to watch out."

"And you know now how fast I am at reacting."

"How was I supposed to know that?"

Holly reached up on her toes and kissed his nose. "You're right, you wouldn't." Holly pulled out of his grasp as she walked out of the room shaking her ass.

"Oh, you are gonna get it." Ben ran after her scooping her into his arms as he rushed them both to the bedroom.

"Hey, hey, hey now, precious cargo here." She placed her hand on her stomach.

"You've always been." He leaned over capturing his lips with hers. "I love you, Holly."

As Ben started kissing along Holly's jawline, she leaned her head back giving him better access.

She couldn't be happier than she was at this exact moment. Things with Jimmy were working out, the clinic situation had been taken care of, and her little peanut was happy and healthy protected inside of her.

She opened her eyes to see Ben looking down at her with the corner of his mouth turned up.

"What's that look for, Mrs. Richman?"

"I'm happy."

"Me too." Ben pulled his shirt over his head tossing it behind him. "And we're about to be much happier."

Holly burst out into giggles.

"Oh, do you think that's funny?" Ben arched his brow at her. "I'll show you funny." He started tickling her causing Holly to thrash around on the bed.

"Stop, stop," she pleaded.

"Not on your life." During the onslaught of tickles, Ben somehow managed to remove Holly's shirt *and* bra.

"How'd you do that so fast?" she asked after realizing she was indeed topless.

"Eye on the prize, babe." He winked.

Holly rolled her eyes. "At least you didn't rip them this time."

"The night's still young." Ben grabbed onto the waistband of her pants pulling them down her legs exposing her sex.

The way Ben looked at her when she was naked always sent Holly into overdrive. Every person deserved someone that looked at them like this. Ben's eyes held so much passion and desire, it drove her fucking wild.

Ben reached around her grabbing one of their pillows. "Over," he demanded. He flipped Holly onto her stomach taking the pillow he'd grabbed propping it under her hips.

Holly looked at him from over her shoulder. "What about you? You've still got your clothes on."

"Not for much longer." Ben unbuckled his pants before jumping from the bed and tossing them to the side.

"That's better." Holly wiggled her ass in the air. She loved this. So, fucking much.

Nothing could stop them when they got to this point.

However, just as Ben hopped back onto the bed Holly heard a bark.

Ben sighed loudly. "I forgot to shut the door."

This caused Holly to burst into laughter. "You might as well get used to the interruptions," she said. "Soon, there's gonna be more than just us in the house."

"No," Ben growled. "I'm just gonna have to remind myself to close the door." Ben grabbed his pair of boxers tossing them all around in the air getting the dogs' attention before throwing them out into the hall.

Holly had to bite her lip when she saw Twitch run after the dogs a few seconds later, once he realized they were now going after the piece of clothing instead of them.

Once the door was shut Ben crawled back onto the bed. "Now, where were we?"

Holly pushed her ass into the air.

"Oh, that's right." Ben got behind her before bending to kiss her exposed back.

"While we have the house to ourselves, we might as well make the best of it."

"Huh?" she said, looking over her shoulder at him confused.

He gave her a wicked grin before entering her in one fast movement causing her to moan loudly.

"Loud, Grace. I want to hear you scream my name."

She sent him back a grin that matched his. She pushed her ass making him enter her deeper. "My pleasure."

Chapter Eighteen

TWO MONTHS LATER

TODAY WAS THE DAY.

And, not just any day, this was *the day*. Everything Ben and Holly had worked toward was finally coming together. And Holly couldn't be more excited.

Today, Jimmy came to live with them.

Of course, his social worker, Carol, would still be making frequent checks, but as of this morning, Jimmy was officially their foster child. It had been two months getting all the foster certifications, and everything else, but all the wait was worth it.

Holy freaking crap on all the crackers!

Holly placed her hand on her growing stomach. Who knew so much could change in the blink of an eye?

Holly looked around their home and sighed. She wanted to pat herself on the back. They'd spent a great deal of time making sure everything was in order. They redecorated one of the guest rooms for Jimmy, which Ben had a blast doing.

Seriously, when they went into their local toy store, Ben's face lit up like he was a kid in a freaking candy shop.

It was cute. A little disturbing, especially when he pouted after Holly told him to put back a couple of items that were more for *him* than Jimmy. But still cute.

They had everything in place.

But maybe...

Holly jumped from her spot on the couch and ran to the spare bedroom that would now be Jimmy's room. Waffles and Ripley ran alongside her with Twitch trailing them.

Poor little Twitch he was always one step behind.

Once Holly got to the room, she did another once-over.

Bed: check.

Clothes: check.

Toys: double check.

As her eyes scanned the room, she noticed Waffles had moved to the corner. He was on his back already snoozing with his tongue flopped out. Typical Waffles.

That was fast. Wait a second!

"A dog bed!" Holly yelled. "We need a dog bed in here! Why didn't I think of it sooner?" She smacked her forehead with her hand. Once the room was finished, Waffles and Ripley had taken turns with who owned it. Ripley normally won since she easily pushed Waffles out into the hall. It was quite funny to watch them fight over the room.

Holly ran back into the living room where they had an abundance of dog beds that none of the dogs used — since they'd rather sleep on the couch — and brought one of the beds back into Jimmy's room.

After she placed it in the corner, she sighed in relief. "Crisis averted."

Then her eyes shot open. "The nursery!"

Holly ran into her and Ben's room grabbing the expensive dog bed they bought a few months ago that was only ever used by Twitch, and brought it to the nursery.

Holly placed the bed in the opposite corner of the crib. Proud of herself, she stood in the middle of the room and looked around. Holly then smacked her forehead with her hand. "Why in the hell did I just do that?"

The nursery was nowhere close to being done. And now,

in a disheveled room there was a dog bed just chilling on the floor. "I need to get a grip."

As if Waffles wanted to agree with her, he barked.

"Thanks, Bub."

Waffles barked again.

Deciding to ignore him, she went back into the living room to wait patiently. *Why in the hell am I all over the place?*

Oh yeah, that's right, her and Ben were about to bring a child into their home.

Holy crap.

This was real.

Holy. Freaking. Crap.

Holly took a deep breath as she sat on the couch. This was it. There was no going back now. She placed her hands on her stomach. "Are you ready for this, Peanut?"

Holly was instantly rewarded with a small bump to her hand. Damn, every time that happened, she still freaked out a little. In a good way, well, after the first few times that is.

I'm gonna take that kick as a yes.

She still couldn't believe there was a baby growing inside of her.

The first time Peanut kicked, Holly thought some part of her body had broken. It wasn't strong, but it was enough to get her attention. And got her attention did it ever.

Holly and Ben were lying in bed when it happened.

At first, Holly could swear her bladder exploded and she'd peed herself. Then after feeling it again, she couldn't stop herself from envisioning an alien creature jumping out of her stomach before doing a tap dance on the bed.

Ben thought it was funny.

Holly not so much.

However, once her irrational fears were gone of being ripped in half, or eaten from the inside out, she loved feeling Peanut, even if it was small little bumps.

So did Mildred.

The old bat would follow Holly around work begging the little one to kick. It was hard to explain to the board of directors the day they came in why a crazy old lady wouldn't let go of Holly's stomach.

Although, as much as Mildred annoyed Holly, she'd really helped her and Ben out. Between Ben's lawyers and Mildred's contacts, they were really able to get everything in order for Jimmy to live with them.

Holy crap, Jimmy was coming today!

There had to be more that she could do. "Maybe he'd want cookies. That's what parents do, right? They make cookies. I can do that." Holly jumped from her seat and ran into the kitchen.

"This can't be so hard." Holly pulled out her phone before searching *easy fast cookie recipes.* Once she found one that only had a few steps she moved around the room searching for the ingredients.

With Waffles, Ripley, and Twitch weaving in between her legs, she did her best to stay focused. Calling the fire department was not on her list of things to do today.

Holly looked down at her fur-babies. "I need you all to simmer down now. Mommy's going to try and bake some cookies."

Ripley and Waffles both cocked their heads.

"Don't give me that look."

Then that dang judgmental dog of hers sent her such a side-eye it almost knocked her on the floor. "Waffles don't you dare judge me. I can do this."

He huffed.

"I can!"

Holly could swear Waffles rose his tiny brows at her. *Well, I'll just show him.* Ignoring her holier than thou dog, Holly turned to the oven and set it to preheat.

Carefully she read the instructions and started placing the ingredients in the bowl. "Softened butter? What the hell is that?" Holly looked at the recipe. "What do you do, sit on it?"

She heard Waffles bark from the other room.

"Stop judging me!"

Waffles barked again.

"No treats for you!" She then heard a dramatic whine. *Serves him right.*

After going back to her recipe, she looked at all the steps involved. This one seems too hard. *Seriously, softened butter was stupid.* Deciding to backtrack she quickly found another recipe with only a few steps.

Perfect.

Looking at her bowl of already mixed ingredients she shrugged. *I'm sure it's close enough.*

This recipe also called for melted butter rather than softened. *That I could do.* She threw the butter in the microwave.

How long do you put butter in for?

Hitting three minutes she waited.

When it hit the thirty-five-second mark the popping started growing louder. Waffles and Ripley followed by Twitch ran into the kitchen to investigate.

As the noise got louder, they started barking and jumping all around the room begging her to do something.

"I know, I know, I don't know what to do!"

It's like bombs were going off in her microwave.

Holly quickly grabbed the lid of a pot and shielded herself as she released the latch opening the microwave door.

"Ahhh!" she screamed as loud as she could as she jumped back hiding her head behind the lid. After a few seconds, the popping subsided so Holly carefully looked past her shield to see the bowl sitting in the microwave as if nothing had happened.

Holly wiped her brow. *See, that wasn't so bad. I could do this all the time,* she thought. *Cookie master, here I come.*

Waffles and Ripley, on the other hand, we're running

around like it was World War III. Deciding they were just being overly dramatic, Holly grabbed two potholders and carefully removed the butter and placed it on the counter.

"Damn that's hot." *Of course, it's hot dumdum it nearly exploded in the microwave.*

Once the butter was in the bowl with the other ingredients, Holly gently started mixing. When she read the recipe further it called for baking soda. She looked through their cabinets but came up empty. "That's the same thing as baking powder, right?" *Ehh, it'll be fine.*

Holly finished mixing in the ingredients deciding to forgo the salt too. *Who puts salt in cookies? That sounds horrible.*

She looked down at Waffles who was once again giving her a severe side-eye. "Stop judging me, you judging McJuderson. No one needs your type of negativity in their life."

Holly carefully spooned out droplets and placed them on the cookie sheet.

After they were all on the baking sheet, she took a good look at them and grimaced. They did look a little weird. One of them was even spreading outwardly like a blob trying to eat the other blobs. She shrugged. "I'm sure they'll be fine."

She placed them into the oven and set two timers. One on the stove and one on her phone.

See no fire department this time. I've got this. Call me Chef Holly from now on.

She'd rather not add this to Ben's ever-growing list of incidents with her cooking.

Holly's phone chimed signaling she got a text message. Mindlessly she placed her hand on her stomach as she read it.

Grace, I'm pulling into your Dad's. We're going to stop at the store and then we'll be home. Don't do anything stupid.

Holly glared at the phone. *Why would I do anything stupid?* She sent back.

Grace...

Oh, he was going to get it. *Do not Grace me!*

We'll be there soon. Have you heard anything from the social worker?

Before she could respond the doorbell rang. "Oh God, it's happening. It's really happening!"

Holly ran to the front room stumbling over the dogs as they ran next to her. The moment she got to the door she swung it open with her arms held wide to greet them.

"Waffles!" Jimmy ran right past her and straight for the dogs.

"Nice to know up front where I rank on the importance list," she laughed, causing Carol to laugh along with her.

"Don't feel so bad. All Jimmy's talked about since everything finalized was Waffles, Ripley, and Twitch. I guess the times we've come for supervised visits really resonated with him."

Outranked by the pets. "At least we have that going for us." Holly placed her hand on her belly.

"How are you doing?" Carol asked.

"Pretty good. Heartburn makes me pray for death, but other than that I'm good. Still want the donuts, though."

Carol laughed.

"Mrs. Holly, can I go play outside with the dogs?" Jimmy ran to her with his big expressive eyes pleading.

"Call me, Holly, squirt, we've talked about this." Holly softened as she looked at the little brown-haired boy with the green eyes that had captured her heart. "How about we wait for Ben to come home and we can all go outside and play? He'll be here soon."

"Oh, man." Jimmy turned back to the dogs. "Sorry guys."

"Why don't you grab your stuff from the car, and we can put it in your room?"

Jimmy's eyes brightened. "That's right! I get my own room now!"

It was funny how attention spans changed so quickly with kids. Like a flash, he was running to the car grabbing his belongings. It was heartwarming to watch as Waffles and Ripley run along with him as he grabbed his things.

On Jimmy's last visit to the house, they'd shown him where his room was going to be. You'd think the kid had won the lottery or something. Her smile spread from ear to ear as Holly turned to Carol. "Thank you."

"I didn't do anything, Mrs. Richman."

"But you did." Holly's heart pounded in her chest as Carol looked at her with a warm smile.

Life is perfect.

Ben pulled into the driveway with Henry in the passenger seat. His heart raced and his palms were sweaty.

This is it.

This was their moment.

Ben saw Carol's car parked in front of their house. He knew the second he walked through the front door his life would be forever changed.

"Son, I can't tell if you're excited or gassy," Henry joked.

Ben laughed as he looked at Henry with a smile on his face. "This is it," Ben answered.

"It is. And, how do you feel about that?"

"It's about damn time." Ben jumped out of the car, with pure adrenaline. He felt more excited than ever. He ran around the passenger side and carefully helped Henry out. Sure, he was eager to get through the front door but he knew so was Henry.

Henry hadn't been able to meet Jimmy yet. All of the supervised visits had been conducted at their house.

Ben imagined Henry was just as excited to potentially meet his first grandson as he was to finally have Jimmy home with them.

Once they made it to the front door, Ben pushed it open as his heart slammed against his chest. There in front of him was Jimmy on the floor wrestling with Waffles and Ripley with Twitch jumping on him whenever he got a chance. Then he saw Holly on the couch holding her extended belly. When she caught his eye, she winked before her smile overtook her whole face.

This was home.

"Ben!" Jimmy jumped from his spot on the floor and ran toward Ben wrapping his arms around his waist giving him a tight hug. "Oomph." Fuck, his heart nearly exploded in his chest.

"Hey, little guy!" Ben squeezed him back before rustling his hair. *Yep, this is what could bring a man to his knees.*

"You're here! We can go outside and play with the dogs now!" Jimmy ran toward the back door but Ben stopped him. "Hold up a second, squirt," he laughed. "I want you to meet someone."

Jimmy moved his focus to Henry. "Hello," he said shyly.

"Hi," Henry answered. Ben could hear the emotions in Henry's voice. "I'm Grandpa Henry."

Jimmy cocked his head to the side. "I've never had a grandpa. Mine died before I was born."

"Well, then." Henry puffed out his chest. "I'm glad I came around."

Jimmy face morphed into a toothy grin.

"I'm Holly's dad."

Jimmy turned to Holly who gave him an encouraging nod. "That's right. He's my dad."

"That's cool!" Jimmy then surprised them all by running

to Henry wrapping his arms around his waist. "It's nice to meet you, Grandpa Henry. Can we go play with the dogs now?"

Ben bit back his laugh through his emotions. Leave it to kids to have a one-track mind.

Ben glanced over at his wife. The smile she had on her face melted him.

Yep. This was home.

"Yeah," Henry answered. "I can't play too well with them. See I've got some issues, but I can watch you play along with the pups."

Jimmy gave Henry the once-over assessing him. "That's okay. I can play with them for both of us." Jimmy grabbed onto Henry's good hand as if he knew, and carefully pulled Henry toward the backdoor.

Holly and Ben stared at them in shock.

Holy shit. Yeah, they wanted Jimmy to feel comfortable with them and Henry, they didn't expect this.

"I have to tell you both, since that first meeting at the dog park, Jimmy has changed considerably. He smiles, he talks nonstop about both of you and the pets." Carol's face softened looking at them. "I know this isn't a done deal yet, but I have to say, I became a social worker for cases like this. The ones where in the end everything falls perfectly into place."

Joy filled the room as Holly moved into Ben's arms. He couldn't agree more.

Then he heard it. It was faint, but he definitely could hear something. "Babe, what's that beeping noise?"

"What beeping noise?"

Ben sniffed the air. "Is something burning?"

"Shit! My cookies!" Holly raced from his arms into the kitchen. Ben saw her glare at the oven timer that was still set to ten minutes. He had to bite his lip to stop from laughing. Clearly, Holly never hit start on her cookies. And seeing that her phone was on the counter, the ringer turned almost all the way down, she didn't stand a chance.

"Oh no!" Holly pulled the cookies out of the oven.

Instantly, his stomach churned. He didn't know cookies could look like that. Wait, she did say they were cookies, right?

"They're ruined!" Holly turned to him, tears in her eyes.

Damn pregnancy hormones. Then again cooking was never her strong suit. Pregnant or not. "No, Grace, they're fine. They are just a little well done."

"Well done? These are beyond well done. They aren't even cookie shape. They're like this big ole blobby thingy." She looked back at him the tears now threatening to escape. "I followed the recipe. I promise... Well, kinda."

"I'm sure they taste fine, Holly." Ben swallowed hard as he looked at the cookie sheet. "Now, don't take this the wrong way, but I have to ask, with your track record what made you want to bake cookies in the first place?"

"That's what moms do! They bake cookies. I wanted to bake Jimmy cookies!" she cried.

"What's all the calliwacking going on in here?" Henry asked, coming in from the back yard. "We could hear the squawking from all the way out there."

"Holly tried to bake cookies," Ben answered.

"Why would you do something crazy like that?" Henry asked appalled, looking at his daughter. "Wait are those the cookies?" Henry's face morphed into disgust.

"Yes!" Holly growled. *Damn the mood swings are strong.* He placed his hand behind his neck. Did he just get whiplash from that?

"They don't look like any cookies I've ever seen." Henry scrunched his nose.

"Hush your face, old man."

"What did you say, young lady?"

There was that whiplash again. Tears appeared in Holly's eyes as her body deflated. "Sorry, Dad."

"That's more like it."

Jimmy stood beside Henry as he tried to make sense of the situation. He had Twitch in his arms, as they both looked at the pile of cookies.

Henry looked to Ben then back at the cookies. He knew what his father-in-law was suggesting in order to ward off Holly's tears.

One bite, that's all you have to do, Ben told himself. He looked back at Henry, who took a small step back. *What happened to team effort?*

When Ben tried to take a piece of the pile'o'cookie from the sheet, it didn't budge. *Did she use cooking spray?*

Knowing Holly, she probably hadn't.

Fuck.

Ben grabbed a kitchen knife and chiseled out a small piece. He brought it to his mouth before taking a deep breath. *Please don't kill me.* He shoved it in his mouth.

Holy fuck! Nope. Nope. Nope!

He couldn't do it. He spit it out so fast he was sure he'd won a world record.

"Ben!" Holly cried.

"I tried, I really did, babe." Ben used the back of his hand to wipe the god-awful taste out of his mouth. *That's it. Holly is now officially banned from the kitchen.*

Jimmy's laugh brought Ben from his thoughts of death by poisoned cookie. He saw Henry bent whispering something into Jimmy's ear.

Ben was positive it had something to do with *never* eating Holly's cooking.

Good advice if you asked him.

Ben pulled Holly into his arms, but she jumped back glaring at him. He bit back his smile.

Carol laughed. "This is going in the books as one of my best placements."

The corner of Ben's mouth turned up. He agreed.

Waffles trotted into the kitchen cocking his head at Ben, judging.

Don't look at me that way, Bub. I was trying to be nice to your mother.

Ben held up a piece of the whatever the hell this thing was – he refused to call it a cookie, in Waffles' direction. The appall on Waffles' face had Ben laughing.

I'm right there with you, Waffles.

Chapter Nineteen

"WHAT ARE we doing at the police station?" Jimmy asked Ben as they made their way up the steps.

Ben couldn't hide his smirk even if he tried. Although, he was moderately sad he couldn't get John on board for this bonding experience. John had to *arrange some things.* Whatever that meant. John had been strangely absent the past few weeks, but nonetheless, he was excited to finally put his plan into motion. "Let's call it a harmless prank."

Jimmy cocked his head to the side trying to understand Ben's logic. "What does going to the police station have to do with a prank?"

"You've been with us a few days now, so you'll understand when I say Holly overreacts with a dramatic flair."

"Like Lord Waffles."

Ben's grin spread from ear to ear. "Yes, exactly like Lord Waffles."

"So, are we going to prank Holly at the police station?"

Ben looked at Jimmy's curious expression. There was a part of Ben that said not to corrupt little Jimmy, but there was a bigger part of him that screamed pranking Holly was of utmost importance.

A good responsible adult would say forget it and take Jimmy out for some ice cream, but then... ehh, a little adventure never hurt anyone. "Holly got a little, how should I say it... high-strung when she met a particular officer a while back which ended with her in handcuffs and a promise to never go near the officer again."

"Are we going to get her in trouble?"

The concern on Jimmy's face had Ben questioning his decision. "Not really. I'm going to see if that same officer wouldn't mind playing a tiny prank on her. Nothing that will get her in trouble." He hoped, Holly did tend to go half-cocked at times...okay, all the time.

Jimmy stopped walking up the steps as he looked at Ben biting his bottom lip. "What about the baby she's carrying in her belly? Would you be pranking the baby too?"

Whoa, Ben had to take a step back. The concern Jimmy had for their baby had his heart tighten. How could this little boy have gone through so much hurt and still be so caring? Jimmy deserved the world, and even if it was the last thing he did, Ben promised to give it to him. "I'll make sure the officer understands it's just a little prank and not to cause any harm to her or the baby."

"Good!" Jimmy face morphed into joy. "I want to meet Peanut."

Holy shit we hit the jackpot. Ben ruffled his hair. "Me too, squirt."

Ben held the door open letting Jimmy through. "Hi Emma, it's good to see you again." Ben smiled at her as they made their way to the reception desk.

"Doctor Richman!" Emma jumped from her seat startled to see him.

"Ben," he corrected. "How many times do I have to tell you, it's Ben?" Emma's gaze dropped to the ground.

"Hey, it's okay, you're a friend now, Emma. Holly hasn't

stopped talking about your lunch dates." He smiled warmly at her.

Panic flashed through Emma's eyes. "Holly talks about me?"

Shit. "Only good stuff," he was quick to add. Holly hadn't gone into much detail about Emma's past, but he knew it wasn't good.

He also knew that John hadn't left Emma alone. He wasn't quite sure if that was a good *or* bad thing? Hell, he and John were shooting some hoops a few weeks ago and Emma was all John could talk about. *"Emma's beautiful... Emma has a strange dog... Emma has these dark brown eyes you can get lost in... Emma this and Emma that."*

He wondered if that's how he sounded when Holly came into his life.

It was nauseating.

But there was something John wasn't letting on to. Every time the word dating came up, or anything about relationships, John would get this stormed look in his eyes.

Ben wanted to know more, but he knew when John was ready to talk, he'd come to him.

"This must be Jimmy," Emma said, changing the subject.

Ben pulled the little boy in front of him. "You'd be correct. Jimmy meet Emma, she's a family friend."

"Hi," Jimmy said as he looked a little unsure at Emma.

"Do you want to know something really cool about her?"

Jimmy snapped his attention back to Ben as he nodded his head excitedly. "Yeah!"

"She has a dog the size of you."

"No way!"

"Yes, way, she has a Great Dane. And he's this tall." Ben held his hand up to show how tall Bruce was.

"That's so cool." Jimmy turned to Emma. "Do you ride him?"

Emma burst into laughter at Jimmy's question. "No, I'm afraid I'd hurt him."

"Why?"

"Uhh..." Emma looked down at her body and then back to Jimmy. She then looked at Ben at a complete loss.

"Sometimes Great Danes can have really bad back problems, squirt," Ben replied.

"Ohh." Jimmy gazed at Ben in wonder. "You know all about animals."

"That's what happens when you become a veterinarian."

Jimmy's next words had Ben's throat tighten. "I want to be a veterinarian just like you when I'm older."

An arrow right through the heart. *Holy shit.*

"That way I can know all about the animals too and take Lord Waffles and Ripley with me to work."

"Ben is the best vet around," Emma chimed in.

"Then I'll be the best vet around too."

Emma smiled warmly at Jimmy. "I bet you will."

"Can I meet your dog?"

Emma looked at Ben. "I'm sure one day we can arrange it."

"You bet, squirt." Ben pulled Jimmy into his arms. There was still so much to learn about him, but there was one thing he knew for certain, Jimmy had a heart of gold. Even after losing his parents and being shuffled around in the foster system.

Jimmy's newfound joy probably had a lot to do with Lord Waffles. Ben smiled.

"What can I do for you two boys?" Emma asked with a bright smile on her face. "Are you here to see Detective Bower?"

"Not exactly, we are actually here to see Officer Jones if he's around."

Emma gave him a sideways look. "Should I be worried?"

"Not at all." Ben smirked.

"I feel like I should be worried."

"We're going to play a tiny prank on Holly, but not on the baby."

Emma narrowed her eyes at Ben. "Is that so?"

Ben held his hands in surrender. "Nothing too crazy, you know just some good old-fashioned bonding between me and Jimmy."

"Mmhhhmm," Emma said before looking at her computer. Ben was going to have some explaining to do, he could see it now. "Officer Jones actually got in not long ago, he's probably at his desk," Emma remarked still giving him the eye.

Clearly, once you were Emma's friend you were under her protection, and if that look she was giving him said anything, it was he better keep this short and simple or her and Holly were going to murder him.

Good to know.

Ben hurried Jimmy along the way. "Thanks, Emma."

Maybe this was a bad idea.

As they rounded the corner Will appeared. "Ben! It's good to see you. What are you doing here?"

"You too, Will."

"Hey Jimmy, do you remember me?" Will asked, crouching down to get on Jimmy's level.

"Yeah, you were the one that came to ask me all the questions."

"That's right," Will softened. "How are you doing, Jimmy?"

"Did you know Mr. Ben and Mrs. Holly have a dog that thinks he's human? He's so much fun, and then there is Ripley, she's really smart and sleeps with me at my feet every night. Twitch does too because Twitch doesn't leave Ripley's side. Waffles comes in every once in a while, but if I don't pet his belly enough, he gets mad and leaves in a huff. It's a lot of fun. And, I have my own room." He beamed at Will.

"It sounds like you're having a good time."

"The best. I really like living with Mr. Ben and Mrs. Holly."

"We like you living with us too, squirt. But you can just call us Ben and Holly. You know that." Ben crouched pulling him into his arms. Giving him a squeeze. He knew it was hard for him. He hadn't opened up about his parents yet, and Ben suspected it would be some time before he did, but while Jimmy was learning to trust them, he would do whatever he could to make him feel comfortable.

"I know."

Just then Officer Jones walked by. "Exactly the man we came here to see." Ben stood, grabbing Officer Jones' attention.

The officer turned to face them, his brow arched. He looked at Jimmy and then back to Ben. "What can I do for you?"

Ben pulled Jimmy to stand in front of him. "Jimmy and I were wondering if you wouldn't mind helping us play a prank on Holly."

"Just a tiny one and only on Holly, not the baby," Jimmy reiterated.

That got Officer Jones' attention. "You're wife?"

"Yes."

"What kind of prank?" Ben saw Officer Jones' smile start to appear.

"How about we sit down for a few minutes and discuss it?"

A wicked smile formed on the officer's face. "My pleasure." He turned leading Ben and Jimmy to his desk leaving Will shaking his head as he walked into his office.

Holly was late. Super late.

She was supposed to meet Ben and Jimmy at her dad's over thirty minutes ago.

And Holly was blaming her lateness one hundred and twenty percent on Mildred. If the woman hadn't stopped going on and on about babies and then running after her to feel her stomach, she would have gotten her work done in time.

But no, Mildred blocked her path every single step of the way today. If Holly didn't know any better, she would have thought she did it on purpose.

And now... Now, Holly was late and the worst part was Ben had sent her a text letting her know they'd picked up donuts.

So, in the grand scheme of things Mildred stood between her and her delicious donuts. And that wasn't okay.

You don't keep a pregnant woman away from her tasty treats. That was just wrong.

Holly looked in the back seat. She would have already been at her father's if she didn't have to run home and grab his holiness, and Ripley.

God forbid they had dinner at her dad's and the dogs weren't there.

Sure, Jimmy would have been upset but it was the meltdown from her dad she didn't want.

No one denied him his visitation to his grand dogs and lived to see another day.

As Holly saw her father's house come into view, she looked down at her belly. "Peanut, I swear please on all things peanut buttery and delicious, please I beg you, take most of your genes from Ben's side."

That's when she heard the siren and saw the flashing lights out of the corner of her eye.

"You have got to be kidding me!" Could today get any worse? Not in her book. She looked over at her father's house that housed the three men she loved... but more importantly her donuts.

Holly pulled over onto the side of the road directly in front of Henry's house. The moment Waffles realized they were stopped and at grandpa's he started to whine. She narrowed her eyes at him. "Could you not?"

Waffles glared at her, before huffing his response.

Universe, if you have any mercy inside of you, I beg you to take me now. I'm done with today, Holly pleaded as she looked to the roof of her car.

"License and registration, ma'am."

Holly jumped as soon as the all too familiar voice hit her. "Holy fuck!" She turned slowly to see her archnemesis Officer Jones cocking his brow in her direction over his dark sunglasses. "Excuse me, ma'am?"

"Uh oh," Holly started to stammer.

"License and registration," he said again.

This cannot be happening. Play it cool, Hol, maybe he doesn't remember who I am.

"Threaten anyone lately?" he asked, causing a cold sweat to break out on the back of Holly's neck.

He remembers.

"I'm not sure what you're referring to," she did her best to sound calm as she reached for the glove box.

"I have to ask you to keep your hands where I can see them."

Holly snapped her attention to Officer Jones. "Well how in the hell do you expect me to get you my registration if you won't let me go into the glove box?" Waffles barked from the back. "Exactly!" She caught Waffles' eye in the rearview mirror and nodded at him in solidarity.

"Ma'am, have you been drinking?"

Oh, hell fucking no!

"Have I been drinking?" Holly pointed to her belly. "I'm

almost six and a half months pregnant. Do *you think* I've been drinking?"

Cop or not she was going to strangle him. How dare he insinuate she'd be so careless to harm her child? Her blood boiled.

"I'm going to have to ask you to step out of the car, ma'am."

"If I step out of this car it's only gonna be to punch you in your throat."

Officer Jones pushed his sunglasses to the top of his head as he stared her down. "Is that another threat? Are you threatening an officer?"

Holly unbuckled her seatbelt as fast as she could before throwing open the door forcing Officer Jones to take a step back. "It's a promise."

When Holly saw a smirk appear on Officer Jones' face, she cocked her arm back.

"Grace!"

Unfortunately, as she geared up for the hit, the sound of footsteps running in her direction accompanied by Ben's voice distracted her. On her unsteady footing, she turned toward the house too fast.

Before she knew it, she was tumbling over.

Holly couldn't even blame it on her new center of gravity. Nope.

Look out ground, here I come.

Officer Jones was fast, though. Within seconds he had her in his arms, catching her before anything happened.

"Fuck!" Ben ran to her. "You weren't supposed to get hurt."

"What are you talking about?" Her adrenaline rushed through her.

"And you wonder why I bring up the damn bubble wrap every other day?"

"Benjamin Richman, you are not wrapping me up in that shit. I'd suffocate you with it first."

Ben shook his head before taking her from Jones' grasp. "Thank you for catching her."

"Anytime." He nodded. "I didn't think she'd actually try to hit me though?" He arched his brow at him before giving Holly the once-over.

"Me either."

Just then, Holly could hear little footsteps running their way. "You tried to hit a police officer?" Jimmy asked, once he was next to them.

Oh crap.

"Ummm." Holly was at a loss for words. She was blaming her reaction on the pregnancy hormones. Normally she would never have threatened anyone, no less actually move to take a swing.

"No," Officer Jones stepped in. "She was playing around."

Did he really just save her? *Thank you, Officer Jones! Maybe he isn't so bad. Huh? You know what I don't even know his first name. Maybe I should ask him—*

"Oh, like how we pranked her?"

Holly watched as Ben's eyes widened at Jimmy's declaration. *Prank?* Holly's eye's narrowed on the Officer, she took it back, she didn't care what his name was. Better yet, she was going to murder her husband. She turned back to Jimmy. "What did you say?"

"Way to let the cat out of the bag, squirt."

"This was your idea?" Holly sent Ben an evil glare.

"It was a bonding experience." Ben shrugged before winking at her.

Oh, I'm going to kill him. Didn't he understand he almost gave her a heart attack? "And you thought it was a good idea to recruit this big lug to help you?" Holly jerked her thumb over her shoulder to point at Officer Jones.

"Excuse me?"

"Lay off it, Mr. Scary Police Officer, dude." Holly snapped her attention to Jones. "You'll get your wish and be able to arrest me seeing as your about to be a witness to murder."

At that, Ben burst into uncontrollable laughter as he pulled Holly into his arms giving her a smacking kiss on the lips. "Love you, Grace. You make each day better than the last."

"Hate you."

Ben kissed her lips again. "No, you love me."

"Sometimes."

"All the time."

"You're not supposed to hit people or murder them," Jimmy announced, bringing their attention to him.

"That's right, squirt." Holly moved out of Ben's arms to talk to Jimmy. "I don't know what came over me. You never raise your hands to anyone, especially not a police officer. They are here to help us. We respect them." Holly wanted to pat herself on the back. This was her first 'mom' moment. She looked past the fact she almost tried to punch out a police officer and decided she was doing a good job.

"I think you should go in timeout."

Holly's mouth almost hit the ground.

"I agree," Officer Jones said which caused Holly to dart a glare in his direction.

"No more peanut butter glazed donuts for you," Jimmy announced proud of his punishment decision.

"What?" she cried. "You can't do that."

"I think Jimmy just did." Ben tried but failed to hold back his laugh.

"Why is it everyone is against me?" she cried as the image of her donuts melted away from her.

"You're fun entertainment." Ben pulled her into his arms as he continued to laugh at the situation.

"Jimmy," Henry called from the porch, who'd been

watching the whole show. "Come help me eat the rest of the donuts." Henry smirked.

"Okay!" Jimmy ran back to Henry with his sights set on her treats.

"I'm gonna murder you," Holly growled narrowing her eyes at Ben.

"Not while Officer Jones is here." Ben looked at Jones. "Thanks."

"Anytime, now go enjoy your family." Jones whistled as he walked back to his police car.

"I really am going to kill you," Holly mumbled.

"No, you won't," Ben replied. "I have two donuts hidden for you."

As Holly looked into Ben's eyes and saw his playfulness and love, her heart melted. Sure, she was still going to kill him for siccing Officer Jones on her in the first place, but anyone willing to hide her donuts deserved all the love. "I love you, Ben."

"I know you do." Ben whistled for Waffles and Ripley, who had been pacing in the back of the car during the whole ordeal to follow them into the house. "Let's get your momma those well-deserved donuts. Just don't tell Jimmy."

"Why not?"

"I need to stay his favorite parent."

"Sorry to inform you of this, but that title goes to Waffles." Holly laughed along with Ben. "Now bring my car into the driveway." She shoved her keys at him. "If you're a good boy I'll reward you later."

Ben placed his hand on her stomach as he brought his lips to hers. "I'm counting on it."

Chapter Twenty

HOLLY DRAGGED herself into the library. It had definitely been an eventful few weeks, to say the least. Holly wanted to believe she was immune and everything would be perfect, and most of the time it was. She wouldn't deny that. She loved her new life, but... she'd be a liar liar pants on fire if she didn't say it wasn't hard.

Plus, her sleep had been damn near non-existent since Jimmy moved in a few weeks ago. Add that to the fact Peanut now considered her insides a punching bag and it was a recipe for no sleep and a grumpy mood.

Holly pulled herself to the desk before plopping down. Her hand went to her stomach as it did most of the time.

This morning had been particularly rough. And she was still feeling the aftermath.

Ben had woken early to make Jimmy waffles.

Yes, waffles...one of her favorite foods. Before becoming a host to the creature overtaking her body, the sweet smell of the deliciously fluffy goodness would've had her mouth watering like it was Niagara Falls.

Not anymore.

On the contrary, the moment the delicious waffle smell hit

her nose, it was like a violent punch to her stomach. Holly ended up running to the bathroom so fast it made her own head spin.

And that was exactly where she stayed.

The. Whole. Morning.

Jimmy and Ben ate their breakfast in peace while Holly tried having a heart-to-heart with Peanut. It did no good, though. Try as she might to get Peanut to understand waffles were her friends not the enemy, anytime she opened the bathroom door and got a whiff she was back hunched over the toilet.

See, rough morning.

Waffles, my fluffy delicious waffles, why do you have to be so traitorous? Holly sighed as she started rubbing her belly.

"Oh, oh!" Mildred appeared out of nowhere and ran right toward Holly with her eyes focused on her stomach. "Is Peanut kicking?" Once she was in front of Holly, she pushed Holly's hands off her stomach before replacing them with her own.

"No." Holly rolled her eyes. "You do realize this is creepy, right?"

Mildred started moving her hands around Holly's belly searching. "It's only creepy if you make it creepy."

Holly cocked her brow as she pushed Mildred's hands away. "*You're* making it creepy."

"You're grumpy again."

"And you're annoying."

"You do know, each time you say that all I hear is, 'Mildred, you're the most amazing person in the world never change, right?" Mildred's eyes brightened as she looked at Holly. "Never stop telling me."

Ignoring her, Holly groaned as she sat further into her chair closing her eyes. *Universe, I know you think this is funny, but with the morning I've had strangling this old bat and receiving nothing but bad karma is looking more and more worth it.*

"Are you gonna tell me?"

Holly opened her eyes to see Mildred now perched on the side of the desk giving her a once-over. "Tell you what?"

"The amount of times we have this conversation is unsettling." Mildred shook her head. "It's a back and forth we don't need to have. I ask you what's wrong, you get all huffy and pretend it's nothing, then I threaten you and you give in. It's very tiring."

"You're telling me."

Mildred ignored Holly as she pulled out her pen and pad. "Spill."

"Just so you have shit to tell your *knitting* buddies? I don't think so."

Mildred tapped her pen on her chin. "I do need more gossip. It is after all my week to bring the juicy stuff." She wiggled her brows at Holly. "But I've already got all I need from an incident I was lucky enough to witness with that hottie fireman and his lady friend in a compromising position over in the romance section, on Tuesday." She scratched her chin. "I think he said his name was Hank, but I could be wrong. Anyway, see you're safe. This is you and me. What's got your twat in a knot?"

The things that came out of Mildred's mouth didn't surprise Holly anymore. That was a new one, though. Holly shook her head with a deep sigh. "I don't know. I think I might be overwhelmed."

"As you should be."

"Gee, thanks."

"Missy, what have I told you about that tone with me? *And* might I add that whole respect your elder's thing?"

Holly sent her a toothy grin. "Not to do it."

"Exactly!" Mildred winked her way before adding, "Respecting me is only a hassle."

Holly burst into a laughter. "Don't I know it."

Mildred put her pen and pad back into her apron before pointing at Holly's belly. "You're huge, your—"

"Wow," Holly interrupted.

"Don't sass me. You know I'm talking about the fact you look like you're about to pop."

Holly glared at her. "It's not my fault this little one in here only wants donuts. It's been seven and a half months of this." Holly crossed her arms over her chest in a huff. "It's just donuts though, Peanut won't let me eat waffles."

"Your dog?"

"No," Holly cried. "The food. The delicious, fluffy goodness."

"Waffles are overrated."

Holly held her hand over her heart. "Blasphemy."

"And might I remind you, on top of being seven and a half months pregnant you just started parenting a seven-year-old boy. Of course, you're overwhelmed."

"I don't know how people do it," Holly replied. "Jimmy is great, he really is. He's sweet, he helps us all the time, but then he gets these moments where he shuts down and I don't know what to do."

"That's understandable."

"But I want to fix it." Holly thought back to the night before when Jimmy came in from the backyard upset. She ran around the house trying everything she could to cheer him up, but nothing worked.

Not even Lord Waffles.

"You can't," Mildred stated as a matter-of-fact. "Jimmy has a lot going on in his mind. The best thing you and Benny boy can do is give him a safe place where he can feel his emotions."

Holly let out a deep breath. "I know you're right."

"But, you don't. Jimmy lost both his parents in a horrific

way. It doesn't matter how much time has passed from that, he's still going to have to come to terms with it."

"It hurts my heart when he shuts down."

"That's called love, dear." Mildred softened as she looked at Holly. "Have you talked to Ben about this?"

"No." Holly closed her eyes. "I don't want him to know I'm freaking out."

"That's silly. Talk to him."

"I can't. I don't want him to think I can't handle this."

Mildred shook her head as she tsked at her. "I never pegged you for an idiot."

"Hey, I'm not an idiot. I take offense to that."

"Don't you think Ben is having the same feelings you are?"

"Ben's not pregnant."

Mildred rolled her eyes. "Okay, fine, he probably isn't having the exact same feelings as you, but they're probably pretty close. Remember the key to a good marriage is communication and right now you both have to work on that. You've taken a child into your home all the while preparing to bring another one in."

Damn, score one for Mildred.

Holly sat back as Mildred's words sunk in. "When did you get so wise?"

"Today I have my Psychologist Mildred hat on." She shrugged.

Holly laughed with a shake of her head. "Have you been reading the self-help books and case studies again?"

Mildred winked. "You can't leave me to my own devices."

"I know."

"Next week I'm thinking of picking up woodworking books."

"Why?"

"Your baby shower is in a few weeks. I need to have something for you."

"Why don't you knit me something in your *knitting group?*"

"That would be boring. Nah, I think I'm gonna whittle you something." Mildred hopped off the desk and started heading toward the craft section of the library.

"Don't hurt yourself!"

Mildred turned back giving her the eye. "For that missy, I'm going to whittle you a cock."

Holly's eyes widened. "What?"

"A Cockatoo. What did you think I meant?" She winked.

"With you? I never know."

Mildred laughed as she turned back in search of whittling books.

Holly closed her eyes as she felt the start of a headache. Mildred was making her a tiny dick out of wood.

She knew it.

"What's wrong?" Ben froze the moment he stepped into the bedroom that evening and looked at Holly. She sat on the edge of their bed with her hand over her stomach with tears in her eyes. "Babe?" He rushed to her side dropping to his knees in front of her.

Holly worried her bottom lip refusing to look at him.

Fuck. He scolded himself. The moment Holly excused herself for the night he *knew* he should have gone after her. The past few weeks had been a lot. Ben had never taken the time to sit down and talk with Holly. And, now he was kicking himself.

The moment she arrived home from work he saw she was at her breaking point. "Holly please talk to me."

When she finally looked at him, it was like a sucker punch to the gut. She had a fear in her eyes, that broke him. "Baby..."

"I'm sorry," she whispered.

He cupped her face in his hands. "Why are you sorry? Talk to me."

Holly averted her eyes away from him, but he held onto her chin forcing her to look his way. "Grace?"

A tear fell down Holly's cheek. "I feel like I'm doing everything wrong, Ben. Jimmy's fine and then he's not. Then I get more heartburn and I think I've done something to hurt the baby. I haven't written a word in months. I should be able to handle everything that comes my way. As Dad likes to say, we're Flanagan's. Flanagan's can handle anything. I mean technically I'm a Richman now, but it's all the same. You're really strong, so I should be really strong, too. And I'm scared to death that telling you this you'll be disappointed in me. You'll think I'm not cut out for all of this even though we thought we were. I love that we have Jimmy here. I love that we have this little one." She placed her hand on her stomach. "But right now, I feel like I'm drowning and no matter how hard I try I can't keep my head above water."

Ben pulled her into his arms holding her tightly. His heart fucking broke at her words. How in the hell hadn't he seen this before? He was pissed at himself. With focusing on Jimmy getting settled, he neglected to see Holly struggling.

He felt like shit. But more importantly, he now knew he wasn't alone. He pulled back looking Holly in the eyes, trying to convey everything he felt. "Holly, baby, I would never be disappointed in you."

"I'm failing."

"You're not." He kissed her lips. "Can I tell you a secret?" He kissed her again. "I feel the same way. One second I'm ecstatic we have Jimmy and this little one coming. The next, I feel like I'm running on empty and I'm terrified, Holly. I can't shake the feeling I'm going to be a horrible dad."

"What?" Holly asked in shock. "You'd never be a horrible dad. It's not in your blood, Ben."

"You know how my mother was. I worry every day I'll end up like her. I can't help having those thoughts."

"Ben," Holly cried, tears spilling from her eyes. "Don't ever think that. You are nothing like her."

"But I can't help it, much like you can't help how you feel. Every decision I make I second-guess if I'm making the right choice. For Jimmy, for you, for Peanut. Every time I see Jimmy shut down I wonder if I could've done better. Or, if there is something else I could do." He kissed her forehead. "We took on a lot. I've never been happier in my life. There is absolutely no disputing that, but going from just us and the pets, to having a seven-year-old and you being pregnant is an adjustment."

"I wanted everything to be perfect."

"It is," Ben answered, looking deep into her eyes. "Because we have each other."

The room fell into silence for a few minutes until Holly spoke. "I didn't know you were feeling the same way."

Ben looked at Holly and saw the love pouring out of her eyes. "I'm sorry I didn't bring it up. We were bound to get a little overwhelmed." He gave her a half-smile. "Next time we ever get this way we talk about it, okay?"

"I love you, Ben."

"I love you, too."

"Do you think Jimmy is happy here?" Holly worried her bottom lip.

"I'd like to think so." Ben placed his hands on her belly. "And I'd like to think once this little one gets here they'll be happy too."

"I worry a lot."

"I know you do."

"I want to be a good mom. I want to be there for Jimmy. And, I want to be there for you." Holly looked at him, tears forming in her eyes again.

"You're always here for me. Jimmy loves you and I love

you. So does Peanut." Ben grabbed the hem of her shirt lifting it over her head. Ben kept his focus on her eyes as he unclasped her bra tossing it behind him.

"What are you doing?"

Ignoring her, Ben grabbed the waistband of her pants pulling them so she was forced to lift her hips. Once she was fully undressed, he stood doing the same.

"Ben?" She cocked her head to the side.

"Shh." Ben scooped her into his arms, bringing her to her side of the bed. He then gently tucked her into the sheets before getting into bed himself. Once he was positioned, he pulled her close to him wrapping his arms around her.

They needed this.

They needed the time in each other's arms.

As silly as that might seem, he knew. He kissed her forehead. "Promise me, whenever you feel like you're drowning, you'll talk to me. I'll be your life vest." He kissed her wedding ring. "You're mine. And *I* promise whenever I feel like I can't handle this, I'll do the same."

"I promise."

"This is you and me against the world, babe. Not us separately against the world."

Holly nodded.

Ben pulled her closer to him feeling her skin against his as he held her in his arms. "I love you, Grace."

"I love you too, Ben."

After a few minutes, Holly fell soundly asleep in his arms. And for the first time in weeks Ben felt that no matter what happened or what would happen, as long as the both of them were on the same page, they could get through anything.

Chapter Twenty-One

AFTER BEN and Holly's heart-to-heart a few weeks ago, everything seemed to fall right into place. They both had made it a point to have a conversation every night before bed. Jimmy had settled in considerably well, and their love for him only grew more and more as the days went on. And thankfully, Jimmy loved Henry. Once every other week Henry and Jimmy had a sleepover that also included the dogs.

It gave Holly and Ben a guaranteed date night. Which in turn only made them stronger.

And Ben was downright grateful for that.

But right now, Ben wanted to be as far away from their house as humanly possible.

Who in the hell knew all the work that went into planning a baby shower? For freaking real.

As Holly, Emma, and Mildred added the finishing touches to the party, Ben had stolen Jimmy and got the hell out of there.

No offense to all the ladies going above and beyond to make it perfect for him and Holly but damn. First, you had Mildred trying to sneak in dick lollipops onto the dessert table. Emma was putting up streamers and then saying they looked like shit and ripping them down only to put them back up again *in the same spot.*

Waffles was causing havoc trying to steal the presents.

Seriously, he took one of the gifts that was on the floor and carried it to Jimmy's room and ripped it open. Ripley and Twitch were running around like it was endless play time.

Then there was Holly.

Ben lost count of the number of times she'd run into the wall, countertop, tripped over the rug, banged her knee against the coffee table, you name it, she did it. At this point, he didn't think his heart could take a second more. If he watched Holly nearly impale herself on a spatula one more time, he'd lose it.

"Are we going to get Grandpa Henry?" Jimmy asked, from the passenger seat of the SUV.

"Yep, and John."

Jimmy looked at him with a wide smile that brightened his eyes. "I like Mr. John. He does weird things."

That's an understatement.

"And he always seems to be in a fight with Lord Waffles," Jimmy giggled.

"That's 'cause John's a child most of the time."

"Like me?"

"No," Ben answered. "I'd say you're more mature than he is."

"It's fun to watch when he gets into fights with Waffles."

Ben winked at him. "You only think that 'cause Waffles normally wins."

"True."

"Are you excited for the party today, squirt?"

"I guess so." Jimmy looked out the window.

Ben watched him from the corner of his eye trying to think of something to say. "You like Mildred, I'm sure she will make you laugh."

"She does." He kept his gaze out of the window.

"You okay, squirt?"

"I'm okay."

Jimmy wasn't okay, but Ben didn't know what else to say. Maybe he could lighten the mood. "How about after we get Grandpa Henry and John we stop by the donut shop?"

Apparently, that's exactly what Ben needed to say.

Jimmy's face shot toward his with a massive smile on his face. "Can I get the cream-filled one?"

"Sure."

"I used to never get donuts at my other houses. But with you and Holly I get them all the time."

Ben grimaced. *Great, let's start him young on unhealthy habits.* "Don't tell Carol that."

"I'll think about it." A mischievous grin appeared on Jimmy's face.

"Why you little..." Ben tried not to laugh as he placed his hand over his heart in shock. "Are you playing me? Was your end game a donut all this time?"

"Maybe."

Ben shook his head impressed as a slow smile spread across his face. If he wasn't positive before, he was now. Jimmy fit in perfectly with them. "Where did you learn to get this good?"

"Waffles."

"Figures."

It only took around thirty minutes to get Henry and John, along with gathering the donuts as a surprise for Holly.

However, Ben should have known nothing was ever as simple as it would have been for anyone else.

Nope. Not even in the slightest.

Ben lost track of the number of times he had to threaten John to stop going into the donut box. It was like he had *two* seven-year-olds in the car.

John actually had the gall to look into the rearview mirror at Ben after he'd sworn he hadn't touched any, with copious amounts of powdered sugar on his face.

Like he said. Two seven-year-olds.

Throw in Henry trying to bribe Jimmy in sending up some donuts his way too. Foolish Ben for thinking having John sit in the back seat with Jimmy would have been fine.

From now on the donuts go in the trunk of the car.

Thankfully, they were pulling onto his street. He just prayed there was at least one donut left for Holly.

As he pulled into the driveway, Ben was reminded why he left in the first place. Mildred had run out onto the porch with a diaper on her head that had a drawing of a crown on it.

What in the absolute fuck was he about to walk into?

Universe, save me now!

Holly looked around the living room and did her best not to freak the fuck out. She should have known better than to leave the planning to Mildred. Thank God, Holly had gotten Emma to agree to help.

Sure, Emma was a little frightened after meeting Mildred the first time — wasn't everyone? But nonetheless, she agreed to help rein Mildred in.

Foolishly Holly thought having Emma as co-planner would have given her a simple quiet gathering as they celebrated baby Peanut.

But no.

Not one freaking bit.

And Holly knew better. Take for instance, right now John and Ben were in a battle to the death. Sure, she knew they were competitive, like hardcore competitive, but this, this was over the top. She had never heard so much trash-talk in her life. Holly had to apologize to Martha, Will's wife, and then send Jimmy out back to shield his young ears.

Want to know the kicker? All this hustle and bustle was for the title of *King of the Baby Shower* which included their own diaper hat with a crown drawn on it.

That's right. All the winner got was a freaking diaper crown.

Sure, it was decked out pretty nicely, Holly had to admit and all but it was still a diaper.

Holly watched as Ben and John duked it out in the new game. The one where if you got another person at the party to say the word, *baby,* you got a stupid little clothespin. The one at the end with the most clothespins won the crown.

By the looks of it, Ben seemed to be in the lead, but not by much. And if the look John was sending Ben was any indication of how things were going, Holly was ninety percent sure there was about to be a full-on brawl between the two.

Lord help her when they start the 'guess the baby food' game. She knew there was a food fight in her future.

Looking past the insaneness that was her husband and John, Mildred's husband kept sneaking to the dessert table and munching down the goodies. Right now, the table was nearly empty. The only reason she knew was because she usually met him at the table sneaking in her own treats.

At this point, the party was about to run out of desserts, her husband and John were minutes from a fistfight, Waffles thought everything in the room was his and that was that, and finally there was a crazy old bat wearing a diaper on her head.

Welcome to my life.

"Come on, Emma, don't be a poor sport, play along. What's Holly got in her belly?" John begged Emma as he cornered her in the room, his evil glare at Ben forgotten.

Holly watched as Emma looked right at her, shook her head with a smile on her face and looked back at John. "About half a donut."

Which was true since Holly still had the other half in her hand. Holly laughed. *One point, Emma. Zero points, John.*

With a growl and then a pout John shot his attention to Holly. She then lifted her donut in the air before taking another bite.

"That's not fair."

"All is fair in a competition." Emma smirked.

"You're not even playing."

"I'm playing. My goal is to make it so you don't get my clothespin but Ben does." Emma fingered the tiny clothespin on the collar of her shirt.

"Really?" John's eyes narrowed as another growl escaped him. "I'm filing this away to bring up later. And make no mistake, Emma, I *will* be bringing it back up." He leaned in closer. Holly couldn't make out what he whispered in Emma's ear but with her face going completely red, she had an idea.

Just to make sure though, Holly pulled out her phone sending herself a text message to remind her to interrogate Emma.

Inquiring minds want to know after all.

Emma stepped back before clearing her throat. "You talk an awful lot of game for a dentist."

"Do you want to know what's the best part of me being a dentist?" He stared at her lips. "I'm damn well educated in all things dealing with the human mouth... especially the *tongue*."

Emma swallowed.

Time to step in... Holly started making her way over to them.

"I'm up to five!" Ben hollered from the other side of the room as he placed another clothespin onto his sleeve.

"Shit!" John jumped back from Emma scanning the room. When he saw Mildred's husband still had his clothespin, he set his sights on him. Before leaving, however, he turned back to Emma. "This isn't over."

Oh, the lunch date this week was going to be an interesting one. Holly added more notes to the back of her mind to bring up as she stopped next to Emma.

"Ignore him," Emma said, looking at her.

"Not on your life, but I will wait until our weekly lunch date to bring it up."

Emma paled before searching the room trying to avoid Holly's eyes.

"Uhh, this has been fun." Emma bit her bottom lip desperately trying to change the subject.

"Sure, let's go with fun," Holly replied.

"If you think this is a good time you should have seen what I originally had planned," Mildred said, coming up to them still wearing that ridiculous diaper on her head.

"I'm pretty sure what you had planned was considered a bachelorette party, *not* a baby shower." Emma's eyes twinkled as she smirked at Mildred.

"If done right, one causes the other doesn't it?" Mildred looked Emma up and down.

Do I now need to worry about a fistfight between these two?

"In your eyes, Mildred," Emma answered, with a shake of her head.

"Hey, it's not my fault you all don't know entertainment when you see it. I was all set to have some hunky men in uniform show up and try to arrest us." Mildred got this dreamy look in her eyes, before she turned to glare at Emma. "But this one went behind my back and canceled it."

Emma took a small step behind Holly shielding herself. "She scares me."

"Me too." Holly smiled before turning back to the old coot. "I would have canceled it too. A baby shower does not need a striptease." Holly turned to Emma. "Thank you for looking out for me."

"Anytime. Speaking of looking out." Emma nodded her head toward John. "Let me go help him. I think Will's about five seconds from arresting him."

Holly turned her head to see John bouncing on his feet begging for Will to answer his question. "You're right. Will does look like he's about had it."

"Wait a second," Mildred jumped in, cocking her brow at Emma. "I thought you hated him?"

"I never said that." Emma's eyes widened.

Mildred did that creepy silent thing as she gave Emma the once-over. Then a wicked smile appeared on her face. "No, dear. Indeed, you didn't."

Then in a flash, Mildred was gone.

"What the hell just happened?" Emma asked as Holly stood there in shock.

"I'm not sure but I think Mildred just looked into your soul and found out all your secrets."

"It did seem that way didn't it?"

"As it normally does with her."

"Pumpkin," Henry yelled, getting Holly's attention. "Come on it's gift time. Stop running your chompers and get your butt over here."

Holly rolled her eyes. *Parents...* She placed her hand on her stomach. *Don't ever let me say shit like that, okay, Peanut?* She looked back at her father with a shake of her head. "We told everyone not to bring anything. We didn't need it."

"And yet we still did!" Mildred squawked from the couch.

"Yeah, you don't show up to a baby shower empty-handed. That's not how this works," Martha agreed, as Will placed his arm around his wife.

"Fine. Have it your way." Holly shook her head as she made her way to the seat that was placed in the front of the room. Ben quickly plopped down next to her. "Do you see how many clothespins I have?" he asked, showing off his arm like it was a trophy.

"Yes, babe. You did such a good job." Holly gave his knee a pat.

Ben puffed out his chest. "I've got two more than John."

"Hey, this game isn't over until the old lady says it is." John glared at him.

"Who you callin' old, buddy?" Mildred stared John down. "For that you lose a point."

"Hey now, that wasn't in the rules."

"I make the rules. You've only lost one, you want to make it two?"

John mumbled something as he threw himself into the nearby chair in a huff.

Mildred turned back to Emma giving her the *look*. "I didn't say anything." Emma held up her hands.

"Just checking."

Out of the corner of Holly's eyes she saw Ben puff out again. *Oh, for the love of all things.*

"Here you go, Holly." Jimmy held out the gift Waffles had ripped apart earlier to her.

My heart. "Thank you, squirt."

Jimmy sat at her feet as she opened the present. It was a light green crocheted baby blanket from Emma. "Thank you, sweetie."

Emma's face reddened. "You're welcome. I made it myself."

"You did?"

Emma placed a stray piece of her hair behind her ear. "Yeah. I kinda picked up crocheting a while back."

"It's beautiful." Holly squeezed it. She felt tears coming to her eyes. *Damnit! These damn pregnancy hormones. They will be the death of me.*

"Thank you, Emma. That's really sweet." Ben smiled at her.

"Can you make me a blanket?' John asked.

"I'll make you a muzzle."

"If it comes from you, I don't care *what* it is." John's whole face brightened.

"Knock it off you two." Mildred glared at them. "Keep going."

In order to avoid the wrath of Mildred, that's exactly what they did. Slowly, her and Ben opened their gifts one by one thanking everyone as they went.

That's when Holly came to the last box. Not thinking

much of it, she ripped it open, pulling the top off. The second her eyes focused on what was inside she snapped the lid back on.

Oh, no. Please no.

Holly carefully peeked inside. *Holy shit. I'll kill her.*

Holly held onto the box with a death grip.

"What is it?" Ben asked, trying to take the box from her.

"Yeah, Holly." Mildred winked at her. "What's in the box?"

Holly narrowed her eyes at the crazy old woman before turning to Ben shaking her head. *Please drop the subject.*

Ben cocked his brow at her before easily prying the box from her grip. When he opened it, he erupted in a deep belly laugh that filled the whole room.

Holly snapped her attention to Mildred as everyone started asking what was going on.

Inside the box was indeed a tiny wooden cock. And, no it was definitely not a bird.

Holly glared at Mildred, and all that crazy old woman did was wink at her.

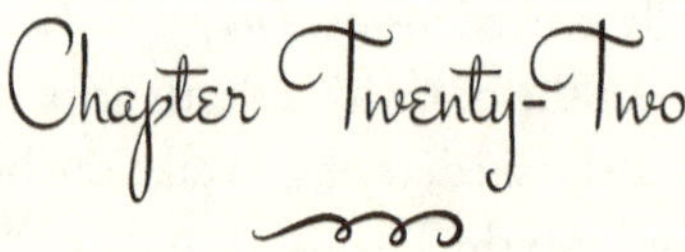

Chapter Twenty-Two

HOLLY PLACED her hand on her stomach as another pain raced through her. She was getting really tired of it. She knew it was nothing more than stress, but over the last three days the pain had gotten worse. At this point, she was ready to murder someone.

She was ungodly huge. Being able to see her toes: nope. Hadn't seen them in months.

Bending over to pick up after Jimmy was done playing: negatory. Bending was *not* an option.

Holly looked around the living room at dog toys *and* human toys thrown all around.

Maybe this was just going to be her life from now on.

It could be worse.

A crippling pain shot through her lower back. "Effe me," she growled. Holly looked to the ceiling. *Remind me to kill Ben when he gets home. If this is what it's like being pregnant, he's never coming anywhere near me with his dick again.*

She tried standing up as straight as she could. *Kill me now!*

"Holly, do you need some help?" Jimmy asked, running into the living room. He quickly picked up the dog toy Holly was trying to grab and handed it to her.

"Thanks, squirt." She ruffled his hair.

Waffles started running around the living room trying to get Jimmy to chase him. "Hold on, Waffles, we gotta make sure Holly doesn't need anything else." Jimmy looked at her expectantly completely ready to do whatever she needed.

Her heart melted.

Jimmy was terrific in so many ways. He was always by her side helping her with anything she needed. If he saw her struggling with anything and Ben wasn't around, he was there in an instant. When she tripped over an invisible rock, Jimmy always seemed to grab her hand or arm to steady her.

He was a little Ben.

And then there was his nighttime ritual. Holly and Ben would tuck him in, making sure Ripley and Twitch were nestled with him. Jimmy without fail, would hug Holly resting his head on her stomach, giving it a squeeze telling Peanut he'd be there in the morning and he was only a few rooms away.

Even though Holly knew it was coming, she still ended up a blubbering mess by the time she got to her bedroom.

Jimmy fit perfectly into their family.

Holly smiled warmly, even with all the pain she was in.

Life was good.

Then Waffles started barking.

Holly rolled her eyes. *Well, it's as good as it's gonna get.* Waffles ran full speed at Jimmy trying to get him to play.

Waffles…

As if he knew, Waffles turned his attention to Holly. He barked once, then trotted toward the back door offended.

Holly rolled her eyes even harder this time. God forbid anyone threw a wrench in anything Waffles wanted.

Waffles looked at Holly over his shoulder.

Sorry me being pregnant is an inconvenience to you.

Waffles huffed agreeing with her.

Holly narrowed her eyes at her dog. *I'll remember this.*

"When's Ben coming home?" Jimmy asked, distracting her from the argument she was having with Waffles.

Jimmy looked down to see Twitch rubbing against his legs so he plucked him into his arms.

"Soon, I hope." Holly looked past Jimmy to glare at Waffles some more.

Jimmy looked at Twitch as he scratched under his chin. "Uh, do you think when he gets home we can go to the dog park? I kinda promised Waffles and Ripley we'd go today."

That's where the attitude from Waffles was coming from. She glared at her dog who was now plopped onto his butt staring her down.

"Oh, you did now?" she asked still in the stare down with Lord Waffles.

"They are kinda hard to say no to when they give you that look." Holly broke her standoff with her dog to see Jimmy biting his bottom lip. When she looked back at Waffles, he was now giving *her* the look. *Why you little shit!* "Are you trying to manipulate my boy?"

Waffles huffed.

He was. Oh, let me at him! Waffles turned his nose up, defying her. "Young man, you do not manipulate your brother. Jimmy doesn't have to do anything you say." Holly crossed her arms over her chest. *Take that, Waffles.*

Oh, he took it all right. He sent Holly an evil look before walking over to Jimmy. The bastard then fell over onto his back demanding scratches.

Jimmy was instantly on his knees giving in to the little devil's demands. To make matters worse, out of the corner of his eye, Waffles had the audacity to look at her as if saying *he* was the one in charge here.

"I'm telling your father." Waffles barked at her. "Don't back sass me."

Waffles flipped over onto his front with a huff before

staring her down again. This caused Jimmy to burst into laughter.

"Don't encourage him."

Jimmy looked at her with the exact same look Waffles got in his eyes when he was causing havoc. "I'll think about it."

Oh my God, there is two of them now. Wait, three when you add in Ripley. Holly plucked Twitch into her arms, who'd been sitting on the floor after Jimmy let him go. *At least I have you.*

Twitch then jumped out of her arms and ran over to Ripley who was on the couch watching the show.

Wonderful. Holly shook her head. "You hang around Waffles too much."

"That's 'cause I love him." Jimmy smiled brightly at her.

She leaned down and kissed the top of his head. "He loves you too. Why don't you go outside and play for a little while until Ben gets home?"

"Okay!" You didn't have to tell Jimmy twice. He took off running toward the back door with Waffles and Ripley by his side.

Poor Twitch. He sat at the back door. He then looked back at her. "Oh, now I'm good enough for you?"

Twitch's head flicked as he stared at her. "Fine. Come here little one." Twitch ran to Holly. "They'll be back in soon then you can go back to pretending I don't exist while they're in the house." Twitch started purring in her arms.

Figures.

"I've got them, Grace!" Ben rushed through the front door nearly scaring Holly to death. She placed her hand over her heart. *I think I just peed.*

Then Ben's words registered. "Wait, what did you say?" She stared at him with bated breath.

"I've got them." Ben held up the papers in his hand.

"Are you kidding? Don't play with me Benjamin, it won't end well for you."

Ben pulled her close before giving her a kiss. "Not even a little bit, Grace. Here are the approved adoption papers for Jimmy."

Holly screamed in excitement. "Is this really happening?"

"You bet your sweet ass it is!" Ben brought his lips to hers once more kissing the ever-loving daylights out of her.

They had worked so hard to get to this point. They'd had countless appointments with their lawyers, supervised visits with the social worker, you name it, and it all came down to this moment.

This was what they had been waiting for.

Jimmy was going to officially be theirs.

Forever.

"What are we waiting for? Let's go tell him." The moment Holly took a step toward the back door she froze causing Ben to stare at her with his brows pulled together. "What's wrong, babe?" He cocked his head to the side.

That's not pee.

"Uhh, Ben, I think my water just broke."

Chapter Twenty-Three

HOLY FUCK!

Ben stared at Holly who was completely frozen with her legs spread slightly apart. He gave her the quick once-over, but his mind wouldn't catch up. There was no way in hell he heard her right. Holly wasn't due for another two weeks.

Two weeks.

Yet, Holly stood there her eyes wide, her mouth partly open, and her face pale.

Maybe it was a cramp? Yeah, that's what it was. Ben looked her up and down again. *No, this was it.* His heart slammed against his chest.

The doctor said two weeks. That meant they had two weeks. That was fourteen days.

Doctors can't do the whole *oops* thing. There were no takesie backsies in this situation.

"Ben?"

He snapped his attention to Holly, who hadn't moved a muscle. "He said we had two weeks! Two. Weeks." Ben's eyes widened. "Doctors get paid to be right about this stuff. Where the hell is the accountability?"

"Are you always right?"

Ben puffed out his chest. "Are you questioning my medical knowledge?"

"No." She shook her head. "I'm saying sometimes things change and right now Peanut has decided they want out. Two weeks be damned."

Ben made a mental note to send the doctor a very strongly worded email about their timelines once the baby was here.

Holy fuck their child was about to be born!

"Are you just gonna stand there?" Holly asked, still not moving.

At her words, Ben finally snapped into action. *Holy fuck it was happening.* In an instant, Ben started running around the house like a madman.

He ran to their bedroom where Holly's hospital bag was packed. Thank fuck he'd made her do it last week.

He then ran into the bathroom. When he got there, he had absolutely no idea why he went in there to begin with.

Fuck it.

He knew he didn't have time to question anything. So instead, he threw open the medicine cabinet, and with an aggressive arm sweep, he tossed everything into her hospital bag.

Better to be safe than sorry. It didn't matter he'd also tossed into the bag his aftershave. Deciding not to care, he zipped up the bag, threw it over his shoulder and sprinted into the living room. That's when he saw Holly's new favorite blanket. The one Emma had made. Quickly he snatched it into his hands before throwing it around his neck.

Ben ran full speed out the front door. Once he got to his SUV, he tossed everything inside before taking off around the house to the backyard.

"Ben! You're home! Now we can go to the dog park." Jimmy's face lit up.

"Not this time, kiddo," Ben yelled as he ran full speed toward him. "It's go-time."

Unfortunately for Ben, Waffles thought anyone running in the backyard meant it was time to play. Instantly Waffles swerved in between Ben's legs causing him to lose his footing.

Before Ben knew it, he was on the grass in a complete daze at what happened.

Was this how Holly felt?

Ben looked at Waffles who was giving him the side-eye, like *he* was offended it wasn't really play time.

Can anything be easy in their life? Waffles barked at him before prancing his way toward Jimmy. Yes, prancing, like the diva he was.

Ben shook his head as he stood. Quickly he brushed himself off before he turned his attention back to Jimmy.

"We gotta go, kiddo."

Without thinking Ben threw Jimmy over his shoulder before running through the backyard, taking the steps up to the house two at a time. All while ushering Ripley and Waffles into the house.

Through all the chaos and barking, Ben managed to get inside before locking the backdoor.

With Jimmy still on his shoulder he ran through the living room and back out the front door. When he made it to the car, as gently as he could he tossed Jimmy in the back seat before buckling him.

Once he was secured Ben ran around to the driver's side door before hopping in. He turned on the car and peeled out the driveway in route to the hospital never once looking back.

"Uh, Ben?" Jimmy spoke from the back seat.

Ben's heart raced as he rounded the corner of their neighborhood. "Yeah?" Right now, his only focus was getting to the hospital.

"I think you forgot something."

Ben's brows pulled together. No, he hadn't forgotten anything. He'd planned this out in his head a hundred times. He had their hospital bag, Holly's blanket that Emma made, and then... "Oh, fuck!" Ben slammed on the brakes causing the car to come to a screeching halt.

Holy fucking shit. He hit his hand on the steering wheel. He'd seen this in movies tons of times, but he never thought it actually happened in real life.

He fucking forgot Holly.

With a U-turn that he was sure was illegal on how fast he peeled around the corner he raced back to the house.

Holly looked down at Waffles. "Do you think he realized he forgot me?" she asked. Waffles barked before walking into the living room plopping down onto his stomach ignoring her.

"Love you too, Waffles."

Holly was a tad freaked out. Okay, she was way more than a tad freaked. She was about to push a human out of her va-jay-jay. A human. That's cause to be terrified. Regardless though, she found herself chuckling at seeing Jimmy thrown over Ben's shoulder as he ran through the house. Holly and Jimmy had even shared a "what's going on" look before Ben carried him out of the house.

"Why were you not in the car?" Ben yelled, slamming through the front door.

Holly crossed her arms over her chest as she arched her brow.

"Don't give me that look, Grace. You could have gotten into the car."

Both of her brows shot to the ceiling as her hands went to her hips.

"Unknot your twat, buster, *you're the* one that forgot me. I just stood here and watched the show."

"Unknot my twat?" His brow raised.

A smile spread on both of their faces as they both said at the exact same time, "Mildred."

That's when another contraction hit her. *At least I now know I'm not dying.*

Ben was by her side in an instant. "You could have come to the car."

"And miss the show? Not on your life. It's not very often I get to see the calm, cool, collected Ben lose his fuckin' shit." Holly looked him up and down. "Why are your knees dirty?"

"Waffles tripped me."

"Really?" Holly smirked. "I thought you were too smooth to let his holiness ever get the better of you?"

Ben glared at her. "I'm gonna let that slide, but only 'cause you're about to give birth to my child."

"*Our* child."

Ben ignored her comment, scooping her into his arms bridal style. "I can walk."

His eyes narrowed at her. "Then you could have walked to the car."

"Good point." Holly wrapped her arms around Ben's neck as he carried her. "Do you think it was dumb to have waited until the baby pops out to find out what we're having?"

"That's what's running through your head right now?" he asked.

"Don't get snippy with me."

Ben shook his head. "Let's just get to the hospital." Carefully Ben got Holly into the car. It didn't help Jimmy was in the backseat laughing so hard he was snorting and threatening that he was about to pee on himself.

Ben sent Jimmy a glare too.

Poor Ben.

"I'm gonna pee!" Jimmy snorted again.

"Don't go joking about peeing on yourself." Holly looked at Jimmy. "I thought I had."

"Eww."

Preach it.

Holly gritted her teeth as she felt another contraction. *Oh, my God, I'm about to have a baby.* "Emma!"

"What about her?" Ben asked as he pulled out of their driveway.

"I promised her I'd call as soon as I went into labor." Holly grabbed her phone dialing her number. Emma swore to Holly she'd be there when the baby was born. She'd be the level head in case anything went wrong... like you know forgetting Holly.

Holly's call went straight to voicemail so she tried again. Nothing.

Oh God, what if something happened to Emma. What if —

"Holly, what's wrong?" Ben grabbed her hand. "Are you having another contraction?"

"Emma's not answering her phone."

Ben squeezed her hand tighter. "Calm down, Grace, it's okay. Maybe she's got no service."

Holly's heart pounded against her chest.

"Can you do me a favor and call John and let him know we're on the way to the hospital?" Ben asked.

Holly nodded as the realization started to sink in again. She was about to push out a child... She wasn't ready. Nope, not at all. "On second thought, I think we can turn around and go home."

"Excuse me?"

"I think all I did was pee on myself. Yep. That's it." Holly started bouncing her head up and down. "That's exactly what happened."

"That was your water breaking."

"Nope. Pee."

"Holly..." Ben looked at her as another contraction hit. *Stop it, Peanut! We aren't ready!*

"Holly you're holding your stomach and wincing."

"It's gas."

"Holly."

"Fine. Jerk." She took a deep breath before looking at her

phone again. It took John four rings to finally pick up. *"Hello?"* he panted into the phone.

"Why are you breathing so hard?" Holly asked as she bit her bottom lip. This wasn't a full-on contraction but it still felt like there was a monster inside of her and it was clawing its way out.

"Why are you calling?" he countered in typical John fashion.

"What's with all the attitude from everyone today?" Holly snapped.

"I'm right in the middle of something here, Holly. You better be havin' that baby or I promise you, you thought I was a pain in the ass before you haven't seen—"

"Of course, I'm pushing out a child. Why else would I be calling?" She narrowed her eyes. That's it, John was officially off their Christmas card list. And this year she had a good photo planned. It involved her, Ben, Jimmy, all their pets, and elf costumes. It was gonna be freaking epic.

"Oh shit! I thought you had two weeks."

"Well apparently doctors lie. Even though it's their job and all, they can say whatever the hell they want."

Holly heard rustling on the other end of the phone. *"Fuck. Okay, we'll be right there."*

"Who's we?"

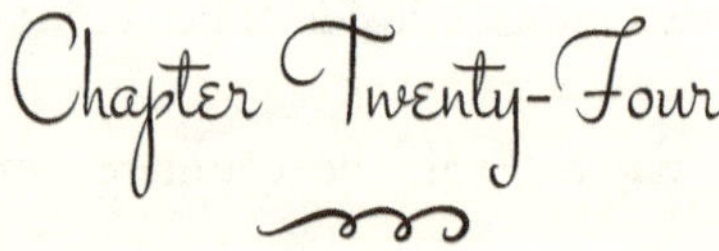

Chapter Twenty-Four

HOLLY WASN'T sure who was freaking out more, her or Ben. From the looks of it, she was leaning more toward Ben right now. At least she got happy drugs once she was admitted into the hospital.

Thank God.

Although, they weren't that happy since she was still in pain.

The moment Ben pulled into the hospital and hauled her out of the car, she was taken to the labor and delivery unit where they started an IV and told her she needed to wait. Unfortunately for her, she was too far along for the epidural, but not far enough to push.

She closed her eyes. *Universe, I thought we had this heart-to-heart already? Will you ever give me a fucking break?*

Holly clenched her hands as another contraction hit.

Nope. Read you loud and clear, Universe.

"How in the fuck do they think you're not ready?" Ben growled, looking at her. "You're wincing every few minutes."

"Language." Holly glared at him, before darting her eyes to Jimmy.

"That's okay, Ben said the same word when he realized he

forgot you." Jimmy sent her a playful smile before looking at Ben.

"Oh, he did now?" Holly's eyes narrowed at her husband.

"Yep."

"I'm gonna remember this, kid." Ben snapped his attention to Jimmy, who shrugged.

Throw me a bone here universe and take me now. Holly threw her head back onto her pillow looking at the ceiling as she felt a sharp pain once again. *I mean Ben is right. Sure, I got meds to help but this kinda sucks. Okay, this really sucks. How in the hell do people pop out more than one kid?*

Ben grabbed onto her hand squeezing it. "Do you want me to force them to give you an epidural?"

"You can't force them to do anything." She gritted her teeth as the contraction went through her.

"I can try."

"It's fine. They said I was too far along. So, it wouldn't help anyway." With her luck, she'd get the thing, push out the kid, *then* end up going numb from the waist down.

"Do you want me to see if they can give you more pain meds? There has to be something they can do."

"No." Holly squeezed his hand. How had she gotten so lucky to have Ben? Even now he was trying to ease her pain any way he could. She looked at him as the contraction died down. There was so much concern in his eyes. "I just want this baby out."

"Two weeks my ass," Ben mumbled.

"Language!" Holly closed her eyes again. "But, you're not wrong."

"Is Peanut coming soon?" Jimmy asked, drawing Holly's attention to him.

"I hope so." *Even if I have to crawl up there myself and get Peanut out.*

Jimmy nodded before sinking back into the chair, looking down at his hands. Holly was about to say something when another pain started to creep in. Her heart raced as a new wave of panic washed over her.

This was it.

There was no going back now.

She was about to push a human out of her. A human she and Ben would be one hundred percent responsible for.

Holy crap on ten million crackers. I'm not ready!

As Holly was about to fall into a complete panic attack, John burst through the door. "Is it happening?"

"Does it look like Holly's pushing out a kid?" Ben scoffed.

"Hey, I don't know how these things work, for all I know she could have popped out the thing on the way to the hospital." John crossed his arms over his chest in defiance.

"Did you sleep through human anatomy in school?" Holly rolled her eyes at him. That's when she saw Emma emerge from behind John. To her surprise, John gave Emma a *knowing* look. "I know all about the human anatomy, so I didn't need to go."

"You were the *we*?" Holly asked, trying to make sense of what other dimension she was sure as hell she was in. Then John's words registered. "Oh my God!"

Emma jumped forward with her hands held up. "It's not what you're thinking."

"What am I thinking then?" Holly's voice raised.

Emma bit her lower lip as John straightened puffing out his chest. Holly moved her attention to Emma. *Oh missy, as soon as this kid comes out, you and I are having a conversation.* She looked John up and down as the pride radiated off him. *A long conversation.*

Emma must have read her mind since her eyes widened as her face lost its color.

That's right! Be prepared.

Just then another contraction hit Holly causing her to scream out in agony. This time it was by far the worst that she'd had. *Holy fuckity fuck. This one's bad. Why the hell was I so adamant that I was fine this morning? Why? Why am I like this? Maybe then I could have gotten the epidural.*

"Is the baby coming?" John asked.

"No. I'm singing the song of my fucking people."

"Language."

Holly snapped her head to Ben. When she saw his smirk, she didn't know whether she wanted to give him a point for calling her out or punch him in the throat.

Punch. Yeah, she was definitely going with punch.

Emma ran to Holly's side distracting her from the plot to kill her husband. "What do you need? Why aren't you pushing? What did we miss?"

Those were some damn good questions. Holly threw her head over to Ben. *Let him do the talking. It's his fault I'm here in the first place.*

"When we first got here, they said she was too far into labor for the epidural but not far enough to push," Ben answered. "They need to wait until her contractions are about two minutes apart."

"I'm not a doctor or anything but by the weird face thingy she is doing I'm gonna say she's two minutes apart," John announced.

"No shit." Holly snapped her attention to him. She then looked at Emma. "Remind me to poison him once I'm sprung free from this place."

"I won't eat your cooking again." John crossed his arms over his chest. "Been there, done that. Learned my lesson."

"Then I'll run you over with my car."

"You'll have to catch me first."

"Children..." Ben warned.

"Get used to it, Ben," Emma remarked, trying her hardest not to smile but was failing.

"You think I would be by now."

Holly squeezed Ben and Emma's hands as her contraction

intensified. That's when she remembered. "My dad! We have to call my dad."

Jesus effeing Christ. How in the hell had I forgotten to call my dad? I haven't even had the kid yet and I'm already failing.

"Taken care of," Ben said, drawing her attention to him. "I called once you were in the room. John had already left so I sent a taxi to get him."

Instantly some of Holly's unease left her as she observed Ben.

He stared down at her with so much love it was almost overwhelming. She needed to remember no matter what was happening she had him and they would get through everything together. He was her rock.

"I'm proud of you," he whispered using his other hand to cup her face, making sure to keep her attention on him. "Thank you for giving me this gift."

Just like that, everything was okay again. "I love you, Ben."

"I love you too, Grace."

"Uhh, Holly?"

Holly turned to Emma who was now biting her lip.

"Umm, Mildred's on her way too."

Holly brows shot to the ceiling. "She is?"

"Yeah, after John said you were in labor I kinda panicked and called her."

Holly threw her head back. Great, this was all she needed, Mildred yapping her jaw about how Holly wasn't pushing right or some crap like that. Holly could see it now. *"You gotta push that baby out like it's the only thing standin' between you and your man's dong again."* Holly recoiled. *Oh God, I'm even thinking like Mildred now.*

Before Holly could really let that thought sink in, the doctor, the one who had been on call when they came in walked into the room. "How are you feeling?"

"How does it look like I'm feeling?" Holly snapped.

"I did hear talk from the staff about this room." The doctor smiled brightly at them.

Can I add him onto the list of people I can murder, Universe? I'll make it quick, you won't even know what happened.

"We think Holly's contractions have progressed," Ben said chiming in.

"Let's take a look here, shall we?"

Just then a frantic Mildred and Henry ran into the room. "Is my grandbaby here yet?" Henry asked.

"Where's the baby?" Mildred echoed.

"Fucking shoot me now!" Holly yelled as another contraction hit her body.

"Language."

Holly snapped her attention to Ben. "You can take that language and shove it right up your ass."

"Young lady," Henry remarked, drawing her attention.

"Labor makes you fun," Mildred said, bouncing on her feet with delight.

The doctor looked around the room. "It was fun for a few minutes. However, I'm going to have to ask all of you to go wait in the waiting room. There's too many people and not enough room."

Holly looked around as she bit her bottom lip in pain. She couldn't agree more.

As her eyes moved around the room, she focused on the spot Jimmy had been sitting, only this time it was empty.

She scanned the room again.

A wave of panic swept through her.

He was nowhere to be found.

"Mrs. Richman, your heart rate is skyrocketing. Are you having another contraction?"

"Where's Jimmy?" She shot her eyes to Ben who also started looking around the room.

Another contraction hit her. *Fuck! No!*

The doctor took one assessment at Holly and placed his gloved hand under the sheet to check her. "It's time."

"The fuck it is!" Holly snapped her legs together effectively locking the doctor's hand in place.

"The baby is coming, Mrs. Richman."

Holly glared at him through the pain. "Let's get one thing straight here, doc." She gritted her teeth. "I'm not pushing a watermelon outta my hoo-ha until I know where my son is."

"Mrs. Richman, while you're still having the contraction you need to push."

With all her strength she held her legs together pulling herself up to the doctor at her waist. She didn't know how but she was able to grab onto his scrubs pulling him close. "This kid isn't gonna see the light of day until my son is in front of me. You get me?"

"That's my girl! Show that doctor who's boss," Mildred gleefully exclaimed fist pumping the air.

Ben was fast. In seconds, he unclasped Holly's hand from around the doctor's collar.

Holly turned to Ben, tears in her eyes as she fought her body's natural reactions to push.

"Found him!" John announced, walking Jimmy back into the room. Holly darted her attention to him, the relief of seeing him was quickly overthrown when she saw the tears in Jimmy's eyes.

Oh no, what happened? "Come here," Holly said, reaching out for Jimmy. "Baby, what's going on?"

Jimmy slowly walked into Holly's grasp. Ben ran around the bed and kneeled down next to him in seconds.

Jimmy looked up into Holly's eyes tears now flowing freely from him. "Once Peanut is born, you won't need me anymore."

"What?" Ben asked.

Jimmy started to choke up. "You'll both forget about me and send me to another home." His sobs grew louder.

Holly's whole world fell apart as she watched her son fear losing them. Had she really been that bad of a parent to Jimmy that she didn't instill in him no matter what happened he would always be theirs, no matter how many children they had? Jimmy was their son. End of story. She pulled him into her arms. "Jimmy, no, never. You are never ever going somewhere else. You are *my* son and no one will ever take you away from me."

"B-but, once Peanut is here you'll forget about me."

"We can never forget about you, squirt. When you came into our life you made it better." Ben pulled him into his arms.

"We love you, Jimmy. To us, you have always been our son, from that very first time we saw you on the camera." Holly looked at Ben. "Do you have the papers by any chance?"

Ben nodded. "Actually, I do. I stuffed them in my back pocket when your water broke." He quickly handed them to Holly.

"Put him on the bed," Holly said, scooting over so Jimmy would have room.

"Mrs. Richman, I need to advise you that this—"

Holly cut him off with a glare so evil the doctor took a step back holding his hands up.

Once Jimmy was right next to her, with Ben standing nestled next to both of them she unfolded the papers. "Do you see this here?"

Jimmy nodded.

"These are your adoption papers, baby. We were on our way into the backyard to tell you it was official when my water broke. With these documents here, you became our son. A Richman. We adopted you, squirt."

Jimmy stared at the papers for a few seconds before looking back to Holly. Tears were in his eyes but he was no longer sobbing. "Does this mean I can finally call you mom?"

Holly's heart exploded at his words. She pulled him into her arms hugging him like her life depended on it. She never thought he'd call her mom. Not with everything he'd been through, but hearing those words come out of his mouth was everything she'd always hoped for.

"Mom, mom." Jimmy flailed around. "Can't breathe."

Holly pulled back looking at him as tears fell from her eyes. "I'll never get tired of hearing that."

Jimmy smiled as he turned to Ben biting his lip. "Dad?"

"Every day for the rest of your life, kid." Ben scooped him off the bed and into his arms. "Love you."

"I love you, too, Dad."

"Oh no!" Holly yelled as another contraction hit her. This time with so much force she couldn't fight not pushing.

"That's it. We can't wait another second. Mrs. Richman, you're pushing or I *will* call for a cesarean section. You're risking your child's life."

Holly paled. How in the hell was she messing up so much already? "Let's do this."

Everyone was quickly ushered out of the room by the nurses as Ben stood at the head of the bed holding Holly's hand, giving her words of encouragement. As the contraction shot through her body Holly pushed like she'd never pushed before.

Within a few minutes, the room erupted in cries.

"Congratulations, it's a girl!"

Chapter Twenty-Five

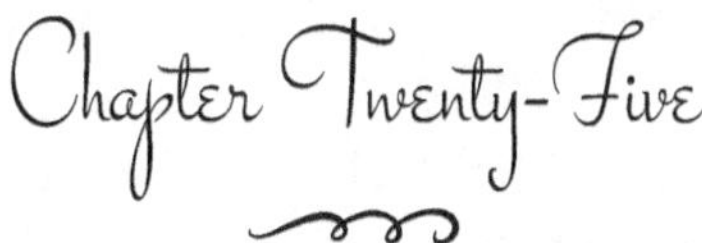

BEN HELD his daughter in his arms as his heart pounded against his chest. She was perfect in every single way possible. He never truly understood what a parent meant when they talked about the feeling of holding their child for the first time.

Now, he did.

Ben looked down at her with so much love, it was overwhelming. This was their child. Their little girl. Life couldn't get much better than this.

He looked up from his daughter to see Jimmy peacefully sleeping on the chair in the corner.

Today he was given one of the greatest gifts ever given. His children.

He looked down at this daughter one more time. *Welcome to the family, Peanut.*

Ben turned his attention to Holly. He saw her staring at him with a silly smile on her face. "She's amazing, isn't she?" she said, looking at their child in his arms.

He nodded. "Beyond any doubt."

Everyone had gone home once the baby was born leaving

just the four of them. Everything went from completely chaotic to peaceful.

He looked back at his baby girl, tears in his eyes. "Thank you." Ben turned his attention back to Holly.

She beamed at him as a lazy smile appeared on her face. "I love you, Ben."

"I love you too, Grace." He moved his attention back to the little girl in his arms.

"Do you think she'll have your eyes?" Holly asked, looking at him.

"I hope she has yours."

"There you two are," Henry said, shuffling into the room with a cup of coffee in his hand.

Ben looked to the door. "I thought John took you home?"

"I told him I called a cab." Henry shrugged.

"You lied to him?"

"An omittance of truth." Henry handed Ben the cup of coffee. "Figured you needed this."

"Thanks." He took it before placing it on the table next to him.

Henry walked over to the side of the bed kissing Holly on the cheek. "You did good, Pumpkin."

Holly smiled at him. "Thanks, Dad."

Holly turned to Ben reaching out her hands asking for the baby. Carefully, Ben stood before walking to Holly placing their baby girl in her arms.

"Dad," Holly said, holding up their child for him to see. "I would like for you to meet Helen Richman."

Henry took a step back. "Holly?"

She started nodding her head as tears appeared in her eyes. "You didn't?"

Holly wiped away the tears falling down her cheeks. "Ben and I talked about it. If we had a boy we were going to name him after his father, a girl, mom." Holly looked down at their baby. "She looks exactly like a Helen if you ask me."

Ben plopped his hip onto the bed placing his arms around Holly's shoulder cradling her and the baby in his arms. "She does. She looks *exactly* like a Helen."

"I—I don't know what to say," Henry stammered, staring at all of them as tears formed in his eyes.

"Would you like to hold your granddaughter?" Holly asked, holding her up.

"You don't have to ask me twice." Henry as quick as he could ran over to Ben's vacated chair and plopped onto it. As best as he could he positioned himself to safely hold Peanut.

Once Ben saw he was ready, he gently took Peanut from Holly and placed her in Henry's arms.

When she was situated Ben went back to Holly placing his arm around her, holding her tightly.

Here in the room was everything he ever dreamed of.

Jimmy slept soundly in the corner, officially their adopted child.

Henry held their daughter.

And he had Holly in his arms.

Ben shook his head. If two years ago, someone told him this is where he would be in his life, he would have laughed at them. But now, now he couldn't see his life any other way.

Ben looked at Holly, her smile spread from ear to ear, which he knew matched his own.

He knew his heart felt full when Jimmy came into their life, but this. This was different.

This was beyond a fullness.

This was perfect.

He leaned over kissing Holly lightly on the lips. "I love you."

She smiled back at him. "Not as much as I love you."

"I'm your grandpa, Peanut," Henry cooed, drawing Ben's attention away from Holly. "I've waited a long time for your mom to give me grandbabies. And in one day she gave me two."

Ben watched as Henry spoke to their daughter.

"I'm the cool Grandpa," he stated. "I'll always be there for you whenever you need me. I'll be here. For you *and* your brother."

"The cool grandpa, really?" Holly laughed.

Henry looked at her. "You know it. I'll make it my mission to stay up on the trends."

"Oh, this is gonna be fun." Ben laughed along with Holly.

"I can learn those texting machines if I need to, or the internet box. I can do it."

Ben chuckled.

Yep, this *was* perfect.

Henry turned back to Peanut. "She's beautiful."

"She is," Ben agreed. "Just as beautiful as Holly."

"Thank you for naming her after your mother." Henry caressed Peanut's cheek.

"There was never a doubt," Holly answered.

Henry looked up at them with a new twinkle in his eyes, as his lopsided grin appeared. "You know, she definitely came into this world with a bang."

"That's Holly's MO." Ben pulled his wife closer. "I was a little worried for the doctor there at one point."

"Me too."

"Hey, you don't get between a mother and her children." Holly crossed her arms over her chest.

Ben leaned over kissing her hairline. "You've always had that possessive gene in you, Grace. I pity anyone that tries you."

Henry's chuckle went through the room. "And you have Mildred on your side. She's a force to be reckoned with. I can still hear her taking bets on if Peanut was gonna be a boy or girl." Henry shook his head. "You know, she was trying to hustle the staff, right?"

"I'm not the least bit surprised," Ben answered.

"I'm still not sure how her husband doesn't murder her," Holly replied, closing her eyes.

"Love is funny that way, isn't it?" Henry looked back down at Helen before turning back to them. "How do you two feel?"

"Amazing," they said in unison.

Henry smiled back at them. "It's a wonderful feeling, right?"

"It is."

"There is one thing I can't wait for, though," Henry said, giving them both a lopsided grin.

"And what's that?" Ben asked, cocking his head to the side.

"Introducing Peanut to Lord Waffles."

Chapter Twenty-Six

FIVE MONTHS LATER

LIFE WAS A FUCKING CHAOTIC MESS.

But Holly wouldn't have it any other way.

It might have been a mess, but it was her mess, and she'd never been happier.

Holly looked around her living room. On the floor, Jimmy was wrestling with Ripley, with Twitch trying to hold his own. In the corner of the room, Waffles was climbing up the cat tree looking for treats.

Peanut was crying so Ben was rocking her in his arms.

And the whole room looked like it had exploded with toys — human and dog, clothes, blankets, and food. You name it. It was in her living room.

Still, even through all that, Holly had a goofy smile on her face.

Glancing around her home she noticed Waffles had made it to the second level on the cat tree. With a deep sigh, she pushed her three-day unwashed hair out of her face and made her way over to him. She plucked him from the cat tree and placed him on the floor, much to his protest.

Waffles stared up at her in disgust as he huffed loudly at her.

"What did you do to him?" Ben asked, coming over to Holly. Peanut still in his arms as she cried.

"I took him off the cat tree." Holly wiped off the front of her shirt. There were vomit stains, and something else, but she wasn't quite sure what it was. She decided it was best to ignore it.

"Did I forget to put the gate around it again?" Ben asked, looking behind her at Waffles.

"No, you did. He thinks when there's madness going on, he can get away with pushing it to the side."

"Typical Waffles."

"Never a dull moment."

Jimmy's laughter rang throughout the room as he continued to play with Ripley and Twitch. He kept squeaking one of the dog toys driving Ripley to bark.

Then Peanut started to cry louder.

Holly caught Ben's eye. Simultaneously a smile spread across their faces.

Chaos never looked so good.

Ben leaned forward kissing Holly on the cheek. "Love you, Grace."

"Love you more."

"I'm gonna take this one to the nursery and see if I can get her down for a nap."

"Good luck." He was gonna need it.

"If it works, you and I are sneaking off to the bedroom for five minutes."

Holly's eyes brightened. "That's all you're gonna give me, big guy? Five minutes."

Ben growled at her causing Holly to throw her head back and laugh.

"I bet I can make you come no less than three times and still have a minute to spare," he whispered into her ear.

"Talk is cheap."

"Oh, Grace. You're gonna get it."

"Maybe."

Ben kissed her again. "Be ready." He turned on his heel making his way down the hall with Peanut still crying.

Never a dull moment.

She'd give Ben a few minutes before she sent Jimmy out back with the pups to play.

Hell, five minutes was all she needed.

Holly walked to the kitchen and reached for her trusted donut box. Once she had it, she took out her prized possession.

That's when she noticed Waffles plop down on his butt staring her down as he eyed what was in her hand.

Not surprising, Waffles then lunged for her treat. Holly was too quick for him this time, though. She yanked it away from him. Waffles plopped back on the floor sending her a severe side-eye.

Holly took a bite as she laughed. "Not this time, Waffles."

Waffles huffed in annoyance.

"This peanut butter glazed donut is mine!"

Just then Ripley came running into the kitchen with Jimmy chasing after her. Holly being completely taken off guard, tried swerving away but ended up losing her footing.

Before Holly knew it, she was on the floor staring at the ceiling.

That's when Waffles casually walked over to her and plucked the donut from her grasp.

He looked down at her as he happily chomped on the last bite.

Instead of fighting it, Holly rested her head on the kitchen floor.

She counted to five the moment she heard Ben's footsteps.

"Holy shit. What happened? I leave you for two minutes and you're already on the floor," he asked, dropping to his knees checking her out before helping Holly to her feet.

"Waffles. Waffles is what happened."

Once Holly was fully upright, Ben shook his head. "That's it."

Holly knitted her brows together as she watched Ben leave the kitchen in a huff and head into their garage.

"What are you doing?" she called out.

When he reappeared in the kitchen he held up his hand. "It's time to try the bubble wrap again."

Stumbling Into the Holidays

STUMBLING THROUGH LIFE BOOK THREE

Chapter One

"HOLLY RICHMAN, do *not* make me call the fire department again. Put down that spatula. *Now!*" Ben crossed his arms over his chest as he glared down at his wife. "You made those poor firefighters leave their Thanksgiving meal 'cause you *wanted to baste the turkey.*"

The corner of Ben's mouth turned up as an amused twinkle appeared in his eyes. "Who knew flames could shoot out of an oven that far?"

Seriously, though, there were a good few seconds Ben thought their house was going to catch fire or at least their kitchen.

However, the moment the words left Ben's mouth, Holly's jaw dropped. "You said you weren't gonna bring that up again. You *promised!*" She narrowed her eyes on her betraying husband. "How could you?"

He cocked his brow as he pointed to the scorch marks on the wall. "No. I *said* when the marks fade or get painted over, only *then* I wouldn't bring it up." He walked to the scorch marks before smirking her way. "And there is no way in hell I'm ever letting you paint over them."

"You jerk."

At Holly's angry growl, Ben tried to hold it together. There was nothing better than riling Holly up first thing in the morning. To him, it was always a damn good day when he could get under her skin. Maybe that's why it was one of his favorite activities.

What could he say? An annoyed Holly was *always* a fun Holly.

However, before Holly could retort, he grabbed her shoulders, dragging her and the scowling expression of one Holly Richman into his arms. At her annoyed grunt, Ben laughed as he brought his lips down to hers. "Love you, Grace."

"Screw you."

As he ignored her annoyance, Ben leaned in lightly brushing his lips to her ear. "It'll be my pleasure. I think Jimmy has Helen in the back room. Wanna see if we can do a quickie?"

When Ben heard Holly's breath hitch, he smirked before nibbling on her earlobe.

Well, this morning just got a hell of a lot more interesting.

Sadly, for him, though, Ben's win was short-lived. Instead of doing what he wanted to do, which was to lift Holly onto the counter and have himself his own Thanksgiving feast, Holly lifted her foot before stomping on his. *Hard.*

"Oww! What the hell, Grace?"

"I don't think so." Holly pulled away and crossed her arms over her ample chest. "You don't get to make fun of me then go to pound town on my lady bits," she whisper-shouted at him.

"Pound town?" Ben arched his brow.

"Yes. Pound town. What else do you want me to call it?" Holly's lips thinned as she glared daggers at him. "I should sic Waffles on you."

With her threat, both of Ben's brows lifted in surprise. "Oh, really?"

Instantly, that famous twitch Holly got in her left eye

when she was annoyed appeared. Was it wrong of him to want to laugh? Probably, but did that stop him? Hell no.

"Fine. Jimmy then."

Ben recrossed his arms over his chest as he cocked his head to the side, eyeing her like she was crazy.

"Okay. Whatever. My dad."

When he didn't move, Holly threw her hands in the air. "Fine, you jerkface. I'll do it myself."

Ready for Holly's tantrum, Ben had his arms open before the words were out of her mouth. As he caught her with ease, he held her against his body, molding her curves to his front. "You know, Grace, if you'd put this much effort into your cooking as you do trying to get me, you probably *wouldn't attempt to* burn the house down as much."

"You assho—"

"Mom!"

Perfect timing.

As their son Jimmy walked into the kitchen carrying his little sister Helen in his arms, the corner of Ben's mouth turned up. As carefully as he could, he gently placed Holly back down so she wouldn't topple over. He knew if he didn't make sure her feet were on the floor, her ass would have been there instead.

It might be fun to mess with Holly, but seeing her fall over wasn't in his plans today.

Holly shot Ben a dirty look telling him this was far from over before she shifted to their kids. However, the moment Holly turned with a little *too* much force, she almost slammed her hip into their kitchen island.

It took everything inside of Ben to not burst out laughing when he saw Holly shoot the island the same glare she'd given him only moments ago.

"Mom?"

With one last death stare at the island, she turned to

Jimmy. "Yeah, baby?" As she reached out to take Helen, she sent Ben another glare for good measure.

"What?" Ben smirked, crossing his arms over his chest.

"I've got her." Jimmy maneuvered so Holly couldn't take the little girl. "I changed her diaper but I think she's hungry. She's still really fussy. Even Ripley can't calm her down."

Ben's heart warmed as he watched Jimmy hold his baby sister close to his chest. From the moment they'd brought Peanut home from the hospital, Jimmy wanted to be fully involved. He took his big brother role very seriously. At first, he wasn't as excited about changing diapers, but he insisted on doing it anyway.

Jimmy had come so far since the night of the break-in at the clinic.

Even though Helen was only seven and a half months old, Jimmy was already extremely protective of her.

As Ben leaned back onto the counter, he watched a look of horror appear on Jimmy's face as he saw what Holly was still holding in her hand.

"Mom, why do you have a spatula?" Jimmy's huge eyes widened as he turned to Ben. "Dad, is she cooking again? Please tell me she's not trying to cook. I thought we talked about this? Grandpa Henry was here and everything."

Ben pointed to the scorch marks on the wall with a smirk. "I think she wants to go for round two."

Holly gasped. "Both of you can kiss my butt!" She glared at her betraying family before she plucked the baby from Jimmy's hands. "At least I have you, Peanut. You wouldn't make fun of your Momma, would you?"

Although the moment Holly had Helen positioned in her arms, the baby looked over her shoulder and right to her father. Instantly, Helen's eyes sparkled as she reached out her little arms trying to get Ben's attention.

"Not you too!" Holly's lips thinned as the little girl made a cooing noise to Ben making her desire clear.

Damn, I love my family. Ben pushed himself off the counter before gently grabbing Helen from his wife's arms. "She's a smart girl, Grace. What do you expect?"

"All of you are jerks." Holly stomped over to the fridge to grab a bottle of milk she'd placed there earlier in the morning. "I get zero respect here."

To no one's surprise, the moment the fridge door cracked open, Waffles, Ripley, and Twitch all came running into the kitchen.

"Oh, come on!"

Waffles, ever the one in charge of their gang, took a small step in front of the others. He then pushed himself onto his back legs, making him look like a meerkat, a trick Holly taught him years ago. Ripley instantly followed suit, with Twitch trying his best to do the same all while his little head bobbed from side-to-side.

"Are you freaking kidding me? When I open the fridge that does *not* mean you automatically get something." Holly narrowed her eyes at Waffles who dangled his tongue out of the right side of his mouth.

"No, it's much worse." Jimmy ran over to Waffles scratching him behind the ears. "Mom's trying to cook. *Again.*"

Within seconds, all three animals dropped to the floor and quickly hightailed it over to Ben's legs to hide behind him. Holly's eyes immediately followed the traitors as she glared daggers at their four-legged fur babies. "How could you?"

Waffles, the jerk himself, trotted in front of Ben before he plopped his happy Corgi butt on the floor giving Holly a side-eye to end all side-eyes.

"Put that attitude away, Waffles, or you'll never get another treat again."

Great, now there is gonna be another standoff.

Ben put twenty bucks on Waffles in this sparring match.

He'd been on the other end of Waffles' judgmental looks too many times and already knew how this was going to end.

On second thought, maybe he should make that forty bucks instead?

A smug expression appeared on Waffles' face as his eyes moved to Jimmy who already had his hand in the treat jar.

Immediately, Holly spun toward her son. "Don't you dare, mister."

Jimmy ignored her with a shrug as he quickly tossed each dog a treat before giving a small cat treat to Twitch. When he looked back at his mom, the corners of his mouth turned into a smile. "What? They all did a trick. You always say we should reward good behavior."

This kid is good! It was like he was made for our family. Who knew messing with Holly would end up being a family tradition? I can't wait to tell Henry about this.

Holly's brows shot to the ceiling in shock at Jimmy's audacity. "And you think *this* is good behavior?" She waved her hands through the air pointing at Waffles.

A playful smile appeared on Jimmy's face as he answered her, "They distracted you enough to put down the spatula, didn't they? I think that deserves two treats." With that, Jimmy tossed them all another one.

"That's my son!" Ben held out his hand to Jimmy who cheerfully high-fived him.

"I'm gonna remember this."

"I'm sure you will." Ben strolled over to his wife, gently moving Helen out of the way before kissing the top of Holly's head.

"If you weren't holding Peanut, I'd stomp on your foot again." Holly sent him another dirty look.

"Good thing I'm holding her then, huh?"

"You just wait. I'm gonna get you."

"Mom, violence is bad. You shouldn't threaten people.

We've talked about this before. Unless it's Grandpa Henry, he said *he's* allowed to threaten anyone."

Holly crossed her arms over her chest as she watched him. "Did he now?"

"Yeah. He said since he's the oldest he's allowed to do whatever he wants. Just like Mrs. Mildred."

"Sounds about right." Ben snorted before grabbing the bottle from Holly's hand.

"Mom, you really shouldn't threaten people. It's not nice."

Holly's eyes snapped to Ben as she sent him a death glare.

"Don't look at me like that, the kid's right. Threatening people is bad." Ben held back his laugh. There was nothing better than getting schooled by a child. Especially, when it was Jimmy schooling Holly and not him. Lord knows that'd happened too many times for him to count.

The kid was smart.

Just as Holly's eye began to twitch again, Jimmy barked out a laugh. "Geez, Mom you sure are fun to mess with. Now, I know why Dad likes to call Officer Jones up every once in a while."

Holly's reply was a flat smile as her eyes hardened on her husband. "You really need to stop doing that."

"At this point, my goal is to actually have him arrest you." Ben winked which made Holly's jaw firm in irritation. "I'm glad I'm here for your entertainment."

"Me too." Jimmy sent her a toothy smile.

"I second that," Ben's voice dropped an octave as he eyed her up and down.

However, the moment Holly opened her mouth to reply, his highness barked which caused her to snap her attention to her dog. "You better not be agreeing with them too, Waffles."

The Corgi barked again before turning to Ripley who replied with her own bark.

Holly threw her hands in the air. "You've got to be kidding me."

Okay, time to step in. She's seconds from really losing it.

Ben grabbed Holly's hand dragging her toward him and the baby. Quickly he gave her a chaste kiss on the lips. "We're only messing with you, Grace."

"Yeah, Mom. We love you." Jimmy ran to them giving them both a hug.

"I don't believe you," Holly remarked, as she relaxed in Ben's arms for a split second.

"That's 'cause you keep tryin' to cook." Jimmy laughed as he jumped back giving Holly a playful smile.

"Oh, for the love of all things," Holly groaned, rolling her eyes.

"Come on, guys, let's go before Mom's head explodes." Jimmy ran out of the kitchen laughing as an all too eager pack of animals scurried after him.

Once they were out of the room, Holly turned to her husband. "You taught him how to gang up on me." Holly angrily snapped her arms over her chest staring him down.

"Nah, wasn't me." He shook his head. "That was all Lord Waffles." The corners of Ben's mouth turned up as he pushed their daughter higher onto his shoulder.

"Lord Waffles doesn't call Officer Jones."

"He would if he could."

Holly gaped at Ben for a few moments before completely giving up. As she flicked her eyes to the ceiling, a heavy sigh escaped her. "You're probably right. All of you are jerks and he's the ringleader."

"That he is, now come here and let me kiss you."

"No." She took a step away from him. However, the moment Holly tripped over thin air, she caught herself on the counter shooting him another death glare. "Don't you say a word."

Ben let out a laugh as he winked her way. "Grace why would I say anything about you tripping over nothing?"

"Don't you wink at me. It's your fault I tripped anyway."

"That so?"

"Yeah."

Ben quickly advanced on Holly, making sure to keep Peanut softly at his side. "How's it my fault you tripped?"

"It's always your fault. One moment I'm standing and the next I'm on the floor."

"I wasn't even home the last time that happened."

"Yeah, but Jimmy told you about it so that makes it your fault."

"Sure, whatever, it can be my fault you stumble around like a newborn giraffe attempting to walk for the first time." He leaned in trying to kiss her but Holly darted away from his advance.

"Hey!"

Ben's brows arched. "Am I wrong?"

"No, but you don't need to compare me to a baby giraffe. I've got more grace than that."

Ben nodded. "Okay, sure, you do." After taking another step in her direction, he had Holly in his arms. "Love you, baby."

Even though she protested, instantly Holly melted into his embrace before kissing the top of Helen's head. "Love you both, even though you're a jerk. You too, Peanut. I'll remember this when you're older."

A small chuckle escaped Ben before he pulled Holly in tighter. He knew without a doubt he loved this woman more than anything in the world. As he stood there with her and Peanut in his arms, and knowing Jimmy and their fur babies were playing somewhere in the house, life couldn't get any better.

Ben sighed closing his eyes for a brief moment. When he opened them, that's when he saw it. As he looked over Holly's shoulder, he spotted the scorch marks on the wall, causing a ridiculously wide smile to appear on his face.

The holidays were sure as hell gonna be fun this year.

"You know, Grace, I was thinking maybe for Christmas dinner you could work your magic and make the other wall match? It sure would be a show for everyone invited. I know John's already placing bets on what you'll set on fire."

Holly jerked back cocking her brow at him. "What?"

When Ben jerked his head toward the burn marks, a deep growl escaped Holly as she narrowed her eyes at him. "You and John can kiss my ass." She plucked Helen from his arms and stormed out of the room leaving a laughing Ben behind.

Yep, the holidays were going to be a blast.

Chapter Two

"Oh boy, who twisted your panties in a bunch?" Mildred asked, casually strolling into the library early Saturday afternoon.

Holly's face snapped up before glaring at the old woman in disbelief. *Why is she here? Isn't today her day off?* Holly's eyes went to the ceiling. *Can I not catch a break, Universe?*

"Whoo-wee must've been bad. Your eye's already twitching. Who was it? No, no, wait let me guess. This could be fun." The glee on Mildred's face made Holly want to throw something at her head.

Mildred plopped her hip onto the desk tapping her chin with her finger. "My first instinct is to go with Ben, but with man meat like he's got, you couldn't stay mad at him long enough to still be mad here. Besides if it was him, he'd probably pound your lady bits so hard you'd forget why you were mad in the first place." Mildred winked as she pulled out the pad of paper she kept with her.

"Really?" Holly's brows arched at the old coot.

"Shh, I'm thinking. Now, I don't believe it'd be Jimmy. That boy is sweeter than apple pie. Then there's my little munchkin of course, but what could she do to make you look like that?" Mildred waved her finger up and down at Holly's scrunched face. "Nothing. That little girl is only an angel." Mildred scribbled on her paper. "That leaves Waffles, Ripley, Twitch, and your dad. You know what, I'm going with Waffles. He probably stole a pair of your ripped panties that Ben so devilishly tore from your body the night before. I bet Waffles, the sly dog that he is, dropped them in the middle of the living room and everyone saw them. So now you're embarrassed." Mildred looked at her watch. "Hot damn, I'm good. I got to the bottom of this in less than five minutes. I should get an award."

Holly stared at her in awe. "Where do you come up with this stuff?"

"Don't be jealous I'm a mastermind. When the detective Mildred hat goes on nothing can stump me."

"Well, you're gonna need to go back to the true-crime section and read up, 'cause you're wrong." Holly crossed her arms over her chest as she sat back in her seat. "For your information, it was all of them."

Mildred's eyes shot open as her hand went over her chest. "No! Say it ain't so? Even my little munchkin?"

"Yes. Even your little munchkin." Holly rolled her eyes.

Mildred sat on the desk for a few moments as she thought it over before shaking her head. "Nope. My detective skills are telling me there is only one answer here."

Holly cocked her brow. Whatever the old woman had come up with would probably annoy her but she couldn't stop her next words as the sarcasm poured out of her, "Oh yeah, please enlighten me."

"Yep," Mildred popped the 'p'. "My conclusion is... it was your fault."

"How is it *my* fault? And why is everyone picking on me today?" A pout emerged on Holly's face as her brows pulled together. *Stupid family. Stupid Mildred. Stupid Waffles.*

"You're an easy target. What do you expect? Now, tell me what'd ya do that had even my little munchkin after you."

Holly's expression pinched together. "I don't know what the big deal is. I was just trying to do something nice for my family... That's it. It's not like I was going to burn down the house or anything. I was just gonna make some waffles for everyone. Is that a crime?"

Mildred snapped back in terror. "You were gonna cook?!"

"I *am* allowed to cook. I'm a grown-ass adult after all."

"No, you're not!"

"Am too. I'm married and have two kids. I *am* an adult." *Take that!*

"Sure, whatever, you're an adult, that's questionable but you are *not* allowed to cook." Mildred shuddered in horror as a new wave of disgust washed across her face. "I don't know why you'd even try to...Wait a second, now I get it." Mildred slapped her knee. "You wanted to see that hunky fireman again. *Now,* I understand it. He's the one that's come out to your house a couple of times when you cooked. Remember the chicken tenders? Whoo-wee, he sure is a fine piece of meat. I knew you wouldn't be stupid enough to actually cook." Mildred wiped her brow.

A deep growl came from Holly's throat as Mildred patted herself on the back. "I swear to God, Mildred, I will murder you."

"I don't blame you at all. That man sure is hot stuff. No wonder why he became a fireman." Mildred fanned herself.

"His cat is also one of my husband's patients, so can you stop? This has nothing to do with the fire department. Plus, that *hunky* firefighter told us the next time he needed to respond to the house he was taking our stove with him. So, no. And while we're at it, can you stop bringing that back up? Every time Hank or his wife brings Dog into the clinic, they *remind* me not to turn on the stove."

"That's right, you told me he's the one with the giant cat named Dog."

"Yes, that's the one. I really need to remember you never forget anything I tell you." Holly shook her head.

"He is pretty fine. Remember when I caught him and his wife in the back of the library?" Mildred got a faraway look in her eyes. "You know what, I think I should call the fire station and tell them Holly Richman's trying to cook her lunch in the break room. You and I both know he'll be the first one here."

As Mildred reached for the phone Holly snatched it from her. "You better not! I swear to all things I will murder you and no one will ever find your body."

"Oh, yeah, yeah, let's go with that one. That way Officer Jones can come by instead. He is f-i-n-e. I'm only seeing this as a win-win for me."

Holly threw her hands in the air. Today was not her day. "Why are you here anyway? It's a Saturday. You're normally off."

"My knitting club is getting together in a few hours and I needed some good material."

"So, you came here 'cause you knew I was working?"

"Duh, who else do I get the best stories from? My gal-pals live for your antics. You're their highlight of the week."

"Great, not only does my own family troll me, so does you and your stupid knitting club." Holly went back to searching the internet trying her best to ignore the crazed woman sitting on top of the desk.

"Let me get this straight, your family was making fun of you for cooking, and now you're here at work annoyed at them?"

Holly rolled her eyes. "A little. I'm not really annoyed, but I'm going to get them back for it. Especially, Ben."

"Really, how so?"

Holly turned the computer around to face Mildred. On the screen was a horde of holiday elf costumes. They were in all different sizes, colors, and shapes. They had everything from pointy ears all the way down to green pointy toe shoes with bells on them. Holly's smile widened as she thought of everyone dressed up. They'd probably grumble about it, but dang they would be adorable!

"I don't get it."

"Ugh." Holly's eyes flicked upwards. "Of course, you don't. I'm gonna make everyone dress the same for our holiday Christmas card."

"And that's a punishment?" Mildred cocked her brow.

"It will be when they realize they have to wear the pointy shoes and ears! That's what they get for making fun of me. Oh, and check this out..." Holly clicked through the site with the mouse. "They have the same costume for pets. I can get one for each of the dogs *and* Twitch. We're all gonna be Santa's little helpers' whether they like it or not." *And, I'll be damned if Waffles tries to fight me for putting clothes on him again.*

"And what did Ben have to say about it?"

"He doesn't know yet. And he isn't gonna say anything. This *is* happening. It's our first Christmas together as a whole family and this is what we're doing. And, so help me if any one of them tries to argue, I will bake them cookies and force them to eat 'em."

"You wouldn't?" Mildred's face held a repulsion Holly hadn't seen in a while.

"Try me."

Mildred held up her hands in surrender. "You sure are snarky. Christmas is only a few weeks away. Aren't you supposed to be all jolly and stuff? Did someone pee in your food this mornin'?" Mildred smirked. "Well, at least you didn't cook it."

Holly narrowed her eyes as her lips thinned. "I *am* jolly."

"If you call that jolly, then I'm Mother Teresa."

"*I am jolly*. Can't you see it on my face?" Holly pointed at herself. "See, ho, ho, ho, and all that shit."

"Sure, you're super jolly and festive right now. I see the holidays coming out of your ears." Mildred rolled her eyes.

"I am damn it. It's Jimmy's first Christmas with us and Helen is here now. I'm gonna make this the most perfect Christmas anyone has ever seen and I will kill anyone that ruins this for me. You hear me?"

"Hold your horses there, tiger."

"No. I need this to be good for everyone. Jimmy deserves the world and so does Helen. Poor Jimmy has been through enough and I never want him to feel the way he did ever again. Not to mention, this is Peanut's *first* Christmas. So, it *has* to be special for both of them. I won't accept anything else."

"It will be. Relax. You're stressing yourself out when really you need to be enjoying the season. Instead, you're here hate buying stupid elf costumes for some Christmas card you won't get out in time."

Holly's mouth dropped at Mildred's statement. "How could you?"

"You know I'm right, and good luck getting Henry in one of those things." She pointed at the screen.

"My dad will stuff his butt into a costume or he'll have to suffer my wrath."

"Okay there, killer. Got it. Just make sure I'm around or at least record it for me. I don't want to miss that." Mildred softened as she looked at Holly, sighing. "You're trying to make this Christmas the best holiday you can and you're putting too much pressure on yourself. You're gonna find out it's all too much and then you'll end up blowing up your kitchen...." Mildred nodded but then stopped. "Actually, that'll be good material. I'm here for it. Your meltdowns give me and my gal-pals endless entertainment. Carry on."

"You know what, you're no longer invited to Christmas Dinner."

Holly: one.

Mildred: zero.

"I'm still gonna show up."

She would too. "I'll have Waffles guard the door, so you can't come in."

"Like he's gonna leave the kitchen?" Mildred burst out into a deep laugh. "Man, you crack me up. My knitting club is going to eat this up tonight."

"You're knitting group can kiss my ass. This will be perfect and I will murder all of you to get it that way. Don't make me tell you again."

"So much violence. I think I'm gonna have to call Benny boy and tell him you need a good workout to deal with your aggression." She winked. "I'm sure he can *pound* some sense into you."

"Stop talking about my husband pounding me."

"Hey, it's not my fault you need to get laid."

"For your information, I got laid last night!"

Mildred quickly grabbed her pen and paper and eyed Holly. "Oh, really, tell me all about it."

"You're disgusting."

"No, I'm amazing and you're jealous."

"Why yes, of course, that's the answer. I'm jealous of a horny, million-year-old lady who talks too much."

"So, you admit you're jealous of me then? It's about time really. Now, we can move on from this and get to the good stuff. Like what happened last night."

"Mildred!" Holly threw a pencil at her head, but the crazy old bat caught it with ease.

"Thanks, my pen was running out of ink. I don't know what I'm gonna do with you, missy." Mildred shook her head as she shoved her pad back into her pocket.

"Put me out of my misery."

"Nah, then my knitting club would be boring." Mildred popped herself off the desk before turning back to Holly. "I'm glad we had this little chat. You've given me tons of stuff. Not to mention, you helped me hone one of my skills. I *knew* it was your fault. Told you I was a detective." Mildred sent her a smug look before she sashayed herself through the library headed toward the true-crime section.

"That's it, I'm getting you and your husband elf costumes too, and I'm gonna make you wear them!"

Mildred looked over her shoulder at Holly. "Oooh, sounds like fun. Maybe you should order me two pairs. I bet a little role play will be in order and I have no idea the state the first one will end up in once hubby gets his hands on me."

Holly physically gagged as she shuddered in disgust. "Mildred! There are people in here."

The old woman scanned the room and shrugged. "Maybe it'll give them some inspiration? The holidays are coming up, you know. Everyone can use a little spice in their life. Maybe that could be their gift to each other." Mildred glanced to the right where the true-crime section was and then to her left where the romance books were. "On second thought, I think I'm going to get some inspiration myself." With that, Mildred beelined it straight toward the romance section with an extra pep in her step.

Holly slammed her head on the desk. "Kill me now."

Chapter Three

"WHY AM *I* BEING PUNISHED?" John grumbled as he kicked a plastic Christmas ornament across the floor. "I didn't piss off your wife. *You* did."

Ben rolled his eyes at his best friend as he tossed John a box of holiday decorations. "You piss her off all the time. Consider these brownie points in advance."

"True, but I still don't understand why *I* need to help you get decorations up. This isn't my house."

"You're coming for Christmas dinner, aren't you?"

"Depends who's cooking." John narrowed his eyes on Ben.

John was going to give Ben a migraine and he'd only been there an hour. "Me. Emma's bringing a few sides, and Mildred dessert."

At the mention of Emma's name, John's whole face lit. "Yeah, I'll be here."

Ben threw him another box that was marked *living room decorations*. "You talk too much and besides, didn't I promise you food?"

"The word food is what got me over here." John caught the box.

"I know."

"Speaking of which, where the hell is my food?" John tapped his stomach after putting the box at his feet. "I'm hungry."

"You're always hungry." Ben opened a box taking out two decorative snowmen Holly liked placed at their front door. "I need your help to get everything done by the time Holly gets back from the library."

"Again, just cause you're in the dog house doesn't mean I need to be."

"Shut up and start unpacking that box."

John muttered something under his breath as he did what he was told. "I don't know why I put up with you. And where the hell is my food?"

"Here you go, Uncle John," Jimmy announced, walking out of the kitchen with a bag of potato chips in his hand.

Promptly, John snatched them from the boy. "At least someone loves me." With that, John opened the bag and put the corner to his lips as he dumped the contents into his mouth. When he finished he looked back at Jimmy. "Thanks, kid." John glanced at Ben with a smug expression on his face. "I'm his favorite."

Instantly, Jimmy grabbed the empty bag from John as he narrowed his eyes. "Maybe now you'll stop talking. My sister is taking a nap."

John's hand shot to his chest. "Right through the heart, kid. I'm supposed to be your favorite."

Jimmy shrugged as a goofy smile emerged on his face. "I brought you food, didn't I?"

John snapped his attention to Ben with his brow cocked. "You sure he didn't come from you? 'Cause he acts exactly like you."

Ben laughed as Jimmy winked at him. He wondered that same question at times.

"That's 'cause I want to be just like my dad when I grow up."

Ben's heart stopped. He'd never get tired of hearing that. Since the moment they met at the dog park, Jimmy had always said the same thing. Ben's face softened as he watched his son. "I'll teach you everything you'll ever need to know."

"You sure about that?" John waved his hand up and down pointing at himself. "Why not be a dentist like your favorite uncle?"

"Eww. I don't want to be a dentist."

At the horror on Jimmy's face, John jumped back as his hand went to his chest like he'd been shot again. "Eww. Really, kid? Are you really gonna say eww? If it wasn't for my expertise your mother would have half of her tooth gone. I'm a hero." John puffed out his chest.

"Mom would've looked pretty even with a chipped tooth."

Ben's eyes sparkled as the two bickered. "She did look adorable with it."

"Whatever. I'm a hero." John tossed a Santa hat at Ben's head.

"You touch people's mouths all the time. That's kinda gross." Jimmy shuddered.

"Yeah, and your Dad has to examine animal poop. Whose job's grosser now?" John straightened his shoulders clearly happy he thought he'd won.

However, both Ben and Jimmy eyed each other before shifting back at John. "You," they replied at the same time.

"I get zero respect here," John scoffed before turning back to the box of decorations. "Being a dentist isn't gross. The mouth fascinates me."

"Why?" Jimmy asked, cocking his head to the side as he pondered it. "Why would the mouth fascinate you?"

A huge smile spread across John's face. "I'll tell you when you're older."

Ben laughed before grabbing a piece of garland from one of the boxes. He knew exactly what was coming next.

Jimmy only waited about five more seconds. "I'm older now, can you tell me?"

John shot his eyes to Ben before looking back at Jimmy at a loss for what to say.

"I'm even older now. Every second that goes by I'm older. So, which older is it? Right now older or in a minute older? I'm wasting away here as I keep getting older."

"Ben, a little help here?"

"He's right you know. My boy's a smart one."

"He didn't get that from you." John narrowed his eyes before turning back to Jimmy. "Once you're *way* older you'll realize just how fun mouths can be."

"And that's enough of that!" Ben jumped to his feet. "Jimmy, will you help me put the garland on the mantel? Mom will be super happy to see it all done when she gets home."

"Sure!" Jimmy shouted forgetting about their conversation as he ran to the garland. As Ben caught John's eye, he sent him a death glare.

"What? I was talking about kissing."

"Sure, you were." Ben tossed him back the Santa hat. "Put this on so you can look the part."

"You sure are demanding." John flung the hat down the hall. "I have no idea why Holly puts up with you."

The corner of Ben's lips quirked up. "She likes my mouth."

John gagged. "And you say *I'm* bad."

"You *are* bad." As Ben held up the right side of the garland to the mantle, Waffles waddled into the living room with the discarded Santa hat in his mouth. "That's the spirit, Waffles. Show Uncle John how much of a humbug he is."

The Corgi plopped onto his belly as he nibbled on his newfound treasure, causing John to raise his brow at the dog. "How is that the spirit? He's chewing on it."

Jimmy ran to the box in the corner labeled *Holiday Dog*

Clothes. "No, he's not. He's asking for someone to put it on him." Jimmy rifled through the box until he found the dog Santa hat with the holes for ears and strap to go under his chin.

Once Jimmy grabbed the hat he ran back to Waffles. Before anything could happen, Ben tried to stop him. "I don't think that's a good idea, Kiddo. Last year when your mom tried to put that hat on him, he almost killed her. He's feisty when it comes to clothes now."

"I know what Waffles wants, Dad." Jimmy carefully took the hat and placed it on the dog's head before securing the elastic under his chin. "There, see? Look how cute he is! Mom's gonna love it."

Ben stood there in awe as Waffles let Jimmy maneuver his ears so they would fit perfectly in the holes. However, the moment Waffles' eyes caught Ben's, he saw the annoyance. "Don't look at me that way. I told him you don't like to be dressed up anymore."

Waffles sent Ben a glare before he barked. Then to prove Ben wrong he turned back to Jimmy jumping into his lap to lick his face. "Seems like he likes it just fine to me, Dad."

That bastard. Ben stared at the betraying dog. *Wait until Holly hears about this. Actually, never mind. I'll never hear the end of it. This will have to be our little secret.*

A deep laugh came from John as he watched the two playing on the floor. "Seems like Waffles only listens to one person in this house."

Waffles looked at John huffing before going back to Jimmy.

"And it sure as hell ain't you." Ben shook his head with a chuckle.

"Whatever."

Ben decided to ignore John as his eyes scanned around the room at all the decorations scattered everywhere. It was like the North Pole had thrown up. He quickly glanced down at his watch. They still had a lot more to do before Holly got home. He thought back, he couldn't remember if today was a half-day for her or a whole day. He really needed to get a move on if he planned on having everything done in time. "You two start putting up the tree. I'm gonna grab the last few boxes from the attic."

"Okay!" Jimmy sprinted to the box with the tree in it, dropping his end of the garland on the floor. "Come on, Uncle John. Let's put up the tree!" The excitement from Jimmy was almost more than Ben could take. "This is going to be the best Christmas ever. I can already feel it."

Ben's heart flipped. *I'll do everything I can to make sure of that, kiddo.*

"Yeah, yeah." John dropped a stuffed Santa on the floor which Waffles gladly ran over to and started chewing on. "The sooner we get this done. The sooner we get to eat."

"You just ate a whole bag of chips."

"And you think that's gonna last me?"

Jimmy studied him for a moment, as he cocked his head to the side. "No."

"Exactly."

Ben chuckled as he watched the two of them. At least it was entertaining. As Ben looked around the room again, he saw just how much they still needed to do.

He knew Holly really wanted to make this Christmas special for everyone, he got it. He wanted to as well. This was their first Christmas as a family, and he wanted it to be perfect for all of them just as much as she did.

He wanted these memories to last a lifetime.

A ridiculously wide smile spread across Ben's face. Although, Thanksgiving was a memory they'd never forget. From where Ben stood, he could see the tail end of the scorch marks on the wall. "You two get the tree started. I'll be right back with the rest of the stuff."

"Sure thing, boss." John patted his stomach. "But first, it's time for a snack. Come on, Jimmy, if we've gotta keep working we need food."

"You just ate." Jimmy ignored him as he fussed with the box that had the tree in it.

"Not enough."

Ben rolled his eyes as he made his way down the hall. Leave it to John to always make things difficult.

As Ben walked past the last door, he did a quick peek into the nursery to see Peanut still fast asleep in her crib with Ripley and Twitch curled up on the floor next to it.

That kid can sleep through anything, he chuckled to himself. He didn't know where she got it from, but he was thankful for it. Especially, when John was in the house.

As quietly as he could, Ben shut the door so that it was only a quarter of the way open. He then headed to the hatch for the attic a little farther down the hall.

The moment he got the ladder down, though, he saw Twitch had migrated out of the nursery to see what he was up to. As his little head twitched the cat looked around before his eyes went back to Ben.

"Your guess is as good as mine."

Twitch's attention darted toward the kitchen as the distinct sound of a bag opening rang through the hall.

"You're Uncle John's here." Ben chuckled. "If you hurry you might get a scrap of food before he eats it all. Waffles is already in there."

Twitch looked at him for one more second before he took off running toward the kitchen causing Ben to let out a laugh.

Never a dull moment.

Once Ben got into the attic, he crawled over to the last two boxes of decorations. As he walked carefully across the beams, he made a mental note to eventually put in a floor up there, so he wouldn't have to worry about stepping on the wrong part.

Lord knows the disaster that would happen if Holly ever got a wild hair across her ass and decided to go into the attic.

There would be no question about it.

That *would* be a disaster.

As Ben grabbed the two boxes, stacking one on top of the other he took a step back toward the hatch only for his heart to stop.

At that exact moment, he heard the distinct sound of their front door slamming open, and one angry Holly yelling, *"What the hell is going on here?"* echo through the house.

Unfortunately for Ben, the jolt somehow made him lose his footing as he slipped.

Before he knew it, Ben was falling through the ceiling.

Chapter Four

HOLLY THANKED the Universe today was only a half-day at the library. Especially after Mildred showed up. She wanted nothing more than to go home and relax. Holly wasn't really angry anymore; she was just stressed.

She really did want everything to be perfect. She knew she needed to take a step back and breathe. But it was hard.

A mischievous smile spread across her face as she walked up the steps of her home. She'd be lying if she said she wasn't excited to show all the traitors what outfit they'd be wearing for their Christmas card.

Her smile grew wider as she thought about it.

Holly even paid for expedited shipping so everything would arrive on Monday.

And no one was gonna argue with her about it. Everyone was going to dress up and be happy or they'd have her to deal with.

Her eyes narrowed.

That went for Waffles too. Ripley didn't mind wearing clothes but every time Holly tried to dress Waffles, he'd lose his mind.

Clearly, the jerk now thought clothes were beneath him.

Not this year, though.

That asshole was gonna wear his elf costume whether he liked it or not!

As Holly opened the door her eyes nearly popped out of her skull as the wind was almost knocked out of her. It was like a bomb had gone off in her living room.

A Christmas bomb. One that left nothing but destruction and sparkles in its wake.

There were ornaments all over the floor. One of which was being batted around by Twitch. Waffles was chewing on the Santa plush doll Holly had bought for Ben last year. There were boxes knocked on their sides with lights, garland, and decorations spilling out. You name it, it was happening.

Then to top it off, their Christmas tree was in pieces scattered all over the room. "What the hell is going on in here?"

Before Holly could take another step into the living room though, a loud crash rang throughout the room.

Then there was Ben.

Holy crap on a freaking cracker!

Her husband was now in their living room surrounded by pieces of their ceiling and insulation. Thank all the things he miraculously ended up somehow on their couch.

As Holly raced over to her husband to make sure he was okay, John stormed out of the kitchen a sandwich in his hand. "Holy shit."

Holly ignored John as she skidded to her knees next to Ben. "Are you okay? Please tell me you're okay?"

"I'm fine," he answered, dazed as he blinked a few times.

"Are you sure?" Holly's heart raced as she checked all around and other than the colossal mess that was now everywhere, Ben seemed to be okay. He was extremely lucky he ended up where he did. Oh my God, she was going to have a heart attack. This was it.

This was her moment.

Might as well say goodbye now.

"Dude, you fell through your ceiling." John took another bite of his food as he laughed.

"Did I?" Holly watched as Ben's eyes scanned around the room before glancing up to the giant hole that now resided in their living room.

"Yes, you did!" Holly's heart officially stopped. "What the hell, Ben?"

"Everything is fine." He sat up slowly brushing off the insulation from his body.

"Everything is fine?" Holly's eyes widened at his nonchalant attitude. "*Everything is fine?*"

"Yeah," he replied, his eyes squinting at their ceiling.

Something inside of Holly snapped. "Everything is *not* fine! Ben, you just fell through the ceiling."

Ben did a once-over of his body again. "I really am okay. I'm not hurt at all and I didn't break anything." He patted his ribs to double-check. "Whoa."

"You're lucky 'cause you're about too." Holly punched him in the arm. "Don't ever scare me like that again!"

"Scare you?" He cocked his brow. "I'm the one that fell, not you."

Holly ignored him as she continued, "And yet you wanted to wrap *me* in bubble wrap! I should wrap *you* in bubble wrap! I've never fallen through a ceiling before. Who needs to be accident proofed now?" Holly looked up once again. "Holy crap, look at that hole!"

Ben groaned as he rolled his eyes. "You've never fallen through the ceiling 'cause I don't allow you up there."

John burst out laughing in that can't control it double over in pain kind of laugh. "Holy shit, dude, you fell through the ceiling. This is the best day of my life. I take it back. I don't know why I was complaining about being here. I would've missed this if I wasn't." John laughed harder gasping for air.

As John continued his roaring, Jimmy slowly walked over

to the couch his eyes wide as tears threatened to fall from them. "Dad, are you okay?"

Still a little shaken, Ben reached for their son. "Yeah, I'm okay, Jimmy. Thankfully, I landed on the couch."

Jimmy looked him over before letting out a small breath. "Do we need to take you to the hospital, like we have to take Mom sometimes?"

Holly gasped as she frowned at the little jerk who was sporting a shit-eating grin on his face. "It's been months since I've been to the ER."

Jimmy shifted toward Holly. "That's 'cause Dad can patch you up at the clinic."

Holly's mouth fell open. *Oh my God, how did this get turned back onto me again? I didn't just fall through the freaking ceiling!*

"This is priceless." John laughed harder. "Only thing that'd make it better, is if I had popcorn."

Holly snapped her attention to John. "Shut your pie hole or I'll shut it for you." Might as well call Officer Jones 'cause Holly was going to lose it.

A goofy smile appeared on John's face as his brows shot up. "With pie?"

Holly growled deep in her throat. "If by pie, you mean my fist, then yes."

Just as Holly was about to lose it, Ben took her in his arms. "He's not worth it."

"Am too," John announced.

They both ignored him as Ben continued to hold Holly in his arms. The fact he was okay made her relax but at the same time she wanted to scream.

Holy shit!

Her adrenaline hadn't been this high since Jimmy disappeared at the hospital while she was giving birth to Helen.

Holy fucking shit.

Who falls through the ceiling? That shit only happens in the movies... Then she thought about it. Actually, that *would* happen to them.

Holly took another deep breath as she pulled back from Ben's arms giving him another once-over. He really did look okay.

Thank the Universe.

Then Holly's eyes looked around the room again, mess wasn't even close to what it really was. Over in the corner, she saw Twitch climbing through one of the holiday boxes. She shifted back to Ben. "Why were you putting up the decorations? I thought we were going to do that tomorrow as a *family*."

Maybe it was the adrenaline of watching her husband fall through their ceiling, but somehow, a pang of hurt rang through her. Holly wanted to put up the decorations together. To make a memory that would last a lifetime. And to make sure it was perfect, of course.

"We were trying to surprise you, Mom."

"This sure is a surprise all right." Holly sighed, pulling Jimmy into her arms kissing him on the head. He might be a traitor but she loved him. Subconsciously, her eyes glanced at the hole again. *I can't believe this is happening.*

"Dad, why did ya have to fall through the ceiling?"

"It wasn't my plan."

Jimmy looked at the hole and then back to him. "That's a big hole."

"That's what she said." John burst into another round of hysterics as he laughed at his own joke.

"John!" Holly jerked her eyes to him.

"What?"

Holly shook her head before she turned back at her husband. "It's okay. No one is hurt." Out of nowhere, Holly couldn't help the smirk that appeared on her face as the thought jumped through her head. "Are you sure you're okay, *Grace?*"

"Oh, no you don't. The only Grace in this relationship is *you.*" Ben's brows shot up as he stared at her.

"And yet, I've never fallen through the ceiling."

"'Cause you're not allowed up there, I just told you that! Besides, I wasn't the one who tried to burn down the house this morning."

Holly's jaw dropped as her eyes narrowed on her husband. "I hope the size I ordered is too small."

Ben cocked his head to the side as he stared at her. "What?"

"Mom, Dad," John sarcastically remarked, interrupting them. "This is all fun and games, but is someone gonna feed us?" He pointed at Jimmy. "He's a growing boy and needs all the food he can get."

Jimmy darted his head to John. "You just ate."

"Okay, fine. *I'm* a growing boy." He patted his stomach again.

Holly threw her hands in the air as she jumped to her feet. "You know what? Everything is fine. It's fine. It's all fine." Holly did her best to avoid the land mines on the floor as she walked to the nursery leaving the mess behind her. When she opened the door, she saw a still sleeping Helen in her crib with Ripley standing guard ready to do whatever she needed to in order to protect the baby.

Go figure. That kid would sleep through an earthquake.

"At least you aren't a pain in my ass." Gently Holly woke Peanut after grabbing the baby bag and made her way back into the living room.

Ben stood by the fireplace still brushing the insulation off himself as John continued to laugh his ass off. How in the hell had her day ended up here? She would have looked to the ceiling to curse the Universe but then that would involve her seeing the hole again.

Instead, Holly scanned the room and as she did, she once again saw Waffles chewing on the plush Santa doll.

Wait a second... This time she got a better look at her dog.

Holy shit, Waffles had *the* Santa hat on! Holly's eyes widened. "Is he wearing the hat I got him? Who got him to agree to that?"

"I did," Jimmy answered with a toothy grin on his face. "He asked me to put it on him."

Holly's eyes narrowed at the dog. "He asked you?"

Then to no one's surprise, Waffles sent Holly the biggest side-eye that she'd ever seen.

"Yeah, he asked me to."

Holly's eyes narrowed further on her dog as she recalled the pain in the ass he was last year as she tried to put that same hat on him. "And he just *let* you do it? There were no arguments?"

"None. He wanted it. See, look how cute he is. I'm gonna go through the box again and find Ripley's so they can match."

"You do that," she answered, not taking her eyes off of her betraying dog. "You are going on Santa's naughty list."

"No, you're not!" Jimmy hollered. "Don't listen to her, Waffles. You're on the good list."

A deep growl escaped Holly as her jerk of a dog turned his nose up at her.

That's it.

A person can only take so much in one day.

"You know what, I'm going to Emma's." Holly hiked the baby bag higher on her shoulder making sure to keep Helen securely in her arms. "And when I get back this better be fixed." She pointed at John. "You go get my dad so he can supervise."

"Me?" John cocked his brow at her. "What the hell? I didn't fall through the ceiling. Don't spit fire at me."

Holly gave him a look that dared him to cross her. "Do it."

John folded his arms over his chest. "Only if you tell Emma I said hi."

"I'll tell her you tried to kill my husband by pushing him through the ceiling."

"That works." John shrugged as he winked at her.

That only served to annoy Holly more. "Go get my dad and have all this cleaned up by the time I get home."

"What is it with all you Richman's being so demanding? I don't know why I stick around."

"You love us," Jimmy chimed in. "Stop complaining and let's go get Grandpa!"

As Holly took another calming breath, Ben walked over to her before kissing her on the head and then doing the same to Peanut. "As you wish."

"Don't you go throwing my favorite movie quotes at me." Holly's left eye twitched.

Ben smirked once more as he kissed the top of her head one more time. "Love you, Grace. Don't worry, we'll have this all cleaned up and back to normal in no time."

"Back to normal?" she scoffed. "There is no such thing as normal in this house."

Holly did another once-over of Ben who seemed completely fine. So fine in fact, that Jimmy, John, and Ben all sported the same stupid happy expression on their faces.

Oh God, she lived in a circus.

Even though her heart still raced at a dangerous level, somehow, Holly relaxed seeing Ben wasn't in immediate danger. Maybe it was because Helen was still fast asleep in her arms. Who knew?

There was only one thing Holly knew for certain. She was getting her ass out of there and by the time she got back, there should *not* be a hole in the ceiling.

How was this her life?

"I promise, you'll never know what happened." Ben winked.

Holly eyed him one more time before a smirk appeared on her face. "Make sure of it, *Grace.*" With that, she walked out of the front door.

Chapter Five

"SEE, GOOD AS NEW." Henry puffed his chest the best he could as he stared at the ceiling where the hole once was.

"You didn't do anything," John grumbled, frowning at Holly's dad like he had two heads.

"What do you mean I didn't do anything? I made sure you numb-nuts didn't screw it up," Henry squared off with John.

Ben rolled his eyes as he rubbed his side. It was pretty sore. After all he did fall through a ceiling *and* patched it back up.

"And we finished putting up all the decorations. Well, most of them," Jimmy announced with a smile. "Mom's gonna be so happy. She's been kinda cranky."

"That's my Pumpkin," Henry answered. "She goes a little overboard at times. Last week when you all came over, she was going ten million miles an hour. I still don't know how she ended up on her butt in the middle of the kitchen."

Ben and Jimmy both spoke at the same time, "She tripped."

"Figured as much." Henry laughed as he sent them his lopsided grin. "Like I said, she's a little crazy at times."

Ben smiled at his father-in-law, a man he now considered like his own father. "At times? How about all the time. And right now, even though she's got a screw loose. We still love her."

"True."

Henry cautiously sat on the couch as Waffles took a running leap to sit with him. Poor guy didn't make it, though. Instead, he hit his chest and fell back onto the floor. Just as Waffles was about to sulk away, Jimmy ran over to him.

"Here ya go." Jimmy picked Waffles up putting him on the couch. Instantly, Waffles eagerly cuddled up to Henry asking for belly rubs, plopping onto his back with his tongue hanging out of the left side of his mouth.

Figures.

"I ain't got any food, Waffles. You're barking up the wrong tree."

At that, Waffles huffed before he jumped off the couch giving Henry an evil glare as he trudged away toward the kitchen. "That dog's a piece of work."

"That's the nicest he's been all day." Ben laughed at the side-eye Waffles was now giving Henry. "Thanks for helping, Dad."

"Anytime, son. It was good to get out of the house. It's lonely there sometimes." Henry shuffled in his seat as a puppy dog expression appeared on his face before looking at Jimmy. "All by my lonesome."

Ben knew what was coming next. He'd been around his father-in-law enough times to know exactly what he was hinting at.

"Lonely? You shouldn't be lonely, Grandpa. Maybe I can have a sleepover? We haven't had one of those in a really long time. It could be so much fun and then you wouldn't be so lonely." Jimmy looked at Ben. "Can I, Dad?"

"You come over here all the time, Henry. Not to mention, you talk to Holly or me every day." Ben sent Henry a look, which Henry promptly ignored. Henry then clapped his hands together in excitement eyeing Jimmy. "Why who would've thought of such a wonderful idea?"

"Me!" Jimmy jumped up and down.

"You are so smart. I think you take after me."

"Kid, you just got played," John remarked, rolling his eyes at Jimmy. "I thought I taught you better than that?"

Henry stared John down. "Not as played as you'll be when you find out you have to stop and buy us pizza on the way home."

John's face brightened at the words. "Joke's on you. I was planning on getting second dinner tonight when I dropped you off anyway."

"Yay, second dinner!" Jimmy bounced on his toes in excitement.

Oh God, Holly was going to kill him. "Just don't tell your mother."

"Speaking of Pumpkin. When is she coming home? I wanna see my little Peanut." Henry glanced at his watch. "It's not right for a grandpa to come all the way over here not to see his little grandbaby." Henry narrowed his eyes on Ben. "Took you long enough to give me both of them."

Ben didn't know whether the pain in his neck was from the fall or having to deal with John and Henry all day. "You got your grandbabies, didn't you?" Ben pulled out his phone. "Her text said any minute now. She left Emma's a little while ago."

"That Emma is a good one." A lopsided grin appeared on Henry's face.

"That she is," John mumbled.

As if on cue, the front door opened to reveal Holly and a smiling Peanut happy to be in her mother's arms.

"There they are!" Henry's whole face lit up.

Ben watched Holly's eyes jump to the ceiling before she acknowledged her dad. "Oh, whoa! Look, Peanut, it's like it never happened. Well, other than the smell of fresh paint."

"Nothing did happen. I told you we'd take care of it," Ben joked, walking over to his wife and baby. He quickly gave her a kiss on the lips before kissing their baby on the head.

"Only 'cause I was here to supervise. That idiot almost made another hole."

John snapped his eyes to Henry. "I thought we agreed not to talk about that."

"I didn't agree to shit."

Ben ignored the two children as he grabbed Holly's attention. "How was your day, Sweetheart?"

"It was good. I no longer want to strangle anyone if that's what you're asking. How are you feeling?" She studied his body up and down. "Are you hurting?"

Ben's eyes darkened. "If I say yes, will you kiss the spots I point to?"

"Told ya the mouth was awesome," John chimed in, turning to face Jimmy.

"What?"

"Nothing," John answered Holly before turning back to Jimmy with a wink.

Clearly deciding it was best to leave it alone for now, Ben watched as Holly focused wholeheartedly on her father. "Hey, Dad."

As Henry tried to get up, Holly stopped him. "No, it's okay I'll bring her to you." Holly moved over to her father before carefully placing Helen in his arms.

Henry ecstatic he held his grandchild in his lap, cooed at her. "There's my girl. I missed you today." Peanut's face brightened as she listened to her Grandpa speak.

Before anyone else could say anything, John spoke. "Yeah, yeah, hi Holly, how ya doing? Great. Glad you had fun and don't want to kill anyone anymore. How's Emma? Did she say anything about me? Did you talk about me? Did I come up at all?"

John talked so fast Ben's head spun.

"You sure did." Instead of elaborating, Holly glanced around the room. "Wow, it looks really good in here."

"Thanks! We worked really hard. As Uncle John and Dad fixed the ceiling, Grandpa Henry and I decorated. We left the Christmas ornaments for us to do together, though. Dad said we needed to do that as a family or you'd make him sleep on the couch."

"Aww, that was sweet of him and also correct." Holly kissed the top of Jimmy's head. "Thank you."

"Excuse me!" John interrupted.

"What?"

"What did you and Emma say about me? You can't just leave it at that. I need to know."

Holly got this mischievous spark in her eyes. "Oh, nothing. Or at least nothing to worry your little head about."

John's brows shot up. "What's that supposed to mean?"

Holly's smile went from ear-to-ear. "Exactly what I said."

"Really, after all I did today, you're just gonna leave me hanging like that? I thought I was your favorite."

"Nope." Holly shook her head. "Definitely not my favorite."

"Boy, if I were you I'd quit while you're ahead." Henry bounced Helen on his good knee.

As John realized he was going to lose this battle, he grumbled as he kicked a dog toy on the ground. Holly's eyes followed the toy as it landed at Waffles' feet. Who was staring at everyone in the room like they were the enemy. "Who pissed him off?"

"That would be me," Henry answered with a lopsided grin on his face. "He thought I had food and I didn't."

"That would do it." Holly eyed her Corgi. "Didn't we go over this already? No more treats. You're on a diet."

At the word diet, Waffles fell onto his back in a dramatic show as he whined.

"Nope, not gonna happen." Holly stood her ground.

Waffles grudgingly got up and huffed as he made his way down the hall, but not before swinging his head back at Holly with daggers in his eyes.

"Glad I don't have to deal with that tonight." Jimmy watched as the annoyed Corgi grumbled as he walked away.

"What do you mean you don't have to deal with that?" Holly turned back to Jimmy cocking her head. "Are you kicking him out of your room tonight?"

Jimmy's whole face lit. "Nope! I'm havin' a sleepover with Grandpa tonight and we're gonna get second dinner!"

"I thought we agreed you wouldn't tell her?" Ben groaned as he rolled his eyes. "I don't even know why we bother. No one can ever keep their mouth shut around here."

"That so?" Holly gave Ben a cross look.

"Yep, Uncle John is gonna take us to get more food before he drops us off at Grandpa's."

"Hmm." Holly stared John up and down before turning her glare back on Ben.

"Yeah, the old man played the kid and pretended to play me, but joke's on him. I'm always hungry."

"We know," everyone in the room said at the exact same time.

"Speaking of which, as much as I'd love to kiss up on my baby some more, it's time for us to head home. We got a fun night planned with movies and snacks!" Henry kissed the top of Helen's happy face one more time.

"Did you say snacks?" John's eyes widened at the word. "You know what, my plans have just changed. Jimmy, how would you feel if you're favorite uncle crashed your sleepover?"

"You just want the food," Jimmy answered, giving John the once-over.

"Yeah." John shrugged not denying it. "But we also get to watch movies together. I'll even let you watch the ones your mom and dad won't let you see."

Jimmy's face lit with excitement as he turned to Henry. "I know he's a pain, but can he come too? Maybe we can stay up *all* night and watch movies and then John can make us waffles in the morning!"

Waffles barked from the hall.

"You can't have any, Lord Waffles. You have to stay here and protect Peanut," Jimmy shouted back which caused a cry and another huff to come from Waffles.

Henry glanced at John who had a puppy dog expression on his face. "You make good waffles?"

"I dabble."

"Fine," Henry muttered. "You're buying the snacks, though."

"That's good with me. I hope you're ready to have a whole concession stand at your house. Let's go."

"Make sure you get dad sugar-free candies," Holly remarked, staring down John.

"Sugar-free?" Henry scoffed. "I might be old, but I don't need sugar-free, young lady."

"Don't worry," John stated, beaming at Holly before winking at Henry. "I'll get the sugar-free candy." John pointed at his eye. "Did you see what I did there? The wink's 'cause I'm lying. We're getting the good stuff."

Holly cocked her head at John in awe. "I know you're smart. You have to be smart. You got through school and are a damn good dentist but man I wonder about you sometimes."

"You wonder about me?" John cocked his brow. "Your husband know about that?"

Holly gagged as John turned to Ben. "How are you okay with your wife fantasizing about me? I mean, I know I'm the better looking one out of the two of us, but I'm surprised." John spun back to Holly. "I have to let you down easy. My heart belongs to someone else." John had the gall to give Holly a sad expression.

"I think I'm gonna vomit."

John shook his head. "I know it's got to be hard to stomach me letting you down. It breaks my heart too. You do have an amazing as—"

"That's enough of that." Ben carefully grabbed his daughter from his father-in-law. "Go get your stuff together, Kiddo. John can bring you home tomorrow morning."

As Jimmy took off out of the room, Ben snapped at John. "You wanna go? You talk about my wife's ass one more time and you'll regret it. Don't forget I'm skilled with a scalpel."

John rolled his eyes. "Like you'd even get close to me."

"Boys, can you stop?" Holly pleaded. "I don't want another baby shower incident again."

John's eyes darkened as he glared at his best friend. "I had more clothespins than you and you know it. You stole that crown from me."

"I did no such thing. I won fair and square."

"You're a cheater!"

Before Ben could retaliate, Jimmy was back in the living room with his bag. "I was gone for two seconds."

John puffed out his chest. "You're lucky your kid came back. He just saved you from getting your ass beat."

"Pretty sure Dad can take you." Jimmy quickly kissed Helen on the cheek. "Be good, Peanut. I'll be back tomorrow and we can put ornaments on the tree together. Mom really wants to do that."

Helen babbled her answer before a tiny smile appeared on her face.

Instantly, Ben's annoyance with John melted away as he looked at his children. Okay, not all of his annoyance. The next time Ben got the opportunity he was going to trip John.

Jimmy placed another kiss on Peanut's head before running over to Holly giving her a hug. "Love you, Mom! Dad already said it was okay. We'll be back early tomorrow morning. I promise. Then we can do the tree."

"Love you too, baby." Holly hugged her son before kissing the top of his head.

Henry carefully got up from the couch before walking over to Holly. "Love you, Pumpkin. We'll be back tomorrow morning to help with the tree. Try not to let your husband fall through any more ceilings while we're gone."

"I can't make any promises."

"Time's a wastin," John shouted as he grabbed his stuff before scratching Waffles on the head and then walking over to Ben giving Helen a quick kiss. "See ya tomorrow, little one. While I'm away, work on your mother for me, will ya? I need some details on Emma."

"Not gonna happen." Holly laughed.

As John ignored Holly, he darted his eyes to Ben. "You still owe me food."

"I bought you two meals today."

"And yet, I'm still hungry."

Ben rolled his eyes. Chaos, Ben lived in complete chaos one hundred percent of the time.

As Jimmy helped Henry out of the house John walked behind them pushing them along.

"Don't stay up too late!" Holly hollered after them.

"We won't!" John hollered back as he winked.

"We already know the wink means you're lying." Holly shook her head as her eyes flicked up.

John winked again.

"Oh, for Pete's sake." Holly walked out of the front door and onto the porch. "Be good all of you. And Jimmy you're in charge."

"Hey!" John and Henry shouted at the same time.

"What? He's the most responsible out of the three of you."

"My own daughter, how could you?"

"It was easy." Holly shrugged. "You tried to pull one over on me with the non-sugar free candy."

"Who cares who's in charge. Let's go, I'm wasting away to nothing." John jumped in the car.

With that, Jimmy helped Henry into the passenger seat before hopping into the back and before anyone knew it, John was peeling out of the driveway and was out of sight.

With a chuckle, Holly and Ben walked back into the house closing the door behind them.

Ben carefully watched as Holly surveyed the entire room. "You know what, I'm not really sure what happened here the last ten minutes but the ceiling looks good. You guys did a good job. Thank you."

Ben walked over to his wife, kissing her on the cheek. "You're welcome, babe. And guess what?"

Holly looked at Peanut as she answered. "What?"

"We finally have the house to ourselves." Holly gazed up at him as a wicked smile appeared on Ben's face.

"That we do."

"Let me go put Helen to bed and then we're gonna have a little chat." He gave her a knowing look making Holly's brow quirk up.

"Oh, yeah?"

"Yeah, after all, you left the house *twice* today angry. That's not gonna fly. You and I are gonna have ourselves a nice little chat, and then I'm going to throw you over the back of the couch and fuck your brains out." At Holly's shocked expression, he winked. "Thank God our Peanut sleeps through everything. I plan on using our night alone to my advantage."

With a pep in his step, Ben strolled down the hall with a happy Peanut in his arms, leaving Holly standing there with her mouth hanging open.

Chapter Six

Holly was still in a complete daze from Ben's words, as she stood frozen in their kitchen while he put Helen to bed for the night.

However, as Holly's brain raced with the events of the day, along with what Ben had just said, something inside of her broke.

Yeah, so she'd left the house a few times angry.

That was okay.

It happens.

And well, in her defense, she did watch her husband fall through the ceiling. That would've been a lot on anyone.

Plus, they were putting the decorations up. That was something she was looking forward to doing as a family...

Okay, sure, maybe she'd been a bit of a jerk lately and got angry for really no reason at all. But well... Damn it. It was a lot of pressure to put on the perfect holiday celebration.

Was it so wrong for her to want everything to go off without a hitch? Was it so wrong for her to want to give Jimmy a good memory? All she wanted to do was replace the horrible ones he'd been through.

Holly clamped her eyes closed as she fought off the tears. She couldn't stop the feeling that washed over her.

It was like everything was failing and all at once.

Why am I not the one putting Peanut to bed? Why am I standing here paralyzed when Ben swoops in to be the most perfect father again?

What is wrong with me?

She was failing as a mother.

Holly's chest tightened as the tears she tried to keep at bay finally fell.

Pull yourself together! Holly angrily pushed her tears away with the back of her hand. *This isn't helping the situation. And how are you going to pull off the perfect Christmas if you're over here having a pity party?*

Exactly, you aren't, so get it together.

"Sweetheart, no." Ben appeared out of nowhere cupping Holly's cheeks in the palms of his hands. "Don't cry, Grace."

At his words, she broke into uncontrollable sobs.

Instantly, Ben pulled her into his arms, holding her tight. "Shh, it's okay. It's okay."

"It's not!"

Ben drew back as he lovingly gazed at her. "It's always going to be okay. As long as we have each other we will get through anything."

More tears threatened to spill as she looked at Ben.

"Talk to me."

Holly shook her head.

"Holly, talk."

"It's stupid."

"If it's upsetting you, it's not stupid. What's going on? Don't get me wrong, Grace, you're normally a little high-strung but not like this. Talk to me, baby. We promised each other we'd always talk through it." Ben leaned in kissing her on the lips before wiping away her tears with the pads of his thumbs.

"It's just…" Holly took a deep breath. "I feel like I'm failing again."

"Why?"

As Holly studied her husband's eyes, she saw the amount of love he held for her, ultimately making her feel even worse. "I have to make everything perfect."

"You are."

Holly shook her head. "I'm not. Every time I try to do something it ends up a mess. I freaking hate bought elf costumes. I almost burned our house down. Mildred told me I'm putting too much pressure on myself and the fact that she was right makes me really want to punch her."

Ben cocked his head to the side. "That's a lot to unpack. We'll get back to the hate costumes soon, but first, I can't believe I'm going to say this, but I agree with Mildred."

She gasped. "You can't. I'm your wife, you have to agree with me."

"And normally I do, but babe, you are putting too much pressure on yourself."

"I have to, Ben. This is Jimmy's first Christmas with us. Look at all he's dealt with in his life. I can't let this be a disappointment to him as well. I don't want to cause him any more pain than he has already been through."

"Holly…"

"And then it's Helen's first Christmas," she kept going. "I know she probably won't remember it but I have to try, okay? God forbid something happens to me like it did my mom and—"

"No," Ben interrupted her. "That's not gonna happen, Holly. Stop."

At his words, Holly burst into another round of tears.

"It's okay." He held her tighter as Holly let everything out. The stress she'd been feeling, the pain, the anger. All of it came out in the form of tears soaking through Ben's shirt.

And after what felt like an eternity, she finally managed a deep breath, before calming down.

"You feel better?" He kissed the top of her head.

Holly nodded as Ben wiped away the tears from her eyes. "That's good. Baby, you're just having a holiday breakdown. That's normal."

Holly stared at him, shocked.

"It is. It happens to most people. Especially people that try to control everything, and actually end up controlling nothing." He bopped her nose with his finger.

"Ben..."

"Hear me out. It's not about making everything perfect, Holly. It's about making memories. And we *are* making memories. Stressing yourself out as much as you are isn't going to work. You aren't enjoying the holiday season. Instead, you are two seconds from strangling everyone you come in contact with."

"Am not."

Ben cocked his brow at her.

"Okay, fine. Maybe a little," she huffed.

When Ben didn't say anything Holly's brows knitted together. "Whatever, mister, you just jumped to the top of the strangle list."

The corner of Ben's mouth quirked up as he winked at her. "That could be fun."

"Ben," she growled as a chuckle escaped her at his attempt to lighten the mood.

"See, laughing is better than anger."

Holly took another calming breath, knowing Ben was right. Plus, it felt good to finally get all of this off her chest. It'd weighed her down, which only ended up causing *more* stress on her. "I guess. It's just I really do want to make everything special."

"And you are. Holly, our kids love you." The palm of Ben's right hand rested on the small of her back pushing her closer to his body. "They are happy, healthy, and loved. You already make them feel special." Ben placed his other hand under her chin, making Holly look directly into his eyes. "You're an amazing mom, Holly Richman. I'm proud of you."

As she looked at him, she felt his words.

She knew he was right. Jimmy always told her how happy he was and that he loved her and Helen.

Well, Helen was the perfect little baby. Holly still couldn't believe how well-behaved and happy she was. Then there was Ben. The love of her life. Something inside of Holly relaxed as she watched him. Ben always made things better. She might be in the midst of losing her mind, but somehow, Ben always brought her back down to reality.

Plus, he really was right. It wasn't about making the holidays perfect. It was about making memories.

Memories were what we'd take with us as we grow older through the years, and trying to force everything to be a certain way is only a recipe for disaster. What kind of memories would those bring back years later?

An annoyed Holly and a miserable Christmas. *That's what.* She wanted to punch herself.

Holly shook her head as she really took a moment to let everything sink in. As long as they had each other and their family nothing else really mattered. Thankfully, she would always have her Adonis to remind her. A soft smile formed on her lips. "I love you, Ben."

"I love you, too, Holly." He kissed her on the lips before pulling back. "You good now?"

"I can't make any promises," she answered. "But I'll try my best."

"That's all anyone could ask for." As Holly relaxed in his arms, a cocky smirk appeared on his face. "Do you want to tell me about hate buying elf costumes now?"

"Ugh..." Holly pushed back before grabbing her phone

out of her pocket. "Those stupid hate costumes cost me over three hundred dollars."

"Huh?" He cocked his brow.

Holly shoved her phone in his face. "When I was at work, I found these elf costumes that I bought for all of us. It's gonna be our Christmas card. I thought it would get you all back for making fun of me."

Ben looked at the photo as an ear-to-ear smile emerged on his face. "You're gonna look hot as fuck in that."

"What? No." Holly's eyes nearly popped out of her skull. "You're not supposed to say that, you're supposed to be annoyed and fight me on it."

Ben glanced at the costumes again as his eyes darkened, filling with heat. "Why would I be annoyed? Do you see how short and fluffy this skirt is? It's gonna take everything in me not to rip you out of it."

Holly took a step back, causing her lower back to hit the counter. "No. No. You are not gonna turn this around. These outfits were gonna be my ultimate revenge. You are *not* supposed to get turned on by them. Do you see this? You even have to wear the pointy ears and the shoes with the bells on them."

"Sounds like fun." He took another step closer to her, boxing Holly in.

"You aren't supposed to like *this*." Her eyes narrowed.

"Holly, everything that involves you, I like. Haven't you figured that out yet?" He leaned in, kissing the side of her neck.

Holly's breath hitched as Ben nipped the skin causing heat to pool low in her belly. "Yeah, well. Uhh."

"It'll be fun." Ben kissed the bottom of her jaw. "I can think of all the scenarios I can put you in. What if I'm the Head Elf and I caught you slacking on the job? What are you gonna do so I don't tell the big guy?"

Holly's heart raced. Wait a second, no, this wasn't how any of this was supposed to go. "Ben..."

"That's Head Elf to you." Ben reached her ear, sucking the lobe into his mouth.

"You're not getting it. This is gonna be our *Christmas card.*"

"I get it just fine," he replied, moving back to her jaw. "We'll be the most perfect elf family Santa has ever seen."

No, no, no. My plan cannot backfire.

"I bought one for each of our pets too."

"Good. Now, we'll all match."

Ben peppered kisses along her jaw as Holly continued, "And Mildred and her husband..."

"Okay." Ben's hands migrated to her hips pushing her body closer to his, so she could feel his length.

"And John and Emma..."

"That's fine."

"And my dad."

"Sounds good to me."

"Ben..."

"You're talking too much." With his words Ben effortlessly picked her up and placed her on the counter. "I'm picturing you in that costume and exactly what you're gonna have to do to prove you're serious about working at the North Pole." Ben's hands found the hem of Holly's shirt before escaping under it. As his fingers grazed her skin, her whole body trembled. His hands soon found their target as he cupped her chest. "I love these babies."

"You always say that."

"And I mean it." In a swift move, he pulled her top over her head before tossing it behind him. "I could get lost in these." He kissed the swell of her breasts causing a moan to escape from Holly's lips.

"Shh, little elf, you don't want the others to hear, do you?

We have to keep things professional here in Santa's workshop." Ben's hands found the clasp of her bra, quickly releasing it.

And as Holly's chest bounced free, she smiled, cocking her head to the side. "And getting me topless is professional?"

"Extremely," he answered, moving in to kiss her right nipple, before bringing it into his mouth. As he worked her, his hands went to the waistband of her leggings. "Up."

"Up where?" She threw her head back as he tugged at her pants.

"Push your ass up. These are coming off." Without her even thinking about it, Ben had perfectly maneuvered her leggings so they slid down her legs, along with her panties.

Ben then instantly dropped to his knees once they were gone, tossing her right leg over his shoulder.

"Ben," she moaned. When she looked down, she saw Ben's lust-filled eyes staring back at her. "It's time for me to have my own Thanksgiving feast."

He took one long lick from bottom to top of her core, making sure to keep his eyes on her as he did it. Holly's heart raced as her whole body heated at the sensation. "Not that I'm complaining, but how is this me proving I need to keep my job at the workshop?"

Just as Ben was about to suck her clit into his mouth he stopped, cocking his brow at her.

"Wait no, keep going." *Why did I have to say anything? Good going, dumb-dumb.*

"You're right." Ben stood, but not without taking another slow lick of her lower lips. "You're supposed to prove to *me* how bad you want to keep your job."

"Wait no, that's not—"

"Too late. You've already been extremely insubordinate, little elf. I'm gonna have to mark this down on your performance evaluation."

"My what? You have got to be kidding me."

"That's another mark." He playfully scolded her before leaning in to kiss her neck again.

"Ben..."

He pulled back cocking his brow at her. "That's Head Elf to you."

Holly rolled her eyes as she shook her head. "*Head Elf*, get back down there. You weren't done." She wiggled her hips trying to entice him.

Instead of falling for it though, Ben grabbed her hips dragging her off the counter. "Wrap your legs around me, you naughty little elf. It's time for your punishment."

"What the hell!" Holly did what he said or she would have ended up on her butt on the kitchen floor.

"And now you've said *hell*..." He shook his head. "You really are raking up the punishments. We do not curse here in Santa's workshop." Ben swatted her ass as he carried her through the house.

"Ben, I will—"

"Shh," he interrupted her as he bit down on her neck. "You don't want to wake anyone up. I heard Santa could be quite grumpy if he gets up too early. He needs to be rested for his big night."

"We are really doing this aren't we?"

Ben pulled back looking her in the face. "You sure don't know how to listen. You're just adding to the comment section in your evaluation, you know that right?"

Holly rolled her eyes again as Ben carried her down the hall toward their bedroom. "Are you gonna add in that you have me naked wrapped around you? Speaking of that, why am I the only one naked? This always happens. Why can't you be naked first?"

"You're prettier to look at than me."

"Says who?"

"Says me." Ben smacked her ass, before giving it a tight

squeeze. "Now, stop talking or I'm adding that to the evaluation as well."

When Ben turned the corner into their room, he tossed Holly onto the bed before ripping his shirt off.

Damn, who knew role play could be this fun? Head Elf here I come.

"Ouch! What the crap?"

Instantly, Ben stopped from going to the belt buckle on his pants as he looked at Holly. "Why did you say ouch? I always toss you on the bed."

Holly ignored him as she jumped around on the bed before tossing their sheets back. When she held up one of their Christmas tree ornaments in her hand, he cocked his head to the side.

"What the hell is this?" She pulled out two more from under the pillow.

Ben continued to watch as Holly threw their sheets onto the floor at a loss for words. That's when he saw a whole stash of Christmas ornaments in all shapes and sizes on their bed.

"What the heck is going on here?" Holly picked up another one before looking at Ben.

"I don't know. I didn't put—"

"It was you!" Holly snapped her attention to the door.

As Ben turned his head, he saw none other than their special needs cat twitching his head from side-to-side as he held another ornament in his mouth.

Ben couldn't help but laugh as one of the cat's twitches was too strong, causing the ornament to fly through the air, landing on the floor in the middle of the room. Of course, the little guy then playfully ran after it, batting it around playing with his treasure.

"Are you bringing these up here?" Holly asked, holding up the ornament for Twitch to see.

As if to make matters worse, Waffles appeared from around the corner with his own ornament in his mouth. "You have got to be kidding me. What are you guys doing? Our bed is not your personal playground and these are not your toys!"

Waffles took the ornament in his mouth and tossed it at Holly before crouching down, playfully barking. "Oh, no, mister. We are *not* playing fetch."

At the word fetch, Ripley came running with another ornament in her mouth.

Ben burst out laughing, as his hand went to his stomach. *Holy shit, this is perfect.*

"Where in the heck are you guys getting these?"

Twitch batted the round ornament on the floor hitting Ben's foot. Ben watched the chaos around him as he kicked the ball out of the door as a happy Twitch ran after it. "My guess is the box next to the tree."

Ben turned his attention back to Holly. The same Holly who was sending death glares to their pets as she held up a green and red sparkly tree ornament in her hand. "We do not play with these. They have enough toys. *These are not toys.*"

As she growled, Ben let out another laugh.

And Holly thought this holiday was going to be a disaster. Nope. From where I'm standing this shit is priceless.

Ben plucked the ball from Holly's hand before tossing it out of the room which had Ripley and Waffles happily running after it.

"Ben!"

"Let them have their fun, Grace." His eyes heated as he scanned her naked body up and down. "That way we can have ours."

Holly's breath hitched, but only for a second before she narrowed her eyes at him crossing her arms over her chest.

"You can argue with them later, Holly." His dick was already threatening to explode. "Little elf, right now you need to prove you've got what it takes to keep your job in Santa's workshop. Are you a good elf or a bad elf?"

"A good elf wouldn't let some whack-a-doo dogs and cat eat the ornaments." Holly cocked her left brow at him.

Ben's entire face brightened as a smirk formed on his lips. "And that's why you're one of the best elves here. But before I can let the big guy know that, you've got to prove it to me first."

"Prove what?"

Ben quickly unbuckled his belt before removing his pants and boxers from his body in one fast swoop. He couldn't help the pride that flared in his chest as Holly's eyes darted directly to his dick. No matter how many times she'd seen it, she'd always look at him like it was her first time.

"Thought so." He chuckled as he crawled up the bed toward her.

"Stop using your body to distract me."

"Now, you know how it feels." Ben separated Holly's legs as he moved in between them. "When you sway those hips of yours, I lose my fucking mind. Every time you walk into the room, I have to stop myself from throwing you over the closest surface and fucking you."

"That's not very Head Elf of you."

Ben's body heated as the corner of Holly's mouth turned up as she played back with him.

"I think that's exactly what the Head Elf should do. You've been teasing me all season long, little elf."

"I did no such thing." Holly moved her hands giving Ben better access to her body.

"And yet, my dick says otherwise." Ben grabbed the base of his member, positioning it at Holly's core.

"Your dick should be on Santa's naughty list then, not me." Holly arched her back welcoming him.

As Ben pushed the tip into her core, Holly's eye's closed. "Are you the one that's gonna tell him that?"

Holly's eyes shot open before she twisted her hips causing

him to move. "And you said I talked too much. Shut your face and fuck me."

"That's another naughty word," he tsked, as he slowly pushed into her center. "What am I gonna do with you?" Holly arched her back giving him exactly what he wanted.

He loved the feeling of Holly wrapped around him. As her walls gripped his dick, pulling him into her body deeper, Ben thrust his hips, nearly losing himself in her heat.

Fuck, she was perfect.

Ben's hand migrated to her nub before rubbing in tight circles causing Holly to pant as she rolled her hips. "That's it, little elf. Give it to me."

"Please, more," she begged, sending a new shockwave of desire through Ben.

"Anything for you." He gritted his teeth as he moved faster, feeling his body tighten as he went. Holly met him thrust for thrust as he pushed himself harder into her core. Fuck, it was too much to handle.

As he felt her walls tighten around his dick, Ben pinched her clit. Instantly, Holly exploded around him calling out his name as she came.

He was right there with her. After a few more movements Ben stilled as he emptied himself deep inside her center.

Holy shit.

Ben gasped, trying to catch his breath as he fell next to Holly on the bed.

When his back hit one of the ornaments he let out a chuckle before sweeping his hands on the sheet making the rest of them fall off.

A small grunt came from Holly when she heard them hit the floor. "I'm telling Santa you did that."

"You think he'd believe you? I'm Head Elf after all." He winked at her.

"He better."

Ben barked out a laugh as he shook his head. "Love you, Grace."

"Love you, too, *Head Elf.*"

Holly's hand went to Ben's chest, before flicking his left nipple. And as that same hand then migrated down to his abs, the corner of Ben's mouth turned up. "My plans exactly. The night's young and we've got hours to explore how you plan on improving the workshop's daily toy quota."

Holly instantly pushed his chest, flipping Ben onto his back as she straddled his waist. "I'll show you a daily toy quota."

"If you keep this up, Grace, you'll be Head Elf in no time." A wicked smile appeared on Ben's lips as his hands went to her hips.

"That's my goal."

Chapter Seven

"I am *not* wearing that."

Holly crossed her red and green striped arms over her chest as she tapped her foot on the floor, making the bell chime. She was already two seconds from having a major headache and her father was about to put her over the top. "Yes, you are, Dad."

Holly foolishly thought since Ben had taken so strongly to the costumes that maybe it'd be an easy picture to capture. Then she could actually get this Christmas card out in time and prove Mildred wrong.

Because after her talk with Ben, that was her only goal now.

Holly *had* to prove Mildred wrong.

Okay, if she was being honest, there was a part of her that still wanted to make sure everything went smoothly for the holidays. But to see the look on Mildred's face after she *did* get the cards out on time was numero uno on the list.

That old coot had won way too many arguments over the years and it was about time Holly finally won one.

"You are out of your mind if you think I'm getting in that." Henry sneered at the outfit disgusted.

"Dad, get in the dang costume. You only have to be in it until we get the picture."

"I ain't letting you have evidence of me in that thing." Henry shook his head. "No freaking way."

"Grandpa, it could be fun!" Jimmy grabbed his elf outfit holding it up in the air. "We'll all look the same."

It turned out Jimmy was a lot more like Ben than Holly thought. When the package arrived while they were adding the finishing touches to the Christmas tree Monday night, Holly had come clean and told Jimmy what she'd done.

To her complete surprise, the kid was all for it.

He remarked how neat it would be to dress up like the elves he saw when they went to see Santa at their local mall. Jimmy even went as far as to mention he should send the picture to Santa himself and see if he wanted to hire him for next year. Since he already would have the outfit after all.

Go figure.

Holly and Ben had both looked at each other dumbfounded before laughing. Holly should've known by now nothing ever happened the way she planned it.

"There ain't no fun in dressing up like an idiot."

Okay well, maybe. Her dad seemed to be pretty annoyed with the idea. "You are wearing it for the card and that's final." Holly's arm snapped to her waist, making her green puffy skirt flare out.

"I can't take you seriously when you look like that."

"I look adorable."

"You look like Christmas threw up."

Holly huffed as she took her dad's outfit and tossed it at his head. "Put it on. I'm your daughter. I don't ask for much."

His good brow shot up. "You ask a lot."

"I do not." She glared at him. "Now, put it on."

"You're pretty demanding for someone who doesn't ask a lot."

"Dad, put on the damn outfit. We are making this card.

Get over it." *Why is he being so difficult? Yeah, I originally bought them to annoy everyone, but now it was more than that.*

"I ain't."

"You are."

"And why the hell is he here? Didn't I get enough of him over the weekend?" Henry jerked his head toward John who was on the couch laughing his ass off.

"I needed someone to take our photo." Holly crossed her arms over her chest again, narrowing her eyes at her father.

"And you picked him?"

"He was the easiest. Now, come on, we don't have all night. Put that damn costume on or I'll force you to wear it."

"I'd like to see you try."

"This is the best holiday ever." John burst into more uncontrollable hysterics causing Holly to snap her head to him.

"There is one in there for you too, buddy. Don't make me get it out." Her eyes hardened at John. Her headache was for sure making itself known now.

John instantly stopped laughing.

That's right, buddy.

However, before he could protest, Ben walked into the living room, making Holly's jaw hit the floor.

"I look good, don't I?"

Holy shit, Head Elf indeed. Holly swallowed hard as she looked him up and down. How the hell he was pulling this off, she had no idea. Holly was absolutely sure of one thing, though. As soon as they could, they'd be dragging these out again for a replay of the other night.

Ben caught her eye before giving her the once-over. It was like he could read her mind as his eyes heated. She did think she looked rather cute in her decked-out costume.

"You look like an elf," Henry grumbled at Ben shaking his head.

"A sexy elf." He winked at Holly. "I'd have *all* the lady elves after me."

"No, you wouldn't." John jumped up from the couch.

"Yes, I would." Ben flicked the top of his ear. "I'd drive them wild."

Something flashed on John's face. "Not as much as *I'd* drive them wild."

Holly rolled her eyes as it began. Why was it always a competition between the two of them?

"Holly said she got me one too, I'm gonna put mine on and we'll see who looks better." John reached for one of the other outfits staring Ben down.

"Oh no you don't." Holly stopped John. "You two can play *after* the picture."

"But I wanna show him what an idiot he looks like and how *I'd* look ten times better," John cried.

"You wish. I look fine as hell." Ben winked at Holly once more causing her headache to turn into a full-blown migraine.

With an annoyed scoff, John puffed his chest out. "You know what, you're lucky. Your wife just stopped your ass from being slaughtered."

"No, my wife just stopped you from looking like a fool."

"You're all fools. Especially in that outfit," Henry mumbled. "I am not getting into that *thing*."

"Yes, you are." Holly swung her attention back to her father.

"No, I'm not."

Before Holly could say another word, Jimmy ran into the living room. "Look at me! Look at me!"

After Holly sent another death glare at her father, she turned to her son. *Aww, holy crapolie.*

As Jimmy stood next to Ben, her heart did a flip. They were identical down to the bells on their toes. Holly's heart warmed. Damn, screw Mildred. She was doing this for herself again. This picture was going up everywhere she could hang it. They really were going to be perfect Santa's little helpers.

Holly's eyes darted to her father again. That is if she could get him to stop bitching and just put on the damn thing.

"Ripley likes her costume too." Jimmy bounced on his feet making the bells jingle on his toes. "She let me put it on her."

Ripley trotted into the room showing off her lady elf costume. She even did a twirl making sure everyone got a good look at her fluffy skirt.

Holly couldn't help but laugh as Ripley shook her tail making the bells on the skirt jingle louder. She was definitely cute as all get out. She even had on the matching hat that had pointed ears attached to it.

See, this was going to be the best Christmas card ever.

Holly: one.

Everyone else in the world, including Mildred: zero.

Holly dropped to her knees as Ripley ran over to her. "Who's mommy's little girl? You're so pretty, Rip. Look at you." She scratched her back making Ripley jingle the bells again as she danced. The dog then kissed Holly before barking in agreement.

"You know it too." Holly nuzzled Ripley's neck. "Now, where are your brothers?"

A toothy grin appeared on Jimmy's face as he spoke up, "They're hiding under your bed."

"Of course they are." Holly flicked her eyes up at the ceiling.

Henry made another annoyed noise in the corner, causing Holly's attention to jump to him.

That's it.

A person could only take so much.

"Put on the damn outfit or I'll make you food and shove it down your throat."

"You wouldn't?"

"Try me. If I don't have this photo uploaded to the site by

midnight, we won't get the cards back in time." Holly narrowed her eyes on her father, daring him to defy her. "At this point, it's about pride."

"That's not my problem," he squared off with his daughter.

"It *will* be." Holly shifted to Ben. "Get Peanut all dressed. I'll be right back with the devil and his jester."

Ben winked. "Sure thing."

As Holly stomped out of the room, her elf feet jingled as she walked. She couldn't help but curse herself as she still heard her father complaining and John laughing his ass off.

Why couldn't things ever just be normal for once in her life?

Holly eyed the ceiling. *Don't answer that, Universe. I already know I'm here for your entertainment.*

When Holly turned into her bedroom, she saw Waffles' fluffy butt hanging halfway out from under their bed. "You know I can still see you, right? You aren't invisible if you're only hiding your head," Holly groaned before looking to the ceiling again. *Really, Universe?*

Waffles barked as he tried to squash his fat butt further under the bed.

"I can still see you." Holly tapped her foot, causing the bell to jingle again.

Waffles barked at her.

"Do not speak to me in that tone of voice, young man. I don't get it. You wore your tux fine when your dad and I got married. Now, you see clothes and you run for the hills. What the hell happened? Is your old age creeping up on you? Why do you have to be so grumpy?"

Waffles grunted from under the bed.

"You will come out here right now, put this stupid costume on and have your picture taken." She crossed her arms over her chest. "Stop arguing with me."

Waffles turned so Holly could see his side profile under the bed. She growled the moment she saw that little jerk was glaring at her.

"Get your butt out here now!"

He huffed turning back so Holly couldn't see his face.

"Do *not* make me get you."

Waffles kicked his foot out toward her. "Did you just try to kick me?"

The jerk did it again.

"That's it." Holly dropped to her knees before reaching for her dog. Before she could grab him, though, the asshole managed to wiggle his way out from under the bed. And now it was a game for him as he ran back and forth trying to avoid Holly.

"Stop moving." She reached for him again only for Waffles to psych her out and run the other way.

"You're wearing the elf costume. End. Of. Story."

Waffles stopped dead in his tracks as he glared at her before barking.

When Holly took a step toward him, that damn dog turned his nose up and ran full speed at her.

"No, you don't." When Waffles ran through her legs, Holly quickly snapped them shut effectively trapping the Corgi. "There! Gotcha now."

When Holly scooped him into her arms, the jerk got his claw stuck on her stocking tearing a hole in it. "Really? I planned on reusing these."

Waffles had the gall to stare her down like that was what she deserved. "I'll remember this. You used to love wearing clothes. Then all of a sudden, boom. You were too good for them. What the hell happened? Don't you remember the wedding? You were so freaking adorable. I wanted to eat you up."

Waffles barked again giving her the side-eye.

Out of nowhere, a realization dawned on Holly. "Oh my

God, are you fighting this because I mentioned you looked dashing in your wedding tux and you'd never hurt a fly?"

Waffles glared at her.

"You have got to be freaking kidding me."

He scoffed, letting out a single bark as he nodded.

"Fine, I take it back. You looked like a secret agent in that outfit. No one would've dared to take you on." It took everything inside of her not to roll her eyes.

Waffles scowled at her for one more second before he took a step closer to her, turning his nose up to the dog outfit at the end of the bed.

"Really? Fucking really?" Holly gritted her teeth as she snatched the outfit into her hands. "This is why you've been an ass? All 'cause I said you weren't intimidating enough in your outfit? I swear to everything, Waffles, one of these days I'm gonna murder you."

The dog grunted causing Holly to hold up her hands in surrender. "Kidding. I still get chills when I think of you in that outfit. *Scaryyyy.*"

Waffles turned his nose up once more before the asshole willingly let Holly put the outfit on him.

This holiday was going to be the death of her.

Once he was dressed, Waffles gave Holly another side-eye before letting out another grunt.

"You look handsome."

The dog's eyes narrowed on her as his body went full dead weight onto the bed.

"Dramatic much? I *can* say you look handsome without you thinking you aren't intimidating."

Waffles snorted.

"I did not go through all this trouble just for you to play dead. And news flash, you aren't intimidating to anyone."

Waffles gave her another evil look daring her to say it again.

"Forget it. Twitch, where are you?"

Twitch jumped onto the end of the bed, bobbing his head from side-to-side.

"Do *not* give me as much trouble as he did." She pointed at the dog still playing dead on the bed.

Twitch glanced from Waffles to Holly before walking over to his mother purring. Holly took that as a sign and carefully put him in his outfit. Once Twitch was dressed, she turned to Waffles. "You see how easy that was? You didn't need to make it difficult."

Waffles huffed again, before turning his head away from her.

"Oh my, however, can I stand it? Waffles, I have to take it back. You're not handsome at all. Instead, you're scary. Very *very* scary," the sarcasm poured out of her.

Waffles snapped his head back to her.

"Ahhhh!" Holly threw her hands over her eyes. "Don't look at me. I'll have nightmares for weeks."

At her words, Waffles jumped onto his feet with his tongue hanging out of his mouth as he smiled at her. *Oh for fuck's sake.*

Holly took a deep breath. *Why the hell is this my life?*

"All right, you two. Time to get this movin'." As Holly jumped off the bed Waffles and Twitch eagerly followed behind her.

When they made it back into the living room Ben smiled at her. "That sounded eventful."

Holly glared at her dramatic dog. "You have no idea."

Ben roared out a laugh as Henry walked out of the side bathroom, grumbling.

"Oh, Dad, you're adorable!"

"Can it, Pumpkin. I'm only doin' this 'cause Ben promised me he'd make me two more batches of his buffalo chicken."

"Yeah, yeah, you can have whatever you want as long as I get my picture. I don't care." Holly glanced around the room and realized that everyone was dressed up and ready. Her heart melted. They all looked positively festive and she loved every second of it. She clasped her hands together in glee as she watched Waffles strut through the room like he was some weird badass in his elf outfit. She had to hold back her laugh.

If he only knew...

"Can we just get this over with?" Henry tugged at the collar of his outfit.

Dad's not gonna like it when I tell him I'll make the buffalo chicken instead of Ben. She scowled at him. *Serves him right.*

"Wow," John announced. "Don't you all look jolly?" He smirked, holding up the camera. "Who is ready for this beauty?"

"Shut your face, or I'll shut it for you."

John swung his attention to Henry. "You're not a very nice elf."

"Is it nice if I stick my boot up your butt?"

"You mean your pointy shoe with a bell on it?" John corrected, causing Henry to snarl.

"Come on people, let's get this picture," Holly announced.

Let's not add murder to the holiday memories.

Quickly, Holly arranged everyone in order before placing Waffles, Ripley, and Twitch in front of them. "We're ready."

"Say cheese."

"We all look stupid. Especially Waffles." Henry pulled at the collar of his outfit staring down at Waffles as he did.

That was the exact moment when all hell broke loose.

Waffles let out a bark as he ran around in circles trying to escape the outfit, he *thought* he looked intimidating in.

Jimmy was following behind him trying to get him to stop.

"You've got to be kidding me!" As Waffles ran past her legs Holly tried to snatch him into her arms but missed. Giving up, she snapped her eyes to John. "Please tell me you got the photo before all this happened?" She turned back to her father glaring daggers at him.

"I didn't do anything."

"Yes, you did," she spat before turning back to John. "Did you get it?"

"Oh yeah, I got it." John bit his lip to stop from laughing as he shoved the display in Holly's face. "See?"

As soon as she saw it, Holly threw her hands in the air. "Oh, for the love of all things. Are you kidding me?"

There in front of her was a picture all right. A picture that had her dad tugging his collar away from his neck. Waffles was staring at her father like he was going to kill him. Jimmy's face held a shock on it that she couldn't even describe as he jumped toward their Corgi. Then there was Ben, Peanut, Twitch, and Ripley all gazing happily at the camera.

And last but not least, there of course was Holly.

Her freaking eyes were closed and her elf hat was falling off her head. She wanted to scream. "We have to do it again."

"No can do, Grace." Ben walked behind her examining the picture.

"We are."

"Waffles says otherwise."

Holly snapped her attention to the dog, who now had the outfit halfway off his body as he continued to run around the living room. While Ripley and Twitch ran after him in some weird game.

Holly's hand jumped to her forehead trying to rub away the migraine. "We *cannot* use this. We have to redo it."

Ben pointed at the dogs again. "Waffles is chewing on it. Ripley just helped him get it off."

Holly's fist clenched at her sides as she glared at her father. "Did you really have to say that?"

"I was only speakin' the truth."

Holly threw her hands in the air. "You know what, I give up. We're using this photo. Screw it."

"That's the spirit." Ben smirked.

"Says the only human looking at the camera."

"Peanut's looking too." Ben held the baby up giving her a wink.

Holly couldn't help it as she glared at her husband as her eye began twitching. "I'm never gonna forget this."

"That's the point, Grace." Ben's smile ran from ear-to-ear. "Memories."

Chapter Eight

IT'D BEEN a week since the picture incident. And yes, that was exactly what Ben was calling it now.

The incident.

It took thirty minutes of Holly trying to convince Waffles he was in fact, an evil scary dog for him to settle down. And even then, it was touch and go.

Oh, and Ben couldn't forget how Holly yelled at everyone saying she'd be cooking all the food from now on. That had gone over *really* well.

Ben had to reassure everyone multiple times that he would never let that happen. Although, Henry was still a little worried about the buffalo chicken he'd been promised.

Maybe that was because Holly told her dad that he'd never know for sure if it was her or Ben who prepared it.

The panic on Henry's face would be something Ben would never forget. Especially when Holly warned her dad he needed to watch his back.

Ben was still laughing about it.

Besides, if you asked him, he'd say the night turned out incredible. And that photo, damn, that photo was something else and summed them up perfectly. He even planned on blowing it up and giving it to Holly as one of her Christmas gifts.

Ben smirked as his mind went to Christmas gifts. He turned on his work computer before opening the internet. Off and on, he'd been browsing a couple of lingerie shops in his spare time and he finally found a few items he wanted to buy for Holly as gifts.

Of course, with every set he liked, he added two to his cart.

A wicked smile spread across his face.

Ben knew damn well he'd be ripping them to shreds off Holly's body. When his mouse rolled over a see-through green baby doll nightie, he groaned. "I'm buying three of that one."

As Ben scanned through the online store browsing through the clothes, he found a few tops Holly would probably like as well.

Another chuckle escaped him as he thought back to their recent car ride to look at the Christmas lights around town.

They'd traveled up and down the streets singing Christmas carols as they oohed and aahed at the decorations. At one point, they'd even stopped at the local coffee shop and gotten everyone a hot chocolate.

It only took two more songs and one more street before Holly ended up spilling the contents of her drink down the front of her sweater.

Ben grinned as he clicked 'add to cart' on a top he thought she would like to hopefully replace that one.

Jimmy hadn't let her live it down. Although, he couldn't blame Jimmy because Ben was still bringing it up, too. How could he not? Holly was still annoyed she'd ruined her holiday Corgi sweater.

All in all, though, Ben was happy Holly managed to relax a bit into the season. Of course, she still had her moments trying to control everything, but she'd gotten better.

At least for the most part.

A strung-out Holly was an accident-prone Holly. And Ben had thought she was a walking disaster before.

Nope. He'd been wrong.

Last night Ben tried to count the number of *new* bruises Holly had on her body, but gave up after she flicked him off and told him to shove it.

He'd only gotten to six.

The corners of Ben's mouth turned up. Damn, he loved that woman.

After completing his purchase, Ben clicked over to his calendar. As he looked over his upcoming week, his eyes jumped to the weekend.

That's when he remembered Emma agreed to watch the kids while he and Holly finished their holiday shopping. And since Ben was headed to the store to get the food for Christmas dinner after work later, toy shopping was the only other big thing that needed to be done.

He'd been at work less than thirty minutes and he'd already received about fifty text messages from Holly reminding him of things to buy for Christmas dinner.

Ben rolled his eyes as he felt the phone in his pocket go off one more time. It's not like she'd be the one cooking anything anyway. Ignoring it, Ben turned back to his calendar seeing Emma's name again. He might or might not have also told John about Emma watching the kids. Ehh, what could he say? He was tired of them tiptoeing around each other. He couldn't stop his smile as he imagined the shocked expression on Emma's face when John would magically show up at their house.

It was the holidays after all, and he wouldn't be the Head Elf if he didn't try his hand at a little matchmaking.

Santa would be disappointed in him if he didn't.

Ben's eyes glanced at the clock on the wall in his office. He only had about five more minutes before he needed to see his first client. As he clicked on the day's schedule, he let out a laugh as he saw the pet's name. He clapped his hands together.

Up first, was one of his favorite clients.

As Ben pushed himself away from his desk he couldn't help but wonder what the little guy was wearing today. He walked out of his office greeting his staff as he made his way over to the cages to check on a few of his patients.

Most of them were pretty routine. Some were staying a few days as they recuperated from surgery. While others were there so they could be given certain medications.

And then there was the bane of his existence.

Ben strode over to the grey and black tabby cat, arching his brow at the little guy. "How you doing there, Buster?"

The cat instantly turned his nose up to Ben and whined.

"You know the drill. We talked about this yesterday. Once you go to the bathroom you can leave." Ben stuck his fingers through the cage to scratch the cat's head. "I have no idea why you're fighting this."

Buster pulled back from his hand sending him a glare before blinking at him.

"As soon as we get the samples we need for the lab, you're free to go home."

Buster stared at him, not moving. "I'm giving you a few more hours before I have to take it myself. And neither one of us wants to do that. Trust me."

Buster's eyes widened before he twisted his head to the litter box in the cage with him.

"You're killing me here, Buster." Ben decided it was best to leave the cat alone. With a shake of his head, he made his way over to exam room one.

"Where is my favorite fashionista cat?" Ben asked, as he walked into the room greeting the hairless cat Rupert and his smiling owner Abbie.

"Hey, doc. Long time no see," Abbie replied, holding her hairless cat to her chest.

"But that's a good thing. Means your little guy here has been healthy." Ben gave Rupert the once-over. The cat was dressed from head to toe, and might he add, very festively, too.

Rupert was donned in a Christmas tree sweater that included blinking lights that went on and off to the sound of *"Jingle Bells"*. He also had on a rhinestone Christmas necklace that sparkled as Rupert moved his head from side-to-side showing it off. "Well, aren't you a handsome fella? You're definitely in the holiday spirit."

Abbie placed Rupert on the exam table who gladly took that as his cue to strut back and forth showing off his outfit.

"Very nice."

"Don't encourage him." Abbie rolled her eyes.

"It's kinda hard not to." Ben laughed, watching as the cat's sweater blinked in tune.

"Ugh. He's spoiled rotten and he knows it. He's got everyone wrapped around his hairless paw."

Ben chuckled as Rupert sent him a small nod in his direction.

"My husband, Hunter, is the worst offender. You know that jerk actually *built* Rupert a dresser?"

"That so?"

"Yeah, and now this twerp thinks Hunter hung the moon. Rupert now makes *me* put his clothes away." Abbie sent an evil eye to her cat. "Between Rupert and our newborn, Hunter can do no wrong." Abbie looked at Ben. "You know, he put up *three* trees this year? He said Rupert needed his own, and then of course, since Rupert got one, so did the baby."

Ben laughed again. "Sounds about right. Congrats on the baby by the way."

"Thanks," Abbie beamed at him as pride radiated off her. "It's a hard adjustment with her here, but it's working out."

"I hear you." Ben glanced back to the cat who was still

strutting his stuff up and down the table. "Catwalk time is over, Rupert. You ready for your annual check-up?"

Rupert stopped before blinking at Ben a few times.

"I'm taking that as a yes." Ben carefully removed Rupert's decked-out Christmas necklace and turned off the blinking lights on the sweater so he could complete his examination.

As soon as the lights clicked off though, Rupert hissed, narrowing his eyes at Ben.

"I'll turn them back on as soon as I'm done."

Rupert glared at him even harder.

For fuck's sake. Maybe it's me that attracts the weird animals?

It only took a few more minutes with Rupert staring down at Ben the whole time for him to complete his examination.

After a quick round of annual shots and one more check of his heart, Rupert was good to go. "He's in perfect health as always." Ben placed his stethoscope around his neck.

"Good to know." Abbie scratched Rupert between his ears. "And here I was yelling at your father for giving you too many treats."

Rupert turned his glare on his owner causing Abbie to narrow her eyes back at him.

Wow. Just like Holly and Waffles when they go at it. Ben shook his head with a chuckle as he clicked on Rupert's sweater. "He's a good weight right now. I would try to keep him where he's at." Ben put Rupert's necklace back on, clicking it into place. "That better?"

Rupert bumped his head into Ben's hand telling him his answer.

"Stop encouraging him. You're just as bad as Hunter."

"I can't help it." Ben's smile went from ear-to-ear as he winked at the cat. "He knows how to dress."

Rupert agreed as he did another strut up and down the table showing off.

"I'll see you both next year unless something pops up. And Rupert keep looking your best self."

Rupert nodded at him, agreeing while Abbie put him back in his carrier. "Thanks, doc. See ya next year. Happy holidays."

"Same to you, Abbie."

"Thanks."

Ben gave them both a quick wave as he left the room.

"Buster *finally* went," Ben's vet tech announced, as she held up the bag. "I'm getting everything ready to ship out to the lab right now."

"Thank God. I did not want to do an extraction today." Ben glanced over at the cages, catching Buster's eyes. "It was better for both of us this way. You did great."

Buster plopped onto his side in a dramatic show causing Ben to flick his eyes to the ceiling. *It's definitely me that attracts them. Forget it.*

Just as Ben took a step toward exam room two, he felt his phone vibrate. As he rolled his eyes Ben took it out of his pocket.

Don't forget the cranberry sauce. You know, the one that's shaped like the can. We have to have that one.

Ben shook his head as he quickly sent back a text with a smile on his face. *I was thinking of trying my hand at making my own this year.*

Instantly he got a reply.

No, it has to be shaped like a can!

Of course, he was going to get the right cranberry sauce. Ben smirked as he sent back his reply. Might as well have some fun with it.

That is no way to talk to the Head Elf. You keep racking up those points there, Grace. By the way, if you're so concerned about something shaped like a can.... I'll show you that tonight.

Ben chuckled as his smile went from ear-to-ear as he headed toward the next room. When he felt his phone going off in his pocket, he knew he'd won.

Chapter Nine

Before Holly knew it, the week had flown by. Emma was at the house watching Jimmy and the baby while she and Ben were browsing through the store getting last-minute gifts for everyone.

So far, everyone was pretty much taken care of. However, Holly couldn't help taking one last gander through the toy aisle to see if anything would catch her eye for Jimmy.

You couldn't go wrong with getting extra gifts, right?

Plus, Jimmy deserved them.

Holly studied her notepad one more time, double and triple-checking that everyone had at least one checkmark by their name. "Okay, I think we've got everything we need."

"That's great, Grace," Ben purred, pulling her to his side for a quick kiss before letting her go.

"At least I think so." Holly's face scrunched as she squinted at him. "You got all the food stuff we need, right? And the cranberry sauce, the *canned* one?"

Ben gave her an all-knowing look. "Holly..." he warned.

"What? I'm being serious here."

Ben cocked his brow. "So am I. You know damn well I got

everything. *And* if you recall, we took care of the canned cranberry sauce saga already." He sent her a wink.

"I'm just checking, gosh."

"And I'm just telling you."

"Ben..."

"Don't Ben me." Ben stopped pushing the cart. "Don't go stressing out again, Grace. You're gonna end up running into a wall."

Holly decided to ignore him as she looked at her pad again and kept walking. "No, I won't."

Just as Holly was about to run into a Christmas display, Ben grabbed her arm yanking her away from the disaster. "You were saying?"

A small growl escaped her before Holly turned her glare on the display like it was its fault. When she thought she'd gotten her point across she turned back to her husband. "I was saying you're a jerk. Now, you're positive you've got everything right?"

Ben let out a heavy sigh. "Yes, baby, I got everything we need to cook Christmas dinner."

As Holly watched her husband stroll through the aisle, she bit her bottom lip.

Now or never, Hol. Do it. He already agreed.

She took a deep breath as she gave him the best puppy dog expression she could muster, and spoke, "What do I get to help with?"

Both of Ben's brows shot to the ceiling as she stopped moving. "Nothing."

Holly crossed her arms over her chest. "What do you mean nothing? I thought we agreed I get to help. Remember when we were at my dad's for dinner? You *both* agreed I could help. I heard you with my own two ears."

"We weren't talking about you cooking, Grace."

"Well, *I* was." Her lips thinned. *Damn it! I want to help.*

"And *we* were talking about you entertaining everyone *not* being in the kitchen."

"Ben Richman, I want to contribute."

"With burn marks?" He stared her down causing her to growl again.

"You can make the salad."

"The salad?" Holly threw her hand over her chest like he'd shot her. "How could you? That's the most boring part. Come on, give me something good to make. Please, I promise I'll be super careful about it. You can even supervise me the whole time. I'll listen to every word you say."

Ben scratched the scruff on his chin. "Me being Master Chef and you as my Sous Chef could be fun. Might have to add that to our bedroom games."

"Ben, come on…"

As Ben continued through the toy aisle, he picked something up to show her. "What do you think about this race car? We might be able to kill two birds with one stone and buy one for John too? That way they can race them."

"Do not change the subject on me. I'm being serious, Ben."

"So am I." He showed both of them to her. "Do you think Jimmy would want the green one or the red one?"

"Green."

"Okay, then John gets the red one." Ben tossed both of them into the cart before picking up a silver one. "You think we should get one for Henry too?"

"Ben, I'm talking here." Holly tapped her foot on the floor.

"And, I'm trying to buy gifts for our family." He tossed the silver one into the cart as well.

"No, you're ignoring me. Come on, Ben, I just want *one* thing to contribute, as well. Please? Plus, I really do want to make up for the Thanksgiving fiasco. This would be the best present you could ever give me."

After a few moments of staring at her, Ben sighed. "If it would really make you happy, fine. Emma is bringing the green bean casserole and the sweet potatoes." He cocked his brow at her. "You think you can handle the mashed potatoes?"

Holly's whole face brightened in excitement. "Hell yeah, I can."

"Without hurting yourself?" Ben crossed his arms over his chest as his brows pulled together.

"Yes, *without hurting myself*," she mocked. "How hard could it be?"

As Ben stared at her, Holly could see his apprehension. Okay fine, she couldn't really blame him with her track record, but she could handle this.

Plus, if they turned out good, then she'd finally get to tell everyone *she* made something that didn't have any one calling the fire department or poison control.

"You have to peel them, cut them, boil them, *and* then mash them together. That's a lot of steps, Grace."

"Peel. Cut. Boil. Mash. Got it."

"Holly..." he warned, cocking his brow.

"What? I said I got it." *Geez, it's not like I'm was asking him to help me hide a body. All I want to do is cook some of the food for Christmas.*

Ben shook his head. "On second thought, maybe I should do the potatoes and you can butter the rolls."

"Butter the rolls! That's worse than the salad. At least with the salad, I get to use a knife."

"Who said you'd use a knife? I planned on getting you bagged salad that you'd just have to dump in the bowl."

Holly's lips thinned as she stared down her husband. "You wouldn't."

Ben cocked his head to the side which made Holly throw her hands up. "Nope, you already agreed I can do the potatoes. It's done and over with. That's what I'm doing. No take-backs." She stuck her tongue out at him.

Take that!

Holly: one.

Ben: zero.

"Fine." Ben quickly turned their cart around shaking his head as he walked out of the aisle and toward the other end of the store, causing Holly to run after him.

"Hey, where are you going?"

Ben walked faster as he headed toward his target. "I'm gonna buy another first aid kit. Maybe two."

Holly froze as her jaw dropped. "You asshole."

Chapter Ten

Christmas Eve.

How in the world was it already *Christmas Eve?* Holly looked around their living room still in awe. Where in the hell had the time gone?

One second it was Thanksgiving and the fire department was there, and then boom, it was Christmas Eve.

Just like that.

Wow.

Holly's eyes moved to their living room window. It was already dark out and in less than a few hours it would be Christmas day.

Their first Christmas together as a family. Hell yes!

Holly sat back as the memory of the evening washed over her. It ended up being pretty amazing if you asked her. Jimmy and Ben had spent a few hours making cookies for Santa while she watched.

Holly was only allowed to decorate them, though. A small grunt escaped her. The jerks.

But she showed them. Kind of. When some of the cookies were baking, a few had expanded. And it just so happened that one of those expanded cookies was a Corgi.

Of course, Holly took full advantage of it and made that cookie into an overstuffed Waffles. Would you expect anything less from her?

Nope.

Waffles wasn't a fan, though. When she showed him the cookie, he scoffed before turning his nose up at her and waddled out of the kitchen like she'd offended him.

One point for Holly.

She thought it was hilarious and so did Jimmy. In fact, he loved that cookie so much he wanted Santa to have it.

Waffles still wasn't pleased, but oh well. Maybe he'd be less of a diva going forward...

Probably not.

Once the cookies were set out for Santa, the whole family sat on the couch as they watched a Christmas movie. When it was over, Holly and Ben had tucked both of their kids into bed and read them a holiday story. Holly laughed at Jimmy tossing the covers over his head the moment the story was done. He'd even faked a few snores in there.

If it'd been up to Jimmy, he would've gone to bed sometime in the early afternoon. He kept mentioning how he'd been worried that Santa might pass over their house if he wasn't asleep yet. He even went on and on to Helen about it as she happily smiled up at her big brother with twinkling eyes, gurgling.

Which was fine by her, that girl loved to sleep.

Holly glanced back out of the window, seeing the holiday decorations outside. It really did look like something right out of a postcard. If Jimmy hadn't been asleep for the last few hours, she would've shown him how beautiful it was.

This really was turning out to be a spectacular Christmas.

As Holly's eyes drifted to the stacks of wrapped presents under the tree, a huge smile spread across her face. What could she say? She might have gone a little overboard but, hey, it was the holidays after all.

"I didn't realize we bought this much." Ben finished wrapping another gift before placing it on a pile to his right.

The soft glow from the lights on the tree illuminated Holly's face as she smiled at her husband. "It's okay. They deserve it."

Ben cocked his brow at her. "You do know we ended up buying John a crap ton of toys, right?"

Holly's eyes scanned the room looking at everyone's pile. Damn, there were a lot there for John. She rolled her eyes. She did say it was the holidays after all, and she needed to stick with it. "I guess he deserves it too. Plus, it's easy to buy for him. You just have to think of him as an eight-year-old boy."

Ben barked out a laugh as he plopped back onto the couch after moving another present under the tree. "You're right. And it will keep him and Jimmy both occupied."

"True." Holly smiled sweetly at her husband as he reached for another gift to start wrapping.

See, everything was working out just fine. As Holly sat back on the couch, her eyes caught the clock in the room, causing her to swallow hard. It was getting pretty late, and if she didn't start now it wasn't going to happen...

Was she really going to do this? Holly took a deep breath. Yeah, she was.

The idea popped into Holly's head after working a few extra shifts with Mildred. All the old coot could do was go on and on about couples using this time of year for inspiration in the bedroom.

Not that her and Ben needed any inspiration in that department. They'd been playing out the Head Elf thing quite a lot...

But then again, *that* was the reason why Holly came up with Ben's Christmas gift. Somewhere along the line, as Mildred encouraged her, Holly decided she would wrap *herself* up in a huge red ribbon and let Ben unwrap her as his gift.

She even bought one of those huge bows to go with it.

As she watched Ben wrap another gift, she bit her bottom lip knowing the ribbon and bow were in the bottom of her closet just waiting...

She could do this.

Holly even watched a couple of videos on the internet on the best way to wrap herself. You really could find anything online if you searched hard enough.

And from the tutorials Holly watched, it didn't seem *all that* complicated. Plus, she *really* wanted to see Ben's reaction.

As she sat back on the couch she closed her eyes. She could picture it in her mind. If she did it right, all he'd have to do was pull one end of the ribbon and poof, she'd unravel in front of him.

He'd love it, and so would she.

See, she could totally do this.

Ben finished wrapping another gift and leaned back on the couch with a heavy sigh. "I don't know if these gifts will ever end."

"They will."

"Only if you help." He cocked his brow at her. "You haven't wrapped anything in twenty minutes."

"That's 'cause I was thinking."

The corner of Ben's lip turned up. "I don't see any smoke."

"Jerk."

"Love you, Grace." Ben tenderly pulled Holly to him, giving her a kiss.

"Love you too. And if you *must* know, I was thinking about something for you. I've got something special planned."

That got Ben's attention. "Oh, yeah, and what's that?"

A mischievous smile appeared on Holly's face as she stood. "Meet me in the bedroom in twenty minutes." She looked around the room. "That'll give you enough time to finish wrapping and get everything under the tree."

As Ben scanned her body up and down his eyes filled with

lust. "Yes ma'am." He grabbed another gift by his foot before hurrying to wrap it.

That's one way to get him to go faster and for me not to have to wrap anymore. The stupid tape was the devil. Bastard tape. I think I still have some stuck on me.

Holly laughed as she made her way down the hall to their room. Ben would be done in no time if he kept going at that rate. Holly decided it was best if she got a move on herself as she bounced into her room before shutting the door. Quickly she went over to the closet and pulled out the extra-large bow and ribbon. As she tossed the bow on the bed, she found the end of the ribbon that she needed.

"Okay, all the videos said you need to start covering your chest and then wrapping it around you, so you can tuck the end in." Holly definitely wanted to do the tucking option rather than the tape. The tape option would end really bad, knowing her. Plus, the tape had already made her its bitch a couple of times while they were wrapping the gifts.

Then again, so could this option.

Holly took another deep breath before she ripped off her clothes and started the process. She went slow and precise as she did her best to recall the videos. "Okay, now through the legs and up and over my hip and then once more on the other side, but this time I've got to—"

Her thought was cut short as Holly somehow found herself falling through the air.

Chapter Eleven

For fuck's sake.

At the sound of the crash, Ben sprinted like a bat out of hell toward the noise. He already knew whatever happened wasn't good.

And, he was right.

The moment Ben turned the corner into their bedroom, he saw a naked Holly on the floor tangled from head to toe in a red ribbon, punching the air. His eyes nearly popped out of his head as he watched her flailing around on the floor like she was fighting off an invisible attacker.

Or, you know, the ribbon.

That wasn't all of it, though.

Nope, Waffles was also on the foot of the bed chewing on one of the biggest bows Ben had ever seen.

"What the hell, Grace?" Ben shut their door as he stepped inside, making sure not to wake their kids before running over to the mess that was Holly.

"No, I wasn't ready! Get out."

"Wasn't ready for what?" Ben picked Holly up in one swift move and sat her on the bed, doing his best to untangle her as he went.

"You're ruining the surprise."

"I'm pretty surprised all right." Ben cocked his brow, as he looked down at the woman desperately trying to untangle herself from the mess she was in. Come to think of it, he was pretty sure Holly was only making it worse. "Are you hurt?" he asked, scrutinizing her to see if there were any signs of an injury.

"My ego."

"Grace."

"Don't Grace me!" she snapped, as she tried once more to untangle herself but failed.

It took everything inside of Ben not to laugh. How could you blame him though? There he was, placing the last presents under the tree, only to hear the telltale sign of Holly once again falling somewhere in the house.

Then to be greeted the way he was? Although, he had to admit, Holly did look downright adorable. She reminded him of an angry little elf, who'd failed the wrapping portion of Santa's workshop.

An ear-to-ear grin appeared on his face as he realized he could use this to his advantage. Damn, he loved this woman.

"This is what I get for trying to seduce you," Holly grumbled. "I'm blaming Mildred for this. If she didn't get that stupid idea of *inspiration* stuck into my head in the first place, none of this would've happened."

"What idea from Mildred?"

"I was trying to wrap *myself* up as a gift and give it to you," she spat as she tugged at her arm trying to untangle it.

Ben's body instantly heated at her words as he eyed her up and down. "That's kinda hot."

"Shut up."

This time Ben did laugh. "Baby, you should know by now you never need to seduce me. I'm a sure thing."

He winked at Holly which caused a growl to escape her lips as she flailed her arms around while she still tried to untangle herself from the mess. "I'll show you a sure thing."

This should be fun to watch. Ben crossed his arms as he waited for Holly to finish thrashing around.

Holly gave up after getting nowhere, slumping into a pile of naked Holly and ribbon on the bed. "I'm pretty sure this thing is cutting off the circulation to my right boob. It's also giving me a major wedgie."

Ben barked out a laugh as he found the end of the ribbon and started untangling her. "Grace, oh, Grace. What am I ever going to do with you?"

"Leave me to my misery."

"With or without the ribbon on?" He smirked, provoking Holly to growl again.

As carefully as he could, Ben slowly worked the ribbon off Holly, before tossing it on the floor causing an eager Waffles to run after it. "Are you hurt anywhere?" he asked, examining every part of her body. The moment Ben reached her left ankle, Holly grunted. "Answer me."

Holly narrowed her eyes on him, as she replied, "I've felt worse."

"I know, but how does this feel?" He lightly squeezed her ankle.

Exasperated she gave up again as she sighed. "Not that bad, it's just a little sore. I think the ribbon got wrapped around it when I fell and landed on it. Or who the hell knows?"

Ben shook his head, carefully putting her foot down before walking into their bathroom. After he found what he was looking for, he walked back into their room. "I'm glad I got the extra first aid kit." He smirked her way. "Nothing feels broken. If it isn't better by morning, I'll drive you over to the clinic and do an x-ray."

"The hell you will." Holly crossed her arms over her naked chest as she scowled at the first aid kit. "I take it back. This is *your* fault, not Mildred's. If you hadn't bought that stupid thing none of this would've happened. You cursed me to get hurt."

It was only a matter of time. Ben's brows shot to the ceiling as he stared at his grumpy wife.

"Don't look at me like that."

"Like what?"

"Like you knew I was eventually gonna get hurt."

"Well, it is you."

"You got a death wish?"

"Those are some fightin' words from the only person that's naked in this room." Leave it to Holly to forget that detail.

"I'll use that to my advantage."

"Are you gonna attack me with your pussy?" His whole face lit. "On second thought, I'm good with that."

"Ben..." she groaned.

After scanning her up and down again, he decided it was better to make sure Holly was okay. Before they went any further, Ben dropped to his knees in front of her. "Let me take a look."

As Holly grumbled above him, he rechecked her ankle. It really did appear to be fine, only a tad red. It was more than likely just a bruise and Holly would be fine by morning.

"But I was supposed to take care of *you*. I was gonna be your present," Holly pouted, recrossing her arms over her chest.

"You're always my present."

"Ugh." Holly flung herself back onto the bed as Ben wrapped her ankle. "The videos made it seem so easy. I don't get where I screwed up."

"What videos?"

"The ones I watched on how to wrap yourself up. I had this all planned out. I was even gonna throw in a little *Head*

Elf action, but no, my stupid fat body had to go and screw everything up... again."

Ben stopped what he was doing as he jumped to his feet. "Excuse me? What did you just say?"

Holly's eyes snapped toward him as panic flashed through them. "Uhhh, you look very pretty."

"That so?"

"Yes." She nodded.

"'Cause it's Christmas, I'm gonna let that slide. But you only get one pass." Ben rolled his eyes as he knelt back down to finish up Holly's ankle.

When he was done, he stood. That's when Holly groaned, kicking out her good foot to hit him but missed.

"Now, that's not very nice of you," he snickered.

"No one ever said I was nice."

"You're always nice." Ben crawled onto the bed next to his wife. "You've never once been on Santa's naughty list."

"Then why do you keep trying to report me to him?" Holly stuck her tongue out at him, causing Ben to bark out another laugh.

With a shake of his head, Ben kissed the side of her jaw. Not a day went by he didn't thank the Universe for having his frisbee hit Holly in the mouth. He had no idea how much fun life could be until Holly came along. "You're feisty when you're angry."

"Am not."

"Are too."

"I'm gonna put *you* on Santa's naughty list." The dare in Holly's eyes did something to Ben.

"Depends on what kind of naughty we're talking about?" Lust filled him as his eyes honed in on her chest.

"You're just as bad as Mildred."

"I take that as a compliment."

"You would." Holly dramatically tossed her head to the other side away from him. "I ruined our night."

"No, you didn't." Ben pushed himself onto his elbow, before kissing her cheek. "I still got to unwrap my gift, didn't I?"

"Not the way you were supposed to." Holly snapped her head back to him.

"The way I look at it, I got to be the hero and save the helpless little elf as she rolled around on the floor naked. *Then* I even got to unwrap her. I say this is a win-win. Best damn gift I've ever gotten."

"Stop enjoying this."

"Why? You're lying naked next to me. Only thing better would be if *I* was naked. Actually... let's change that." Ben jumped from the bed and removed his shirt and pants standing there in front of Holly in nothing but his Corgi Christmas boxers.

"Oh my God, where did you get those?"

"Online." He smiled at her. "You'd be amazed at what you can find there."

"Trust me, I know." Holly ignored him as she sat up staring at the Corgi in the Christmas hat, sleeping on a pillow surrounded by presents. "They are the cutest thing I've ever seen."

"I was going for sexy, but I'll take cute." He chuckled.

Just as Ben was about to remove them, he saw Holly's eyes look past his body. Instantly her face hardened. "Do you know how much that stupid bow cost me?" she growled. "Stop chewing on it, Waffles."

Ben swung his head around, for him only to see Waffles chewing on the bow as he'd tangled himself in the same ribbon Holly had just been in.

Like mother, like son.

Ben scanned Waffles once more, making sure the ribbon wasn't hurting him and that he could get out if he wanted, before turning back to his wife. "Let him have his fun, Grace. It is Christmas after all." Ben quickly pushed down his boxers and crawled back onto the bed. "Now, it's time for some fun of our own." He kissed up her body as his hand carefully went to her left ankle cautiously looking into her eyes. "You sure your ankle's okay?"

"Trust me, I'm accident-proof."

"You and I both know that's not true."

"Fine." She rolled her eyes. "But, I'm okay. I had the amazing Doctor Richman wrap it up for me. I don't even feel a thing."

He cocked his brow at her. "I can't tell if that's sarcasm or the truth?"

"Truth. I'm pretty sure my body's used to things like this by now."

"You're probably right." He let out a laugh as he gently grabbed Holly's hips, repositioning her on the bed.

"Hey!"

"As Head Elf, and as long as you really aren't hurting, I plan on accepting my gift."

"Ben..."

Both his eyebrows shot up. "Head Elf," he corrected.

Holly flicked her eyes to the ceiling as Ben grabbed a pillow and placed it under her hips. "Master Head Elf," she mocked. "Don't you think the mood is ruined?"

Ben tapped his finger on his chin. "Master... I can get used to that."

"Oh geez, why did I say that?" Holly threw her arm over her eyes.

"Shh, let me live out this fantasy," he remarked, moving himself between her legs. "And the mood is not ruined. It's Christmas. It's the happiest time of the year."

"Not for sexy times."

"Always for sexy times." Ben kissed the inside of her thigh. "Right now, I'm going to show you just how good Christmas-time can feel."

Holly's eyes widened as she frowned at him. "No, this was supposed to be about *you*, not me."

Ben cocked his brow as he playfully nipped the inside of her thigh causing her to yip. "Wasn't this my present?"

"Yeah, but…"

"No buts, if it's my present then I get to decide how I want to use it. And right now, I want nothing more than to stick my tongue deep inside of my wife." At her shocked face, Ben winked. "Maybe the extra endorphins can help heal your ankle faster."

She flicked her eyes to the ceiling. "I feel fine right now," she protested.

"And you're about to feel a whole lot better." Ben smirked, moving himself to her core.

God, no matter how many times he'd done this, he couldn't get enough. There was something about Holly that always had and always would drive him wild.

As his tongue flicked along her opening, he squeezed her thighs with his hands.

Ben knew without a doubt, making love to Holly was something he'd never get tired of. As he inhaled her scent, he let his tongue seek out her clit as his fingers found her core. While he worked his fingers in and out, Holly moaned causing the sound to rocket through his body.

Fuck yes. God, he loved that sound.

As Holly moved her hips, Ben finally brought her clit into his mouth.

"Yess, please," she panted, her body tightening around him.

The moment he nipped on his treasure, Holly's whole body shook forcing Ben to hold her hips in place, so she wouldn't injure her ankle any further.

After a few moments, Holly finally came down. "That's what I like to call a Merry Christmas, Grace."

Holly laughed as she shook her head at his words. "Only you." When she looked at him with nothing but pure love in her eyes, Ben's heart squeezed.

"I love you, Holly." He crawled up the bed, positioning himself at her center.

"I love you, too," she answered, pushing her hips up forcing the tip of Ben's dick to enter her.

Ben instantly looked down at her with his brow cocked and the corner of his mouth turned up. "Why you naughty girl," he chuckled. "Maybe you do belong on Santa's naughty list."

A wicked smile appeared on Holly's face. "If it would get you to move your body, I'm good with that."

"You little shit." Ben laughed as he grabbed Holly's hips, pushing him the rest of the way in.

"Ben…"

He pulled halfway out before moving back in. "Head Elf," he corrected again, as he thrust inside of her keeping his hands on her hips so she wouldn't jostle her leg, just in case.

"Please, harder," she begged.

Who was he to deny her? As he slid in and out, he felt her walls tighten around him like a vice grip. "That's it, baby. Feel me." He knew he needed to be mindful of her ankle but with Holly moving her hips to meet him thrust for thrust he nearly lost it. "Oh, shit, Holly. Fuck."

"More."

As she met him in his movements, he reached between them seeking out her nub. As soon as he found it, he feverishly rubbed causing her walls to tighten around him harder. "Come for me, Grace. Now."

At his words, Holly shook, doing exactly that. At the sensation of her exploding, Ben couldn't help it as he followed suit releasing himself deep inside of her core. Once he was done, he collapsed onto the bed next to Holly.

Holy shit.

As Holly slowly came down from her high, Ben tucked her into his side. "Merry Christmas, Holly."

"Merry Christmas, Ben," she lazily replied as she snuggled deeper into his side. "I don't know what I did to deserve you."

"I can say the same about you." He kissed the top of her head. "Now, get some sleep. We'll check on your ankle in the morning, but I'm positive you'll be fine."

"I don't even feel it anymore."

"That's 'cause you just experienced two earth-shattering orgasms. Your head's not in the right place."

"Earth-shattering, you think that highly of yourself?"

She stared at him with a smirk, causing Ben to quirk his brow. "You denying it?"

"No, but you don't have to say it like that."

He laughed. "I'm only speaking the truth."

"Yeah, yeah," she remarked, casually molding her body into a more comfortable position on her side. "Hey! Don't look at us like that."

Ben glanced over Holly's body to see Waffles giving them both the most disgusted look he could muster toward them.

"You were the one that wanted to stay in here to eat the bow," Ben reminded him, causing Waffles to glance back at the destroyed bow and then back to them with another look of disgust on his face.

"That's what you get." Holly stared him down. "Next time, don't eat the gift I was using to give to your father."

Waffles turned his nose up to them and huffed his disagreement.

"Waffles. So help me God, I'll—"

"Go to sleep, Holly," Ben interrupted. "He's not worth it. Plus, before you know it, it'll be Christmas morning. Then all the fun can start."

Holly snapped her attention back to her husband, Waffles long forgotten. Her whole face glowed with an excitement Ben hadn't seen in a while. "That's right! When do you think I should start the potatoes?"

Ben flung his head back onto the pillow as a heavy sigh escaped him. "I was hoping you'd forgotten about that."

"Peel. Cut. Boil. Mash!"

We're all doomed.

Chapter Twelve

CHRISTMAS MORNING

WHAT A FREAKING MORNING.

Okay, Holly's night might have also been a factor in her good mood, but dang, she couldn't help it. She was energized.

Holly was the first one up and after she checked to make sure she could put weight on her foot, she hightailed her ass out of bed and quickly donned her *Elves do it better* pajama set she'd bought last minute and jumped on top of Ben to wake him.

When his grump ass *finally* opened his eyes, Holly ran to Jimmy's bedroom doing the same to him. All the while demanding everyone got their butts out of bed and into the living room.

At first, Jimmy had thrown a stuffed animal at her head, but as soon as he realized what was going on, he shot out of bed faster than anything Holly could have imagined.

It was Christmas morning! *Duh.*

Between Holly and Jimmy, it was a race to the Christmas tree.

Of course, Jimmy won, but Holly might have let that happen on purpose. The second she saw Jimmy's face light up as he excitedly looked all around the room, Holly knew it was her who'd really won.

Jimmy's eyes twinkled as he skidded to his knees in front of the tree examining all of the presents. "Santa came!"

"It sure looks like he did, Kiddo." Holly's smile went from ear-to-ear as her heart twisted in pure happiness. As she watched Jimmy bounce from one end of the tree to the other while he laughed, it was everything Holly could've asked for.

When Jimmy turned back to her with the biggest smile she'd ever seen on his face, everything felt right in the world.

Hearing a noise, Holly glanced over her shoulder to the hall as Ben slowly made his way into the living room with a gurgling Helen in his arms.

"Took ya long enough." She winked at him as the corner of her mouth curved up.

Ben cocked his brow at her. "It's five-forty-five in the morning."

"Yeah. And your point is?"

"Nothing." Ben shook his head with a chuckle as his eyes scanned her body from top to bottom. "Elves do it better, huh?" His voice dropped. "That would've done just as well as the ribbon."

Holly's cheeks heated as she glanced down at her top. "This was my plan B."

"It'll be your plan A tonight." He smirked with a wink.

Before Holly could reply, Ben turned to their son. "Merry Christmas, Jimmy."

"Merry Christmas, Dad!" Jimmy dropped one of the gifts he was eyeing and ran over to his baby sister, kissing her on the head. "Merry Christmas, Peanut."

"What am I, chopped liver?" Holly's brows pulled together, hiding her smile as she stared down at a grinning Jimmy.

"Not today." He threw his body with full force at Holly giving her a huge bear hug. "Merry Christmas, Mom."

"That's better." She squeezed him back as she kissed the top of his head. "Merry Christmas, sweetie."

"That sure is a crap ton of gifts," Ben remarked, nodding his head at the tree. "Looks like everyone in this house ended up on Santa's good list."

A boyish smile appeared on Jimmy's face. "Even Waffles?"

At his name, Waffles waddled his butt into the living room and plopped down on his stomach.

Holly rolled her eyes as her dog then flopped onto his side kicking out his back legs. "Yes, even Waffles, although it was touch and go there for a little while."

Waffles lifted his head off the floor staring her down.

"Don't get mad at me. I'm only speaking the truth."

Waffles snorted, then dropped his head back down, ignoring Holly.

I should've made that Corgi cookie ten times bigger just out of spite. The jerk.

The moment Twitch and Ripley came bolting into the room they froze when they saw the tree. Ripley barked as she danced in circles with Twitch trying his best to copy her.

"Good to see you're both in the spirit." Holly smiled at them before turning her glare toward the Corgi, who once again kicked his leg out to hit her. *Asshole.* "Maybe you should learn something from those two, Waffles?"

The dog rolled onto his back dismissing her.

"I guess you won't get the presents Santa left for you. I *think* he might have even left you a new bone."

At the words, Waffles jumped up. His face darted to Holly before he honed in on the Christmas tree.

Before anyone knew it, Waffles took off full speed toward the tree, bulldozing a stack of presents in his wake.

"Oh, for Pete's sake." Holly stomped her foot. "That's *not* what I meant by being in the spirit."

Waffles looked back, giving her the side-eye as he used his nose to nudge a gift out of his way. She had to hold back her growl as Waffles daringly stared her dead in the eye as he did it again.

"You're lucky it's Christmas, mister." Holly crossed her arms as a faint smile appeared on her face. *I don't know why I expect anything less at this point.* Holly let out a laugh as she looked at him.

Just to make a complete ass out of himself, Waffles left the pile and trotted her way. However, the moment Holly reached her hand down to pet him, he faked her out running back to the tree toppling over another stack of presents.

"Waffles!"

The dog then had the balls to pop his head out from under the tree, sending Holly the glare of all glares.

That's it. Waffles is what we're having for dinner.

The moment Holly took a step toward him, Ben grabbed her arm pulling her to his side. "Don't let him get to you. That's what he wants."

Holly snapped her eyes back to her dog. "I'm not gonna forget this."

Ben threw his head back laughing as Waffles smiled at Holly causing her to throw her hands in the air giving up. "Waffles always seems to win, Grace."

"Yeah, and that jerk freaking knows it too." After she gave up, Holly plucked Peanut from Ben's arms. "I'm gonna get the coffee ready and feed this one while you deal with that." Holly hitched her thumb over her shoulder, pointing at the two hell-hounds who were now playing a game of hide and seek in between the presents.

"Anything for you, Grace." Ben kissed her on the lips before shifting his attention to Jimmy. "Wanna help me wrangle up these guys?"

"Yeah!"

An hour and a half later, and after about twelve more arguments with Waffles, Jimmy was opening his last present.

Holly's eyes looked through the room at the aftermath surrounding her, causing a ridiculously wide smile to appear on her face.

She did it.

She freaking did it!

Holly wanted to pat herself on the back.

As she sat back on the couch, Holly kicked her legs up onto the coffee table. As far as Christmas mornings could go, this was by far the best.

"Mom?"

"Yeah, baby?" Holly smiled at her son, who was studying her with his head cocked to the side.

"Why is your ankle wrapped?" Jimmy put down his remote-controlled car and crawled over to Holly's legs to examine them. "I didn't notice it until now."

Before Holly could answer, Ben chimed in. "Mom wasn't asleep when Santa came and she was forced to tackle him to the ground to stop him from seeing her." Ben smirked at Holly trying to hold in his laugh.

"You did *what*?" Jimmy's eyes practically exploded out of his head as he stared at her. "Is that why I heard a crash last night? I was gonna check but I was worried it was Santa and I didn't want him to think I wasn't asleep. I didn't know you *tried* to kill him, Mom. I would have definitely gotten out of bed to save him."

"I did *not* try to kill Santa!"

"Think of all the children in the world, Mom. You would've disappointed them all if you'd hurt him."

Holly growled as she punched Ben in the arm. "That's not what happened. You tell him. I do not need my son thinking I tried to kill Santa."

Jimmy's face turned into a playful smile. "I don't know,

Mom. You've been known to resort to violence. Look how you just punched Dad in the arm."

Holly's jaw hit the floor. "How could you? And on Christmas morning nonetheless. My own son." Her hand went over her chest.

Ben burst into a hearty laugh as he held his stomach trying to control himself.

"Shut up, Ben," Holly snapped, glaring at him. "Tell him I did no such thing."

A wicked smile emerged on Ben's face as he turned to their son. "Even though, it would've been *epic* to witness... No. Sadly, Waffles pushed your mom out of bed and she landed on her ankle."

"Oh." Jimmy shrugged his shoulders, believing that was plausible and went back to playing with his toy. "Makes sense. As long as you didn't go after Santa, Mom. That would've been inexcusable. You'd be on his naughty list for life."

Holly glared at her husband as she held Peanut in her arms. "I'm gonna get you back for this."

"I'd like to see you try, Grace." Ben smiled, taking Peanut from Holly's arms. "It looks like you're ready for a nap. Who knew Christmas Morning would take so much out of you?" Ben kissed Helen's head before walking out of the living room, ignoring a glaring Holly on the couch.

"That's so funny. Mom, check out Waffles," Jimmy distracted her from her plot to seek revenge on Ben, which made Holly's attention go back to the tree.

Her eyes instantly found a fast-asleep Corgi in a pile of discarded wrapping paper with a bone hanging halfway out of his mouth.

Holly's whole face softened as she watched Waffles kick in his sleep. "Isn't that just adorable? Too bad he's not like this all the time."

Jimmy laughed again. "He's even snoring."

"He's doing it to be cute."

"Well, it's working."

"I know." Holly flicked her eyes to the ceiling. "That jerk."

Holly saw Ripley and Twitch slowly inch their way toward Waffles out of the corner of her eye. She knew exactly what was coming next. "Don't even think about it you two." Holly pointed at Ripley and Twitch who were seconds from pouncing. "For once in his life, he isn't being a butthole. Let's keep it like that."

Ripley watched Holly for a few moments before glancing back at Waffles. She saw the exact moment in Ripley's brain when she'd made her choice.

In less than a second, Ripley pulled back before jumping onto her brother with all her might. Followed by little Twitch doing the same.

"Dang it!"

Their attack scared Waffles so bad, he farted as his life flashed before his eyes.

"Eww, Waffles, that's gross." Jimmy laughed, as he waved his hands through the air.

Waffles turned to Holly like she was the one that'd betrayed him. "Don't look at me like that. I didn't jump on you. Your sister and Twitch did."

Waffles darted his scowl toward Ripley, who was now playing with Twitch in the discarded wrapping paper that was once Waffles' bed.

Oh, for fuck's sake.

"Here it comes." Holly let out a heavy sigh.

Waffles backed up, shaking his butt from side to side ready to make his move. Just as he was about to jump, Ben walked back into the room. "They got you fair and square, Waffles."

Instead of going after his sister, Waffles snapped his eyes to Ben.

"I'm sure you'll get her back eventually."

Waffles grunted loudly before sulking his butt out of the room.

"How long do you think he'll play the victim?" Ben asked, as the corner of his lips turned up into a smile.

Jimmy jumped to his feet. "Until we start cooking!"

"You're probably right." Holly watched as Waffles turned back one more time giving everyone an evil look before stomping away.

"I know I'm right," Jimmy giggled watching Waffles leave. "I know my dog."

That he did.

Holly laughed while jerking her head toward the direction Waffles went. "Go give him some pity scratches and get dressed. You and Dad need to get Grandpa before everyone starts arriving."

"Isn't he gonna know I'm only doing it 'cause he walked away upset and in a mood?"

"When is Waffles *not* in a mood?" Holly quirked her brow at him.

"True!" Jimmy chuckled. "Waffles, I'm coming! And you're the biggest scariest dog the whole world has ever seen." With that, Jimmy took off out of the room.

Holly eyed her husband, a small smile on her face as she shook her head. "At least we aren't the only ones having to deal with his highness anymore."

"Jimmy does make it easier in that department. Doesn't he?" Ben plopped onto the couch pulling Holly into his arms.

As he kissed the top of her head, she snuggled into his side. "We did good, Ben."

"That we did."

He tightened his grip around her shoulders as a wicked smile appeared on Holly's face. "Now, when do I start the potatoes?"

"*Fuck!*"

Chapter Thirteen

"DON'T CUT YOURSELF, GRACE." Ben eyed Holly with a warning. "I don't want to go to the ER today." As he studied her up and down, a smile appeared across his face. "Although, they can always check out your ankle while they are at it."

"*I don't want to go to the ER today,*" Holly mocked, glaring at him. "I'm *not* gonna cut myself. And for your information, my ankle is fine. See, I'm standing on it, aren't I?" She bounced a few times.

"For now." He laughed, giving her a look. "The moment I unwrap it, who knows what will happen."

Holly growled. "You aren't taking this away from me, Ben." She pointed the knife in his direction, causing him to hold up his hands in surrender.

"Down, killer."

Before Holly could reply, John walked around the corner into the kitchen carrying the red remote-controlled car he'd ripped open when he'd arrived. "Why does she have a knife?" He fell backward, hitting the wall dropping his toy on the ground. "Oh God, I thought you said she wasn't cooking?" John's eyes quickly shot to Ben. "Did you lie to me?"

"I—"

"Are you trying to kill us?" John interrupted, in a panic turning his angry glare back on Holly.

"Who's killing who?" Emma asked, walking into the kitchen. She and her Great Dane, Bruce, arrived shortly after John did.

"Holly's cooking," John answered, not taking his eyes off Emma as he eyed her up and down.

Ben couldn't help but laugh. Every time Emma walked into the room, John was glued to her. Hell, he didn't know how the guy managed to walk around the house without running into something.

"For real?" Emma shot her eyes to Ben. "I hate, and trust me I *hate* to agree with John but he has a point here." She cautiously glanced at Holly who was now pointing the knife at her.

"Some best friend you are," Holly snapped. "All of you can kiss my ass. Ben promised me I could make the mashed potatoes and that's exactly what I'm gonna do."

When John was finally able to tear his eyes away from Emma, he shot a death glare at Ben. "You're an idiot."

"Do *not* call my husband an idiot." Holly turned the knife toward John. "He trusts me."

John's brows shot up as he stared at his best friend, who shrugged. "I grabbed an extra first aid kit at the store and some supplies from the clinic yesterday."

John instantly flung his hands up. "This is gonna be a disaster," he groaned before turning to Emma. "What did you bring, so I know what's safe to eat?"

At his question, Emma's whole face brightened with pride as she stood taller. "Broccoli casserole and green bean casserole."

"Vegetables, blah." John shuddered. "It'll have to do, though, or..." He glanced at Emma again as his eyes twinkled. "Wanna go out to eat?"

"Don't you dare." Holly waved the knife around through

the air, causing Ben's heart to drop. *Oh shit, this was a bad idea. A very bad idea...*

"Maybe it'll be okay?" Emma shrugged, forcing a smile on her face as she anxiously glanced around the room.

"You remember Thanksgiving." John's eyebrow quirked up.

"Again, he has a point." Emma's eyes moved to the burn marks on the walls. Apologetically she shifted back to Holly, her eyes darting from the spot back to her best friend once more.

"She's *just* making the potatoes," Ben interjected. "Everything else I'm making."

John narrowed his eyes at him. "I've heard that one before."

"She's only doing the potatoes, I promise." And if Ben were lucky, he'd somehow get Emma to make them and get that freaking knife away from Holly.

Ben reached for his pocket, checking to make sure his phone was there just in case. You never knew when you'd need to dial nine-one-one when Holly was involved.

A deep growl escaped Holly as she glared at everyone in the room. "I'm making these damn potatoes, and you all are gonna sit down at the table and eat them or I will shove them down your throat."

"Holly," Ben warned.

"Don't Holly me." She pointed the knife back at him.

Yep, this was a horrible mistake.

"What's all the ruckus going on in here?" Henry walked into the kitchen and seeing what Holly was doing, he froze. "Who the hell gave her a knife?" Henry turned to Ben who let out a sigh.

"Say it ain't so?" Henry pleaded with his daughter. "Pumpkin, you aren't supposed to be in the kitchen. When Ben and I said you could help, the food was *not* what we were talkin' about."

"I'm making the freaking potatoes," Holly spat, narrowing her eyes at her father.

As Henry completely ignored his daughter, he shifted his attention back to Ben. "How'd she convince you to agree to something so stupid?"

Fuck if I know. He held in his smile. "*Well, it probably had something to do with her pussy but still.* Ben shrugged, shaking his head.

"Emma and I were just discussing going out to eat," John announced, walking over to Henry. "Wanna join us?"

"So help me God if you all don't shut up, I will shut you up myself." Holly dropped the knife on the counter, throwing her hands to her hips.

"Hurry grab the knife!" John tried reaching for it, but Holly snatched it back.

Damn. Ben sighed. *He almost had it too.*

"This is Christmas dinner. We are all gonna have a great meal, and you won't die from my cooking." Holly pursed her lips together, making Ben hold in his laugh at her attitude. She might be seconds from stabbing herself or someone else, but she was at least adorable as she did it.

"Says who?" John countered.

"Says me." Holly angrily pointed the knife toward the back door. "Now, go outside and play with Jimmy and the dogs. I'm sure they'd love to chase after the cars. Before I decide to make something else, and I'll force you to eat that too."

"Bruce might be afraid of them," Emma commented, trying to change the subject. "I don't think he's ever seen a remote-controlled car before."

Holly jutted her head toward the back door. "Ripley's out there with him and he loves her. She'll keep him safe."

"He is the biggest scaredy-cat I've ever seen." Henry laughed as a lopsided grin appeared on his face.

"Hey, he is a scaredy-*dog*, thank you very much." Emma

crossed her arms over her chest. "And there is nothing wrong with him."

"Never said there was. I like him."

Emma instantly softened at Henry's words. "Good. He likes you too. Which is surprising since he hates men."

"He doesn't hate me." John puffed out his chest as he pushed his hair out of his face.

"Depends on the day."

"It's Christmas, so he can't hate me today."

When John winked at her, Emma smiled sweetly back at him. "We'll see."

Henry snapped his fingers getting John's attention. "That big old oaf never hates *me.*"

At his words, John growled. "He likes me better than you."

"No, he doesn't."

"John, does everything really have to be a competition with you?" Emma asked, rolling her eyes.

"You remember the baby shower? He and Ben still argue about it," Holly replied, waving the knife in the air again.

"Can you stop doing that?" Emma pleaded. "You're freaking me out."

"She's freaking all of us out." Ben walked over to Holly grabbing the knife from her hand.

"Hey, give that back!"

"You're not even ready for it." Ben stared down at her, as Holly popped her hip out, crossing her arms over her chest.

"Thank God. I was getting worried there he was actually gonna let her cook." Henry held up his race car. "Now, let's stop this squawking and get to the good stuff." He jutted his head to John. "Bet I can beat your ass around the backyard before you can even get your car moving, punk."

"Who you calling a punk, old man?" John growled at Henry.

"You."

"Oh, yeah?"

"Yeah."

Ben grinned as the two men stared each other down. "I don't know why either of you even bother. We all know Jimmy will kick both of your asses. He's my son after all."

"And my grandson."

"I'm his favorite uncle!"

Ben smirked. "And if I were out there, I'd beat all of you."

"But, you're not." John shifted his attention back over to Henry. "I've figured it out. Benny here is too afraid he'll lose. Once again he's all talk and no game."

"Nope. You're wrong." Ben quirked his brow at his best friend. "I *know* for a fact I'd win. But would you rather want me out there kicking your ass or in here cooking?"

John's eyes widened as they shot to the angry Holly who was still pouting. "Uhhh. Shit. Okay, fine. You win this round but right after dinner we're going head-to-head."

"You're on." Ben narrowed his sights on him daring John to say anything else.

However, before John could, the back door slammed open. "Uncle John, Grandpa Henry, come play with me! You're taking too long," Jimmy shouted, as Waffles ran inside as fast as he could before skidding out and then running out of the back door. "Waffles' got the zoomies. Come on!"

"Coming!" Henry hollered, trailing after a runaway Jimmy who raced after Waffles.

John hastily spun back to Emma. "Keep an eye on her." He pointed at Holly. "You're the only one I trust here."

"Isn't that sweet of you," Emma replied.

John's brow cocked as he gazed down at her. "If you want sweet, all you gotta do is ask, Em." As he leaned in, Emma expertly ducked under his advance before turning to Ben. "What can I help with?" she asked, nervously avoiding John's gaze.

Ben couldn't help but send an apologetic look toward

John who quickly shrugged it off. He still didn't know Emma's full story, but his heart went out to her and John. Hopefully, soon enough they could work it out. As Ben decided it was best to break the tension, he sweetly smiled at Emma before nodding his head to Holly. "You can keep an eye on her." He handed Emma the knife.

"Hey..." Holly's brows pulled together. "I don't need supervision. I watched a few tutorials on how to make them already. You were sitting right there when I was doing it this morning."

"Yeah, and you watched tutorials on the ribbon and look how that turned out."

"What ribbon?"

Holly darted her head to John who had his head cocked to the side. "Never you mind."

"How about I cook them with you?" Emma asked, cheerfully trying to help the situation. When Holly didn't budge, she continued, "How about I help only if you need it? That way Ben can be focused on the main dish."

Holly thought about it for a moment before nodding. "Okay, fine. But that's *my* knife."

John groaned. "Can't you just give her like two potatoes, so she can pretend she cooked the food? And after she fucks it up, it won't be a big deal 'cause we'll have more."

"I can hear you."

John grinned at Holly. "I know. I said it right in front of you."

Emma stepped in front of John placing her hand on his chest. And the moment she did, John's whole body melted into her. "Go out back and play with Jimmy and Henry. I'll make sure nothing bad happens in here. You trust me, right?"

John's face softened as he nodded his head slightly. "I'll always trust you." He then flicked his eyes to Holly pointing at her. "It's her I don't trust."

"But, you trust me." Emma pushed his chest. "Go have fun."

John leaned into her once more. "I hope one day you can learn to trust me too." Before Emma could say anything, John straightened. "If you need me, I'll be outside kicking everyone's ass." With that, John trotted out of the door leaving Emma staring at the spot he'd just vacated.

After a few awkward moments, Holly broke the silence. "You okay?"

"Uh, yeah..." Emma swallowed hard, putting the knife down onto the counter.

"You sure?" Holly asked again.

"Yeah."

Ben watched a sad expression flash through Emma's eyes before she quickly pushed it away. And as Holly sneakily reached her hand out to grab the knife again, Emma jumped in stopping her. "Why is your ankle wrapped? What did you do?"

Holly snatched her hand back like she'd been burned before darting her attention to Ben.

"Why are you glaring at me, Grace? I didn't do anything."

Holly's lips pursed together as she shifted back to Emma ignoring Ben's laugh. "I fell."

"Sounds about right." The corner of Emma's lips rose as she playfully winked at her best friend.

And just like that, all the tension was gone as Emma walked over to the potatoes that were in a bowl in front of Holly. "Okay, how about I wash them and then we can start?"

Holly's eyes went round. "Wait, you have to wash them?"

Oh, for fuck's sake. He should have said anything other than the potatoes.

Ben looked to Emma, a plea in his eyes. "You're in charge of her. Don't let her out of your sight."

Emma picked up a potato tossing it in the air before she caught it. "Got it, boss."

It took over thirty minutes for Holly and Emma to wash and peel all the potatoes. At this rate, Holly was going to be an old woman before she actually did anything useful, *or* fun.

Holy crap on a cracker, why are there so many potatoes? And why are they so wet? Holly rolled her eyes. They did *not* need to wash them. They pretty much washed themselves.

When Emma got Holly's attention, she saw the fear in Emma's eyes. "We need to cut them into smaller pieces so they can cook evenly."

"Finally!" Holly reached for the knife but Emma stopped her.

"If you are so hell-bent on doing this, we have to go slow. I don't want you bleeding everywhere."

"I'm not a child."

"But you are *Holly*."

Ben chuckled from the other side of the room.

"Shut your face, Ben." Holly ignored her husband as she shifted her attention back to Emma. "I'll be careful, I promise."

"This is how you do it." Emma took one of the peeled and washed potatoes, tucked her fingers under and cut it in half. "See, if you do it like this, even if the knife slips you shouldn't hurt yourself."

Holly watched closely as Emma finished slicing the potato. It didn't look *that* hard. And it wasn't like this was her first time using a knife. *Cutting potatoes yes, using a knife no.*

"You try, but please be careful."

Holly cautiously took the knife from her friend and did exactly what she'd been shown. Boom, just like that, one potato was tossed in the pot, cut into the perfect size. "See, I told you. I got this."

Go me!

"We'll see." Emma smiled nervously at her. "Just go slow."

And she did. Holly took each one out and carefully did what Emma had taught her to do. One by one, she cut them before she flung them into the pot. Everything was going perfectly, until out of nowhere, Holly felt a sharp claw dig into her foot.

"Ouch." That's when it happened. "Shit! Owwie!"

Holly dropped the knife as she held her finger in her other hand. *Oh crap, oh crap, oh crap. This is it. This is my end. I'm gonna bleed to death, or worse. If I don't bleed to death, I'll never live this down. I'll never be allowed in the kitchen again! Shit!*

Holly looked at her feet only to see Twitch pulling at the wrapping on her ankle. "This is all your fault!"

Twitch raced off as Ben came running from the other side of the room. "What did you do?" He grabbed her hand.

"It was Twitch."

"Twitch didn't cut you. You cut you," he grumbled as he examined her finger.

"You were doing so well, too." Emma shook her head, while simultaneously wiping her hands on her apron. "I'll get the first aid kit."

Just as Emma walked out of the kitchen, the front door slammed open and in walked Mildred and her husband.

And to absolutely no ones surprise, Mildred had on a tacky Christmas sweater. One with Santa bent over with Mrs. Claus behind him saying, *who's on the naughty list now?*

Holly squeezed her eyes closed trying to decide what was worse. Her finger, or Mildred.

Right now, she was going with Mildred.

Kill me now.

"The fun has finally arrived!" Mildred shimmied her shoulders, causing the bells on her sweater to jingle. "Now, we can get this party started."

Chapter Fourteen

AS BEN FINISHED the last bite of his dinner, he sat back in his seat with a smile on his face and a full belly. He couldn't complain about the day, because everything turned out better than he expected.

Even the potatoes.

Ben's eyes drifted to Holly's bandaged finger as he shook his head from side to side. She was one hundred percent going to be the death of him one day.

At least today's accident was only a small cut to her finger. He was just glad it didn't need stitches. Although, he was grateful he'd grabbed those supplies from the clinic just in case. Thank God he didn't need them. Giving Holly stitches was not an easy task as he'd found out early on in their relationship.

Ben flicked his eyes to the ceiling, holding in his laugh. Holly was still blaming Twitch. Of course, there was a possibility of that, but then again this was Holly after all. The number one award winner of tripping over thin air.

At least, for the most part, the rest of the day remained accident-free. Well, he couldn't discount Holly tripping over her feet, nearly tossing the green bean casserole all over the dining room table. But all things considered, that was a typical day for them.

As long as there was no more bloodshed, things were good.

While Ben's eyes moved throughout the room, he caught a glimpse of Mildred's sweater again.

He didn't know why at first he'd been surprised with her choice of clothing. He chuckled. Sure, it was a little hard to explain to Jimmy what Mildred was wearing, but even that turned out okay. Jimmy ended up shrugging and saying something along the lines of, "That's Mildred."

And Ben honestly couldn't agree more.

Mildred's husband was a saint and Ben couldn't figure out how he did it.

At least she was fun as hell.

A pleasant sigh escaped Ben as he observed everyone sitting around the table. He couldn't help the ear-to-ear grin on his face as he sat there.

This was his family.

After his dad died, and well, disowning his mother he never imagined he'd be here, surrounded by everyone he loved. "I know we're all still eating, but I wanted to thank you for coming. It means a lot to spend these moments together as a family."

As Holly glanced at him, a soft smile formed on her face. Ben never wanted this moment to end. This is what the holidays were about. Being together.

"Thanks for inviting us, even if Holly did cook something."

Oh, for fuck's sake.

"Shut your face, Mildred." Holly snapped her attention from Ben to the old woman, glaring at her. "The potatoes turned out yummy."

"Only 'cause Emma helped," Mildred couldn't resist retorting with a shit-eating grin on her face. "I honestly don't know why you even tried, missy? I'm disappointed we didn't get to call the fire department, though."

Holly's nostrils flared as she let out a growl.

Emma dropped her fork on her plate. "Holly did most of the work." She glanced around the room anxiously. "I only took over while Ben bandaged her up."

"And that's why we got to eat them." John sent a death glare to Ben. "I *told* you."

"Shut your face. I put the butter in *and* mashed them. Ya jerks. At least, as good as I could with this stupid thing on my finger." She waved the bandaged appendage around before turning her glare on it. "Stupid finger."

"At least you only cut yourself once, Mom."

Holly's jaw hit the floor as the bandaged finger went over her heart. "Jimmy!"

"What? You did good, Mom. I'm proud of you." His boyish smile lit up the room, causing Holly to toss her napkin at his face.

When he caught it, everyone laughed.

"You did a good job adding the butter and mashing them, Grace." Ben reached over the table, grabbing her hand in his before squeezing it.

Play it cool, Ben. If you give her this one, she'll never ask to cook again.

"Thank you." Holly lifted her chin in defiance. "I really did, didn't I?"

"No one ended up in the hospital. I say that's a win," Mildred announced with another grin on her face. "But we still have to digest the food."

"All of you can shove it. This has been a great day." Holly swung her fork at everyone as Helen burped. "See, even Peanut said so."

"Says the person with the bandaged finger? But sure, we'll go with that." Mildred shifted her attention as she pointed back and forth between Holly and Emma.

"Although, it would've been a hell of a lot better if you had your men dress up in Santa outfits and give me a little show."

All the blood drained from Emma's face. "John's not my man."

"You keep telling yourself that, young lady." Mildred turned back to Holly ignoring the frazzled Emma. "I expected more out of you."

"Mildred..." Holly warned.

"Don't Mildred me. When I agreed to come here, I was promised a show." Mildred's eyes flicked to Ben, expectantly.

Ben shrugged, with a laugh. "John and I do have an elf costume?"

Holly snapped her fingers on her good hand getting Mildred's attention. "You know damn well you weren't."

"You sure?" Mildred's brows pulled together as she faced her husband. "Didn't I say she promised me a show?"

"You talk a lot, dear. I normally just agree." He winked at Holly, as he placed a fork full of food in his mouth.

Mildred leaned into her husband's side kissing his cheek. "And that's why we've been married for the past forty-eight years."

"Has it been that long?" He cocked his brow at her.

"If you want to make it forty-nine, I'd just nod your head. I know people." Mildred gave him *the* look.

"Yes, dear." He shook his head.

Turned out, this ended up being the show for Ben and he sure as hell wasn't complaining. As long as there weren't any more disasters, he'd consider today an enormous success.

For fuck's sake, Mildred was going to be the death of Holly one of these days. Although, it was fun to watch Emma still squirm in her seat.

Lord knows Holly had been on the receiving end of Mildred's match-making skills far too many times to count.

Hell, the old coot *still* texted Ben whenever Holly was in a bad mood at work to *pound some sense into her.* Holly wanted to smack herself in the forehead. She still regretted giving Mildred Ben's number in case of an emergency.

Maybe I should change our cell phone numbers? Ugh, what's the use? She'd end up calling the clinic or worse.... Holly shuddered. *Officer Jones.*

As John and Mildred blathered on about the elf costume, Holly caught Ben's eye. He sent her a quick wink before turning back to the conversation to argue who looked better in the outfit.

God, she loved him. He might be a pain every once in a while, but he really did have her best interest at heart. Even if that meant not letting her in the kitchen.

She definitely lucked out in marrying Ben.

Holly glanced around the room again.

All in all, though, even with Mildred being Mildred, everything turned out really well.

However, as Holly sat back in her seat, she heard a faint rattling noise come from the other room. At first, Holly thought she'd imagined it, but then she heard it again. "Did you guys hear that?"

Everyone stopped talking as they turned to her. "Hear what?" Ben asked.

Then it happened again. "You don't hear that noise?"

"What noise, Pumpkin?" Henry asked, searching around the room just like everyone else was.

"Benny, are you sure it was only a small cut? I think she's lost too much blood and is losing it." Mildred quirked her brow at Ben.

"There it is again!" Holly jumped from her seat and headed toward the noise. The moment she peered over her father's head at the end of the table, she saw the top of their

Christmas tree swaying back and forth in the living room. "What the hell?"

That wasn't all of it, though. No, not by a long shot. Not only was her tree moving, but all three of the dogs were standing on their hind legs inches from the tree examining it.

Even Bruce was toe-to-toe with Waffles sniffing around. That surprised her, Holly could have sworn at the first sign of anything unusual, Bruce would have taken off running and ended up halfway under the bed or something like that.

Guess she was wrong.

As Bruce pushed himself higher in the air, almost reaching the top of the tree, Holly's heart stopped. "Get down. You're gonna knock over the tree!"

Holly should've known better. The moment the words were out of her mouth, Bruce panicked falling face-first into the tree.

It all happened in the blink of an eye. One second the tree was up in all its glory. The next it was on the ground as Waffles and Ripley barked and jumped on top of it.

"What the crap? Stop it you dumb-dumbs." Holly ran into the living room, stopping in front of the toppled-over mess, only to see Twitch poke his head out of the branches bobbing his head from side-to-side. "Oh my God. Was this your fault?" Holly yelled, glaring at her cat as her heart raced.

I should murder all of you.

Twitch blinked at her as the three dogs ran around the room in complete chaos. Okay, well, Waffles chased Bruce that is. And, now it was some weird game and her living room was the battleground.

Holly's eyes darted to her cat who ducked his head back under the branches before popping back up with an ornament in his mouth.

"Are you freaking kidding me?" She stared at Twitch in shock. "Is that what you were doing? Really, Twitch? Didn't we already talk about this?"

She was going to kill the cat, then Waffles, and while she was at it, Mildred and John too for good measure.

"Mom!" Jimmy ran up behind her freaking out as the chaos continued around them.

"Everything is fine, sweetie," she replied, staring at the vacated spot Twitch had just disappeared from. That cat was out to get her today and she was damn well sure of it. "Well, it'll be fine after I strangle the animals."

"Holy shit." Ben laughed as he grabbed the base of the tree putting it back in place. "And here I thought we were in the clear since you'd already cut yourself."

"That was Twitch's fault!" Holly stomped her foot.

"So this was Twitch's fault too?" Ben cocked his brow at her as his hand went to his stomach laughing.

"It was!" That's it. Screw it being Christmas. Everyone was on her list.

"Sure it was," Ben chuckled again picking up a few orna-ments from the floor. "At least nothing's broken. We made sure to put away all the glass ones after the cat started taking them off the tree..." Ben trailed off as it suddenly dawned on him. He quickly glanced back to Holly who was cocking her brow at him. "Oh."

"Yeah, oh," she mocked, pointing at the tree. "He wanted another one to play with."

Just then, Twitch strolled out from under the tree carrying a red and green ball in his mouth as he headed toward Ben and Holly's room.

Instantly, Ben burst out into a deep laugh as everyone made their way into the living room to see what was going on.

"I'm so sorry," Emma apologized as Bruce ran to hide behind her legs. "I'm so *so* sorry. I don't know why he did that. He never even acts like a dog unless he's around you guys. On the one hand, that's a good thing but not if he does this. He's normally scared out of his mind at everything. I have no idea why he did that. I am *so* sorry."

The worried expression on Emma's face made Hollys' heart tighten.

"It's fine Emma. No harm, no foul." Ben sent her a soft smile. "We'll call it even since you made it so Holly wouldn't poison any of us."

That jerk. Holly angrily brought her attention back to Ben. "Who said I didn't?"

"She probably did," John replied. "We should have gone out to eat when we had the chance."

Holly narrowed her glare on John ready to attack. However, from the corner of her eye she saw Bruce still cowering behind Emma.

Oh, no. Her heart broke. *Maiming John can wait. This is far more important.*

Holly cautiously walked over to the big guy. It wasn't his fault. She knew that. "I'm not mad at you, Brucie... It's okay." Holly gently kissed his cowering head. "If I'm mad at anyone, it would be your ringleader. I'm sure this was his idea." Holly darted her eyes to Waffles who looked at her with his tongue hanging lopsided out of his mouth.

With a grunt, Holly decided it was best to ignore her asshole of a dog. As she shook her head, she turned back to Bruce, giving him another kiss on the head. "You're such a good, strong boy. Just try not to let the short one convert you to his evil ways, okay?" Holly gave him one more kiss before she lightly gave Emma's arm a squeeze, hopefully conveying to her it was all right.

Just then, Ripley trotted into the living room carrying the red ribbon and bow from last night making Holly's heart stop.

"What's that?" John asked, going over to Ripley.

"Mom, did Ripley find another present? I don't remember seeing any gifts with a bow that big on it?" Jimmy glanced over at her as panic raced through Holly.

"Ho-ly shit!" John bent over as he burst out laughing

holding his stomach. "Was this the ribbon thing you were talking about earlier?"

"No!" Holly stormed over to her dog, snatching the ribbon and bow from her.

"Is that how you hurt your ankle?" Emma asked.

Holly wadded up the ribbon and bow as she quickly ran to the front door throwing them outside. Once they were gone, she slammed the door behind her. "I don't know what you're talking about. You saw nothing."

John turned to his best friend still gasping for air as he laughed. "Nice, dude. I have to admit I'm impressed."

"Stop talking!" Holly paced the room, sending a death glare to Ripley. *And here I thought you were my good child.*

"Not the show I was hoping for, but this will do." Mildred stepped further into the room, kicking a red ornament as she went. "Glad you took my advice on the inspiration part." She made eye contact with Ben. "You can thank me later."

A wicked smile appeared on Ben's face as he winked at the old woman. "I planned on sending you a box of chocolates the next time you were at the library."

"Make it an extra-large cheese pizza and I'll make sure to keep dropping a few gold nuggets into Holly's brain every once in a while." She winked at him.

"Deal."

For fuck's sake. Holly closed her eyes as she took a deep breath. *Why did I think hosting Christmas would be a good idea?* When Holly opened them she glared at the pain in her ass. "I'm sure your knitting club is going to eat this up, aren't they?"

"They're gonna love this." Mildred walked over to the coffee table to put her drink down. The moment she saw the stack of Christmas cards, she held one up as a mischievous grin appeared on the old coot's face. "Told ya you'd never get them out in time."

Holly growled as she picked up their tree topper, forcing herself to not toss it directly at Mildred's head.

Kill me now.

Mildred pumped her hands in the air as she did a victory dance around the room. "Detective Mildred strikes again!"

Chapter Fifteen

CHRISTMAS EVENING

HOLLY HAD DONE IT. She'd actually done it. She'd pulled off a spectacular Christmas, and no one died.

At least as far as she knew.

As Mildred liked to point out as she walked out of their house an hour ago, she still needed to digest those potatoes. And if anything happened, she'd be calling Holly in the middle of the night. Even though Holly was pretty sure they were in the clear, just in case she planned on leaving her and Ben's phone in the living room.

You could never be too sure when Mildred was involved.

After dinner, everyone bundled up and went for a walk around the neighborhood to look at the Christmas lights. Which turned out incredible.

Holly wanted to pat herself on the back. Even though it was dark outside she'd only tripped twice. And each time Ben saved her from falling flat on her face.

Which was a record for her in the dark.

Then, of course, there was John the whole way around the block laughing at her, which of course included him bragging about his multiple race car wins. Although, Holly had a sneaking suspicion he was just trying to impress Emma.

John had even demanded to be the one to walk Bruce. Something about chivalry and all that.

And when John placed his arm around Emma's shoulder guiding her along the way, Holly noticed the faint hue of red on Emma's cheeks.

Maybe that was the real reason for her second *almost* face-plant. She was concentrating on them instead of where she was going.

At least she was now able to blame someone. And Holly figured that blaming John was just as satisfying as blaming Ben.

All in all, it really did turn out to be a perfect Christmas.

Holly: one million.

Everyone else: zero.

Wait, it's the holidays. Everyone else: one million, as well.

Holly placed Helen in her crib gently tucking her in. "Love you, baby girl. I hope your first Christmas was everything you could've ever wanted." Holly kissed her sleepy baby's head as Peanut gurgled one more time before closing her eyes. "Love you, sweet one."

"It was."

Holly turned to see Ben leaning against the door of Peanut's room. As she did a once-over of him, a soft smile appeared on her face.

"Come on, Holly." Ben held out his hand for her to take which she gladly did. "Let's go tuck our other tired boy into bed." While they walked hand-in-hand to Jimmy's room, the warmth of pure love and joy washed through Holly. Nothing could get better than this. Once they got into Jimmy's room, they saw he was already in his pajamas and in his bed. His green race car tucked in right beside him.

"You can't sleep with that, kiddo."

"Why not?" he asked, eying Ben, nudging the toy closer to his side.

"It'll end up falling off the bed in the middle of the

night, scare Waffles half to death and then, in turn, scare your mom, who would probably end up falling out of bed as well."

"Hey!" Holly punched his arm as she laughed. "Take that back."

As Ben took the toy from Jimmy placing it on the floor, he smirked at Holly.

"He's probably right, Mom."

Holly crossed her arms over her chest narrowing her eyes at both of them, as a smile spread across her face. "Well, he doesn't have to say it. And *you* don't have to agree."

Jimmy sent her a boyish grin. "Yeah, we do."

"Whatever," Holly mumbled, they were just lucky it was still Christmas.

Jimmy fidgeted on the bed, while he glanced up at them, biting his bottom lip. "Uh, Mom, Dad? Remember when we went to the mall and I sat on Santa's lap?"

"Yeah?"

The sweetest smile appeared on Jimmy's face as he spoke his next words. "I told Santa there wasn't anything I wanted for Christmas 'cause I already got what I wanted."

Holly cocked her head to the side as she watched her son. "Really?"

"I got it when you adopted me." His big eyes gazed up at her, revealing all the love he held for them.

"Oh, Jimmy..." Holly choked up as tears threatened to spill from her eyes.

"It's true, Mom. I love all this new stuff, don't get me wrong. But I would've been okay if Santa came and only brought stuff for Helen, Waffles, Ripley, and Twitch. I got the best present already and nothing can ever top that. I got you guys."

"Come here, Jimmy." Ben pulled him and Holly into his arms. The emotions in the room were almost too much for any of them to handle. "I love you, Jimmy."

"Love you too, Dad." He faced Holly. "You too, Mom. Even when you try to cook."

She leaned back cocking her head at her son. "Why do you have to ruin a perfect moment?"

"Every moment with you guys is perfect."

Holly's heart stopped as she watched her son give them a toothy grin that went from ear-to-ear.

Well, damn.

"This is the best Christmas I've ever had. Thank you."

What could you say to that? And here Holly was most of the season flipping out trying to give Jimmy the perfect holiday. Instead, he gave it to her. Between, Ben, Jimmy, her dad, and Peanut she had all she could ever want or need.

She really did luck out in this lifetime.

Hell, even her friends, actually, wait no, her *family* made everything an adventure for her. Even John and his ridiculous need to always have food in his mouth. She shook her head. At least Emma loved to cook.

As Holly watched her son, her heart filled with a love she never knew she could feel. "I love you, Jimmy."

"Love you too, Mom."

Jimmy scooted himself further into his bed. As Holly did her best to keep it together, her and Ben tucked Jimmy in, making sure to both give him a kiss on the head before walking out of his room gently closing the door behind them.

When they made it back into the living room, they saw Waffles on the floor happily chewing on the bone he'd gotten from Santa. Holly already knew Ripley and Twitch were fast asleep in the dog bed by Peanut's crib.

At least Waffles isn't trying to argue with anyone for once in his life. I should stuff his face with bones more often.

Holly plopped herself onto their couch kicking her feet up. Thank God, her ankle really was fine. It hadn't hurt once all day and she was sure as hell lucky she had Ben by her side. His medical expertise might be tailored to the four-legged kind, but it sure as hell helped her more times than she'd like to admit.

Holly let out a deep breath as she beamed at Ben. "This really did end up being a perfect Christmas, didn't it?"

"It certainly did. Even if you didn't get the Christmas cards out on time." He gave her a half smile. "Plus, you didn't break any bones in the process or strangle anyone. That makes it pretty damn perfect if you ask me."

Holly instantly tossed one of their throw pillows at his head. Which the jerk expertly avoided. "I'm never letting you live that down. I'm even gonna hang the photo I got for you in the office tomorrow."

Holly rolled her eyes. That's okay. She'd get him back sooner or later.

Out of nowhere, Twitch strolled into the living room and jumped onto the couch. "You nearly killed me today." Holly held up her bandaged finger waving it in his face.

Twitch ignored her as he bumped his head on her hand demanding attention. Holly sighed as she shook her head. "You might be a pain in my ass but I still love you." She used her bandaged finger to bop him on the nose.

"That's what made it a perfect holiday."

Holly cocked her brow at Ben. "Twitch trying to kill me?"

"No." The corner of Ben's mouth quirked up as he reached over to scratch Twitch between the ears. "The memories. We'll never forget this holiday as long as we live."

"You're right." Holly glanced down at the cat purring away on her lap before turning her attention back to her husband. "Merry Christmas, Ben."

"Merry Christmas, Grace." Ben hauled Holly into his lap, making Twitch jump down as he kissed Holly on the lips.

When Waffles let out a whine Holly darted her eyes to him. "Geez, okay. Merry Christmas to you too, Lord Waffles." Holly rolled her eyes as his highness sent her a side-eye before plopping his head back down onto the floor.

"It's not like I hadn't wished you a Merry Christmas earlier?"

Waffles grunted.

"Can't you be more like your sister? She's in Peanut's room fast asleep *not* annoying the crap out of me."

Waffles picked his head up to scowl at her.

"One of these days, Waffles, I'm gonna—"

He stared her down as a deep noise came from his throat daring Holly to finish her sentence. She gave up shaking her head as she sighed. "Love you, Waffles."

At her words, his tongue fell out of the side of his mouth while he smiled at her.

"Oh, for the love of all things." Holly flicked her eyes to the ceiling before shifting back to Ben. "Why wasn't he on Santa's naughty list?"

"He'd find a way to murder us once he takes over the world," Ben answered, snuggling Holly into his lap deeper.

Waffles let out a small bark in agreement, causing Holly to shake her head as she growled at him in return.

"You might as well give up, Grace. He's never gonna change."

After a few moments, she gave up with a sigh. "You're right."

"I'm always right." Ben kissed her once more. "Merry Christmas, Holly."

"Merry Christmas, Ben."

"And, now it's time for *you* to unwrap *me*." A wicked smile appeared on Ben's face as he picked Holly up in his arms and carried her off to their bedroom only tripping over a runaway Waffles twice in the process.

Epilogue

NEW YEAR'S EVE

HOLY CRAPOLIE!

It'd been a full week since Christmas, and somewhere along the way, Holly came up with the bright idea to invite everyone back over to ring in the New Year together.

Maybe she was a glutton for punishment? She still didn't know.

It only took her agreeing to not walk into the kitchen even once for everyone to be on board. She had to admit she was still a little pissed about it, though. She'd found a New Year's Eve party dip she wanted to make, but she decided to forgo it, wanting to spend the night with her family instead.

Plus, this made it so Emma brought most of the food. And Emma made *fantastic* food.

That bitch, Holly laughed to herself.

It didn't matter, though. Since Holly wasn't making the food it was really a win-win in her eyes.

Holly laughed again. Emma loving to cook was a good thing for John. Well, that was if Emma ever decided to pull her head out of her ass.

All in good time, though.

Holly knew sooner or later they would get together. They were meant to be. Just like her and Ben were.

"I'm extremely disappointed you don't have a life-size cake for someone to jump out of when the clock strikes midnight." Mildred eyed Holly crossing her arms over her sweater. The same sweater that had so many sparkles on it, every time Holly looked at her, she thought she'd go blind. "I was expecting some man chest today."

"Isn't it past your bedtime?" Holly placed her hand on her hip.

"Might be past *yours*, but it sure as hell ain't past mine. Isn't that right, Snookums?" Mildred glanced at her husband who nodded. "Sure thing, dear. Whatever you say."

Holly eyed him as she deadpanned, "You do know, you don't always have to agree with her, right?"

Mildred gave her husband a quick kiss on the cheek. "He learned a long time ago it was better this way."

"Don't we all," Ben agreed, as he slowly walked up to Holly.

"Watch it," Holly warned, before she gave him a quick kiss. "Did Jimmy go to sleep?"

"Yeah, he couldn't stay up no matter how hard he tried."

"Poor kid. There is always next year."

"Yeah." Ben smiled at her, kissing her once more.

"It's not midnight yet. Stop doing that." John gagged from the other side of the living room. "I wanna keep down my food."

"Not my problem," Holly remarked, as she yanked Ben into her arms to give him another big smacking kiss on the lips.

"Watch your hands there, son, that is my daughter you're manhandling," Henry chimed in seeing Ben's hand go to Holly's ass.

"She grabbed me, Henry. I have no control where my hands go after that."

"That's what I'm talking about." Mildred spun around to her husband. "This might be better than someone popping out of a cake after all."

"Do you ever stop talking?" Holly flicked her eyes up.

"No." Mildred shook her head.

"Figures." Just as Holly was about to say something else, Waffles waddled his butt into the room and plopped down in front of her. The moment he leaned over to lick Holly's right foot she snatched it back. "Stop doing that."

Ben chuckled as Waffles tried to do it again. "It's your fault you spilled the cheese dip on your foot to begin with, Grace."

"I cleaned it off." She narrowed her eyes at her dog.

Ben snickered. "Waffles doesn't think so."

"You're killing me here, Waffles." Holly pointed to John who was across the room. "Can't you go bug someone else?"

Waffles looked around the room before turning back to Holly. He then licked her foot one more time.

"Oh, for fuck's sake."

"Language, Pumpkin."

Holly growled snapping her attention to her dad. "Language my ass."

Henry cocked his brow at her as Ben burst out laughing.

"This is why I love coming over here," Mildred announced as she sat down with a bowl of popcorn in her lap and watched them.

"Me too." John grabbed a handful of popcorn from the bowl as he sat next to Mildred.

"Oh, no you don't." Mildred forcefully tugged the food away from John. "You've got your own work to deal with." She jutted her head toward Emma who was on her knees petting Bruce on the other side of the room.

"I'm working on it."

"Not fast enough," she replied. An evil smile emerged on Mildred's face. "Want me to help?"

John's whole face paled. "God no."

"You sure? I know people."

"And that's what scares me." John jumped up, the popcorn completely forgotten as he raced over to Emma's side shielding her from the old woman. When he glanced back toward Mildred, he sent her a glare. "You're not allowed to talk to her anymore."

"Young man, I can do whatever I damn well please. I didn't get this old not to have that right."

John pleadingly looked to Holly who shrugged. "This is her being a *mild* Mildred. I'd just deal with it before she gets a crazy idea in her whack-a-doo brain."

Mildred bolted to her feet. "I got it!" She pulled out her trusted notepad and started scribbling.

"We're all screwed."

Ben chuckled at Holly's annoyed expression. "Maybe she'll forget." He shrugged.

"I doubt it." Holly let out a sigh. "At least for once it's not us. Maybe Emma and John can be Mildred's new subjects at her knitting club."

"That's something you should've asked Santa for." Ben winked, giving Holly a quick peck on the lips.

"Maybe I did," Holly replied with a lopsided grin of her own.

"It's time!" Henry clapped his hands together. "Everyone stop your yappin'. We got us a New Year to ring in!"

Ten, Nine, Eight, Seven, Six, Five, Four, Three, Two, One!

"Happy New Year!"

Ben pulled Holly into his arms as he kissed her like his life depended on it. "Here's to another great year," he whispered, pulling away from her lips for a second, before kissing her again.

Holly's entire face brightened as she lovingly gazed at her husband before going in for another kiss, herself. However, just as her lips were about to meet Ben's, she saw Emma had

John pinned to the wall as they shared a kiss in the corner of the room.

"Whoa." Holly pointed at the two.

"Wonder how that's gonna turn out?" Ben remarked, with a chuckle.

A devious grin appeared on Holly's face. "Only one way to find out."

Before she could say anything more, Ben pulled her back into his embrace planting another kiss on her lips. "Best holiday season ever, Grace."

"It really was. Even if there were some stumbles along the way." Holly's smile went from ear-to-ear. "And, here is to many more holidays with you." Holly sealed her lips to Ben's once more.

Might as well start the New Year off right.

John and Emma's story is up next in the Stumbling Through Life series. In the meantime, did the cat named Dog and his hunky firefighter owner intrigue you? If so, check out Teased by Fire. Or, was it the fashionista cat named Rupert? If so, check out Rupert, his owner Abbie and her archnemesis Hunter in Nothing But a Dare.

There is a sneak peek of Chapter one of Nothing But a Dare on the next page.

Curious what Mildred was talking about when she saw a hunky firefighter and his woman in a compromising position? Check out Hank and Olive's story in Teased by Fire. Sneak peek of Chapter One after the sneak peek of Nothing But a Dare.

CHAPTER ONE

"I DARE YOU."

Hunter James raised his brow at ten-year-old Abbie Collins as she braced herself on the highest tree branch in their neighboring backyards. She quickly moved her eyes from him to reassess her surroundings. From where Abbie balanced, things weren't looking too good. How in the world had she gotten herself into this mess?

And again...

Her eyes moved back to the boy taunting her.

Oh yeah, how could she forget?

Hunter freaking James.

He's the reason she was now in a tree.

Since Hunter moved in next door with his dad and step-mom, he was constantly causing trouble. And somehow, Abbie was always involved.

She closed her eyes as she held onto the tree trunk tightly.

The day Hunter and his family moved in, Abbie and her mother, Kathleen, brought them over fresh baked cookies. That was the nice thing to do, after all. The neighborly thing.

Plus, Abbie had been particularly proud of this batch

552

since she spent hours decorating each one with the word 'welcome'.

Abbie, along with her mother, had considered herself the welcoming committee of the neighborhood.

Ehh, what could she say? She got her nurturing side from her mom. Plus, Abbie absolutely adored making new friends. You could *never* have too many if you asked her.

The more, the merrier.

Maybe it was because Abbie didn't have any brothers or sisters, or maybe it was her need for everyone to feel like they belonged.

After her father abandoned her and her mom right after Abbie was born there was always something lacking. That could've been the reason why her mother always made it a point to welcome anyone that moved in with wide open arms and a plate full of cookies. She needed them to feel wanted since they'd never felt that.

Well, that plate full of cookies was two years ago and every day since meeting Hunter James, Abbie regretted every freaking second of it.

"Are you gonna do it or what?" Hunter taunted from below. "You better hurry, I don't know if that branch will hold you much longer?"

Jerk. Abbie's eyes narrowed at him as she held onto the tree trunk a little tighter. If she could go back in time, she would have added salt to the cookies, or better yet, maybe some arsenic.

"Stop being a baby, Collins."

"I'm not being a baby!" Abbie felt the branch bend under her weight.

Quickly, she closed her eyes as her heart started to pound against her chest. Okay, so she knew she was only about six feet off the ground, and the likelihood of her causing severe damage was slim to none; however, the more she looked at the annoying boy below her, the farther away he seemed.

Abbie took a deep breath before she opened her eyes and looked back at Hunter.

That's when she noticed it.

Hunter was staring at her with that stupid smug smirk on his face. The same one he always got when he thought he'd won.

A growl erupted from deep inside her. *Not today!*

If Abbie were on the ground and *not* a million feet in the air, she'd march right up to him and smack that dang smirk right off his stupid face.

Stupid Hunter.

Stupid tree.

Stupid dare!

For two years now, Hunter James had made her life a living hell.

If he wasn't constantly picking on her, he was daring her to do something she didn't want to do.

And *that* was the exact reason she was up in a tree right now.

"You're too scared, Abbie." Hunter laughed as he crossed his arms over his chest.

"Am not. I just think it's dumb to jump out of a tree unless there is a logical reason to do so."

"Why do you always do that?" He glared at her.

"Do what?"

"Say shit to make you sound all smart and stuff."

"I am smart, unlike you dumb-dumb."

Hunter's eyes narrowed before his lips formed into that smirk. "I dare you."

A Collins never surrendered.

A Collins never backed down.

A Collins never turned down a dare.

At least that's what her mother would say. Okay, not so much the dare part, but the never backing down part. Collins' were strong, and no matter what was thrown at them, they always ended up on top.

No one will ever knock us down.

Not her deadbeat father, and certainly not Hunter James.

And that left Abbie here.

About to jump to her death.

She rolled her eyes at herself. *Maybe death was a little dramatic.* She took another deep breath before looking at the ground. Her breath caught in her throat as Hunter suddenly seemed very far away. *Actually, death could be a possibility.*

"You scared?" Hunter shouted.

"Not as scared as you were when I dared you to jump off the roof into the pool," she snapped.

"I did it, didn't I?"

"Only after I called you a chicken," she yelled back. Why couldn't she have just walked away? Any other normal human being would have, but no. Abbie was now two years deep in some messed up back and forth dare-off.

"And that's what you're being right now. Abbie the chicken!" The corner of his mouth turned up into that stupid smirk again. "That's your new name."

"When I get down there, I'm gonna hit you!"

"You'd have to catch me first."

Abbie's eyes narrowed in on her target. She hated him. With every ounce of her being, she hated Hunter James.

Screw it.

She jumped.

Thankfully something broke her fall.

That something being Hunter James.

"What the hell?" Hunter cried. "You weren't supposed to jump on me, Collins."

"You never specified what I had to do in the dare. If you wanted to make sure I *didn't* jump on you, then you needed to disclose those terms upfront." She huffed as she righted herself making it so she sat on Hunter's chest. She then pushed her chestnut hair out of her face. "It's not my fault your dumb brain forgot that part."

"Who talks like that?" He squirmed trying to get her off. "Has anyone ever told you, you're annoying?"

"Yes, you. Every day."

"You're ten. You're not some genius." Hunter pushed her off him, causing her to land on her butt in the dirt.

From where she landed, Abbie watched as he fixed his clothes before pushing his black hair out of his face, giving her the view of his hunter green eyes that matched his name. "Excuse you, I turn eleven in two days." Abbie stuck her tongue out at him as she jumped to her feet.

"Oh, that reminds me..." Hunter pulled a tiny box out of his pocket. "This is for you."

Abbie took a step back caught entirely off-guard. Then out of nowhere, her heart did this weird flip thing she couldn't explain.

As she stared at him, with her mouth open in disbelief. She quickly tried to scan her body. She was ten, so there was no way she was having a heart attack. Right? When Hunter pushed the box closer to her, her heart did it again.

What the hell? Am I dying? Oh, God, the jump really did kill me. And, of course, this is now my hell. A hell where Hunter James existed.

"Take the box, Abbie," Hunter scoffed annoyed.

Had he really gotten her a birthday gift? She looked at the box and then back to his face. He *seemed* sincere. But then again, this was Hunter after all.

Abbie bit her bottom lip as she took the box. *Maybe this is the end of the feud...or, you know, maybe it was a bomb.* There was a fifty-fifty shot of either one.

Screw it. That was Abbie's motto when it came to Hunter.

She opened the box.

"Eww!" Before Abbie knew what was happening, grasshoppers started jumping out causing her to drop the box.

"Happy Birthday!" Hunter laughed as Abbie danced around trying to get the creatures off. "You're a jerk, Hunter."

"No, I'm not." He took a step closer to her plucking one of the grasshoppers off her shoulder. "I dare you to eat it."

"No way!" Abbie shook her head stepping back from him.

"You scared, little girl?" He pushed the grasshopper closer to her face.

"No, I'm not scared."

"Abbie the chicken. I knew the name would fit."

Screw it!

Abbie snatched the grasshopper from Hunter's fingers before shoving the thing into her mouth causing Hunter's eyes to widen for a split second before his amusement overtook him. "Holy crap. I can't believe you did it."

"Of course, I did," she said disgusted with herself. "I'm *not* a chicken."

"Abbie Babbie, the one with too much flabby," Hunter laughed.

"That's it." Abbie launched herself at Hunter tackling him to the ground. "What's your problem?"

"I don't have a problem. *You* have a problem." He fought from under her.

"Oh, that's really mature." Abbie kept him pinned to the ground. She'd learned a few things from their past wrestling matches. Like how locking her knees around his chest would prevent him from moving for at least a few seconds.

"I *am* a mature person. I'm almost thirteen. That makes me almost a teenager." Hunter looked at her. The moment her eyes locked with his green ones, that strange feeling in her heart came back. Maybe she *was* having a heart attack.

"You're a jerk."

"You always say that."

"That's 'cause it's true."

Hunter grunted before pushing Abbie off him effectively flipping her onto the ground. "Whatever. Why don't you run on home and stick your head in one of those stupid books you always have with you?"

"How is that an insult?" Abbie crossed her arms over her chest. "You make it seem like reading is a *bad* thing. Maybe if you picked up a book every once in a while, you'd actually learn something."

"Oh, like the books *you* read teach you anything?" He cocked his brow.

"Duhh. They teach me all kinds of stuff." Abbie walked to her bag and threw one of her books at him. "I dare you."

Hunter caught it with ease. "You dare me to what?"

"Read a book. Learn something. Stop being such an asshat."

Ignoring her new insult, Hunter cocked his head to the side. "You want me to read *Treasure Island?* This isn't English class, Collins."

"What are you scared you might actually learn something?"

Abbie knew she had him. Hunter *never* turned down a dare from her. Just like she never turned down a dare from him. "I *dare* you to read that whole book, Hunter."

His eyes shot to hers as they narrowed. "Fine." He placed the book under his arm as he turned away from her. After walking a few steps, he looked over his shoulder. "A dare's a dare. Just remember this isn't over."

Would it ever be?

Continue Abbie and Hunter's story in Nothing But a Dare.

CHAPTER ONE

OLIVE QUINN GLARED daggers at her traitorous best friend, Miranda Parker, as the bane of her existence moved yet another piece of his furniture into her apartment. This was all Miranda's fault.

"Stop trying to murder me with your eyes, Olive." Miranda sighed in annoyance as she pushed the hair out of her face.

That only caused Olive to glare harder in her friend's direction. "I will not stop trying to murder you with my eyes," Olive whisper shouted. "It's your fault *he* is moving into *my* apartment."

"What the hell did you want me to do, Olive? I knew I couldn't leave you stranded to pay the rent on your own. You're just pissed I'm moving."

"Damn right, I'm pissed. If I were you I'd check every box you packed for surprises." Olive squinted her eyes harder in Miranda's direction trying to intimidate her.

Miranda shook her head. "How many times are we going to go through this? If I thought I had a chance of getting the job, I would have told you. I would have thought hell would've frozen over first."

"And yet here we are. Hell must be mighty cold right now."

"I'm sorry, okay. I'm freaking sorry."

At Miranda's defeated posture Olive softened. "No, I'm the one that's sorry. You've got your dream job now. I need to stop being angry and just be happy for you."

"It's a lot changing all at once."

Olive looked at Miranda, her eyes filling with tears. "I'm going to miss you. We've been stuck together since the first grade."

"Nothing's changing," Miranda tried reassuring her.

"Everything is changing. You're moving clear across the country and I only found out two days ago. I haven't had time to accept the fact my only friend is leaving me." Her eyes narrowed. "And, to top it all off, you went behind my back and gave your *brother* your room."

Miranda sighed before crossing her arms over her chest. "I don't understand why you are freaking out so much? Yeah, Hank is an ass, but if you both stay out of each other's way, you'll be fine. Plus, I've brought you the best research tool a romance writer could ever ask for. You'll be able to get a up close and personal experience on how he operates. I brought you a gift."

"If you mean the gift of an STD infested man-whore? You can keep it." Olive's eyes widened as everything clicked into place. This wasn't her best friend. There was no way in hell her best friend who she'd known for years would actually be doing this. That settles it. She'd somehow been abducted by aliens and the person standing in front of her was an imposter. *This is it. This is the zombie apocalypse we've all been waiting for.* Olive quickly grabbed Miranda's arms examining them for any sign of an implant.

Miranda snatched her hands back. "Jesus, Olive, what are you doing?"

"Checking to see if you have a tracking device some-where," she said as a matter of fact.

Miranda rolled her eyes. "Do you ever live anywhere other than your fantasy world?"

Offended, Olive crossed her arms over her chest. "Hey, my weird brain is a masterpiece. How else do you think I come up with my stories?"

"I don't know how you function when all you think about is the zombie apocalypse or some strange alien race invading the earth."

Olive pointed at her head. "This imagination makes me money."

"How? Your brain makes zero sense. You don't even write the shit that goes on in your mind." Miranda shook her head. "Olive, you write contemporary erotic romance. Please explain to me how a brain so involved in aliens and zombies writes hard-core romance with alpha males that make all women drool?"

Olive shrugged. "I don't know. I think it's a weird yin and yang thing, you know, balance to the Force and what not."

"Fuck!" They heard from the other room as a loud bang echoed throughout the space.

Olive's eyes narrowed back at her friend as her lips thinned. "He's a big oaf, and he's gonna use his big oaf muscles to make holes in my walls."

Miranda crossed her arms over her chest. "All right, Olive, I get it. You're fucking pissed. Okay. If I were you I'd be pissed too, but there is nothing we can do about it now. Hank is moving in. Right now, as we speak. He needed a place and you need someone that can pay half the rent. End. Of. Story."

Olive knew Miranda was right, but that didn't stop the betrayal and hurt from running through her. Within two days, everything she was accustomed to had been upended. That's a lot for anyone to take in.

"It's not like he'll be here often anyway," Miranda

remarked. "He's always at the fire station, and when he's not, he'll be out with his flavor of the week."

"That isn't the point. With Hank the Tank..." Olive physically revolted. "I hate that nickname everyone calls him."

"It's stupid, I agree."

"Back to what I was saying," Olive started again after shaking the thoughts from her head. "With Hank moving in, I can't be me anymore. Olive Quinn: awkward, hates people, never goes outside or wears a bra. I'll be banished to my room or *forced* to wear a bra. I don't want to wear a bra. Bras suck and stifle my creativity. Oh god, don't even get me started on underwires. Who the hell came up with underwires for bras, anyway? I bet you it was a man. Yup, it had to have been a man. A woman wouldn't have invented something that after a little while, a hard metal wire pokes out and causes you excruciating pain; when all you want to do is walk to the store and buy some snacks. But no, instead I'm walking down the sidewalk discreetly trying to move the wire to a place where it's not trying to puncture through my skin and kill me."

Miranda chuckled. "You have a point about the bra, but you said the same thing about pants and you've grown accustomed to wearing them."

"*Not by choice!* I only wear them because you kept the air on "cold as fuck." If I didn't wear pants these thunder thighs would have gotten frostbitten."

"I keep it cold because you have that weird obsession with the holidays."

"I do not!"

Miranda's brow rose before she pointed to the corner of Olive's bedroom. "You have a freakin' Christmas tree up."

"Yeah, what's your point?"

"It's the middle of *June*. No one needs a Christmas tree up in the middle of June."

Olive held her hand to her chest as if she'd been shot. "How can you say that?"

Miranda instantly rolled her eyes. "It's the *middle of June.* That's how I can say that."

"Haven't you heard of Christmas in July? I'm just a few weeks early."

"Christmas in July," Miranda scoffed. "Olive, you haven't taken it down in the three years we've lived here."

"Damn, Scrooge much? Sorry, my joy of the holidays makes you a bitter humbug."

Miranda held Olive's shoulders. "Please leave this apartment more often and get some fresh air. I really am worried about you."

"Do not shit all over my love of the happiest time of the year. And, stop deflecting on the fact that *you* went behind my back and moved in your brother."

"Think of all the material for your books you'll get now." Miranda swiped her hand towards the bedroom door. "His friends are delicious, what more can you ask for? Hot firemen as your personal research subjects. You can save your computer from all the viruses from those porn sites you..." She made air quotes. "...use for research."

"Hey, don't knock it. Those sites are a golden tool for my line of work."

"Whatever. It's done. Now, let's go back out there and get the rest of my stuff packed away."

Olive huffed before following her friend. "Remember those *research subjects* include your brother the next time you read one of my books." Olive couldn't help the smirk that spread across her face when Miranda's eyes widened. *Take that you, traitorous devil woman!*

"Oh shit, what have I done?"

Olive pushed Miranda's shoulder shoving her towards the door. "Serves you right."

As they walked back into the living room, Olive's heart stopped as she saw a shirtless, sweaty Hank standing in the middle of the room. How in the hell was it possible to look *that* good? He had muscles for days. Her eyes went to his abs as she started mentally counting them. Sure, half the men in her books were described like him, but that was in her mind. Men did *not* look like them in real life. And, why the hell was he looking at her like she was a tall glass of water and he was a man dying of thirst?

Her whole body shivered. She one-hundred percent stepped into an alternate universe.

"There you two are," Hank remarked. "I thought you'd left all the work to us." He nodded his head towards his station buddies that'd agreed to help move Miranda out and him in.

Olive looked around at the men scattered throughout the room. It was like a *Hot Fireman/Paramedic* calendar threw up in her apartment. Maybe this wasn't such a bad idea after all.

She turned towards her friend and smirked, which made Miranda blanch for a brief second before she spoke. "No, we haven't left. We were just discussing something in Olive's room," Miranda announced before making her way to one of the many boxes in the living room.

"That so, and what did you and Olive Oil need to discuss?" Hank smirked in her direction.

"Do not call me that!" Olive glanced around the room for something to throw at his head. She'd grown up with Hank teasing her every chance he got, and if he thought she would just stand by and let him do it in her own home he had another thing coming.

At her annoyance, Hank chuckled. "Oh, I think living with you will be lots of fun, Olive Oil."

Olive turned back to Miranda ready to demand she make him leave when Hank yelled out, "Any of you seen Dog?"

A chorus of *no's* rang out throughout the room which made Olive roll her eyes. "Let me guess, another one of your degenerate friends?" she asked glaring at Hank.

His eyes brightened with laughter as his smile grew wider. "Miranda didn't tell you about Dog?"

Olive's eyes shot to her best friend who now busied herself with removing an invisible piece of dirt from her shirt. "No, I guess that tidbit of information escaped her," Olive sneered.

Hank disappeared out of the room leaving Olive with her brow raised and her arms crossed at his sudden departure. *Well, okay then. Clearly living with Hank was not going to be a walk in the park.*

A few minutes later she heard Hank shout, "Found her!" He then made his way back into the living room. That's when Olive spotted the largest Maine Coon cat she'd ever seen in her life cradled in Hank's arms.

"What is that?"

Hank pat the cat on its head causing the ginormous thing to tilt its face in his direction seeking out more attention, or possibly meat from a small animal being used as a sacrifice. "This is Dog," he said with a grin.

That's when she snapped. "Who the fuck names a *cat* Dog?"

Continue Hank and Olive's story In Teased by Fire.

Also by Molly O'Hare

Stumbling Through Life Series

Stumbling Into Him

Stumbling Into Forever

Stumbling Into the Holidays

John & Emma's story – *Coming soon*

Teased by Love Series

Teased by Fire

Teased by Tinsel

Lucas & Miranda's story – Coming soon

Hollywood Hopeful Series

Hollywood Dreams

Risking It All (Danny and Lexi's Story) – *Coming soon*

Standalone Novels

Nothing But a Dare

Learning Curves

Tents & Tights

Stay Connected

Sign up for my newsletter or check out my website.

If you just want to hang out, come join my reader group: Molly's Badass Babes.

About the Author

Molly O'Hare is a USA Today Bestselling author of curvy romance books.

Molly's obsessed with all things animals, mainly Corgis, and body positivity. She grew up with severe dyslexia: trust her, spelling is not her strong suit. Over the years, she's become a huge advocate of "just because you learn something a little differently than others doesn't make you less." To help herself fall asleep, she'd create stories in her head, always picking up where she left off the night before. Molly figured if she got enjoyment out of her imagination, others might as well. So here we are.

Stay Connected

www.ingramcontent.com/pod-product-compliance
Lightning Source LLC
Chambersburg PA
CBHW061202190726
48288CB00001B/31